CHIP

CONTROL

A NOVEL ABOUT EMPOWERMENT

CHIP
CONTROL

A NOVEL ABOUT EMPOWERMENT

P J SWIFT

First published in Great Britain in 2018
by P J Swift

This novel is a work of fiction. Names, characters, businesses, places,
events and incidents are either the products of the author's imagination
or used in a fictitious manner. Any resemblance to actual persons, living
or dead, or actual events is purely coincidental

ISBN 978 1 9164185 0 9

P J Swift

Summary

When Kate meets Luke (fifteen years her younger) she has no idea that he has a behavioural problem, and beguiled by his charming, persuasive manner, uncharacteristically she falls deeply in love with him. Soon however, Luke's idiosyncrasies begin to manifest themselves causing hurt and a rift between them. Unable to forgive him Kate finds a uniquely inventive and satisfying form of punishment, providing hours of entertainment for herself and her friends until it gets out of control.

Chapter 1

Not a Brief Encounter?

'I'm not the only one cutting it fine,' he thought as he saw her running down the slope towards him; sparks of red highlighting her amber hair in the late, autumn sunshine.

It had always intrigued him how women could run in heels without falling over, and he took advantage of the distance between them to stare in fascination. It was only when she readjusted the slipping strap to the bag on her shoulder that she faltered slightly.

His eyes were drawn to her jacket which seemed to float on her, as the effect of the long strands of fur gave her the appearance of moving in slow motion. It fell just below her waist revealing slender hips and *very* long legs. So, as they both drew nearer to the entrance he gestured to let her through.

'Thanks,' she said mechanically with a winning smile and stepped up to the window, 'A return to London Bridge please. I have this card,' she said holding up a railcard, 'That's for the 10.36.'

'There ain't no 10.36; it's been cancelled.'

'What! What do you mean "it's been cancelled", so when is the next one?'

'At 11.04.'

'But that's half an hour! Where are the notices? I went online and there was nothing there? What's going on? How's a person supposed to know?'

The two men behind the glass looked at each other with blank expressions waiting for the other to speak, then the stocky one shrugged his shoulders irreproachably, but she felt compelled to make her point and carried on, 'I have organized my whole day around this train, there must be loads of people who have been inconvenienced by this cancellation!'

This was met by another shrug of the shoulders – unbelievably frustrating! It was obvious that they were totally uninterested in how the cancellation had affected her plans, and she was just about to find some other reason when a voice from behind her piped up, 'Yeah, she's right you know – it's not on, I've rushed to get here too; still got wet hair – if I'd known I could've taken it easy! You ought to get your fucking act together!'

'Right!' exclaimed the man, 'We're closing!' and promptly pulled down the blind on the window leaving her dumbstruck and amazed.

'How can they do that? I don't believe it! What are we going to do now?' she exclaimed in disbelief although she guessed that it had been the "F" word that did it.

'I'm going up. I'll get my ticket on the train,' was the response. And so she resigned herself to doing the same, however, realising that she had a good half hour to kill before the next train, instead of using the café on the platform she decided to drive into town and get herself a decent cup of coffee – it would make her feel better.

Everything had resolved itself when she returned with her coffee as they had reopened the ticket office so she had been able to buy her ticket, albeit with a certain sullen reluctance from the same stocky man who somehow still connected her with the swearing.....as if!

She had exaggerated slightly, the cancellation was a nuisance but it wouldn't mean any serious change of plan. She was going to visit a friend who, at seventy-eight, had undergone major heart surgery just four days previously, and was recovering in St. Thomas's.

Sunday was Kate's only truly free day to herself and although she had planned a day at home to start a blitz on her living room (long overdue), she had decided instead that her *very* good friend Frank deserved her company and cheer more than her home did. The house could wait – it had for more than two years, another week wasn't going to make any difference! And in any case, this was the least she could do to repay a little of all the kindness, support and generosity of spirit he had shown her through the last twenty-two years. Sometimes she had been at her wit's end, with bouts of depression caused by a feeling of entrapment from lack of funds and bringing up twins on her own. Much of the time Frank had been the only one to talk to and whether or not he understood, he was always there to listen and try to make sense of it all. He was special.

It was the last Sunday in November, and as Kate stood on the platform, she couldn't believe the heat from the sun on her chest and shoulders forcing her to remove her jacket.

'This is like summer,' she thought to herself and realized how lucky she was that she wouldn't be trudging through the streets of London in the rain or drizzle, as had so often been the case.

She sipped her 'up-market' coffee and the thought occurred to her that maybe it was serendipity – after all, if she had got the other train then she would not be standing there enjoying the wonderful sunshine, and drinking decent coffee instead of the stuff from the station snack bar.. All the angst and irritation that she had been feeling thirty minutes ago had completely disappeared; she felt calm and content with memories of standing on other platforms in warm, foreign lands.

One day I'll have the time and the money to go back to some of those places, she considered with a twinge of regret.

'Perfectly timed, only three minutes to go,' she thought as she savoured another mouthful.

The train pulled in almost silently. She remembered how she would cover her ears and back away from the steam trains when she was small; they had terrified her! Even though she had been told that they were perfectly safe it was the noise that scared her – so much hissing, screeching, and rumbling; even the platform seemed to tremble! They were like monsters. Then there was the plight of getting on (and off), negotiating the enormous gap between the carriage and the platform, which always looked far too wide for her little legs. She would cling fearfully to her mother until safely over it, often imagining what would have happened if she had slipped.

Anyway, that wasn't the case now, the new trains were relatively clean and the doors opened smoothly at the press of a button with virtually no gap, at least not at Pembleton-on-Sea. She stepped inside, and seeing that the carriage was practically empty, headed for a table, where she would be able to work in relative comfort if she wanted (she always carried work with her when travelling). However, just as she was about to sit down a vaguely familiar voice said, 'Do you mind if I join you?'

'No, of course not. Please do,' she could hardly have refused given that there were three free seats, anyway she was going to be reading her book and was not likely to be distracted. She had an assortment of reading material prepared as the thought of spending nearly two hours (each way) on a train doing nothing would have been a complete waste of time, and Kate *hated* wasting even a minute!

Her days were full from the moment she woke to when she closed her eyes at night, in fact she often regretted that there weren't three of her: one for earning money, one for mundane drudgery like grocery shopping and housework and one for just enjoying life, having a good time, going out, clothes shopping and making love! The last one was a full time job on its own – she had always said that she didn't have time for a man.

It didn't worry her in the slightest living alone, in fact she loved it; she could do exactly as she pleased, no one to answer to, no need to explain why she had bought another pair of shoes or earrings (two of her weaknesses). She would describe herself as a sociable loner. And besides, there was the cat, always so delighted to see her – her buddy!

She wasn't sure how the conversation started, or who initiated it; but it did. She did, however, remember that he had asked her (nicely) how much she had paid for her ticket.

'Only £14.50 because I have a senior citizen rail card,' she replied quietly, not wanting to broadcast the fact to the whole carriage.

'Really! That *is* reasonable.' More like borrowed off her older sister or a mate, he thought, there's no way she's over sixty, this will be interesting when the ticket inspector comes around.

'I'll be able to get one of those soon,' he said referring to the rail card. 'Are you learning French?' He had seen the course book on the table.

'No, I teach it!'

'Oh, really?!'

'Yes, I also teach Spanish, Italian, German, Maths and English.'

'Wow! That's impressive!'

'Not really. It sounds good, but you know when you live in another country it's not hard to pick up the language.'

He raised an eyebrow skeptically, 'I've met lots of people who have lived in Spain for years and can't string a sentence together.'

'Yes, me too and I have never understood why; it was my first and main objective.'

'So, have you lived in *all* those countries?'

'Yes.'

'How long did you spend in each?'

'My original plan was to spend two years in each to learn the languages, but of course it didn't work out like that. I got waylaid in a couple – things never seem to work according to plan.'

'No, I suppose not.'

'And I spent quite a while in the States and Bermuda.'

'Why on earth did you come back to England?'

'It's a long story and I wouldn't even be able to begin to tell you on this journey!'

'Some of it maybe?'

Kate didn't answer; she just smiled and picked up her book hoping to engage herself in her own thoughts and do what she normally did on a train – use the time profitably preparing lessons or teaching herself another language; Greek and Chinese being her latest challenges.

She had begun Greek years ago at an evening class, but it had petered out due to a lack of students, however she had never lost interest in it and would pick up a book or listen to a CD occasionally; like a musical instrument that gets taken out of its case and played occasionally.

'Is that your name? It looks French?' he had noticed a name written in thick black felt tip pen on the outside edge of a book. She had taken to doing this on all her teaching material as previously so much had gone astray!

'Catalan actually. It's my married name.'

'Oh, you're married. I didn't notice.'

'No, not now – divorced.'

'Me too"

She smiled again and made a gesture with her hands as if to say

'That's life!'

'I have two boys, all grown up now. Do you have any?'

'Yes, two – boys.'

'What ages?'

'Twenty-one and twenty-one.'

'Sorry?' he thought he had misheard.

'They are both twenty-one. I have twins,' she smiled.

'Did you find that a hard work?'

'No not at all, I thoroughly enjoyed it until they were about fifteen, when they turned into monsters!'

Now it was *his* turn to smile, 'Kids eh!'

She returned the smile and took advantage of the pause to go back to her book, over optimistically, as before long he started again – it didn't look as if she was going to do much this trip, or maybe he would be getting off soon?

'It must have been interesting living in all those places; did you go with your husband?'

'No, it all happened before I got married that's why I haven't minded being in one place for a while bringing up the boys.'

'And do they get to see their dad?'

'No, never, he's abroad.' That wasn't the only reason, but she didn't see the need for further explanation.

'I see.'

'And your wife, are the boys in contact with her?' She felt she could ask something personal in return.

'Yeah, when they are in the country. They both usually work abroad, but the youngest is camping out at my place at the moment. It's only temporary though.'

'That's good. I mean – that they see her.'

'You mentioned Bermuda – that must have been wonderful? Whatever made you come back?'

'A man, of course!' she said this with a certain nonchalance as though men had played quite a part in her decision making, and that it hadn't been a one-off.

She considered the number of times she had changed her life for, or because of a member of the opposite sex. 'Had it all been worth it?' she asked herself, 'Or had she learnt anything from the experiences? One thing was for sure, she would *never* go out with, or date a man again; she had had enough of them. She had tried too hard and wasted too much time and energy on them – they all wanted to put her down. They required too much hero-worship, and doing for. Also, she blamed herself for choosing badly and allowing it to happen. Being even a bit intelligent had never worked in her favour, it had just made her discontent and annoyed because instead of pursuing her own goals she had been side-tracked and distracted trying to build and/or keep a relationship; it had all been *so* exhausting and fruitless.'

In retrospect, and what she found incomprehensible, was why had she kept trying! Why had she thought she was ever going to find "the one". She thought she had in Bermuda, but he had died!

People were always saying, "But you have the boys!" As if that were compensation or a reward?

The boys! A constant worry and a drain on resources She should be enjoying life, going on cruises, visiting her friends abroad, not bailing them out from their debts, worrying about a leaky roof, the toilet not flushing properly, or the boiler breaking down! And then she would tell herself that things could be a lot worse; to be grateful for the fact that she was healthy, and so were they.

'I had waited three years for him to get divorced and assumed that it was never going to happen so instead of wasting more time I came back, and *then* his divorce came through! But it was too late, by then I had started a new business here and didn't want to leave it.'

'Really! What kind of business was that?'

'Fast food'

'What? Fish and chips?'

'Sometimes, but mostly burgers, hot dogs and chips.'

'Funny, I would never have placed you in that kind of business. Where was it?'

'Outside one of the night clubs, I only worked three nights a week. I had a van.'

'Really!' he sounded genuinely surprised, 'That was brave of you! There must have been loads of drunks, were you on your own?'

'No, I had a girl working with me. There wasn't *that* much trouble when the clubs turned out, I think that they just wanted something to eat and to go home. It was late and people were hungry and tired.'

He was still curious about Bermuda, 'What were you doing in Bermuda, the same sort of thing?'

'No, I was teaching, but that wasn't the reason I had gone there – I had been offered another job that didn't materialize so I had to become resourceful and looked for something else.'

She went on to tell him about some of her extraordinary experiences in other countries – fascinated, he was quite content to listen.

He had been watching her carefully. He noticed how her earrings matched the understated animal print on her top, its smooth silkiness revealing 'a great pair of tits' and was aroused and shifted uneasily. 'She's gone to a lot of trouble to look good; her makeup, hair and nails – all immaculate! Must be meeting someone,' he concluded.

'Just having a day out or are you meeting some friends?' he thought that keeping it plural sounded less intrusive.

'Both really, I'm going to see a friend in hospital, and may visit my cousin after.'

'Oh, nothing too serious I hope?'

'Well he's just had major heart surgery, but is making a remarkable recovery.'

'I was right,' he thought, 'this guy must be pretty important for her to go to all that effort. She'd certainly cheer *me* up!'

'And what's your reason? Are you meeting up with friends or doing something special?'

'No, nothing special, I'm up here nearly every weekend for The Stroll. We meet in Hyde Park,' and he opened the top of his backpack revealing a pair of roller blades.

'Oh! You skate!' she exclaimed hoping that she hadn't sounded too surprised; she had never imagined that he would be a skater, that was something she associated with teenagers not grown men in their fifties! It was difficult to guess his age, she assumed late fifties as he had referred to getting a senior citizen rail card soon.

'Yeah, love it, and this might be the last one before the spring so I just had to take advantage of the great weather.'

'Yes, that's for sure – it's extraordinary.'

8

Her perfume wrapped around him seductively; he thought he recognized the fragrance, but her skin had transformed it into something unique and intoxicating. She chatted on totally unaware of the beguiling tone and expression in her voice. She spoke clearly, enunciating all the parts of words that he and his friends didn't – almost theatrical, like a news reader or presenter, and *so* enthusiastic about everything. There was a freshness to her. The women he met usually rabbited on about their children and how wonderful they were.

Soon, the familiar buildings of the city had replaced the rural landscape, and she was gathering up her things. He did this tedious trip nearly every Sunday, but this first time he didn't want the journey to end.

Very shortly she would step off the train and walk away, and the chances of them meeting again would be slim. If they hadn't met in the last two years (since he had moved to Pembleton) then bumping into her again would be highly unlikely. He wanted to listen to her for longer and wondered how he could prevent her from disappearing; he didn't feel it appropriate to ask for her number, and he had no real reason to give her his: anyway, why should she want it?

As she stood up he felt he was being cheated in some way; that fate was working against him. This was the first time in two years that he had been in the slightest bit interested in a woman. He had told all his mates that he wasn't interested in a relationship, he had been let down too many times and the last two had been particularly vindictive, and he didn't need the headache. This one though....

'What's your name?' she said as she drew alongside him.

'Luke, and yours?'

'Kate, here's my card,' and she passed him a shiny business card with all her contact details.

'Just in case you hear of anyone who wants to learn a language, or any kids who need tutoring, I'm always looking for business.' She smiled again and then she put her hand on his shoulder and said, 'Enjoy your skate!'

'Thanks,' he replied savouring the moment's contact. His shoulder tingled from the touch, and a rush of optimism surged through him in the realization that he might – just might – get the chance to see her again.

She stepped onto the platform, and as the train pulled out he hoped that she would turn to acknowledge him in some way. Kate had considered waving, but suddenly realized that she couldn't be sure that she would recognize him especially through those dusty windows! She would have looked really stupid waving at the wrong person – or the whole train. So, scanning the platform for signs, she set her sights on the exit and didn't look back. Besides, their paths would never cross again so what was the point?

However, little did she know as she mingled with the station crowds, that the brief encounter would change her life forever.

Chapter 2

The Stroll and London?

The Stroll was a weekly, marshalled street skate through central London, and it gave Luke an opportunity to meet up with friends and other skaters, and talk skating. He went every Sunday, weather permitting.

'You're looking pretty pleased with yourself?!'

It was amazing how his mate Keith could always read Luke's feelings: depressed, worried or feeling great – Keith instinctively knew.

'Yeah, real good today – you?'

'Yeah, all good except for the shoulder.' He had been involved in a nasty skating accident some months previously, and it was taking a long time to mend.

He drew up alongside Luke, and they skated on together with an ease that made walking look difficult!

Skating for more than twenty years, and friends for nearly as long; they had met on their skates – two guys doing their own thing in the same area, gradually got to know each other and realised they had a lot in common. Even though they no longer lived in the same town, the twenty miles between them had changed nothing.

'So... what's put the smile on your face?'

Luke skated on ahead leaving Keith in suspense.

Keith went after him, 'Well, I figure that it's gonna be one of two things,' he wasn't going to let it drop.

'Yeah, like....?' Luke was enjoying the game.

'You either made loads of cash or it's a girl?'

'Damn! He does it every time! How can he know?' he thought.

'Well, come on!' Keith insisted with a hint of impatience in his voice.

'OK, you're right, but which one?'

Keith didn't answer immediately but watched him skate for a while. Luke flipped around, skated backwards with a swagger and smiled enigmatically.

'It's a girl, isn't it?'

'How do you do that? It's *so* annoying!'

'I had a fifty-fifty chance; was lucky, that's all. But you said "never again" – I can't believe it. She must be something *really* special!'

'Yeah, she is – at least I think she is – only just met her.'

'Wha'd'ya mean? Ah, the train! You met on the train?'

'Yup.' Luke had his back to him now.

'So......?'

Finally, he opened up and gave Keith a detailed description of the whole journey.

'Hmm, sounds good, there's only one snag.'

'Oh yeah, what's that then?'

'Well, you're a yob and she's a classy lady by the sounds of it.'

'And ....?'

'Classy ladies usually date classy blokes.'

'Yeah, *usually* they do, you're right; but *she* ain't usual, so maybe she likes a bit of the unusual?'

'Well she'd certainly be getting some of that!'

'Thanks – I'll take that as a compliment.'

'I can't believe she spoke to you looking like that!'

'Too well-mannered I guess; or was it my scintillating wit and personality? Anyway, she gave me her card, didn't she? That must mean something!'

'Good business woman, that's how I see it. Wishful thinking on your part.'

'You can be real cruel sometimes.'

'Well how are you going to handle this? Where d'ya go from here?'

'I haven't got that far yet; I could say I was interested in learning a language.'

'Ha! Ha!' Keith was doubled over by this idea, '*You*! Learn a language! You *hated* school; you're the *least* academic person I know apart from Kai and Stu and .....'

'OK, OK, you made your point, no need to bunch me in with them numpties,' his voice had lost some of its confidence and he dropped back to eavesdrop on something the others were arguing about behind him.

Meanwhile, Kate had reached the East entrance of the hospital, and as with most old-fashioned structures, she found herself in a renovated, modern extension and reception area. The directions to the wards were colour coded so all she had to do was follow the right colour.

The clinical, monotonous corridors seemed to go on for ever, and she wished she had put on lower heels as the joints in her toes were beginning to give her grief.

Finally – Kings Ward, she walked slowly past the bays of beds looking for the familiar thatch of thick white hair belonging to Frank. There was a board with names and a number next to Frank Horton so in no time at all they were both sitting on his bed laughing and exchanging news.

When they had caught up on everything: the details of the operation and what the boys were up to; Kate gave him the fruit and the newspaper that she had brought with her, along with a small book of puzzles and riddles that they spent the next hour trying to figure out. It was fun and stimulating, and she had always admired his sharp mind and repartee.

He was a keen Ukip supporter and knew exactly how many hospitals could be built for the amount the UK paid into the EU each year. He had all the facts, figures and reasons for not staying with Europe at his fingertips; Kate did not necessarily agree with everything but she listened, and it had opened her eyes.

After a couple of hours he was looking a little weary, so she gave him a hug and told him to take care, and as she turned to wave goodbye she couldn't help but admire the advances in modern medicine, and the skills of the practitioners

Frank's operation had been pioneering and it would be some months before he would get the all clear; but she had been amazed to see him looking so well. They both knew that he would not be able to throw himself back into work on the farm; but fortunately the winter months would take the pressure off and hopefully, by spring, he would feel stronger and slowly he would get his life back. The visit had done them *both* good: Kate was consoled and relieved, and Frank knew that he could rely on her loyalty and friendship. She was pleased that she had made the effort.

The exit signs were not leading her back the way she had come in, and quite imperceptibly the architecture changed – she recognized some features that must have belonged to the original structure: a marble covered floor and columns. She could hear the strains of a piano, 'Nice touch,' she thought, 'they should pipe this music through all the corridors.'

There were busts of famous surgeons, specialists and benefactors on plinths, each ensconced in its own alcove with a dedication engraved on a brass plaque. She slowed her pace and studied the faces; they all looked like learned men, people you might trust with your life; but where were the women? Not one – not even a token matron or ward sister, and yet none of the surgeons' patients would have survived without the care and dedication of the thousands of nurses who worked tirelessly and without complaint. At least Hollywood and television had gone some way to preserving their memory.

Suddenly the corridor opened out into an original reception hall with a high, ornate ceiling supported by Corinthian columns; white marble slashed through with grey everywhere – and there it was – a magnificent grand piano with pianist!

An elderly, somewhat distinguished looking gentleman was at the keyboard, and he was playing Beethoven's Moonlight Sonata. She was no expert on classical music but her first boyfriend had been a musician and had introduced her to his eclectic taste, and had gifted her recordings from his collection. He had opened her eyes and ears to so much more than the Beatles and the Rolling Stones – her only musical exposure as a student of art.

There was no audience – no one at all!

'What on earth was he doing here?' she wondered as she scanned the hall for a chair.

She settled on a wide balustrade between two of the columns, and with her back supported against one of them she leant back to absorb the fullness of the music. He was not reading a score, nor did he look at the keyboard, the music was all in his head, and something told Kate that he wasn't English. He smiled at her in acknowledgement, and as she sat down she reciprocated.

She had learned the piano as a child and for various reasons had been unable to pursue it, but she admired the ease with which his fingers found the keys; just as she admired Spanish guitarists and accomplished players of other instruments.

At the end of the Sonata he raised himself slightly from the stool and acknowledged her applause with an indiscernible nod of the head.

'Do you have a request?' he asked with a smile and an intriguing accent.

'I am a fan of John Barry. Do you know John Barry? Or maybe you don't approve? He's not everyone's taste.'

Still smiling, and with a flourish of his overcoat, he recomposed himself and to Kate's delight began to play the theme music to 'Out of Africa'.Although now cynical of romance, she loved films based on real life, especially if the protagonist was Robert Redford!

As she closed her eyes to the haunting strains of the music, she visualized Meryl Streep reaching behind her to hold Redford's hand as he flew her across the plains of Kenya in his monoplane causing the herds of animals to stampede in their wake. She knew nothing about flying but it had always puzzled her why Redford (the pilot) was sitting behind her? Her logic told her that the driver (in this case 'pilot') would be able to see better at the front? It was one of those stories that didn't end happily but compelled her to watch it every time it was repeated. There were few films that had it all!

Kate didn't want to move. She didn't want to look at the time. She was weighing up whether or not to visit her cousin; she wouldn't really be missed if she didn't call in. Her cousin and family were always *so* busy and *so* tied up with their lives; they never contacted her.

In many ways she felt that she was intruding in their world and her visit would be more out of duty and conscience as they were her only blood relations apart from her sister, who she hardly saw either. None of them would weep at her funeral or even care if she disappeared for ever so why was she bothering? She knew the answer, it was because they were her *only* family and felt she must; that old-fashioned, dutiful, Victorian upbringing reared its ugly head once more and played its "feel guilty" card.

She remembered her father trying to persuade her to stay at home once he had had a stroke, 'You should stay here and help your mother instead of gallivanting off abroad.' She had been twenty-two for pity's sake! And just because she wasn't married he expected her to dedicate her life to being a constant companion and support to her mum who, of course, would nurse him. So, each time she would leave under a cloud of guilt with her mum wishing her a wonderful time and yearning to go with her!

It was this sense of duty and guilt that always nudged *Kate* into picking up the phone to London only because she felt she *ought to* and then she wished she hadn't because it was never 'convenient' – 'I can't talk for long because so-and-so is here' or, after five minutes of conversation, ' Oh! I am so sorry but there's the doorbell; I loved our little chat – we'll speak soon, love to everyone, byeeee.' She could predict the length of a call to her cousin and how quickly it would end.

After three more requests, all beautifully executed, Kate decided that however much she wanted to stay, that she would have to pull herself away from the therapeutic music, so she went over to thank him, promising to return another Sunday. The charming gentleman with Slavic looks stretched out his hand, and as Kate responded, instead of shaking her hand, he drew it up to his lips planting a light, lingering kiss on the back, saying that he wished he were twenty years younger. As she turned to leave she speculated on the idea, especially having felt the smooth softness of his lips brush across the surface of her skin.

When she arrived at the flat in Islington they were all there preparing for some party or other, so she had a choice: she could either have a quick cup of tea and leave, or stay for the party (not knowing anyone) and experience the terrors of travelling alone, after midnight, on a train with drunks, thugs and potential goodness knows what. It didn't take too much thought before she opted for the former.

They had all 'acted' so pleased to see her and asked the right questions, but she felt awkward; no one stopped what they were doing, she'd been handed a knife and asked to chop some vegetables – her visit would have been nothing more than a slight diversion, and unless *she* made the effort none of them would ever bother to contact her again. The whole thing was a sham, and the more she thought about it the less she wanted any more to do with them. Why did people try to make her feel guilty by saying "But they are your family!?" If they were only interested in her and the boys when it suited them, then why should she feel as though she had to keep up the performance? She remembered her clairvoyant saying to her that no one in her family had actually bothered (or taken time) to understand her. How right she was! Kate didn't want them at her funeral; she would write a list of guests and include it in her will; she knew who her friends were and she only wanted them to see her off, assuming that they were still alive.

She was still annoyed when she boarded the train, 'Why had she bothered?' she asked herself, she felt no real love for any them; she had learned years ago not to waste affection where it was not reciprocated. She got more warmth and affection from her cat! And when she had really needed moral support and help a few years previously – where had they been then?

'Ah, well.....' she plugged in her earphones, 'I went. That's that!' and, much to the amusement of the people nearby, she started repeating phrases of Mandarin to take her mind off family matters.

Normally Luke would have got the train at Victoria but he had decided to go to Charring Cross in the off chance of meeting her again. He scanned the platform and walked the length of the train but he came to the conclusion that she must have stayed on at her cousin's and would catch a late one. The train was still at the platform so he considered hanging around the station to wait and see if she turned up and then act as though it was a coincidence, but he was not good at killing time and she might not leave from Charring Cross? He could be hanging around for hours to no avail when he could be watching motor cross at home, besides it was getting cold. He found a fairly empty carriage and sat down resigning himself to a routine, uneventful journey. He put in his earphones and reflected on the morning's encounter.

Chapter 3

Making Contact

As Luke opened the living room door heat hit him in the face from the fireplace. His son was outstretched on the leather sofa.

'Hi Dad. How was it? Great weather!'

'Yeah, yeah, all good, same crowd. What did you do?'

'Slept 'till 12.00, then Sal and I went to the open mike session at Coffee Bean, and tried the new pizza place.'

'Any good?'

'What – the pizza or the open mike?'

'The music.'

'There was a new girl – a singer – pretty good, she had an unusual voice, kinda husky, sexy; great for jazz, otherwise just the regulars.'

'What was her name? Do you remember?'

'Elli, Ella...Elaine, sorry Dad no,' he had a terrible memory for names. Faces – no problem, but he always wrote names down to remember them.

Luke walked over to the window, dropped his backpack on the floor next to him and stood looking at the lights of the town. The night was crystal clear.

'Something interesting happened on the train this morning,' he said still staring out of the window.

'What was that?'

'I met a lady.'

'Woo......'

'Yeah big woo. She was good company and completely transformed my journey. It didn't drag like always, in fact I couldn't believe where the time had gone; before I knew it we were at London Bridge and she was getting off, but she did leave me her card!' he brandished it and smiled almost triumphantly.

'She must have really fancied you then? Let's see the card.'

'Hmm, I like to think so but no. I think she had business on her mind; she teaches and works from home. I told her that I had a brother and sister with children but she doesn't know that they don't all live here. I really would like to see her again.'

'She was *that* nice?'

'Yeah, real interesting. She didn't talk about her kids all the time because she had a life before them. She's travelled a lot and not just on holiday, she's lived in different countries and speaks the languages! And to top it all she's stunning!'

'Wow! I haven't heard you talk about anyone like that for ages.' While his father had been talking, Joshua had been studying the list of credentials on her card, 'I suppose you realise that this woman is seriously intelligent? She has two degrees *and* teaching certificates!'

'Yeah, pretty much. I told you, didn't I?' Luke sounded mildly indignant.

'If you do contact her, what will you say?'

'I don't know, I haven't figured that out yet. I could say that I'm interested in learning a language?'

'Hmm, which one? You're not exactly academic.'

'You put it nicer than Keith. He just called me a yob and basically told me that I didn't stand a chance.'

'That wasn't very nice of your best mate.'

'Well he just says it as it is, that's Keith.'

'Which language would it be then?'

'Italian appeals to me, I love the sound of it – musical. We could go along together then it wouldn't look so obvious.'

Joshua thought for a second, 'Yes, but it isn't as useful as Spanish, and Spanish would be more helpful to me when I go back to the States. Also, loads of countries speak it, think of all the Latin American Spanish speaking countries?'

Luke's other son lived and worked in the States. He had married an American from Maine and worked for his father-in-law's real estate business, and had managed to get Joshua a job working for a charity in the same town. He had worked for Oxfam in some pretty difficult situations and was back in the UK doing a business and management course in the hope of improving his situation.

'Or I could just ask her out?'

'Yeah, but where? It would have to be somewhere classy if you want to impress her; not the pizzeria.'

'No, you're right. You go out here more than I do – any ideas?'

'What about that place down the hill, it's been taken over by new management?'

'Do you mean behind the pub? It's pretty seedy especially at the weekend full of drunks.'

'No, you can go in the side door, you don't have to walk through the pub any more and they've replaced the windows, there's a wonderful view over The Channel – you can see the lights in Calais, it is quite romantic and I've never seen it crowded.'

'Sounds perfect. That's it! I'll ask her for a meal, I'll leave it a day – don't want to look too keen.'

'Well good luck Dad, you've got nothing to lose, she can only say "no".'

He wanted to send a text the next day so he waited as long as possible and sent it in the evening. 'Hello! This is Luke (we met on the train on the way to London last Sunday) and I was wondering if you'd like to have dinner with me one evening soon?' He reread it to make sure he hadn't made any mistakes, reminding himself that she was a language teacher, then pressed "send".

He hadn't expected an immediate response but became concerned two days later when he still hadn't heard anything! He checked the number on the card; the numbers were the same.

'Strange,' he thought, she hadn't struck him as the sort of person who would ignore an invitation, and even if she had declined he was certain that she would have replied one way or another. So, after some thought he decided to send an email, and if he didn't get a reply to that then he would let it drop.

Kate was just finishing a bunch of photocopies when she heard a ping on her mobile; she reached across and opened her mail. When she saw the message she smiled, 'Well fancy that!' she said to herself, 'Who'd have thought it?' and she tried to put a face to the message but couldn't! She was annoyed with herself for not being able to remember *any* of his features, she could, though, recollect the gear he had on; it had been very casual, almost scruffy, but then he *had* planned to go skating. She thought she remembered long hair.... anyway she would have to answer him, it would be rude not to.

She poured herself a glass of wine to mull it over. Perhaps dinner with an 'ordinary' guy was just what she needed and would do her good? She wouldn't have to try too hard; she could just be herself, and enjoy the meal.

She wished that Megan (her closest friend) hadn't chosen that moment to go half way across the world on holiday; she would have liked to have sounded her out and she didn't really know anyone else intimate enough to discuss it with. Also, she would probably be waking her at three in the morning, because she had no idea what time it was in Thailand.

Chapter 4

Megan

About two years previously, Megan had turned up for German lessons and the two women very quickly realized how much they had in common. For instance, they both loved art; Kate had studied art (before languages) and Megan had been taking sculpture classes for years and was quite proficient. They also discovered a mutual love of dance which led to them trying a local ballroom dancing session. This, in turn, led to Salsa classes and then to Rock 'n Roll so they found themselves constantly in each other's company having fun and laughing a lot. Megan even joined Kate's pottery class, in fact every single evening of the week was taken up with some kind of activity.

'How long do you think we can keep this up?' Megan asked her one evening over a spritzer. They were both (deceptively) sixty-four.

'For as long as we can,' Kate chuckled, 'or until we drop!' She raised her glass and as Megan reciprocated their glasses clinked.

For Megan, Kate had delivered her from a humdrum existence of feeding a husband (and sometimes other visiting members of the family), walking the dog, housework, and gardening.

She had a small business organizing underwear and costume jewellery parties; but she didn't advertise, it was all 'word of mouth' and because she and her husband, Harry, were involved in so many charitable organisations her reputation had grown and although the work was sporadic she looked on it as pocket money – a bit of a bonus.

But more importantly, Kate had introduced her to a way of life that had escaped her until now! She felt free – liberated! Up to that moment she had spent evenings in on her own, drinking gin and tonic and watching crap on television by herself.

Harry was out *every* evening playing darts or bowls with 'the lads' or attending a committee meeting, and assumed that Megan was happy to vegetate at home. Occasionally, wives were included in social gatherings, and until she had met Kate that had been enough for her.

Not anymore! Megan was having the best time of her life – she had been sucked into a whirlwind of pottery throwing, dancing, and drinking and whatever else took her fancy. She looked to Kate as her mentor in life. She admired her: the way she had managed to teach herself several foreign languages; bring up two children entirely on her own; buy a house and look so glamorous! She had never met anyone like her – all of Megan's other friends seemed to be resigned to their lot, children all grown up and independent, they did as they were expected by their husbands.

Kate felt they were suspicious of Megan's new found friendship as they watched in awe, and whenever she joined them all for a day out or a mea she tried to be relaxed and convivial, ensuring that she spent more time in the company of the women rather than their husbands, in an attempt to gain trust, not jealousy!

She did her best but she was always going to be the single, more attractive woman with an exotic past, among a bunch of drab, boring, middle-aged couples, with all the husbands secretly desiring her but trying to look uninterested for fear of an argument later.

Megan was proud of her glamorous friend's exciting, if dubious, past which had done nothing other than keep her young. She looked at least fifteen years younger than her years, and this, combined with a natural enthusiasm and freshness meant that she still had pulling power.

Megan would watch her in admiration at the dance sessions flirting and teasing the men, most of whom were spoken for but who were all secretly hoping to get a moment alone with her, and fantasizing about what they would do. Once she asked Kate, 'Can you show me how you do that?'

'Do what?' she'd said innocently.

'Flirt like that, I'm completely out of practice. I don't even know what to say to a man any more.'

'Jesus, was I flirting? Who with?'

Megan couldn't believe that she was oblivious to the fact.

'Hell, I was just having a good time – enjoying myself!?' She looked at her friend in amazement.

'Well, it looked and sounded like flirting from where I was standing.'

'Really?' Kate said incredulously, 'You know I've been accused of that before, by boyfriends and had no idea what they were talking about. Maybe what I see as being "friendly" others perceive as flirting. I don't know what I can do about that! Or maybe it's pure and simple jealousy. My ex would imagine that I was flirting with every man alive – I couldn't even to talk to one!'

'Blimey, I can see why he's your ex.' Megan sympathized.

Months went by filled with dancing and competing in quizzes (another favourite pastime) that they often won because each of the team had a specialty, as well as good general knowledge.

Kate had not only improved Megan's lot but Harry's too; he approved of Kate's influence, it had taken the pressure off at home, he was no longer made to feel guilty when he went out in the evening because now, invariably, Megan left the house before him and arrived home when he was in bed!

Nothing had changed at home; the house was just as clean and there was always good food on the table. In fact, he could only see benefits from her newfound friendship as she was a happier person to live with and he couldn't remember the last time she complained or nagged him.

Kate liked Harry too, he came across as an easy going, content individual and she found him very interesting to talk to. He was really knowledgeable about current affairs and she could discuss a contentious subject with him in a civilized manner, he wasn't out to make her change her mind, although he usually did because he was so well informed, and his arguments were so convincing. She had never seen him get angry or raise his voice and she quite envied her friend for having what seemed to be an uncomplicated relationship with a supportive, empathetic partner.

However, it wasn't until about four months into their friendship when Megan had had a bit too much to drink one evening at home and took Kate into her confidence because Kate had been extolling

Harry's virtues and telling her how lucky she was.

'We haven't made love for over 35 years!' Megan blurted out unexpectedly.

'Why on earth not? Has he got a problem?'

'Yes, I'd say!'

'Well, what? Is he impotent?' although knowing that they had had two children she couldn't see how that would have started so long ago. She had read about impotency problems in older men but that didn't explain thirty-five years of inactivity.

'Probably now because he hasn't used it for so long!' Megan replied almost jokingly, 'but there's more to it than that.'

'What do you mean?' Kate wasn't being nosy, she just wanted to understand and felt privileged that Megan had chosen to share such an intimacy with her, also if her friend was in the mood for opening up she felt duty-bound to try and help her.

'You have to promise not to let what we're talking about leave these four walls,' Megan's tone was deadly serious and she was worried whether she had already said too much.

'Look, Meg, if you don't want to tell me everything then I'll understand, but if you need to get something off your chest or want to talk it through then I'm here to listen and to help in any way I can, and it goes without saying that whatever you say tonight goes no further, I promise.' And Kate reassuringly took hold of her hand.

Megan nodded and managed a weak smile, 'Thanks, because I have never discussed this with anyone.'

'Not even Susie?' (Susie was Megan's oldest friend).

'No, no one.'

'OK, well maybe it's what happens to all couples after years of marriage – the novelty has worn off and you just need to add a bit of spice to it?'

'No, it's not that,' she said emphatically, 'we're talking thirty-five years, maybe more, I've lost count!'

'Have you tried sexy underwear? What about a blow job?'

'You've got to be joking, he wouldn't let me do that, he thinks it's disgusting. He thinks ALL sex is disgusting! And I tried the underwear once on Valentine's, it was a complete waste of money – he laughed!'

Kate raised her eyebrows and took a sip of wine as she imagined the scenario.

'But you have two kids! He can't always have been that way?'

'It started as soon as he knew we were having Olivia. That was it! We never made love again, I tried to interest him, I mean I made all sorts of overtures and did my best to get him aroused but he would just push me away which made me feel *awful,* so I stopped making the effort, it was too soul-destroying.'

'Christ, yes, I can imagine. It sounds unbelievable,' she took a couple more sips as she tried to imagine 35 years with no sex; she couldn't. 'Didn't you look for sex elsewhere? You must have been racked with frustration, especially in your thirties if you were anything like me. I had more men than hot dinners in my thirties!' she exclaimed with pride.

'No,' Meg replied with regret, 'I was always *so* busy. We were never without a business – a shop of some kind and it was all consuming. Apart from the fact that there were two children to bring up and I had to take them to all their after-school and weekend clubs, and shop, and clean, and cook blah, blah...'

'Yes, of course, I can see how difficult it must have been and in a town like this it would have been very hard to keep it under wraps even if you could have found the time. Didn't you ever talk about it?'

'Well, I tried, but it was useless; I always got the same response: "What for? You've got the children you wanted, we don't need to do it any more", or that it was a "disgusting act".'

Kate had never heard anything like it. She might have read something similar in an agony aunt column but she was detached from that, after all she didn't know the people who wrote in. But this was different, this was *her* friend and as far as she could see she had suffered for most of her married life from a lack of sexual pleasure; but worse still, been made to feel guilty or ashamed about it! Kate remembered telling her about some of her own sexual exploits and how much she had enjoyed them and realized how insensitive she had been.

'Have you considered that he might be gay? You know that years ago, thousands of gay men got married and had children to cover it up, and even when it became legal it was still taboo and no one "came out" for fear of ridicule or being ostracised. Didn't you tell me his father committed suicide?'

'Yes,' Megan sounded close to tears so Kate thought it would be a good idea to change the subject, because now that it had been broached she could bring it up at another time.

'Where's that brilliant word game you've got? Let's have a go at that – bet I beat you!'

'Do you mean Boggle?'

'Yes, come on, where is it?'

Megan got up rather reluctantly and came back with the game placing it on the coffee table; she found a couple of pens and note pads to record their answers on, and after vigorously shaking the box, they set to writing down as many words as they could in one minute.

They ended up laughing and the subject of unrequited sex was temporarily shelved, but Kate wouldn't forget their conversation – it had made an extraordinary impression on her.

Chapter 5

Unsolicited Advances

They carried on all through the summer acting like thirty-year-olds and feeling like them.

Then, one mid-September evening, during a session of table football in the pub, (they would invariably end up there because the rock 'n roll finished too early for them to go home), Megan suggested going away for a long weekend somewhere. She had seen a very reasonably priced, three night stay in Prague and she thought it would be fun to get away from the confines of the area and have a bit of an adventure.

Kate wasn't sure about spending entire nights in her company and was even less happy about the prospect of sharing a bedroom with her as there had been a couple of isolated instances when Megan had thrown what could only be described as a hissy fit!

The first had been in a hotel bar when she complained that Kate wasn't listening to (she meant 'ignoring') her because Kate's attention had been diverted by two guys over Megan's shoulder, who had caught her eye and were showing interest.

The second was when she accused Kate of not saying good night 'properly' when she had dropped her off!? Kate had been completely baffled by the word 'properly'; she wondered what she had meant as she replayed the moment in her mind. She had said "goodbye" and "thank you" (for the lift) that was a matter of course, so what else had she been expecting? And for the first time a thought crossed her mind that maybe Megan was hoping for more than just a friendship. Kate had told her about her casual 'experiments' with other women, and now she wondered whether Megan was looking to Kate as an answer to her sexual deprivation.

Kate had shuddered at the thought, all *that* was behind her, in fact *all* sex was behind her (she hoped), she had had more than her fair share and she simply couldn't get excited about it any more.

So, when Megan mentioned the trip to Prague, and Kate didn't respond enthusiastically, she sensed the overwhelming feeling of disappointment in both her face and voice. Megan had the ability to make her feel really guilty whenever she didn't say "yes". It didn't happen very often but occasionally Kate needed time to prepare lessons or to catch up on something at home, so a couple of times when she had turned down invitations, she would have thought that the dog had died by her reaction. On several occasions Kate had given in just to avoid the guilt.

However, this wasn't a meal and a game of Boggle, this would be *three* nights sharing a room abroad! If anything went wrong she wouldn't be able to retreat to her house at the end of the evening, and she wondered how she would cope if Megan came onto her!

She could feel the pressure from her stare hoping for a positive response, so in the end Kate said, 'It could be a good idea, and Prague is exquisite.' Her response seemed to appease Megan and they started another game of football. The rest of the evening panned out the way it usually did with Kate thrashing Megan at table football, and then both of them thrashing the quiz machine.

The next morning Kate picked up the buzzing phone, 'Hello!'

'Hi, it's me. I've booked the holiday,' Megan sounded cheerfully upbeat.

Kate didn't answer immediately as she wasn't sure if she had heard correctly, 'What?'

'I've booked the long weekend in Prague. The one we talked about yesterday. It's exciting, isn't it?'

Again, Kate was struggling to know what to say, 'What do you mean?'

'The weekend that we decided on yesterday!' Megan sounded surprised by her friend's reaction.

'But I never said to go ahead and book it!' There was panic in Kate's voice.

'You said it was a good idea!' retorted Megan.

Kate's mind was racing now as she tried to recollect her words; yes, she did say something about it being a good idea.

'I think I said it *could* be a good idea, I never expected you to go ahead and book it!' Kate refused to believe that a perfectly innocent conversation about a weekend break had turned into a reality over night, and was alarmed by the way it had all escalated out of control. How could Megan have done this without consulting her?

'But I didn't *agree* – you didn't say you were going to do this!' now Kate's voice was somewhere between panic and hysteria.

'Well it's done now. I've paid with my card. Aren't you excited?'

'Not really, it's a bit of a shock, I don't know if I really want to go to Prague.'

'Of *course* you do. You told me it was beautiful,' Megan insisted, 'you can't have changed your mind since yesterday!'

Kate felt like a trapped animal and didn't like it, 'I never agreed to go anywhere last night. I don't understand. Why on earth would you go and pay for something like that when we hadn't discussed it!' She felt hysteria turning to anger.

'Why are you shouting?'

'Because I'm angry. You've gone ahead and committed me to something that I had no intention of doing!' Now she was aware of the sound of her voice, but didn't care, 'You'll have to cancel it!'

'I can't. I've paid!' Megan's tone had changed now, and she wasn't happy.

'Well I'm not going – I think what you've done is reprehensible. You've gone too far. You can't force me to go and I am not!' and she hung up.

The phone rang almost immediately. There was no way Kate was going to answer, she knew it was Megan and as far as she was concerned the conversation was over, besides, she was far too upset to speak coherently. She marched up and down her living room muttering expletives interspersed by outbreaks of 'How could she?' with only the cat for an audience who raised her head in the off chance of food being involved.

Kate considered opening a bottle of wine (she kept an emergency supply in the garage), but when she looked at the clock, thought better of it. It was times like this that she wished she smoked. Her neighbour would have lit up and a few puffs would have helped to pacify her. She had asked several smokers what they got from it, but none of them had come up with a satisfactory explanation. She had tried it herself when she had been a student but it had done nothing for her so she gave it up; spent the money on alcohol, and had never looked back.

She switched on the kettle and decided on a hot drink, something decaffeinated – she was hyper enough.

When Megan realized that Kate was not going to answer her mobile she tried the landline. After eight rings the answer machine kicked in and Kate heard her own voice followed by Megan's pleas of, 'I'm *really* sorry Kate, I obviously misunderstood. Can't we talk about it? *Please* pick up. I feel terrible. We can sort it out; I know we can.' Megan didn't hang up, she was waiting for Kate to answer because she knew she was listening.

Kate didn't trust herself, if she spoke to her again, now, she might be abusive and that wasn't her. Other people made her like that, and in turn, made her angry and upset. It would take her hours to calm down, maybe all day.

'Alright, I expect you are too upset right now but *please* ring me later or perhaps we can meet for a drink? Anyway, I'll leave it up to you. Speak soon?' And with that she signed off.

Out of the corner of her eye Kate could see the red led light flashing on the machine which would annoy her all day and resurrect her feelings of resentment, so she went over and deleted the message, then she tried to get back into the rhythm of her day although she knew it would be futile because the situation was not going to go away and would play on her mind no matter how hard she tried to distract herself.

Later, in the afternoon she found a text message, 'Shall I pick you up for Salsa?'

Kate stood with the phone in her hand, she really wanted to go to the class but she wasn't ready to confront her friend. She punched the words with annoyance into her phone, 'No, sorry, not up to it,' she didn't get any response but then she didn't want one. She wasn't sure when she would feel like talking to Megan again and wondered whether she would go on her own.

The week went by in silence, not for want of trying as Megan had left loads of messages, and Kate was miserable not dancing; she had decided to stay away for fear of a showdown.

The following couple of weeks went by uneventfully. Kate missed her friend but she knew that she hadn't cancelled the trip as she had sent her a couple of texts hoping for a change of heart and to recover their friendship, but Kate couldn't see any way of patching things up with the holiday hanging over her.

Two of her students took dance classes, Argentine Tango and Flamenco, that she knew wouldn't interest Megan, so she filled two evenings a week with them and she went to Lindy hop out of town on another which brought some stability back into her life.

Of course she regretted what had happened and sometimes longed for a return to the fun, carefree evenings that they had shared together, but at the same time she was relieved in the knowledge that the holiday had been avoided.

Luckily Megan and Harry lived a few miles out of town, so there was little chance of crossing paths. Once Kate thought that she saw Megan pass her in her car going in the opposite direction, but that was the only time until just before Christmas.

Chapter 6

The Showdown

It had been just short of three months since they had argued on the phone and Kate was thinking that maybe it was time to build bridges, so two days before Christmas she decided that she would pop a card through their door as a gesture of goodwill.

As she was looking through her box of cards the doorbell rang.

When she opened it she saw Harry standing there with two large bags packed with presents.

Kate couldn't believe her eyes. She just stood there in shock and disbelief. She wondered where her voice had gone?

Harry broke the silence, 'Megan would like you to have these,' he said with the faintest of smiles, and holding out the two carrier bags.

'Thank you, I really wasn't expecting anything. This is so uncanny as I was just about to write your card.'

He didn't reply but turned, walked around the car and as he opened the door added, 'By the way, that was a terrible thing that you did to Megan, unforgivable, I have no idea why she asked me to deliver these,' and he gestured towards the bags.

His words didn't quite register as Kate was still stunned by his unannounced arrival and seeming generosity, but before he had a chance to pull away she came to her senses.

'Hey! Woo! Hang on there a second !' she shouted as she ran around the front of the car and as Harry rolled down the window she could feel herself fighting her anger.

'How dare you come round here to lecture me on *my* behaviour when you know absolutely nothing about what *really* happened, and even if you did it would only be Megan's version. Besides, none of this would have happened if you had paid her more attention.

Look to yourself for blame!' Kate's words shot from her mouth like bullets. Her face felt hot and flushed even though an icy wind was blowing down the lane. She left him negotiating a tight five point turn; went inside and slammed the door behind her.

She hadn't lost her temper for months in fact, not since the row with Megan.

What was it about those two, she thought, that got her so worked up? She didn't like it! Her Libra ascendant needed balance and harmony, not people on her doorstep unjustly accusing her of god knows what! She had been cornered and felt compromised. Why did he have to say anything? If only he had just left the parcels and gone, then peace and friendships would have been restored, and Happy Christmas to all!

She left the bags in the hallway and glowered at the box of Christmas cards on the kitchen counter as she popped the cork on a bottle of cheap, fizzy wine. Taking two large gulps she put the lid on the box of cards and virtually threw them back on the shelf above her PC. A card was not going to be large enough for everything she had to say to them! So, armed with the bottle and glass, she marched into the 'classroom', grabbed a handful of A4 copying paper, sat down, pushed her sleeves up her forearms, and with pen poised thought about her opening words.

Years ago a friend had told her that if she ever received a letter from her she would tear it up without reading it, having been witness to some of Kate's epistles in the past.

It didn't take long for her to fill up the pages once the alcohol started to take effect, she didn't need to search for inspiration, that had been triggered by her innate sense of justice and a need to clarify some issues that had lain dormant for too long.

She wasn't going to take this lying down, Harry had never been at the firing end of her passion, so he had no idea what was coming his way when he drove out of the snow-covered lane that day. She felt sorry for Megan because she had held out an olive branch (more like a whole tree when Kate counted how many gifts were in the bags!) and Harry had ruined it all at the last minute by admonishing her. The moment had been magical till then; she had been touched by the gesture and a feeling of warmth and goodwill had consumed her; she had nearly hugged Harry! Thank goodness she hadn't!

Twenty minutes later, she was on page six and she was still writing furiously, she had not stopped to consider syntax or punctuation, she just wrote it as it was (or had been). When she finally read it through the bottle was nearly empty and the paper felt like Braille, she had pressed on it with such vigour.

She put the carrier bags into a large black plastic rubbish sack and tied it securely attaching a label "Please deliver this package to your neighbours Harry and Megan"

She wasn't going to return the presents that afternoon, especially after having consumed nearly a bottle of 5% wine! She would deal with it the next day.

Chapter 7

The Truth

When the neighbour knocked on the door Megan must have looked as surprised as Kate had been a couple of days before. She hauled the bag inside having thanked the neighbour and recognising the writing on the label Megan's heart soared with the realisation that Megan had been thinking about her too.

She eagerly pulled open the bag but froze when she saw what was inside, 'What on earth..?' she muttered.

Then she saw the letter addressed to both of them, sealed in an envelope; by this time Harry had come downstairs. '

Was that the postman?' he asked.

'No, it was Pat from next door.'

'Anything wrong? Did he need anything?'

'No, he didn't need anything, he just delivered this.'

'Well, what is it?'

'It looks like the presents that I gave you to take down to Kate.'

'What do you mean?'

'Well look!'

By now Megan had taken everything out of the bag and placed it on the floor including the envelope addressed to them both. She looked quizzically at Harry holding up the envelope.

'That's strange!'

'Yes, strange indeed,' she repeated, 'Why on earth would she have sent them back!' she said looking accusingly at her husband.

'Well, she did seem a little agitated when I left.'

'Agitated! What do mean by agitated? Why should she have been agitated?'

'Well, I did say that I didn't approve of the way she had behaved towards you.'

'What! Why? We agreed it was my fault!'

'Because I thought it needed saying; you were terribly unhappy when she wouldn't talk to you.'

'But that was because she felt compromised! I don't understand you! All I asked you to do was deliver the presents, but you had to go and open your mouth, anyway there's a note here – maybe it will enlighten us?'

'OK let's open it and have a look, she's addressed it to both of us.'

Megan opened the envelope and read aloud, in it Kate had explained that the reason she was writing was because of what Harry had said, otherwise she would have received the presents graciously and they would all probably be having a Christmas drink together.

Basically, she expressed her concerns about Megan's possessive attitude and how she had felt cornered. Then she went on to explain how, in her opinion the whole problem had evolved from Harry's selfish attitude leaving Megan alone nearly every evening and not satisfying her in bed.

When Harry realized that Megan had disclosed details of their non-existent sex life he was visibly shaken. All the colour drained from his face and he was forced to sit down. He sat there cradling his head in his hands. Eventually, he looked up, 'What on earth possessed you to tell her?'

'I don't know; it just came out one evening when we had both had a few too many. Kate was extolling your virtues and telling me how lucky I was, and I just got fed up with it and told her.'

Megan's explanation did nothing to ease the anguish that she could see etched on his face; betrayal seemed to have suddenly aged him.

'I'll make a cup of tea,' Megan jumped up and scurried from the room, she didn't want to talk about it–not in broad daylight and sober! 'Bugger!' she muttered under her breath, why did she have to mention *that*? Kate had really landed her in the shit.

'Here you are, and I've put a slice of fruit cake on the side, that should make you feel better.' Megan placed them gently on the table by his side wishing she could find an excuse to go out, but they had cupboards full of food in preparation for Christmas.

Harry didn't acknowledge her or move, he was sitting in the armchair staring at the window. He felt numb, no one had known about their "relationship", *no one*, not even his best mate Richard. Of course, all the club members made the usual sort of jokes about not remembering what the wife's tits looked like, and "it had been so long they'd forgotten how to do it"; and Harry would often contribute something witty, so none of them had any idea how he *really* felt.

He had managed to keep it under wraps all these years, so on the surface they came across as any 'normal' couple. They had got on with life like most couples did. They were friends! Okay, maybe he could have spent more evenings in, but she had *her own* interests, just not in the evenings – at least not until Kate had entered their lives and filled the void.

Megan sat in the other armchair watching him with some concern as five years previously he had had a heart attack, and although he was scrupulous about taking his medication, the threat of another always hung around in the background, and it was exactly this kind of worry or shock that could set one off.

Harry looked down at the tea and cake and said, 'I think I need something stronger.'

'I think we both do!' she said and with that she picked up both mugs but left the cake; went straight to the kitchen, and poured the contents down the sink. She took two glasses from the cabinet and rapidly reappeared to the cheery sound of ice cubes in malt whisky chinking against the cut glass.

Harry accepted the glass with the liquor like a sacrament, and after holding it up to admire the rich golden hue, he drew it slowly to his lips, took a measured sip, closed his eyes and swallowed. He had the crazy thought that when he opened them everything would be back the way it was, and none of this would have happened: Kate wouldn't have returned the gifts; there would be no letter lying on the coffee table; Megan wouldn't have told Kate about his lack of passion in the bedroom department and they would be sitting there reading a heart-warming Christmas card in Kate's handwriting thanking them for their generosity and saying how sorry she was for everything that had happened. Kate and Megan would have a long chat on the phone; they would both cry, and life would return to the way it was four months ago. If only!

'You don't have to worry – I swore her to secrecy,' Megan remembered most about that night; the important bits anyway, 'I'm positive she won't say anything to anyone, she promised.'

Harry gave an unconvinced, cynical chuckle. He reached for the remote and pretended to focus on Countdown.

Megan saw no point in pursuing the conversation as his body language said it all, so she took her drink and retired to the kitchen in the hope of lifting the mood with a hearty dinner.

And that was how they left it, for a while anyway. But the dragon had been woken and Megan couldn't leave it alone. She felt he had too much too answer for so she couldn't help herself, especially as she had little or nothing to do in the evenings. She wasn't like Kate – she couldn't just go off on her own and look for something else to fill the void. Friends and family encouraged her to get out and try new things, but it was no fun on her own. So, while Harry spent his evenings out of the house, she slipped back into the habit of drinking and brooding about her plight, until he got home and then have a go at him about the lack of sexual attention, reliving the return of the Christmas presents and generally admonishing him for her frustration and discontent.

'After everything I have given up for you, all those hours of unpaid, unforgiving labour in the businesses, at home and for your clubs and committees; creating table decorations, producing buffets and dinners, and you can't get your dick up to give me a few minutes of physical satisfaction! I might as well get a blow up doll!' The alcohol contributed to the aggression.

Harry would try to escape by locking himself in the bathroom, but once she had worked herself up she couldn't stop, and continued the onslaught through the door.

'Kate thinks you're gay. Are you gay?' When he didn't reply she shouted louder, 'Well, *are* you?' If she had had more to drink than usual she would accompany her verbal assault with a series of loud thumps on the door.

Eventually, tired of talking to an unresponsive zombie she

reluctantly got into bed, falling asleep to the monotones of the shipping forecast. Sometimes she left the radio on all night because it distracted her when she couldn't sleep, and helped to drown out his snoring.

Chapter 8

Nearly Forgiven

Megan made no attempt to contact Kate until an email arrived the following March informing her of the birth of a grandson. Kate, now well established in a different milieu, was unsure how to react as she didn't want to upset her new found stability, so she decided to sleep on it.

A new day and a new perspective. Kate had concluded that sending congratulations and nothing more would be the right thing to do, and would prove that there was no animosity, at least not on her side.

Kate's acrimony had calmed almost as soon as she had delivered her letter along with the Christmas gifts. It was her way of clearing resentment. She often wrote people letters and never sent them. She found the simple process of putting pen to paper gratifying enough, and imagining the impact of her words on her recipient usually appeased her. When she had finished, she would put it in an envelope and address it but invariably leave it on the kitchen counter or the computer desk unsent. She had gone through the motions and most of the time that worked, because the letter would get covered by something else, so in her memory she had 'told' them what she thought, and it was there to send if she ever changed her mind.

Anyway, that was not the case now as she pressed 'send' to her one-word text message of "Congratulations".

Kate was even more convinced she had done the right thing when she received no reply; not for several days, when, out of the blue Megan asked her to meet for lunch!

This created a new dilemma. Should she? Shouldn't she? Would she be reopening a can of worms? What to do? Again, she decided to leave it a couple of days before answering, it would give her time to analyse how she really felt about reactivating their friendship. In the end, curiosity got the better of her and she committed herself to 'Yes!'.

Megan was already sitting at a table when Kate arrived.

'Hello! Well, it's been quite a while, hasn't it?

'Yes, it certainly has stranger!' Megan replied with a broad smile.

The first thing that struck Kate was the change of hair colour and length, 'Hey, what's with the hair colour?'

'Oh, I don't know, I just felt like a change.'

Kate made no comment, she wasn't going to start their reunion with personal criticism. It wasn't subtle or flattering; jet black and well below shoulder length and did nothing for her.

She smiled and said, 'Well, we all feel like that occasionally.'

'It was Lisa's idea (Megan's daughter) – she thought it would make me look younger. She chose the colour and put it on for me,' she said flicking it back over her shoulder flirtatiously, reminiscent of Miss Piggy.

Kate thought the opposite – it aged her, although again she kept that thought to herself. In her opinion if women of a certain age wanted to keep their hair long then they should wear it up, or have it stylishly cut short, otherwise it usually did them no favours. Five months ago, Kate would have told her what she thought, but she knew that this time she would have to hold her tongue.

'So, you're now officially "granny",'

'Yes, and he's a sweetie!' Megan exclaimed and brought up the latest photos on her phone. Kate made the appropriate noises and comments and prayed that neither of her two got anyone pregnant, the last thing she needed in her life now was a grandchild.

They caught up on family issues, work, health and hobbies and it seemed like nothing had changed.

'Look!' Megan said with conviction, 'I know everything that happened was my fault. I was too clingy and controlling. I spoilt it all, I know, I am so sorry. I've learnt my lesson! It'll never happen again, I promise.'

'Hey, forget it! Water under the bridge – it's really good to see you and catch up.'

'Yes, it is, you're right.'

How are Harry and Lisa?'

'Good. She's got a new man so fingers crossed,' she smiled, 'You know that we're selling the house?'

Kate wasn't sure if she had understood, 'What? You and Harry? *Your* house?'

'Yes.'

'Where are you going?'

'We're not sure yet, but we're separating so we'll be getting our own places.'

Kate nearly choked on her soup. When she'd collected herself she knew there was no disguising the astonishment in her voice, 'Separating!? You and Harry? Jesus! Who'd have thought it? *I* certainly wouldn't. But why?'

'Harry was fed up with the situation as it was and so was I, truth be known.'

'My god! I can't believe it, I thought you two would rub along together for ever.'

Megan looked down at her plate and shrugged her shoulders. She didn't feel it was the time to elaborate on the issue. She was so grateful to Kate for agreeing to meet her and she didn't want to upset the apple cart by apportioning blame.

Never for one second did it occur to Kate that she had played a role in their demise, she was stunned and disappointed by the news, 'I'm sorry,' she said inadequately.

'I'd like to stay in Hillside if possible, I do like it here.' Hillside was a small community outside Pembleton.

'Have you seen anything you like?'

'No, there's nothing really suitable on the market. I think Harry's probably found somewhere, his mate Gerald is lending him the money because he doesn't want the property to be snatched up by anyone else and we haven't had any offers on ours yet.'

Megan showed little enthusiasm at the prospect of buying her own place in fact, she seemed quite indifferent, not at all the attitude that Kate would have expected from a prospective new home owner. She remembered how exciting she had found buying a new home herself but saw none of that in her friend. She appeared to be totally disinterested.

Having renewed their friendship, they were soon back exercising together. Not *every* evening as before, but they saw each other at least three times a week and sometimes as many as five. It was as though nothing had happened, and the letter was never mentioned. So, that is where they stood when Kate met Luke, the best of friends again, and Megan in a new home of her own, not in the area she had anticipated as she had left everything till the last minute, so when they had found a buyer she took whatever she could find, suitable or otherwise.

Chapter 9

First Date

Kate hadn't been out for a meal (with a man) for ages and the idea intrigued her, after all it would only be dinner, nothing else, she told herself when she had decided to take Luke up on his offer.

She had poured herself a glass of wine for some Dutch courage before replying to the email and by the time she had accepted the glass was empty, and after a couple more messages they'd arranged where, when and how. He would pick her up (by taxi) on Saturday at 7.30.

She was surprised to find herself looking forward to it – the unknown, something to spice up her life. What would she wear? Plenty of time to think about that, she thought, as she switched on the tele.

Suddenly it was Saturday and she was wading through the clothes in her cupboards, far too tightly packed together to be able to see what she had. She wanted to impress, so she picked out a little Italian number in rust red; a shortish dress with a sleeveless, loose gilet decorated with appliquéed flowers in the same material that didn't need ironing. It had turned a few heads in the past and when a couple of women had asked her where she had found it, she loved being able to say, 'Italy'.

She glanced up at the clock as she applied the varnish to the last nail.

'Good job I started to get ready early,' she thought blowing madly at the ends of her fingers, even then she smudged one putting on her shoes. 'Damn!' she muttered, 'No time to redo it.' She heard the text arrive, 'At the end of the lane.' She tried not to panic and replied, 'On my way,' grabbing the Paco Rabanne bottle she quickly sprayed her neck and wrists, slipped her mother's eternity ring onto her ring finger (right hand) and checked the hair in the hall mirror on the way out.

As she turned the key in the outside of the door she could see a small, black vehicle parked across the top of her lane (technically a mews); she loved living in what used to be a stable for horses. Shortly after moving into the flat above, she had gutted the ground floor changing it into living space. It had been *her* project and although it had cost more than budgeted and the builders had driven her crazy, she was delighted with the result.

She had transformed one of the stables (28m long) into her living room with open-plan kitchen and breakfast bar. She had been converted to open-plan everything in the States. Why shut yourself off from the people you have invited by being isolated in the kitchen?

The ceiling was over four meters high, so plenty of space for her art work. Kate was an avid collector (not expensive, well-known artwork – just good prints or originals from boot fairs or second-hand shops) and had covered the walls with some of her own work and stuff she had collected over the years.

She had kept most of her parents' antique furniture even though it wasn't popular taste, but it brought her comfort being surrounded by their possessions.

The car didn't resemble a taxi so she hesitated before opening the back door and couldn't see anyone else but a driver!?

'Bit weird,' she thought as she opened the rear door.

'Good evening,' said the driver. Kate peered through the darkness and realized that he must have decided to bring his own car so she closed the door and quickly changed to the passenger seat at the front.

'Hello,' she said feeling a bit embarrassed for not having recognized him, 'Sorry, I was a bit confused, you said that you were coming by taxi?'

'Yeah, sorry about that, none available, Saturday you know, and I was in a bit of a hurry. I'll leave it there and we'll get one back then I can have a drink.'

'That's sensible,' she felt awkward and strangely nervous, 'Have you had a good week?' It was something to say and always worked.

'Yeah, pretty good thanks and yourself?'

'Yes, busy but good. Where are we going?' She could see that they were heading out of town and didn't want to go too far, after all he was an unknown quantity as such and although she could handle herself she didn't want the evening to turn into a fight for survival. This was not what she had intended and just as the seeds of doubt were germinating, he signalled and turned off left towards the sea front at the bottom of the hill.

'I thought we'd try the place behind the pub, it's been taken over and I've had some good feedback on it.'

'Sounds good to me. You're in charge.'

Kate was relieved when he found a space right by the door because she didn't want to walk far in her heels, they were higher than what she was used to, but made her feel more attractive. She'd picked out a pair exactly the same shade as her dress as she had seen the effect they had three months previous at a friend's anniversary.

The other side of the door was a long corridor and a sign 'restaurant' to the right which led them to a small, freshly painted, glass-enclosed dining area. There was only one other couple dining and a waitress appeared from nowhere to show them to a corner table by the window overlooking the sea, as dark and shiny as a vinyl.

The lights on the coast of France winked at them twenty miles away and as she sat down, Kate wondered if they could see *their* lights and how many couples over there were dating for the first time?

'This is lovely,' she said appreciatively feeling very relaxed.

'Glad you like it,' he smiled.

The waitress asked if they would like a drink.

'I would like some wine with my meal,' Kate had lived on the Continent for more than ten years and enjoyed wine with, and without food, it had been part of her life for so long that it would have been inconceivable for her not to have wine with her meal. 'But I would also like some fizzy mineral water if that's alright? But what about you, you might not like wine?'

'Yeah, no problem, a bottle of wine sounds good.'

'Would you like to see the wine menu?' the waitress suggested.

Luke knew that he would be out of his depth with a wine list, and although he had no wish to embarrass himself so early in the evening he knew that turning it down would be tantamount to admitting ignorance. Fortunately, before he could reply Kate took over the situation,'No, that won't be necessary thank you,' and asked, 'Do you have a white, house white?'

'Yes, we have a Pinot and Sauvignon?'

'Pinot will be fine thanks,' she said and Luke was relieved that the moment had passed. He wouldn't have known a Pinot from a Sauvignon and they were all impossible to pronounce!

There was no denying that he was nervous. He had dated a beautiful, intelligent, sophisticated lady who was at least eleven years his senior but looked five or six younger than him! He was in unfamiliar territory. She was unlike any other woman he had ever dated, and for the first time in his life his usual mien of confident bravado had deserted him. She was "worldly" and he had never met a woman with so much experience of life.

He had always been the one with experience, the one who oozed confidence and who awed others with his wit and wisdom, but then the others had all been younger and a holiday on the Costa Brava would have been the extent of their exposure to foreign travel, so his adventures of long distance lorry driving had kept them riveted for hours.

He was not at all at ease in this situation and he certainly wasn't going to mention lorry driving, not wishing to expose his lack of education, which she had probably guessed already from his appalling accent and lack of grammar.

He wondered why she had accepted – curiosity or boredom maybe? He might ask her later after some wine. Meanwhile, the waitress returned with the menus and poured the Pinot into his glass for tasting. Another challenge! He had seen other people doing the sniffing and swirling business and thought what prats they looked. He and his mates would always take the mickey and have a good laugh over it, so he tried to minimize the gestures and keep a straight face.

That's fine thanks,' he nodded.

They picked up the menus and started chatting about food.

'Are you having a starter?' she asked. Kate found herself eating far less than she used to and sometimes (depending on the size) a starter would be so satisfying that she couldn't eat a main course.

'Yeah, I think so, you are, aren't you?'

'Yes, something light, not too filling.....' She looked down the list, 'Ah, grilled scallops, I love *all* sea food. How about you?'

'I don't eat it as much as I used to,' he was not going to admit to not having seen a scallop; he thought it was a piece of meat covered in breadcrumbs. He continued, 'I think I'll try the stuffed mushrooms and then the steak. What are you having next?'

'I'm going to have fish again – the turbot and caper sauce, it is such a wonderfully firm fish!'

The waitress took their order, and as they sipped the wine conversation flowed more easily although, as far as Luke could see, she had been in her element since they has sat down.

She looked stunning in that red dress and each time she crossed and re-crossed her legs she exposed another few millimetres of shapely thigh.

And the shoes! The shoes were playing with his mind; from the moment that she had walked down the lane towards the car to when he followed her down the corridor in the pub, and even now seated next to her he kept having to check them out. She had allowed the back of the shoe on her crossed leg to slip off her heel and was swinging it tantalisingly from her toe.

He was fascinated by the shape and design of high-heeled shoes and how they transformed the wearer into a temptress. He knew it wasn't just him, most men were gripped in the power of high heels. They seemed to change the shape of a woman's body; the legs, the butt, the arch of the back, everything seemed to stick out more, even the tits! He would have liked a law to be passed forcing all women to wear short skirts and high heels. He was sure that the world would be a happier place to the clickety-clack of women weaving their way through the crowds on their 3 inch heels. It worked for Miss Piggy!

He was brought back from his reverie with a question, 'I was wondering why you decided to email me instead of texting?'

'I don't think you got my text messages, that's the reason I emailed you.'

'Really! What number did you use?'

Luke pulled her card from his wallet, 'The number on your card,' he read aloud, '07583 416 702.'

'Did. you say 416?'

'Yes.'

'No, it's 415 not 416.' Kate refuted.

'But it's here on your card. Look!' Even as Luke handed her the card she was convinced that he was mistaken.

'I don't think it can be. It must be 415!' But as she focused on the card she couldn't believe it; he was right!

'Oh, my god! You're right, it *is* a 6 and I've never noticed! I wonder how many I've handed out? I shall have to change it. How careless of me, I suppose it's because I've recently got a new number. *So sorry*, I'd better check everything else.' Luke watched her scrutinise the information, and was surprised that she had no need of reading glasses.

'Hmm, it seems to be alright otherwise. Thank goodness you pointed it out to me or god knows how many more I would have given out. I wonder if I've lost any business because of it?'

'Yeah, well I didn't think you were the sort of person who would totally ignore a message, that's why I tried an email.'

'Well, I'm glad you were so tenacious because this is very pleasant, and in a way it's serendipity,' it was one of her favourite words and she used it whenever she could, remembering the times she had found herself in a sticky situation that had turned around in her favour.

Luke wondered what 'serendipity' meant and wasn't even sure about 'tenacious' although he had heard it before, so he just smiled and agreed, but he made a mental note to find out later.

The rest of the evening was spent in light conversation quizzing each other about hobbies and pastimes, family backgrounds, tastes in music, work history and besides speaking five languages fluently, Kate dabbled in astrology so she revealed some surprising truths about himself. It was very superficial because he didn't know what time he was born so she couldn't find his ascendant (an all important component of a birth chart) although she did discover his age.

She was surprised to find that he was fifteen years younger than her because he had struck her as being older, especially as he had spoken about being eligible for a senior citizen rail card in the near future. She knew that he was a Chinese snake from the year that he was born and she would look into that later. She had never dated a "Snake" before and wondered what kind of people they were?

The food wasn't Michelin Star but very tasty, well presented and cooked with care and they both enjoyed the meal.

'This was a good choice,' she remarked.

'It was my son's suggestion actually; he goes out around here a lot more than I do.'

'Still a good choice.'

'Yeah.'

Three hours later Luke asked the waitress to order a taxi and paid the bill in cash, (Kate had noticed that he'd been carrying a lot of cash on the train when he'd paid for his ticket). She also noticed that he'd left a generous tip, which met with her approval because she couldn't stand a mean man.

As he helped her on with her coat she could feel his breath on the back of her neck and he, in his turn, took advantage of those few seconds to inhale her perfume, the same fragrance that had captivated him on the train. He asked her if she would like to see him again, to which she promptly agreed.

Chapter 10

Second Date

The following day, being Sunday, Kate was having a lazy morning tidying and doing laundry when she checked her phone and saw that he had left a message, 'Thank you for your company yesterday evening – I hope you enjoyed yourself as much as I did!'

Kate replied, 'Yes I did, it was lovely, thank you.'

Another message arrived almost immediately – 'Do you enjoy walking?'

'Yes, very much.'

'I was wondering, seeing as it is such a nice day, you might like to walk down to the sea front with me to pick up the car?'

Kate glanced at the clock, 'Yes, sounds good. When were you thinking?'

'In about an hour?'

An hour...an hour, she tried to get her brain into gear, would that give her enough time?

'How about an hour thirty?'

'Yeah, good I'll text when I arrive.'

'Great! See you later.'

She almost threw the phone down as she peeled off her PJs and turned on the shower. The next hour was spent tearing around the house: feeding the cat; painstakingly applying make-up; styling hair; choosing something to wear and hanging out washing.

This took longer than it would for the average person because she refused to use a tumble drier so she spent time pulling each garment into shape before carefully hanging it up so she wouldn't have to iron anything! In fact, Kate boasted to her friends and students about how little she ironed; she was proud of the fact that the iron only saw the light of day once or twice a year max! None of them could believe it because she always looked immaculate, and many had adopted her strategy and had said how grateful they were for the tip because it had saved them so much time *and* electricity.

Before she knew it, a text popped up on her screen, 'Hi! – I'm at the end of the road.'

Kate pulled the front door to behind her and saw him standing at the end of the road with dogs! He hadn't mentioned dogs!

The animals were very excited to meet her and although she wasn't a huge dog fan, she took an immediate liking to them. For a start, they weren't too big and looked intelligent, she was pretty sure she could see poodle in them and the brown reminded her of milk chocolate, the same colour as his boots – good, sturdy walking boots with a warm sheepskin lining – 'He means business,' she thought.

She was glad that she had put on sensible (but fashionable) footwear because she got the idea that he took walking seriously.

When the dogs had calmed down a bit they crossed the main road in the direction of the sea front. Kate noticed that there were no leads, he wasn't even carrying one but the dogs obediently crossed when told and not before, she was impressed.

'I thought we'd go the long way around if that's alright?' He looked down at her shoes and was relieved to see that she was not wearing heels.

'Yes, I'm up for the exercise – we'd better make the most of this weather, there won't be many more days like this,'she agreed enthusiastically.

Kate enjoyed walking on her own and did a lot of it. She would stick in her earphones and learn (or practise) a language; it didn't worry her when people stared as she repeated phrases in Chinese or Greek out loud. She didn't care – she wasn't hurting anyone and she hadn't been arrested! And she didn't have to try to keep up with anyone. Her ex had had long legs and always walked faster than her; walking with him had been more like a marathon than pleasure!

She could see that this was going to be a totally different experience. For a start, Luke's legs were shorter and was not in a hurry.

When they reached the lower promenade Kate leant against the railing to take in the scene.

There was a light breeze but the sea was calm and families were out on the exposed rocks hunting for signs of life. Occasionally she could squeals of childish excitement when something scuttled across a pool.

Three little girls were being chased along the beach by a slightly older boy swinging a long string of shiny, black seaweed around above his head in a threatening manner. They were screaming and calling out, 'Help! Mum! Dad! Gareth has got some slimy stuff – tell him to stop!'

Their parents, some distance away on the adjacent beach, shouted out to him but it had no effect whatsoever, and Kate could see from the expression on his face that he was enjoying himself far too much to relinquish the sense of power the seaweed had given him..

'Strange' she thought, 'how even at that age they enjoy the power thing.'

Fascinated, she had to stop to see the outcome of the pursuit remembering all the times that her sister had chased her, and recalling the fear that she might trip and be thrashed with the cold, wet strip of kelp. She was rooting for the girls to escape.

'I hope they get away,' she said out loud and heard Luke chuckle next to her.

Did he think she was silly to get involved?

'Scatter!' the tallest one shouted.

Suddenly, they split and ran in different directions, and momentarily the boy vacillated wondering which one would be the easiest prey, just like a lion chasing gazelles.

He went for the middle one, being slightly heavier than the other two, she was the most out of breath and losing momentum. The others were ordering him to stop – no way! He was gaining ground when it happened ... she tripped!

'Aarr!' he let out a sound like a pirate brandishing his cutlass and brought the nasty, rubbery stuff down onto the girl with such delight, who was trying to protect herself with her hands over her face. She had curled up into a ball, knees to chest crying out, 'Not on my face Gareth. Not on my face!' By now there were tears and *all* the girls were crying.

Luke heard Kate muttering under her breath, 'Horrid little boy, how spiteful!'

'Hey! They're only playing – kids!'

Kate didn't see it as play. She saw a bully taking advantage of a vulnerable little girl and she wanted to go down there, grab the stuff from him and tell him what she thought. Or better still, give him some of his own treatment and see how he enjoyed it! She was considering shouting from where she stood, but fortunately the parents had homed in on the situation and had pulled him away. The other two girls clung to Dad's trousers in tears speaking at the same time through their sobs, while Mum comforted the one on the ground who refused to move until Gareth was ordered to take the seaweed down to the water's edge and throw it out to sea. He took his time to rejoin the group knowing that now he would be in the doghouse for the rest of the afternoon, but he thought it had been worth it.

Eventually, after a lot of consoling and reassuring, and with the promise of ice cream, the little group made their way slowly up the beach towards the cafeteria with Gareth keeping his distance; no ice cream for him, but he didn't care.

'Well, that's the drama over!' declared Luke, and as they resumed their walk Kate could hear the girls' pleas over her shoulder.

'But he *will* be punished, won't he Daddy?'

'He won't be allowed to use the Ipad this week, will he?'

'Or the Nintendo?'

'Will he still be allowed to go to Sean's party?'

The girls were full of ideas for chastisement, and she smiled to herself with some satisfaction knowing that he was outnumbered three to one and they were not going to let him get away with it.

Throughout the whole incident the dogs had behaved impeccably, they had barked a couple of times with indignation, as they obviously understood right from wrong, and which only made her warm to them all the more. In fact, she felt herself changing her mind about dogs, which surprised her, as she had always been a 'cat' person and she loved the way they kept looking over their shoulders to make sure that Luke was still there.

The time passed remarkably fast as there were so many people out making the most of the wonderful autumn sunshine, and people watching was another of Kate's favourite pastimes.

The car was where he had parked it the previous night, and hadn't been vandalized or incurred any fines. After settling the dogs in the back, it took Luke about three minutes to reach Kate's house.

'Do you mind if I don't ask you in?'

'No, it's good. I have to get back anyway.'

'I've really enjoyed this afternoon, thank you,' she smiled; that smile had captivated him from the start.

'Yeah me too. Are you free anytime tomorrow?'

'Well, I always try to get out for some fresh air in the middle of the day, so I walk down to the Polish café for a light lunch. It gets me out of the house and means that I get some exercise.'

'OK. Would you like to meet for lunch?'

She didn't take long to answer, 'Yes, I would like that.'

'Right, I'll meet you outside the chemist next to Smiths?'

'Sounds good,' she replied.

Once inside, she flopped onto the sofa and Cat immediately jumped up beside her for attention. He always welcomed her home if she spent any length of time out, and Kate appreciated the acknowledgement if only from a cat! So, while he purred loudly, Kate contemplated the last 24 hours and felt strangely optimistic about their lunch date.

Chapter 11

Midday Rendezvous

It was another crisp, sparkling, autumnal day when Kate crossed the main road in front of W. H. Smith and spotted Luke with his hands in his pockets, she only ever saw older men wearing gloves, she supposed it had something to do with street cred.

'Hello!'

'Hello! How are you? Where are the dogs?'

'A lot of places won't take dogs; it just makes life complicated.'

'Well I was very impressed with them yesterday.'

'Who thought up their names. Did you call one of them cocoa after the drink because of his colour?'

'Kinda, spelt different though.'

'What? like the clown?'

'I don't know about no clown?'

Kate realized that she was showing her age. Every Christmas her parents would take her and her sister to Bertram Mills Circus in London and there was always a clown called Koko; he was very famous when she was a child, so she didn't pursue the subject.

'Did you get back in time to watch the motor racing yesterday?'

'Yeah, ta.'

She was quite hungry now as she had a really bad habit of skipping breakfast and would get so wrapped up in what she was doing that she would forget to eat, so she was delighted to find no queue when they walked into the café.

The girls behind the counter knew her order before she opened her mouth.

'Soup with two slices of wholemeal toast?' one of them said. Kate smiled and nodded.

Kate turned to Luke, 'What are you having?' He was still studying the boards on the wall behind the counter.

'I think I'll have a panini with ham and salad please.'

'Would you like any dressing on that?' the same girl asked.

'Yeah, just a little ta.'

They sat down by the window, steamed up with condensation, and watched as blurry images of people went about their business.

The panini were freshly prepared to order so her soup arrived first as there was always a huge pot simmering away, and as she sipped her soup he asked about her work.

He knew that she spoke five languages because they were listed on her business card.

'Are you fluent in all those languages on your card?' he asked her, 'Silly question; I suppose you must be if you teach them?'

'Yes.'

'That's impressive.' He said with genuine admiration.

Kate always enjoyed a compliment, but she didn't feel as though she really deserved it as acquiring her languages had been interesting and fun.

'A lot of people say that, but it's not so hard if you live there and immerse yourself – you *have to* pick it up,' she said modestly.

'Yeah but you must have a gift to be able to pick up *five* just like that! Didn't you do languages at school?'

'We did French but we never learnt to speak a word! In fact, I failed my exam, I didn't have a clue what they asked me in my speaking exam, and I hated the fact that none of us could communicate in the language. The only advantage I had when I arrived in France was that I knew all my irregular verbs because we were made to recite them every lesson!'

'But how did you learn the grammar? Did you get lessons in the country?'

'No, I just picked it up, by ear. I can't explain why I found it so easy but I tried only to mix with native speakers and found a boyfriend who didn't speak any English at all so I learned to communicate quickly. Once I became fairly fluent I started looking into the structure of the language but for some reason that always came later. Someone told me that it was because I was musical, and that people with a musical ear had a natural aptitude for languages.'

'Yeah, well, I think it's a gift and I'm pretty impressed.'

Kate shrugged as though it was of no consequence, but she took it as a compliment and it made her feel good, after eleven years bereft of any praise or appreciation from the previous oaf in her life.

'The most amazing thing is how much I have learnt about my own language, stuff they never taught me at school; either that or I wasn't listening,' she added with an impish grin.

Ah, that smile again, he thought, it completely won him over, she was no longer the teacher but the fun-loving globetrotter. It invited trouble. He wasn't surprised when she talked about boyfriends (in the plural); he imagined there had been more than a few and wondered how he was going to measure up to them, and what on earth she was doing there – with *him*?

They met the next day, and the next; in fact they met for lunch every day that week and took two long walks with the dogs at the weekend. Luke worked nights mostly, so he was always available and didn't seem to need much sleep.

He had the sort of job her boys would have loved, driving deluxe cars. He delivered luxury cars (for hire) to exclusive clients, often the rich and famous. And picked them up when they had finished with them. Occasionally he had to go abroad, but he enjoyed working at night as there was less traffic on the roads, and it left the day free for him to pursue his passion for rollerblading. A friend of his owned the company so things were pretty flexible.

Kate wasn't tiring of his company, nor he of hers, and they texted each other continually when not in each other's company.

When she had told him how much she hated cooking he immediately volunteered to make her something special, extending an invitation to the Tuesday evening after her salsa class. Apparently, he enjoyed it! Now Kate was in admiration – a man who loved cooking, was it possible?

Tuesday came around very quickly and she took extra care getting ready. She'd found a slim fitting mini dress in cream lace in a charity shop; it was the perfect excuse to wear it. A couple of people at salsa commented on how good she looked, so she was fairly confident that it would have the desired effect on Luke.

The front door bell set the dogs off and it only took Luke seconds to answer. He was on the ground floor so Koko came bouncing out of the flat door first to greet her with Kiki right behind him, tail wagging profusely. Luke managed to get in between them and kiss her. They had exchanged a few kisses after lunch – nothing deep – just superficial signs of affection, which was enough for Kate as she wanted to take this one slowly. She had been burnt too often in the past and had no intention of getting emotionally (or physically) involved too quickly.

Once the dogs had calmed down and they were all inside he closed the flat door and led her through into the living room.

The first thing she noticed was the fake coal fire roaring away in the open fireplace, the second was the distinct lack of furniture, nothing like her place, Kate had crammed every possible space of her house with something – the walls were covered in pictures (real or otherwise) and there were books everywhere, of course! Talk about a contrast, she thought.

An enormous white, leather L-shaped sofa took up most of the room.

'Do you want to take your coat off?'

Kate looked around for somewhere to hang it, and ended up throwing it on the sofa.

'Love the dress!' He said approvingly, 'Did you wear that to salsa?'

'Yes.' Did he think she had changed just for him?

'Cor! I bet you drove them crazy!' Kate was pleased with the reaction.

'Come and join me in the kitchen for a minute – I'm just finishing off,' he suggested, leading the way.

'Hmm, smells wonderful!' she was looking forward to it now.

'It's goulash. I hope you like it?'

'Yes, love it. My grandmother had a hotel in London and the chef was Hungarian so I grew up with it.'

'I'm impressed again, most people have never heard of it and certainly wouldn't know that it was Hungarian.'

It was a small, clean but practical kitchen. Kate wondered where the bedroom was.

'Do you like dumplings?' he asked, ladle poised at the ready.

'I love them, but what size are they?' Luke dipped the ladle into the cauldron of bubbling mixture and fished out a beautiful, puffy dumpling about the size of a golf ball.

'Oh, I shall have to have two of those,' she said eagerly.

He took two deep dishes from the cupboard and carefully ladled out the rich brown mixture, topped with a couple of dumplings.

'Do you mind taking the glasses and the wine?' he gestured towards a bottle of rosé, 'We're eating in the living room – I don't use the dining room much because it's quite large and not very warm. '

'No problem, that's fine by me,' she said following him through.

They sat on the sofa and with plates on laps, sipped rose, ate and chatted, while Koko and Kiki curled up together on a rug by the fire.

When they had both wiped their plates clean with chunks of baguette he offered her seconds.

'I'd love to because it was delicious, but I'm afraid I don't have the space.'

'But I can refill your glass?'

'Yes please,' and she lifted her glass towards the bottle.

'I'm sorry but there's no desert.'

'That's fine, I don't have a sweet tooth and hardly ever eat one.'

'Yeah you mentioned it at the restaurant. Shall we see what's on?' He reached over for the remote and scanned through the channels, 'That's a good film – have you seen it?'

'Which one?'

'Angels and Demons.'

'No I haven't. Isn't it a Dan Brown book?'

'Yeah, have you read it?'

'No, but I should imagine it's good.'

'Well it makes a bloody good film!'

'You've seen it then?'

'Yeah.'

'If you've already seen it, won't you be bored?'

'No, it's definitely worth seeing again, besides it's all filmed in Rome so you'll probably recognize lots of it.' Kate had talked about the time she'd spent in Italy and evidently he had been listening!

'OK, as long as you don't mind?'

As he switched on the names of the main protagonists were still showing on the screen, so she knew they hadn't missed anything.

The next two hours were spent in virtual silence apart from the occasional interjection, as Kate was transfixed to the screen.

When the credits rolled up she agreed that it had definitely been worth the watch and wanted to sound him out.

She had been told by numerous friends and ex boyfriends how critical she was, but she just couldn't help herself.

She marvelled at how casting directors had to know absolutely every actor ever born! Some actors were so perfect for the roles – take Elizabeth Taylor as Cleopatra, or Sylvester Stallone as Rocky and the unforgettable Johnny Depp as Captain Jack Sparrow. And she couldn't imagine anyone else taking Hugh Grant's role as Charles in Four Weddings and a funeral. There were *so many* films that had been made by the choice of actors. And she loved the special effects enhanced by a new digital age, Avatar being one of the most memorable.

Between them they picked it apart, mostly agreeing but enjoying to disagree. Kate admired the validity of his criticism and was impressed by his attention to detail, maybe it was because it was his second viewing but he had noticed things that had completely escaped her. Unusual for a man, she thought.

They finished the bottle of wine and snuggled on the sofa in front of the fake fire. Kate felt warm and safe as Luke's arms encircled her and he whispered in her ear '*I really* like you, I want to look after you – treat you like a princess.' Kate squeezed his hand in response, she was surprised by how much his words affected her, a familiar queasiness inside reminded her how easily she could be inveigled and didn't want to promise anything in return, besides, she had heard *so many* promises from *so many* men in her life that she was loathe to believe anything they said any more. But she was loving the thought.

They spooned on the wide, leather sofa, Luke holding her close as they watched Q.I. She was totally relaxed and didn't feel in the slightest bit threatened as he had made no moves on her, and although she didn't want to leave she knew she had work to prepare for the next morning so she made noises about leaving.

Before she had time to get up he turned her face towards his and kissed her gently on the lips. Kate responded turning the rest of her body in towards him and she wanted to stay; he didn't smother her like most men, letting her breathe and when he brushed her lips lightly with his she moved in for more. Suddenly, the dogs were awake and barking loudly and Kate heard the key turning in the flat door.

'My son!' Luke said with a flicker of alarm in his voice.

They quickly pulled apart and tried to resume an air of composure, sitting upright with a few inches of respectability between each other.

The living room door opened and an attractive face peeped around it, 'Hi! Alright if I come in?'

'Yeah, come on in Josh, I'd like you to meet Kate,' and as Luke jumped up Kate extended her hand over the back of the sofa.

'Pleased to meet you, Dad's mentioned your name, it's nice to put a face to it. Look, I don't want to disturb your evening so....'

'Na, you're not disturbing nothing, Kate was just about to leave.'

'Yes, your dad's right, I was literally about to put on my coat,' she added as she stood up and reached for her coat.

'Hey, don't leave on account of me – I'm going to bed.'

'No, really, I have stuff to prepare before tomorrow, and it's getting late if I want to get it done,' she said reassuringly.

As Luke helped her on with her coat Koko and Kiki jumped up anticipating action, so she had to make a bit of a fuss of them. They wriggled with pleasure and followed her out in the hope of more, stretching their heads as high as they could, because jumping up was forbidden.

'Are you sure you're alright to drive home? I could call a cab?'

'No, I'm fine. I know I'm probably over the limit but I've eaten and I feel fine. What is it – two minutes? And there's hardly anyone on the streets at this hour.'

'You sure?'

'Absolutely. Please, don't worry, I'll text you as soon as I get in'

Before she stepped off the threshold he pulled her towards him, and as he kissed her she could feel the emotion ripple through her body leaving her weak in the knees.

'Thank you for coming over, I've really enjoyed this evening,' he said almost in a whisper.

'Thank *you*,' she replied emphatically, 'so have *I*, and I thoroughly enjoyed the meal.' She could smell the cologne on his neck.

'We must do it again, soon?' he said in the form of a question come invitation.

'That would be lovely,' she said looking into the grey-blue of his eyes. He kissed her once more.

'Drive carefully!'

'I will!' she replied sliding into the car.

He waited by the front door with the dogs at his side until she pulled away.

As soon as she was inside and had bolted the door behind her she sent a text: 'Back home – no problem xxx' adding a smiley face. A message came straight back, 'Good (forgot to ask) Still OK for lunch tomorrow? xxx'

'Yes, and thank you for a lovely evening xxx'

'My pleasure – any time, as I said, I love to cook xxx'

She went straight through to the classroom, and as she switched on the light Cat got up, stretched and greeted her.

'Hi Cat!' Kate tickled her under the chin and she followed her around the table hoping for more, but Kate wanted to prepare her work for the next day and didn't have time to fuss over her so she jumped down in search of food.

Once the copier had warmed up she set to copying the relevant material for the next day. She hated having to rush in the morning and slept better knowing that everything was ready.

As she stood there, staring at a Jack Vettriano print of the Singing Butler on the wall above the copier, she wondered what would have happened if Josh hadn't turned up; how far would they have gone? She certainly hadn't been thinking of putting on her coat.

She switched on the television to distract herself and landed in the middle of Captain Corelli's Mandarin. More perfect casting she thought; she couldn't imagine any other faces in place of – Nicolas Cage, Penelope Cruz or John Hurt! She'd seen it *so* many times that she didn't have to focus – just let it run in the background; she'd be finished soon anyway and as it was already past midnight she didn't want to get involved in a lengthy feature film that she hadn't seen before.

Chapter 12

Lunch and Lust

'I'm sorry about Josh coming back last night, he knew you were coming round so he'd arranged to go out.' Luke said apologetically but with under tones of regret as he reached across the table for her hand.

'Hey, it was nearly midnight, how was he to know? Anyway, it was nice to meet him and who knows what would have happened if he hadn't come back?'

'Yeah,' he added wistfully recalling the moment; he could have stayed on that sofa all night rather than break the spell.

They both knew that they were ready to change to a higher gear in the relationship, however, there were logistical problems:

One of Kate's boys was still taking advantage of a free ride, 'I'd ask you back to my place but I don't really want my boy to know about us yet; not until I am sure where it's going.'

'Fair enough, I understand. I have a problem my end too, I started major work on my bedroom just after we met and it's going to take another couple of weeks to sort out.'

Kate laughed, 'Well, we'll just have to be patient, won't we?'

'It's going to be hard because I meant what I said last night. I haven't been interested in anyone for years; I haven't wanted to be. You're the best thing that's happened to me for ages.'

Kate wasn't sure how to respond because he sounded genuinely sincere and she didn't want to discourage him.

Past experience had taught her that men who declared their feelings and intentions so early in a relationship were usually shallow, and she couldn't reciprocate because although she was enjoying the 'affair' she was not prepared to commit herself.

She was flattered and was loving the attention, because the last 'pig' she had wasted *eleven years* on had shown more love and care to his dog than he ever had to her. He had been her last effort, depleting her of all energy and emotional resources to such an extent that she hadn't even looked at another man never mind talk to one!

'I'm very flattered and I really like you. I enjoy your company too, and I can't remember the last time that I have felt so alive, but I am not sure about my feelings – I have a lot of past history to deal with and I am going to need time before I can entrust you with my emotions,' Kate searched his face for clues.

'Sure. No problem. We've all got history, me included. Don't worry, I can wait; it's meant to be, it will give us time to get to know each other better. It doesn't bother me. It's all good.'

She found his faith heartening and was relieved that her lack of it hadn't disappointed him. Their little chat had cleared the air, and as they ate lunch he talked about his plans for Christmas. They had both made arrangements weeks ago so they already knew that it would be spent apart, but he wanted them to see each other as much as possible over the holiday period, and so did she.

There were less than three weeks left and although Kate had been buying bits and pieces for her boys she still had a lot to think about; she hadn't even written her foreign cards, in fact everything had gone on hold since her first date with Luke! He had become all consuming! It had been insidious, she hadn't noticed it happening because she had been so happy, and with her best friend and playmate away on holiday, she had filled her absence with his presence. She hadn't stopped dancing but she had made an effort to meet up with Luke whenever she could, which meant every spare moment, so non-urgent obligations had been shelved.

Now she found herself panicking slightly knowing that she didn't want to give any of it up but at the same time wondering how she would cope. He had suddenly become part of her life and she didn't want it to change.

Chapter 13

Megan's Return

Megan arrived home on the Sunday (almost three weeks after that momentous train journey) and she texted Kate as soon as she touched down.

'Hi! How's everything? xxx'

'Yes, all good thanks. You? Xxx'

'Yes, glad to be back xxx'

'Good holiday? Xxx'

'Yes thanks, but looking forward to getting back to the dancing etc xxx'

'OK. Speak soon xxx' Kate would ring her later from the land line as she was on "Pay as You Go" and saved her talk time for essential calls. She hadn't thought it appropriate to tell Megan about Luke, she would wait until they were together – the following evening at Rock 'n Roll.

They were having a drink at the pub afterwards, and Kate let Megan tell her all about the holiday, which hadn't been such a tremendous success as she had spent most of her time babysitting.

'You know it's quite dangerous to go away and leave me on my own,' Kate said thinking it was a good way to broach the subject.

'Oh yes, why would that be?'

'Well I met a guy.'

Megan looked at her to see if she was joking – clearly she wasn't, 'Where? How?' she asked requiring more information.

'On a train.'

'On a train! But you never go on trains!' Megan exclaimed in disbelief.

'I know, but I did, just after you left,' and she went on to describe the unusual turn of events that had taken place up to that moment. Megan didn't said a word throughout; she just sat there looking into her drink. Kate wanted her friend to be happy for her but all Megan could see were obstacles; she didn't want to share her, not now they had patched things up and were enjoying each other's company again so much.

'Damn!' she thought, wishing that she hadn't gone away, 'But then Kate would probably still have gone up to London by train that day, so maybe it was fate.'

'Hey, look! It isn't going to change anything between us, I'm here aren't I? He doesn't want me to give up any of my classes. He likes me dancing, singing and drawing, honestly Megan he's so tolerant – not at all clingy or demanding. We haven't even been to bed yet!' Kate tried to lighten the mood, 'Come on, let's play a couple games of football.'

There was a football table in a screened off corner of the lounge and they always had a few games. Unlike Kate, Megan was very competitive so she enjoyed the battles spinning little wooden men around on metal poles in an attempt to shoot a small, hard ball into a goal at the other end of the table. Kate too loved the game; it was such simple unadulterated fun! There was no intellect required – it was just a test of reflexes embellished with aggression.

She usually thrashed Megan but that evening she decided to let a couple through to make up for the news about Luke. It was weird how she felt guilty, almost as though she had betrayed Megan in some way. They weren't lovers! They were just good friends, but Kate's conscience wouldn't leave her alone so she was trying extra hard to lift her friend's spirits.

As they walked back to their table Megan's demeanour had changed, she was laughing and joking and the rest of the evening was spent on the quiz machine which paid out enough money to cover their drinks, so when Megan dropped Kate off they were both on a high and looking forward to resuming their lives in pursuit of fun and entertainment.

The only adjustment made, was that Kate wanted to go and see Luke straight after their Zumba class as that had become the arrangement during Megan's absence, and if she resented it, she concealed her disapproval.

Kate was finding it hard to suppress her enthusiasm for her new–found romance and it had altered her persona. People who didn't know her that well (at the classes) had noticed a difference but couldn't quite put their finger on it. She had always been sociable and would put on a good front even when she woke with depression, she would pretend, put on an act, sometimes going over the top so much with the "bubbly and bouncy" that people would ask her what she was on.

Recently though, she seemed to have even more energy and passion for life than before, but at the same time she had adopted a glow of serene contentment similar to that of an expectant mother, although that would have been impossible for Kate given her age.

Megan had noticed it too and felt more than a pang of jealousy, she felt that she was losing her friend to an unknown source and didn't know how to stop it. Kate had told her about how they hadn't been able to sleep together because of the bedroom situation and how D-night was drawing nigh and how the anticipation was killing her.

In fact, Megan was finding it difficult to stop herself saying something malicious as Kate went on and on about Luke; Luke this and Luke that. What he did and how he did it better than anyone else; what he said and how he said it more romantically than anyone else; how he had better taste than anyone she had ever known (and that was like half the world, if the stories of her encounters were to be believed!).

He was "witty, intelligent, athletic, good-looking, talented......."

'Good God!' Megan thought, 'Is there an adjective she hasn't used!' She tried to switch off when Kate started a monologue of all his attributes, as it left her feeling dejected and unappreciated.

He and Kate had been meeting every day for lunch and arranging long walks with the dogs at the weekends, weather permitting, but they were both counting down the days to when the bedroom would be ready, and they could take their relationship to another level.

At the moment they were doing an exceptional job of controlling their passion; of course they held hands and kissed, and a couple of times events nearly went the whole way on the sofa, but it was unrequited passion and Kate was hoping for the romance of a full blown love affair with all the trimmings; trusting it went well on the night.

Chapter 14

D-night

That night finally arrived. Luke picked her up and they drove to a small restaurant overlooking the fishing harbour. It was one of Kate's favourites because of the view it offered: boats rhythmically swaying on the high tide, their lights reflecting the spreading ripples like quicksilver

He had booked a table at the window but within the warmth of the fireplace.

When the waitress appeared, Luke knew to order a white wine spritzer with soda and no ice in a tall glass for Kate, and a Budweiser for himself, although he rarely touched alcohol. He was as nervous as hell and hoped it didn't show. When he looked across the table at Kate she seemed completely composed and he felt fluttering in his belly as he watched her sip her spritzer in the glow of a candle.

It took very little time to order as there were only two other couples dining, and the menu was uncomplicated.

Kate was thoroughly enjoying the homemade duck and orange pâté, savouring every mouthful, but she couldn't help notice the speed at which Luke was consuming his whitebait, barely taking a breath between each tiny fish and clearing his plate before Kate had started on her second piece of toast.

'Are you alright?' she was concerned as he normally took his time to eat.

'Yeah, just hungry, that's all. Bin paintin', laying carpet and shiftin' furniture all day and forgot to eat,' he smiled, 'Just wanted it all to be perfect.'

'I'm sorry.'

'Hey, it's not your fault!'

'No, I mean, I'm sorry you had to work all day, and that you haven't eaten.'

'Don't worry, I'll be fine as soon as I've had some food.'

When the waitress had removed the plates, they gazed through the leaded windows at the ever-changing reflections of the lights bobbing on the surface of the water, and had it not been for the row of shiny (mostly new) cars parked outside, the scene was timeless.

Her parents could well have been sitting there sixty years previously admiring the exact same scene. It looked unchanged – even more so in the dark.

Kate had good memories of days on the sands, digging enormous holes that were as deep as she was tall, and then watching them fill with water as the tide came in. They (her cousin and sister) would build boats that they could sit in and pretend to navigate, and castles, elaborate ones with turrets, ramparts, a moat and a drawbridge. They were Halcyon days and a part of her childhood she wanted to remember with warmth.

She had nothing against change per se, and she understood the necessity for it, but some of the monstrosities that had sprung up in place of the beautiful Georgian and Victorian buildings had made her want to cry.

There had been a period when money had influenced the judgement of the planning committee, and corruption was rife. Most of it had happened when she was abroad which made it all the more striking because when she returned for a holiday, glass, concrete and steel structures had replaced familiar red-brick classical facades. The local inhabitants hadn't notice it so much, or if they had, they had been powerless to do anything about it. Kate would hear the rumours each time she returned about builders bribing council officials and everyone being in everyone's pocket.

She had nothing against "modern" and admired some of the ultra-modern designs that had transformed the London skyline, however she would have preferred to find her home town untouched by new-fangled ideas.

The waitress reappeared with the main course and Luke attacked that with the same gusto as the whitebait, Kate had never seen him devour his food with such voracity and asked him again if he was alright. This time, even though he said he was hungry, he didn't finish the dish and as he laid down his knife and fork Kate had barely started on her fish.

He looked uncomfortable and began fidgeting. Kate enquired again.

'I've got a stomach ache – must have been the sauce,' he said in a subdued tone.

'I think you may have eaten a little quickly,' she suggested.

'Maybe. Do you mind if we leave, I don't feel good at all.'

'No. Of course not,' now she was concerned, as they had eaten several meals together and she had never seen any adverse reactions.

'One of the fish must have been off,' he said miserably

'I don't think so. You wouldn't have reacted so quickly. I'm pretty sure you ate too quickly on an empty stomach. At least that's my theory.'

'Yeah, and the nerves,' he was annoyed with himself, 'I'll be alright if we can get out of here,' there was a sense of urgency in his voice.

He didn't wait for the waitress to bring the bill but handed his wallet to Kate saying he needed some fresh air and would wait outside.

As Kate had barely touched her fish, she asked for a doggy bag (in this case a pussy bag) and paid as quickly as possible, leaving a decent tip.

Through the window, she could see him almost bent double leaning against the car, but when she joined him he held open the door on her side and seemed fine to drive, however she couldn't be sure if he was concealing the pain.

'Are you feeling a bit better?' she asked still concerned.

'Not really,' he replied under duress.

As soon as they got inside the dogs bounced around with joy but Luke could only throw himself prostrate on the sofa in agony, now he was actually groaning and grasping his stomach with both hands!

'What can I do?' she asked feeling completely inadequate.

'Nothing. It'll pass – just give me a minute.'

'It must be a form of indigestion. I have some Gaviscon at home. I'll go and get it – I'll only be a second. Can I take your car?'

'Yeah, keys are in my jacket pocket.'

Kate took the keys and left. She hadn't driven Luke's car before so had to search for the light switch. It was a lot smaller than hers but quite powerful and Kate was home in minutes. She tore upstairs to her bedroom because she remembered putting a small bottle of Gaviscon in the bedside cabinet, (remnants of a previous boyfriend who had permanent indigestion.) She didn't check the date on the label because it was going to have to do.

When she re-entered Luke's flat he hadn't moved from the sofa and the dogs were lying nearby on the floor with what Kate interpreted as a worried expression.

'I found it!' she announced with a sense of achievement, 'Here, take a couple of gulps from the bottle, it's brilliant stuff, I've seen it work in minutes!' she said convincingly.

He did as he was told, nothing could make it worse he thought to himself, 'Yuck! Ba! That's disgusting!' he groaned.

'Never mind, just give it a few minutes to work. Lie down again!' she ordered.

He fell back again obediently with a groan while Kate patiently sat at the other end waiting for the magic to take effect. As he lay there writhing in pain she wondered why all the little firemen (as seen on tele with their hoses squirting out white, soothing liquid) weren't doing a better job of putting out the fire? After all, they did advertise *instant* relief!?

This was *not* how she had imagined their first night together; she enjoyed a game of doctors and nurses, but not the real thing!

Suddenly he rolled off the sofa, got to his feet and staggered out of the room muttering, 'Back in a minute,' leaving Kate, Koko and Kiki looking quizzically at the closing door.

Kate assumed that Luke had headed for the bathroom and thought it best to leave him in peace, she just prayed that the Gaviscon would do its job and that the night she had so been looking forward to was not completely written off.

She grabbed the remote and switched on the television, Johnny Depp and Daniel Radcliffe were being interviewed on a sofa – she watched but wasn't really listening.

After what seemed like an age, he reappeared looking a little worse for wear, but standing upright and apparently no longer in pain!

'Better?' enquired Kate.

'I think so. I just got rid of the dinner down the toilet. It must have been that stuff you gave me.'

'Not exactly what is advertised,' she thought, 'but a result.'

'I still think it was something I ate. I don't think I'll go back there again.'

Kate felt a tinge of disappointment as it was one of her favourite restaurants, 'Personally, I think it was the way you rushed your food, especially on an empty stomach.'

'Yeah, could've been, anyway it was a bit of a waste, it's all down the karzi now.'

'But you're feeling better?'

'Yeah, definitely, just feel like someone's punched me in the stomach!'

'We don't have to do this tonight if you don't feel up to it?'

'Hey, I've been waiting three and a half weeks for this. I may not be firing on all cylinders but I'm up for it if you are?'

'Me? Absolutely! After all the suspense and anticipation why wouldn't I be?'

Feeling as he was, he would not have felt totally dejected had she said 'no' giving him the opportunity to recover before having to prove himself as a lover. However, not wanting to completely ruin the evening he would have to 'man-up' and do his best as he didn't want to disappoint her, and sickness aside he still desired her.

'Well, as long as you're not expecting too much.....'

'No, we don't have to do anything if you don't feel like it – we could just spend the night together and see how you feel in the morning,' Kate felt this was a sensible solution and one that wouldn't put him under any pressure, although she was sure that once in bed together there would be no holding back. Her thoughts were confirmed seconds later ....

'Hon, if you're in my bed I won't be able to keep my hands off you!'

That's exactly what she had planned, she wasn't going anywhere, 'Good, that's settled then!' she said decisively.

They both got up and made their way downstairs. She was amused to see that he had hung a purple ribbon across the door, frame to frame, and as he passed her a pair of scissors he said, 'Please do the honours.'

'Woo, I've never been asked to open anything before,' Kate moved forward and with a single snip the ribbon gently floated away, 'I now declare this bedroom open and fit for purpose,' she giggled as Luke reached around her and opened the door, 'Tarah!' he exclaimed in the absence of a fanfare.

He smiled allowing her access, and as she stepped forward fresh paint filled her nostrils. She had tried to envisage what it would look like, but hadn't been able to settle on a colour scheme.

Now though, she could see how the pale, charcoal grey and lilac swathed in the soft glow from a tall corner lamp worked perfectly. He had left the lamp on to create a welcoming effect. She admired his taste, noting how the shade of lilac in the curtains blended with that of the duvet cover. She most definitely approved.

'You've done a superb job – I love it!' she said in a laudatory fashion.

'I'm glad you think so,' he was pleased with the appraisal, it meant a lot to him to impress her.

'Do you want to use the bathroom or shall I go first?' She asked almost formally.

'No, you go ahead, I've already had a spell in there,' he smiled.

'Thanks, I won't be long.' She picked out what she thought she would need from her bag and disappeared to the bathroom – white-tiled, clean and practical.

After having showered, she wrapped herself in her crimson, silk kimono, and quietly let herself back into the bedroom, slipping into the bed beside him.

'Hmm, it's lovely and toasty in here,' she whispered snuggling up to him.

'Yeah, I switched on the duvet.'

'Switched on the duvet?' she repeated as a question.

'Yeah, it's heated, I prefer it to an electric blanket.'

'I agree, it's a wonderful idea; I didn't even know they existed.'

He leaned over and kissed her, not passionately but gently, reassuringly.

She loved his kisses which was unusual, because Kate had

always considered kissing a waste of time, but there was something intangible about the way Luke kissed, arousing her like no one else.

Still under his spell she felt his hand reach around her waist pulling her in closer.

At last she could run her hands all over his body, although slight in stature he was sinuous and firm; not an ounce of unwanted fat anywhere, unlike the bunch of middle-aged blokes she'd dated in the past. They had all let themselves go – all loose and flabby as though a beer belly was their right! This was like an early Christmas present.

It crossed her mind that his experience might not be so satisfying.

Even though she knew she looked good in clothes and could still wear figure-hugging gear with confidence, there were parts of her body that she would no longer expose in public and her bikini days were long gone!

Dancing toned certain areas, but not all, and because she had what was considered to be an 'ample bosom'; great when supported by a good bra but she had stopped looking in the mirror naked a long time ago. She tried to block her physical inadequacies from the magic of the moment. If she was to enjoy the night she would have to push all doubts to the back of her mind and relax.

She needn't have worried when she felt a hand on her shoulder gently waking her.

'I've made you a cup of tea. It's here on the floor.'

Kate managed a sleepy, 'Lovely, thank you.' Slowly, she was engaging her brain, lack of sleep was making her very sluggish. She turned over, and with the realization of where she was, she felt comfortable and safe.

He slipped back into his side of the bed with his own cup and she could hear him taking thirsty gulps. She reached over her side of the bed (eyes half-closed) and groped for her own mug and managed to take a couple of sips without sitting up and without dribbling, 'Aah, that's *so good*,' she said appreciatively. She couldn't remember the last time anyone had brought her a cup of tea in bed – pure luxury!

She was trying to recollect the events of the evening/night. Had it been two or three times?

Did it really matter? She just knew that she felt *wonderful*, tired but wonderful!

Luke put his cup on the floor next to him, and then by flipping his body a full one hundred and eighty degrees so that he was on top of her, he looked straight down into her eyes.

There was no mistaking what he wanted and no way she could resist, so the morning was christened with another climax!

It was Saturday and, as neither of them had anything of any urgency to do, they slept in till eight o'clock which was late by both their standards.

Luke was first up, 'What do you want for breakfast?' he asked, in nothing but an apron and boxers.

'Breakfast!' Kate didn't usually do breakfast, she was never hungry enough, or just so busy that she would forget, 'Wow, I *am* being spoilt. I don't know – what do you have?'

'We have everything, whatever madam desires,' he said like the maître d' of a posh West End hotel. 'We have a choice of cereals,' and he reeled off the names of several famous brands. 'However, if madam would prefer a Continental breakfast we have plenty of toast, butter and jam. But if madam is exceptionally hungry we can offer her the full English without sausages, mushrooms or tomatoes.

'Hmm, the full English sounds nice.'

'Certainly, and how would madam like her eggs?' keeping up the performance.

'Fried, if that is not too much trouble?'

'No trouble at all madam and how would that be? Sunny side up, easy over ...?' he continued with a long list of American expressions for eggs that Kate had heard of but never understood.

'Madam prefers a squidgy yellow, hard white and no slime,' she said with a giggle.

'Certainly, and is that with two rashers of bacon and beans?'

'No thank you, just the eggs please on a slice of brown toast if you have any?'

'Of course madam, will whole meal suffice, I'm afraid that this establishment doesn't have brown bread.'

'Yes, perfect, thank you,'

Once he had left, Kate slipped on her kimono and headed for the bathroom. She quickly showered, brushed her teeth and hair, and considering the lack of sleep she was not unpleasantly surprised by the reflection in the mirror.

She got back into bed to warm up just as Luke appeared with a plate held aloft; a crisp, white tea towel over his arm which he laid on top of the duvet before placing the plate down in front of her.

'Woo, that *does* look good!' Kate was loving the attention and couldn't remember the last time anyone had made such a fuss of her. She picked up the knife and fork and eagerly tucked in. She was surprisingly hungry.

A moment later Luke had joined her with an identical plate of eggs.

'How are you feeling?' she asked between mouthfuls.

'Yeah, good thanks. Still a bit sore but no sickness,' he smiled 'These eggs are perfect, compliments to the chef.'

'We aim to please,' he smiled again, 'I want to spoil you rotten – treat you like a princess.'

'I can't think why,' she sounded genuinely perplexed.

Luke put his plate on the floor and slipping his hand inside the top opening of her kimono he said, 'Well I can think of at least two!' and he brushed his lips over a nipple. Kate caressed the nape of his neck and leant back against the pillows consumed with pleasure.

When he had paid equal attention to both sides he said, 'I think we ought to get dressed or we may be here all day.'

'Yes,' she reluctantly agreed, although the alternative seemed increasingly inviting.

It took Luke seconds to get into his jeans and a sweater whereas Kate had more layers, so, as he left the bedroom he asked if she would like a coffee.

'Yes, I'd love one.'

They sat on the bed and while Luke watched her apply makeup, they made plans for the evening.

Luke always went rollerblading on a Saturday. He had a group of friends in another town and in the winter they met at a sports hall every Saturday afternoon and evening without fail.

Kate and Megan were going to a Fancy Dress dance arranged by the Rock 'n Rollers. There was going to be live music and a guest singer and people came from miles around. They had decided to go as St. Trinian's schoolgirls! White shirts, *very* short, navy skirts

(Kate had found one in a charity shop and cut it dangerously short), badly knotted ties and torn tights. She had found a great wig with plaits (very panto) that made her look twenty something! She hadn't done anything that crazy for years.

The last time was when the boys were tiny, when out of the blue, her best friend had persuaded her to do a kissogram for a friend's fortieth birthday as the one they had booked had cancelled at the last minute. She did a dance of the seven veils announcing herself as 'Madame Soleil clairvoyant extraordinaire'. After her performance, which left her veil less but respectable, in a black lacy basque, fishnet tights and high heels. She spent the rest of the evening telling fortunes with the Tarot Cards. Actually, it had been so much fun that she contemplated registering with an agency and doing it part time. But fortunately, or not, her career had taken another pathway.

When Kate was ready Luke drove her home, arranging to meet at his place later that night after they had both finished their social activities.

Luke was first back so he made sure the heated duvet was switched on, and lit some candles for atmosphere while he waited up for her.

Chapter 15

The Run up to Christmas

When Megan picked her up they were both in great spirits. Kate had never understood the need for drugs in order to have fun. She was quite capable of getting the most out of life on alcohol which, in her eyes, was not a drug!

She had been given the opportunity to try cocaine and weed several times in the States and the Bahamas but they had done absolutely nothing for her, so she saw no point in pursuing something that was not only expensive but also addictive, and had no advantages.

Alcohol, on the other hand, did it all. She had had to watch her intake as she knew it had taken control in the past, although, since she had been dancing, she barely touched it, drinking spritzers or lime and soda!

Of course, Kate couldn't contain herself once Megan asked her about the night's activities.

She listened with fascination to the events in the restaurant and was amazed that he had recuperated enough to perform in bed, but once Kate began to extol his skills in love-making she switched off and wriggled uneasily in the driving seat. In the end, she said, 'I don't think you'd better tell me anymore, we don't want an accident, I'm losing concentration.'

'Yes, I'm sorry, that was very insensitive of me, it's just that I want to tell someone and you're the nearest and dearest at the moment,' she said apologetically.

'No, it's my fault. I want some of what you're having, and your description is a bit too graphic! Or my imagination is too wild! Maybe a bit of both?'

Megan could not help but notice the difference, 'So that's what an injection of sex and passion can do,' she said to herself feeling cheated and longing to have a go.

'I can't deny that I am incredibly jealous,' Megan admitted.

'Oh, please don't be. I just want you to be happy for me. Just wait, you'll find someone. You know what they say: there's someone out there for everyone.' She reached over and put her hand on her friend's shoulder changing the subject to the evening ahead and making Megan laugh by suggesting some possible matches for her from the crowd of regulars.

'How about:"Clammy hands", "Yeti", "Hal" (short for halitosis) and "B.O."' – they had invented names for nearly everyone.

Once there, they just had fun. Kate tried not to mention Luke although she wished he liked rock n roll, it would have been the icing on the cake being able to share it with him. She knew there was no way that she was going to take up roller blading – far too dangerous at her time of life, even though she reckoned she could have been good at it.

She had carried her ice skates all around Europe with her when she had been working in various countries and other people told her she was good. Once she even helped out with a lesson when one of the teachers didn't turn up. Had she been twenty years younger nothing would have stopped her; but she had become 'sensible' in her sixty something years, and as a self-employed person she could not afford any broken bones or torn ligaments!

It was the first time she had worn a skirt to the club so it caused somewhat of a sensation, mainly due to the length (or the lack of it). Guys who she had never danced with before were inviting her, and for the first time in years she realized that she still had pulling power, or at least her legs did! One of them told her that if she always wore a short skirt she would never get a chance to sit down.

Anyway, she was going to make the most of it.

Her last 'boyfriend' of *eleven* years had treated her as a commodity – a piece of furniture, and he had never once paid her a compliment! She used to make a real effort when they went out, but he never seemed to notice, so eventually, (after about five years) Kate didn't bother any more. However, once he *did* remark that she had worn the same trousers for the last twenty odd times they'd seen each other which Kate saw as a result, as *any* comment on what she was wearing was an achievement in her books.

She had tried to dump him *so many* times but he kept turning up like a bad penny. She had wasted eleven years of her life with a chauvinistic, manipulative, controlling pig. He hadn't an ounce of empathy and the only person he loved was himself (and maybe his dog). Things would have worked out beautifully if Kate had cleaned, cooked, opened her legs when required and told him three or four times a day how wonderful he was, without expecting anything in return. She was angry with herself for having allowed it to go on so long, but she had been so busy bringing up kids and trying to keep afloat that he became a habit.

Fortunately, she had never moved in with him, on the other hand it probably wouldn't have lasted as long if she had. She did however, drive out to his place in the country every weekend, making the trip five times – sometimes six!

It took about twenty minutes each way, much of it along windy, narrow, country lanes. She hated it as invariably they would get 500 yards from the house and realise they had forgotten something important so she would turn around, unlock the door, go back in, retrieve the item and set off again only to repeat the process a few minutes later.

No one seemed to appreciate the effort involved in getting the kids' act together. She certainly wasn't doing it for herself, that novelty had worn off long ago. And when she did arrive, although he always seemed pleased to see her, he never once told her how much he appreciated the effort. The dog got more attention than she did!

Kate blamed herself for not having read the signs. His one and only wife of twenty-seven years and mother of his two children had walked out one day, leaving a note on the table saying, 'I have left'!

She had waited until the day after she buried her mother, then she had packed one case, left a brand new car in the drive (that he had recently bought for her) and ran away with the local village drunk, fifteen years her elder (nearly seventy!) and with a long, white Gandalf-like beard.

They lived together in a caravan in his back garden because his wife wouldn't move out, or allow the 'new' woman in the house! And eventually they moved abroad.

When Kate first heard about this she thought that the woman must have lost her senses but later on, when her eyes were opened, she admired her and understood how desperate she must have been to get away.

Anyway, that was all in the past, as fortunately he found a replacement which had given Kate the freedom to start a new phase in her life.

Her boys were busy doing their own thing and they didn't require any looking after, so that was when she embarked on filling every spare moment of her time with dancing, drawing, photography and painting, and hadn't regretted one minute of it.

Megan pulled up in front of Luke's flat and magnanimously told her to enjoy herself. Kate said she would while hauling an overnight bag out of the back, and was ringing the bell almost before Megan had pulled away.

The dogs went mad as soon as they heard the doorbell and it seemed like an age before Luke opened it, looking drowsy and dishevelled.

'Sorry hon. Fell asleep; good job they heard the bell,' he said referring to the dogs, and kissed her. All the while she was being jostled as Koko and Kiki vied for her attention, but soon settled down once she had made a fuss of them.

Kate dropped her coat on the sofa and Luke let out a long, low whistle, 'Geez, you must have had blokes queueing all night in that skirt!' he exclaimed.

'Yes. That was the idea,' she said teasingly giving him a twirl.

'Hey, come here Mummy Longlegs!' he said pulling her down onto the sofa next to him, leaned over and for a while just stared, his face millimetres from hers.

'You haven't a single wrinkle,' he declared in admiration. Kate was thinking that maybe he needed an eye test or that he was too near, or that the lighting was poor. Either way it made her feel good and she would take any compliments coming her way.

'Well thank ye, kind sir,' she said in a West Country accent.

Seconds later she was at his mercy as he kissed her-she could have lain there forever; there had only ever been two men whose kisses had reduced her to jelly the other, a Greek waiter, who had driven her to the top of the cliffs in his Alpha Romeo and tried to seduce her. She had been so frightened by the effect he had had on her at the time that she never saw him again! She had been very young and felt extremely vulnerable; he could have done anything he wanted to her that evening in his car, but fortunately, fear had stopped her wanting to find out.

She didn't want to pull away now, she wanted more! She was a lot older and a lot of water had gone under the bridge, besides, she had nothing to lose and nothing to be afraid of. She had never taken hard drugs but she imagined that they could have the same effect – dangerous and delicious! She loved losing control "safely", and wondered if it was the same for him. She had kissed *so many* men and couldn't figure out why there had only been two who could do it for her! She made a mental note to talk about it to Megan.

'Let's go to be...,' he said almost panting when their lips eventually parted. Kate had been on the same wavelength and had interrupted before he finished, 'Yes,' she said breathlessly.

In no time, she found herself cosseted between the warmth of the covers and his naked body. If anyone had told her a couple of months ago that she would be lying in a man's bed yearning for a night of love making she would have called them crazy, but there she was and she wouldn't change it for anything!

The morning brought its own rewards, followed by tea in bed, and breakfast à la carte.

They spent the whole day together walking with the dogs, having lunch in a pub, playing darts and enjoying each other's company; she hadn't felt so optimistic about the future for years.

Normally she dreaded the approach of winter and Christmas, but not this year.

The next couple of weeks they spent as much time as they could together, weekends, lunchtimes and nights, whenever Luke wasn't working.

She had had to turn Megan down a couple of times and she sensed that familiar tone of disappointment and resentment, but

Kate felt no guilt (not like before) because her loyalty had shifted. She couldn't help the way she felt about Luke; he had become part of her life and although she still enjoyed Megan's company, Luke had taken priority.

Chapter 16

Reading the Future

It was a weekday and Kate had left early to go in hunt for some presents that she still hadn't managed to find. She noticed that an empty shop a couple of minutes from where she lived had opened up and there were intriguing signs in the window: "Palm Reading, Tarot cards, Psychic medium...." She supposed that they had moved in over the weekend as there was a lot of activity going on inside; shelf stacking, furniture shifting, emptying of boxes, hanging art work etc.

Kate had always been drawn to the occult and cartomancy; she had a couple of friends who were truly psychic and unbelievably accurate, so she was fascinated by the new business right around the corner and as the sign on the door said 'open', she decided to have a look inside.

There were three people working feverishly at getting the place shipshape. A good-looking young man, a thirty something lady with chiseled features and rainbow-coloured hair and an older lady who was adjusting the angle of a picture.

'Hello! Please come in!' the lady with colourful hair said smiling in a welcoming manner. She abandoned whatever she was doing and walked across the shop towards Kate.

'I'm sorry about the chaos, but as you can see we have only just opened and we're still trying to organize things.'

'It looks fascinating,' Kate replied, 'Actually I would like to book a reading if that's possible?'

'Yes, absolutely. When were you thinking of? You are our first customer so any time is available at present, in fact, you could have one now if you have time?'

Kate looked at her watch, ' How long will it take?'

At that moment the lady with colourful hair involved the older women in the conversation, 'Is that alright with you Sylvia?' she asked the older lady who had been listening in.

'Yes, no problem, it usually takes about 45 minutes.'

After they discussed the price, Kate made a snap decision to go ahead and was relieved when the lady led her into a small, more intimate room at the back, as she would have been reluctant for the others to hear all about her life.

There was a powerful odour of jasmine emanating from a joss stick, an abundance of candles, two of which were lit, a small, circular table covered in Indian silk and atmospheric music gently playing in the background; almost as though she had been expected.

Sylvia sat in one of the two chairs inviting Kate to face her in the other.

Kate knew the routine as she had seen more mediums than she could remember, with only one really disappointing result, a complete charlatan, who Kate had refused to pay as she knew enough about the business to realise that the girl was learning herself and making most of it up.

So, as she sat there shuffling the cards she looked around trying not to think of anything in particular.

An hour later, Kate emerged in the bright December sunshine, and as she wandered into town she mulled over everything Sylvia had told her. She was impressed by what she had seen in her past but there was no doubt that what she had told her about Luke had left her stunned and puzzled.

Sylvia had immediately seen him in the cards, which was unsurprising as he featured so strongly in Kate's life, but what she had said about his feelings for her had astounded her.

Sylvia told her that he was head over heels smitten with love, that he would do *anything* for her and that she saw marriage! Adding that she had never been wrong in predicting marriage and that Kate would be married by the summer!

It was not at all what she had been expecting, and the revelation that Luke's feelings were stronger than he pretended, frightened her slightly. She liked him a lot and there would be a void in her life if he weren't there.

As she walked she tried to analyse her feelings – she didn't *want* to fall in love, nor did she really want anyone to fall in love with her, but she was loving the attention. She thought they were 'cool'. Why did it have to get serious? Marriage! Christ! She wasn't ready for anything like that! They hardly knew each other! How could she have made a prediction like that? They were enjoying each other in and out of bed and that was the way Kate wanted it to stay, at least for now.

She wandered around the shops, but her mind was elsewhere and she returned home empty handed.

That evening she went through the motions of teaching but she found it hard to concentrate, so when she heard Megan tooting the horn outside to pick her up for rock 'n roll she was looking forward to the distraction.

'Have you had a good day?' Megan asked cheerfully

'Unusual,' she replied fixing her seat belt.

'Oh?' Megan sounded intrigued.

Kate was wondering how much she should tell her when they drove past the shop.

'See that new place over there – it's just opened up.' Kate pointed it out but as Megan had her eyes on the road she only caught a glimpse of it, 'What is it?'

'It's an occult shop, card reading and all that.'

'Woo, just up your street and right around the corner, you'll be living there!' she said jokingly.

'Well it's certainly handy,' Kate didn't want to admit to having already been inside so she kept quiet. The last thing Megan would want to hear about would be marriage. She had plenty of other people she could talk to about the card reading without rocking the boat in their relationship.

Megan dutifully dropped her off at Luke's house afterwards and the next morning she awoke in his arms. It wasn't the sex that she looked forward to because to be frank he was no Casanova and didn't make the earth move, although she was never going tell Megan that, as far as she was concerned he was Superman between the sheets. It was the consideration and respect that he showed for her that she loved, such a contrast to the last prick who had treated her like a piece of meat with two eyes.

They ate breakfast together, chatted about Christmas and discussed their plans for the day. Luke wanted to meet her for lunch but Kate had a jam-packed day and hated letting him down. She was so used to the crestfallen expression on Megan's face that Kate looked for telltale signs but he seemed casual about it, he wasn't clingy or possessive, if Kate said that she couldn't see him for lunch he didn't make a big deal out of it; he just shrugged and said that they would meet up later and told her, "To have a good day.'

She loved the relationship – she did her thing, and he did his. He obviously trusted her, and she felt she could trust him.

Chapter 17

Christmas

The days leading up to Christmas flew by.

Knowing Kate's aversion to cooking, Megan had very kindly invited her and the boys for Christmas lunch.

There was quite a party: Megan's daughter and grandson, a friend with no family who would otherwise have been alone, and Kate with her two boys.

Megan loved cooking for people and Kate was grateful to have been let off the hook. She didn't mind washing up but she had been put off cooking by having to produce food for the kids day in day out for eighteen years. It got worse when her last boyfriend expected a roast *every* Sunday and she had to start cooking at three thirty in the afternoon! Talk about messing up a day. What can you do if the whole day revolves around cooking at three thirty, or even three o'clock? Men and their bloody stomachs, that and sex, did they ever think about anything else?

She remembered, when she was working in Madrid, that her Spanish boyfriend would turn into a monster when he was hungry and couldn't find anywhere to eat.

After they had digested the meal they opened their presents and played games; it was one of the most enjoyable Christmases Kate had had for years, and she made sure that Megan understood how much she appreciated it.

Kate spent the rest of the evening at Luke's after his family had left, and they opened the presents they had bought for each other in front of the fire.

It had been difficult buying for him, but in the end she had settled on an interesting piece of art work that he had admired when they were walking past a local art shop one day; it had been pricey but worth it when she saw his reaction, and as he pointed out, every time he looked at it he would be reminded of her.

He had been equally, if not more thoughtful, and had bought her a number of smaller gifts: some perfume, a beautiful silk scarf, an 'I Ching' book (she had mentioned mislaying hers), some art materials and a CD of Under Milk Wood read by Richard Burton, something she had always wanted but never got around to buying.

They watched a DVD in bed and made love – a perfect end to a perfect day.

On Boxing Day, she and the boys had been invited to her sister's for an evening meal, and although they had nothing in common Kate felt guilty if she didn't make the effort, and sorry for her nephew as it couldn't have been much fun, just the two of them.

He was no conversationalist and her sister usually spent the whole time complaining about life, and listing all the parts of her body that ached or pained her.

However, Kate was determined to try and liven up the evening with some fun and games so she took a box of party games to play.

Her nephew was an intellectual; an expert in robotics, ICT and creating programmes which she admired, even though most of the time she didn't have a clue what he was talking about.

'How's the research going?' Kate asked politely, apprehensive of his response, but tired of the boys' trivial chatter and witticisms dominating the conversation; they certainly lifted the mood even if it was all complete crap.

'Hmm, yes, it's good – all good, in fact we're working on something that could interest you.'

'Really?!' Kate tried to sound encouraging, but anticipated a bunch of technical jargon.

'Yes, we're developing a tool for use in education'

'Okay?' she said sceptically.

'Yes. It's a handwriting pen fitted with a minute chip but controlled by a programmed hub that can be manipulated or changed by the teacher.'

'Okay, I think I understand but with what purpose?'

'Well, we are constantly hearing about the lack of handwriting skills in young people, some handwriting is so poor that the examiners are marking down simply because they can't read it, so we have supplied a number of schools with the tool as a trial, and so far we've had very positive feedback.'

'Yes, that *does* sound like a good idea, but how does it work?'

'Basically, the teacher sets a handwriting exercise but controls the pen or pens from a master pen, so as the teacher writes on her screen the pupils' pens follow the shapes of the letters made by the teacher. In other words the child, and this can be introduced at a very early age, is trained to form perfect letters without realizing that the pen is actually doing all the work.'

'Okay but what happens when the pen is taken away and they have to manage on their own?'

'Well it's a gradual process. The pen trains the hand and mind to form perfect letters, it's a bit like practising the same tennis stroke the correct way until it becomes a habit. Once the mind remembers the movement it automatically sends a message to the hand and it becomes a habit; the child can be weaned off the pen incrementally until he or she is forming letters alone. Apparently, according to the feedback it has done wonders for their confidence and the children are writing legibly and are proud of their work.'

'Don't the kids get bored with the repetition?'

'No because after each exercise we reward them with a short game; educational of course. And after a number of exercises they get a longer game.'

'Yes, you're right it does sound positive although I don't think I would be able to use it because the kids only spend an hour with me so I usually leave them to do that kind of thing at home. But I could tell a couple of friends who are still in mainstream.'

'Well, as soon as we have enough positive statistical information we're going to approach the Ministry of Education with the hope of supplying every school in the country.'

'It's a big project then?'

'At the moment it looks like it has incredible potential, but obviously it depends on the results of the trials.'

'Yes, of course, that makes sense. Could it be adapted to other areas?'

'Yes, we are doing trials with various sports by fitting the chip into tennis rackets, golf clubs, even football boots – the chip copies the movement created by a similar chip fitted to the trainer's boot, shoe or racket until their brains learn to do it on their own.!'

'Hmm, spooky. Could it replace teachers?'

'No, I can't see that happening, because an expert is always required to initiate the process. However, once robots take over they may no longer be needed,' he said with a wry smile.

Kate had found their conversation fascinating and understood his enthusiasm for it. She could envisage all kinds of uses for his chip, 'Could it be used to teach music?' she asked intrigued at the possibility.

'It's funny you should ask that because it's next on the list. Yes, we are really keen to do that, in fact, we are working on it now.'

'The applications seem limitless?'

'It certainly looks that way at the moment, but of course we have to rely on funding so we can't run as many trials as we would like to.'

'That's a pity.'

'Yes, but that's the way it has always been. We may find a millionaire who needs help developing his children's skills, or who has a child with learning difficulties and is so grateful that he injects a whole load of money into the project, otherwise we have to be patient and work within our budget.'

'Well, I wish you the best of luck.'

'Thanks, although it's got so much potential that I can't see how it can fail,' he said confidently.

The boys had started a word game while Rob and Kate had been talking, and were laughing at their own jokes. Kate's sister sat with a bemused look on her face as most of their conversation in "teen talk" went above her head and required interpreting.

Kate came to the rescue, 'Hey! You two! Calm down! Auntie Pat can't understand – talk sensibly.'

'No, really, don't worry it's quite amusing in a weird kind of way,' she said jovially.

The evening continued with a series of games until the contents of the box were exhausted. At about midnight they said their goodbyes, and that would be that for another year as far as Kate was concerned, as she never deliberately sought out her sister's company. The refrain: "You can choose your friends but you can't choose your relations," came to mind as she drove away

Chapter 18

Truth and Trust

Kate was happier than she had been for years; but she was by no means complacent, she knew how quickly life could change, she'd been there too many times in the past.

She wallowed in time spent at his place, lazy evenings in front of the fire and indulgent mornings of being pampered with tea in bed and a breakfast cooked to perfection, he had even bought mushrooms and tomatoes to please her. He made her feel special and she was going to make the most of it for as long as she could, praying it would never end.

He had time off over the holidays and Kate's classes had dropped off, so the extra time wasn't wasted especially as they were blessed with unusually fine, mild days.

Living by the sea was a bonus, the coastal area offered an abundance of walks and trails and the dogs would collapse in front of the fire at the end of a day's exercise with what Kate interpreted as a look of complete contentment.

One morning, Luke sat on the bed next to her while she was applying her war paint, and said, 'I think you've probably guessed by now that I earn more money than from just delivering cars?'

'I haven't really thought about it,' she replied in an off-hand sort of way. However, Kate *had* thought about it and sometimes wondered where all the money came from; he always had a pocket full of notes and never used a card and *insisted* on paying whenever they went out.

Of course, she adored being treated and had tried to pay her way at first, but soon gave up when she realised that she wasn't going to win. And she stopped feeling guilty when there seemed to be a never-ending supply of cash.

He continued, 'It's because I respect and trust you that I want you to know that I don't *just* deliver cars; I have something else going on the side. I'm telling you this because the other night when you did my Tarot cards much of what you said was accurate. But I also want you to know that I don't hurt anyone with what I do.'

Now he had her complete attention; she was intrigued. It was true, she *had* done his cards the other evening, it was something she had been doing for more than thirty years, mainly for party entertainment. She was not clairvoyant but weirdly, and she had no explanation for it, the readings that she gave were usually accurate! The cards would astound her with their accuracy and she had learned lessons in the past (to her detriment) when she had chosen to ignore them!

She had told him that she could see two or three men close to him in the form of business partners and that there seemed to be something that they were doing together that would culminate around the end of February and looked very successful. However, the card for March forecast some kind of catastrophe and while she was trying to figure out exactly what, Luke said that he had heard enough and had asked her to put them away, so he was left with an extremely positive reading up to March, but Kate never got the opportunity to tell him what she saw after that. She didn't insist on giving him the bad news, as often, when people's lives changed the future would be affected, so not infrequently what she saw three months ahead could change considerably.

The other evening he had given her no indication as to whether what she had said had in any way been valid, so she had assumed that it had been one of those readings that just hadn't worked. She knew that it didn't work with some people, whether it was because they were disbelievers or that something blocked the cards, she wasn't perceptive enough to know. She had friends who *were* and could say why – but now she realised that the cards had been truthful and that maybe he hadn't been ready to divulge this other business and that had been the reason for his non-committal responses at the time.

The strange thing was that when Kate did her own cards later on in private, the same foreboding card appeared in the same place and she decided to dismiss it as an unfortunate coincidence, although in the back of her mind she knew that anything injurious or pernicious that affected Luke would automatically have a deleterious effect on herself

He didn't elaborate any more but simply repeated that he didn't hurt anyone with this other business and as Kate didn't feel that it would have been appropriate to probe, that was how it was left.

However, when she confided in Megan about the conversation, she immediately said, 'Drugs! It *has to* be drugs! Kate, you don't want to get mixed up in that! You have to get out!'

Drugs or no drugs Kate was not prepared to give him up and refused to believe it.

'Well?' Megan continued, challenging her, 'What else could it be?'

Kate hated being put on the spot and took her time to answer, 'I don't know. I only know that he said that he didn't do anyone any harm,' she said emphatically in his defense.

'It worries me, I don't like the sound of it at all. Promise me you'll be careful.' There was genuine concern in her voice, and although Kate didn't doubt her sincerity, she knew that there was no way that she was going dump him based on an assumption.

And anyway, whatever it was, neither she nor her life had suffered as a consequence, on the contrary 'it', and he, had enhanced her life, she hadn't felt so alive for years. Moreover, there was no cash flow problem – that had been another thing that had bugged her about the last idiot; 'mean' was an understatement. It wasn't as if he had been short of a penny.

How she *hated* mean men, she would rather be on her own and muddle along budgeting the best she could than tag along with someone who resented every penny they spent on her. She still asked herself how and why she had put up with her ex-boyfriend for *so* long, and found it difficult to justify the wasted years.

'Yes, of course I'll be careful,' she answered almost indignantly, 'but I don't think he's involved in drugs and even if he were, it's probably only soft stuff and what's wrong with that? Practically everyone does that.'

'Well, I don't! and neither do you, and I don't know anyone who does.'

'No, but that's a generation thing, nearly everyone under a certain age does; it's recreational.'

'Hmm,' was all that Megan added disapprovingly.

'Well, until I find out for sure I don't think we should speculate.'

'Fair enough. I just worry for you.'

'Yes, I know,' Kate felt that her concern was genuine although she wondered about an ulterior motive.

The subject was dropped and not mentioned again.

Chapter 19

Near Contentment

Life went back to normal after the holidays: meeting for lunch, spending cosy evenings in front of the fire, eating breakfasts together, going for long walks, dancing and drawing for Kate, roller-blading for Luke and work.

They hardly saw Josh, he seemed to have a circle of very understanding friends who he used for accommodation while he was in England. He knew that he always had a bed (albeit on the floor) at his dad's place but he was a gregarious, young man and enjoyed the company of people of his own age so when he was offered a bed elsewhere he took advantage of it. Also, all his mates knew that they were always welcome in Spain where he worked part of the year, and it suited Luke and Kate who were still "honeymooning" and desirous of privacy.

Because they both had a lot spare time on their hands until after the New Year, Luke had offered to cook dinner again but this time he had asked Josh to join them. The idea pleased Kate as he obviously wanted them to get to know each other better, which was all good in her eyes.

After her salsa class, she let herself in with the key Luke had given her, and had to practically jump over the dogs to get inside. She adored them, and the thought of owning one had crossed her mind more than once.

Josh appeared at the top of the stairs, 'Hello,' he said warmly, 'Let me take your coat,' and he laid it over the back of the sofa. 'Dad is still adding the finishing-touches, would you like a glass of wine?'

'Yes, I'd love one.'

'Please take a seat for a few minutes, I'm sure he won't be long.'

'I ought to pop down and say hello'

'I wouldn't if I were you, things are pretty intense down there at the moment.'

'OK,' Kate had a mental image of pots and pans piled up in the sink and various unwashed utensils strewn over the work surfaces. It smelt wonderful. Josh reappeared with a glass of rosé and a bottle of beer for himself and sat down on the other end of the sofa.

For the first time, she was able to observe the young man who came across as highly confident and articulate. He was completely at ease chatting away ten to the dozen about his jobs in various parts of the world working for humanitarian organisations, and Kate was able to contribute knowledgeably having lived abroad for years herself.

'Excuse me but I think I ought to check on Dad,' he said getting to his feet.

'Sure, shall I come too?'she offered and started to move.

'No, please, it's fine. Don't move – I'll be back in a few.'

After he left the room Koko laid his head on her knee probably in the hope of keeping her anchored as everyone seemed to be leaving, and she reassured him by tickling him behind the ear and saying how beautiful he was. He responded with frantic tail-wagging.

True to his word, Josh reappeared with two over-sized plates of food which looked like Greek mezes. The dogs were immediately ordered to their beds at the far end of the room because the plates had to go on the floor, and like a magician, Josh produced napkins, knives, forks and condiments from his pockets!

'Back in a moment,' he said disappearing again. Minutes later they both came back laden with little bowls of sauces and dips and bottles of drink.

It amused Kate to eat off the floor, it was like having a picnic. They helped themselves to an assortment of small bundles of food cooked to perfection in filo pastry, each one a surprise to the taste buds.

Kate wanted to try everything without looking greedy, and was full of praise and admiration for the cook.

'We're lucky,' Josh volunteered, 'because when he doesn't get it right it all ends up in the bin and then it's baked beans on toast!'

'You're joking!' Kate was sure he was.

'No! No joke, I'm perfectly serious. I can't count the number of times that food was chucked.'

Kate looked over to Luke in disbelief and saw him nodding in agreement.

'But why? Why on earth would you throw it all away?'

When Luke had swallowed he said, 'It has to be perfect – I won't serve it unless it's perfect. If it ain't perfect it goes in the bin.'

'But most meals can be salvaged, they don't have to be chucked.' Kate suggested.

'Not Dad's, if it's not perfect it can't be saved.'

She carried on eating considering what Josh had just said. She had *never* thrown food that she had prepared in the bin, and as far as she could remember her boys had eaten everything that she had put in front of them. She had had plenty of dinner parties (mainly before the boys were born) and never had to apologise for a disaster, nor could she remember one. Burnt bits were scraped or cut off, and torn or broken pancakes had been eaten. She wouldn't have called herself a brilliant cook and things hadn't always turn out like the magazine picture, but she had always managed to retrieve something or revamp it.

'If it's wrong it can't be fixed. You should have noticed by now that I'm a perfectionist,' he said putting down his plate.

'With some things yes, I have. But I didn't know you went to such drastic measures with the cooking,' she thought about the perfectly fried eggs that he served up every morning for breakfast and wondered how many had gone in the bin, and didn't really want to know.

The meal had been a great success; it had given them the opportunity to get to know each other better, and Kate hoped that she had made as good an impression as he had on her.

He was a charming, good-looking, intelligent young man and she had thoroughly enjoyed his company.

At about half ten he excused himself saying that he had to meet up with some friends and would probably spend the night at their place.

Before leaving he made sure to make a fuss of the dogs, and Kate could see that they too had a special relationship.

Luke, and Kate snuggled up on the sofa and watched a late thriller before going to bed, while the dogs warmed by the fire.

Chapter 20

Auld Lang Syne

Luke was always paying for meals so Kate had decided to pay for New Year's at one of her favourite restaurants and had bought Luke a voucher as part of his Christmas present; there was going to be live music and she was really looking forward to the evening and was pleased to be able offer him a meal for a change. They would drive down and walk back leaving the car to pick up the next day.

Kate drove round to his place and let herself in, there was the usual performance from the dogs, but no sign of Luke so she went downstairs only to find him ironing!

'This is a nice domestic scene,' she said with irony.

'Oh, Hi, I've just finished.' And with that he slipped on the crisp, newly-ironed shirt, tucked it into his trousers, adjusted the belt, looked in the mirror and seeming satisfied with the reflection, picked up the navy overcoat from the bed and swung it over his shoulders like a toreador about to enter the ring. 'You look nice,' he scanned her head to toe, 'I love the shoes.'

She had chosen a simple black dress covered with tiny sparkles and the shoes had the same sparkly surface. She had gone for understated bling.

He looked immaculate as usual.

They were full of anticipation on the way to the restaurant. One of the main reasons for her having booked there, was because she knew that a group of musicians that she particularly admired would be playing. As they approached She could see the lights and quite a number of people standing up around the bar.

Luke held open the door for her.

It was not a large place so it was possible to take in the whole area from where they were standing. The group of people at the bar all seemed to know each other and there was no one else sitting down. It appeared that they were the only others dining.

'I'm not sure about this,' he said

'What do you mean?' Kate wondered what had upset him.

'Well, it looks like this is a private party and we are the odd ones out, and look over there,' he pointed to the area behind the group of people by the wall where there was a long table covered in buffet style food.

'I hate that kind of thing even if it is only for the first course and it looks like we are going to be out on a limb here. Where's the music?'

'Good point.' Kate looked over to the area where the group normally set up but couldn't even see a music stand. 'I'll find out.'

Kate had been to the restaurant several times and had become fairly friendly with the owner, 'Brian,' she said loudly to be heard above the noise that the people were making.

'Yes, can I get you two a drink?

'Well actually Brian I was wondering where the music was?'

'Oh... yeah.... Right....They couldn't make it.'

'But that was part of the deal; in fact, that was the main reason for me booking this evening. If you remember the conversation we had, you agreed that if for any reason there wasn't any music then I would have a full refund?'

'Yeah, yeah, absolutely. But I don't have any money in the till – I haven't taken anything yet.'

Luke interrupted, 'OK then mate so when can she come and get her refund because the whole thing is wrong here, we weren't told that there would be a private party and *us,* or that it would be a buffet.' '

'The buffet is only with drinks before the meal. There's a proper menu,' Brian said defensively.

Luke had taken over the situation, 'Well, this ain't what she paid for, and we're going to feel really uncomfortable and won't be staying. So, what about this refund?'

'Maybe if you come back later,' Brian suggested.

'Yeah, we'll do that,' Luke responded almost threateningly. 'Come on sweetie,' he said to Kate in a totally different tone of voice and with that they left.

Outside on the pavement, they found themselves restaurant less which was going to be a bit of a problem on the 31st of December.

'I don't know what we're going to do now,' Kate said, disturbed by the way things were turning out.

'Don't worry about it, we'll find somewhere. And if we don't – no matter, I'll rustle something up at home and we'll watch tele.'

She wondered how he could be so blasé about it. This was their first New Year together and she wanted it to be auspicious. She was determined that they would not end up watching everyone else celebrate on television, and she racked her brains.

'You like Chinese, don't you?' she said optimistically.

'Yeah, but I've never eaten Chinese here, the only decent one I know is in London!'

Not very helpful, she thought and then remembered one that had recently had a makeover at the other end of town. 'I know somewhere!' she said hoping that the evening would not now be a total washout.

They jumped back into the car as it was at least half mile up town. Luke pulled into a space right outside. Kate saw this as a positive omen, she was a great believer in fate – what would be, would be.

On entering, a softly spoken, elderly Chinese gentleman in a DJ approached them, 'Can I help you?'

Kate took the initiative, 'Yes please, I know it's short notice, and we haven't booked but we were hoping to have dinner. Do you have any free tables?'

'Is it just for two?'

'Yes,' they replied in unison.

'In a few moments,' he said with a strong accent, 'some people just leaving. Please take a seat.' He indicated a bright red sofa behind them. 'Can I get you a drink?'

'No thank you, we will wait,' Kate replied relieved that they had found somewhere not totally booked up.

The décor was typically oriental, lanterns decorated with red and gold dragons and long crimson tassels, hung alongside western style Christmas decorations also in red and gold. Kate was trying to work out why the partnership of styles didn't jar, when the elderly gentleman beckoned them over to an archway.

'This way please,' and they dutifully followed.

They walked down a long aisle with alcoves on either side accommodating no more than four occupants. Each table was completely cut off from the ones either side by a partition allowing almost total privacy. It was reminiscent of some Dickensian style pubs she had seen in films where shady deals took place, or card sharps played for huge sums of money.

There was nothing sinister about this interior however, the booths created a feeling of intimacy perfect for a romantic dinner together. Luke had been adamant about not staying at the first place, he had taken an immediate dislike to it and although it hadn't been exactly what she had expected, he hadn't been prepared to even give it a chance.

As they sat down she saw him smile; all that remained now was for the food to meet with his approval and she would be able to enjoy the evening.

'This is the best Chinese food I've had outside London. These spring rolls are totally fresh and the prawns too – I'm really enjoying this,' he said helping himself to a fourth one.

'Yes, I agree,' Kate sounded relieved, 'I came here ages ago with a Chinese friend and it was excellent then too, but you can never tell because places change so quickly. I'm glad it's the same.'

'Yeah, so glad we didn't stay at the other one. What a dick; make sure you get your money back. Do you want to go back when we finish here?'

'I don't know, we'll see.'

'Okay hon,' Luke reached across the table for her hand. It was moments like these that Kate savoured.

The rest of the meal was cooked to perfection and Luke's mood had lifted, so when their fortune cookies arrived they laughed at the forecasts which could have applied to anyone in the restaurant.

Kate paid with a card convincing Luke that it was supposed to have been part of his Christmas present, and for once he didn't put up a fight.

They left the restaurant at about half eleven and decided to go across to the pub to see in the New Year.

It was packed with people ready to see out the present year and welcome in a new one. Kate never really saw the point of it unless it had been disastrous. She had had a good year and didn't want it to end, and didn't see how the new year could in any way improve on the old one. But the atmosphere was jubilant and even if they all woke up crying the next day everyone seemed determined to celebrate the moment.

Luke fought his way to the bar to get the drinks leaving Kate amidst a crowd of drunken revellers feeling awkward and vulnerable.

A scrawny woman with died, black, ratty hair came up to her and said, 'Who d' ya think you are, a fuckin princess or som'in?' Dumbfounded and wondering whether the woman was actually speaking to her or someone else she looked around, but could only see blokes so she replied, 'No, why is that?' curious to know what was going through the woman's mind.

'With ya diamond brooch an' all,' she said pointing a bony digit at the bling on the lapel of Kate's long, black coat and breathing alcohol and onions all over her. Kate tried not to inhale and stepped back and the woman turned away.

'You okay?' Luke asked handing her a spritzer, 'What did that woman say?'

Kate could sense that he was on the offensive, 'She was admiring my brooch,' Kate smiled reassuringly.

'Well, she's right, it's very attractive but then so is the owner,' and he kissed her briefly on the mouth. She wallowed momentarily in the compliment.

They stood in a corner watching the inebriated crowd shout at each other, even though they were only centimeters apart. In unison, encouraged by the television, the whole pub started a countdown to midnight that terminated in an enormous cheer and an outbreak of kissing.

It always amazed her how, on the stroke of midnight, total strangers went around kissing and hugging each other indiscriminately like long lost friends. She didn't like the idea of a total stranger kissing her, and definitely *not* on the mouth.

Sensing that Luke felt the same way she pulled him back into the corner, strategically placing him between herself and the frenzy.

They stood and watched the bizarre performance from relative safety hoping that no one would notice them until it was all over.

There was one guy with unwashed, grey hair and stubble, completely pissed out of his mind who was searching for women to slobber over. His last victim, a petite, attractive, oriental brunette, was wiping her mouth in disgust; her expression saying it all. He was stumbling from one victim to another like some kind of Neanderthal on the prowl.

Kate tried to make herself small, which was difficult given that her heels made her at least two inches taller than Luke. She saw the primate look in her direction but thought better of it when he realised she had protection, and turned in the direction of easier prey.

'Well, we've seen in the New Year, what do say we head home?' Luke turned and kissed her on the forehead.

'Hey! Where's my New Year's kiss?' Kate said feeling cheated. Luke took her face tenderly in both hands and whispered, 'Happy New Year sweetheart,' he kissed her passionately on the mouth transporting her into a world of their own where drunks and cavemen didn't exist.

'And thank you for a lovely evening,' he added as he led her through the throng of people outside into the fresh, crisp night air.

They walked fairly briskly back to his place, not giving the cold a chance to get to them.

Kate gave Kiki and Koko an official New Year's kiss, then they went to bed to properly celebrate.

Chapter 21

New Year

New Year's Day and sunshine was streaming through a gap between the curtains, when Kate felt Luke's hand on her shoulder.

'There's a cup of tea here,' he said putting it on the chair next to her, 'and it's a perfect day for a skate. Keith rang and he wants to meet down the seafront. We can take the dogs if you would be prepared to walk with them?'

'Yes, of course, sounds good,' she managed drowsily.

They took their time eating breakfast together comparing notes on the events of the previous evening, but were eager not to miss out on the wonderful winter sunshine.

The promenade was packed with people also keen to make the most of the extraordinary mild, sunny advent to the year.

There were families accompanied by dogs of all shapes and sizes which thrilled Koko and Kiki who wanted to say hello to all of them. Kate didn't mind stopping for all the sniffing and greeting; she was in no hurry, in fact it amused her and she enjoyed indulging them, they were beautiful animals with gentle temperaments.

As she sauntered along Luke and Keith skated, weaving their way through the forest of people, enjoying the glorious weather of uninterrupted blue sky to the horizon.

Kate couldn't ever remember seeing so many cheerful, smiling people all together by the seaside; it was quite a spectacle. Occasionally, people would stop, kiss and wish each other Happy New Year; it was like a continuation of the night before, but without the zombies.

'What an auspicious start to the year,' she thought, determined to enjoy the unfamiliarity of human warmth, she resolved to soak up as much of the atmosphere and winter sunshine as she could, and reap the benefits.

They all met up at an open area surrounded by wooden benches where Luke was allowed to show off his 'moves'. He called it 'Slalom', although Kate could draw no parallels to skiing. It was more like figure skating except on wheels. He was very adept and there was obvious skill involved, but as an accomplished (ice) figure skater herself she saw it as a fun hobby, and four wheels on a rough surface looked a lot more stable than a thin blade of steel on a smooth icy one. She knew that had she wanted to take it up, with enough practice, she would be able to master the activity, but she wasn't prepared to risk injury as a self-employed person of sixty-two!

Kate sat down on one of the benches in direct exposure to the January sunshine, and watched him build a small crowd of admirers; mostly kids on roller skates, but there was a man in his early forties standing chatting to Keith while his young son on skates spent most of his time getting up from the ground!

It turned out that the man was French, over on a work contract for at least a year, and had brought the family with him. The boy's English was already better than his dad's, who still seemed to be struggling, so when Keith asked Kate to interpret for him she needed no persuading and jumped at the chance to use her languages, aware that just like a musical instrument, if you didn't use it you'd lose it. Besides, much of the teaching became very repetitive and she rarely got the chance to converse with native speakers unless she was on holiday, or on the phone to her friends abroad.

Like most Frenchmen who had a certain 'je ne sais quoi' for British females, Kate could see his attraction. He was tall and slim and had an air of distinction. He was typical of his breed who had acquired a level of higher education probably from one of the more eminent engineering schools, and who considered themselves superior to the rest of humanity. Had Kate not been fluent in French he would have looked down on her with contempt and/or pity.

However, as it was, the minute she opened her mouth his demeanour changed. Nothing impressed a Frenchman more than a foreigner (especially an English person) who had mastered their language.

Once, Kate had been told by a friend observing her engaged in conversation on holiday in France, that she could get anything she wanted from a Frenchman. Kate had found his observation fascinating, totally unaware of the power she wielded.

She had learned, years before, while working in Paris never to completely lose her English accent. Her boyfriend of the moment had warned her that she was beginning to lose it which, apparently, detracted from her charm.

It turned out that an English person speaking French with an English accent had the same sexy, debilitating charm as a French person speaking English with a French accent. Unbelievable as it may seem but true! So, whenever Kate had needed information or help from a French person she had learned to turn on her English accent, and amazingly, it had always produced the desired effect!

It turned out that Jean-Claude was interested in improving his skating technique and although he didn't have his skates with him he was an avid skater, having only quite recently taken up the activity on account of his son's passion for it.

It was a rare treat for Kate to see a Frenchman admire *anything* British and yet here he was captivated by Luke's skating skills, and her ability to articulate coherently in his own language!

Kate loved France and everything about it, she would even forego the rudeness and bad temper of the Parisians in order to indulge in the delights of their city.

When the French rabbited on about how they have the best wine, the best cheese, the best fashion, the best this and that, Kate would always smile and nod because basically it was true, however she managed to defend the UK with, 'But you don't produce whisky! And what about The Beatles and James Bond?'

'Ah, oui! Vous avez raison!' he replied with a broad smile, and from then on it was a contest; for every British product that Kate extolled, he came up with a French one equally as good, if not better.

She roped in Keith and Luke for suggestions –

'Burberry!' suggested Keith.

'Louis Vuitton,' Jean-Claude retaliated triumphantly and added, 'Picasso!'

'Sorry, he doesn't count, he was Spanish,' Kate spotted quickly.

She could tell that the others didn't know that.

'Okay, les Impressionists alors!' and he reeled off a list of them beginning with Monet. Kate thought of the Pre-Raphaelites and Turner but instead challenged with, 'Shakespeare!'

'Yeah, and Dickens!' shouted Luke doing a kind of pirouette on one foot.

Jean-Claude came back with, 'Baudelaire and Molière!' both of which sounded better to the ear but were no contestants in Kate's opinion.

The competition continued with song writers, composers, scientists, engineers, sports people; each side trying to outshine the other in a lighthearted, patriotic way. In the end, they resorted to the internet and it got out of hand, so they agreed on a draw.

It had been an amusing if not intellectually challenging interlude, which Luke and Kate kept up all the way home.

'Why didn't we say Churchill?' Luke said disappointed with his own lack of imagination.

'Yes, that's a good one, but he would only have come back with De Gaulle,' Kate said.

'Na, Churchill won the war!'

'With a lot help from the Americans,' Kate added.

'Hey! Whose side are you on anyway?'

'Well, both actually, both countries have achieved so much *and* contributed so much, it's difficult to take sides. I mean, where would we all be without penicillin?'

'Yeah, you've got a point there,' he conceded.

It had been a beautiful day and one to remember.

Luke dropped her off at her place as she had to feed the cat and do some stuff in the house, saying he would pick her up later.

Sure enough, he drew up at the top of the lane on the dot and as Kate got into the passenger seat he asked, 'What's that you've got?' She had grabbed a DVD at the last minute, one of her favourites, 'The Reader' with Kate Winslet and Ralph Fiennes, and was positive he would like it.

She was right, he had been riveted from start to finish and apart from a couple of gasps of astonishment at the twists in the plot he didn't move.

'How did she manage to get to that age and hold down a job without ever learning to read or write?' he said at the end.

'Well don't forget there was a war, on and if she came from a tiny village or an isolated farm I don't suppose she had much schooling, if any, and if she was brought up in the countryside she wouldn't have needed an education in the countryside. She would have only needed to know how to cook, clean, milk cows and make butter and cheese. It doesn't really explain the reason why she never learned, but I think there were loads of illiterate people all over Europe.'

'It just seems amazing that she managed to conceal it for so many years,' Luke said.

Kate agreed and added, 'Well, I suppose that as a tram conductor she never needed it.'

It wasn't a film with a happy ending and left them with unanswered questions, but based on a true character it was deserving of all its accolades, and prompted her to ask what kind of books he was interested in; a subject that, strangely, had eluded them up to that moment.

'I don't read books,' was his reply!

'Pardon?' Kate thought she hadn't heard properly.

'I don't read books,' he repeated, 'I've never read a book.'

'But you must have!' she said refusing to believe it, 'What about when you were at school?'

'Nope!' was his response.

Kate couldn't leave it alone, 'But you would have had to study books for literature?'

'No, not me. I didn't do it. I didn't do any exams; spent most of my time avoiding school and got out as soon as I could.'

'Really!' she said, genuinely surprised by this revelation. Admittedly she hadn't seen any books anywhere, but she found it hard to believe that someone who spoke so intelligibly on so many subjects had never read anything. She admired him for his wit, and considered him to be one of the most intelligent men she had ever met, and she had more than a few to compare him to! She sat watching the flames flickering in the fire wondering what life would be like void of literature, and decided she couldn't.

An idea came to her, 'What if I brought a book round and read it *to* you?' she suggested.

'What – you mean like in the film?'

'Hmm, sort of,' she replied, and watched his reaction.

'Yes, why not,' he appeared to be happy with the idea, so when she got home she went through the book titles on her shelves, trying to find something that would appeal to him.

She settled on 'The Little Prince' (something short with a message) and read it to him in bed. However, when she asked for his opinion, he said that he had enjoyed listening to her voice but hadn't really understood it, leaving her with the feeling that it had been a waste of time and effort.

The next day was a public holiday in lieu of the New Year falling on a Sunday, so they had another lazy day except for some food shopping as the supermarkets were all open.

Kate hated grocery shopping. She went under duress and never did "a big shop". She saw no point in buying food in advance that she might not fancy at the end of the week; let alone unpack it all at the other end!

She had had a large freezer and she ended up wasting so much food that she got rid of it, so when she changed her refrigerator she opted for one that had a small freezer above the fridge (perfect for one person) where she would freeze the odd item that she found on offer.

"Eat for today" had become her motto. She loved the reduced section in the supermarket or the corner store, and sometimes lived for days on reductions, especially when something that appealed to her was there.

She knew almost all the times when the various shops reduced their food and would try to make sure that she could visit at least *one* of them every couple of days. She approached the designated area with anticipation and excitement often imagining that someone else, who happened to be walking in the same direction, was trying to get there before her, so she would tactically change her route and walk faster arriving before the imaginary "bargain thief".

It always amazed her by the amount and quality of food that other people didn't want to eat leaving real bargains for the thrifty shopper, like fresh salmon or trout: she loved fish. Occasionally, but rarely, there would be nothing there to whet her appetite so she would leave empty-handed and slightly deflated, and would resort to the reserves in the mini-freezer.

So, when Luke asked her if she wanted to go to the supermarket with him, she didn't know exactly why, but she felt quite privileged, besides it was a dull, drizzly day and she would only have spent it indoors catching up on photocopying and preparing lessons.

It was about midday when they left his place and although they had eaten eggs for breakfast, that had been more than four hours ago, so, they both felt the call of food when they walked past the cafeteria.

'Do you fancy something to eat first?' Luke suggested.

'Yes, that's a great idea,' Kate replied instantly.

They ordered roast chicken and cleaned their plates. For a supermarket dinner it had been exceedingly good and they left feeling satisfied and ready to do battle in the aisles.

Whenever Kate went supermarket shopping she would just go places in no particular order, but it rapidly became clear that this shop was not going to be done randomly. Luke had his own method, although he had written a list, he insisted on doing all the aisles in order even if there was nothing in one of the aisles on his list. There were twenty aisles! Kate braced herself for a long shop.

They were sauntering down aisle five when Luke froze and swore.

'What's the matter?'

'Those people coming towards us. They're the parents of that bitch who emptied my flat!' This was the first time Kate had ever seen him panic or flustered. Was that fear she saw on his face? She watched in fascination as he nimbly manoeuvred himself behind her, making sure that she was blocking their view. Kate wondered what *exactly* had gone on, after all she only had Luke's account of events and it had obviously been an acrimonious split, so the girl's parents would only ever have heard *her* version, which would naturally have been biased.

He had told her about the relationship that he had with a girl a couple of years previously, when he had taken up with a girl in the late autumn who had moved in with him. Everything had been going swimmingly until his life got busier in the Spring with the warm weather beckoning him out skating and fishing (another of his favourite pastimes). So when she began to complain that he was leaving her on her own too much, the relationship turned sour. He spent *even more* time away from the flat in order to avoid being nagged or having to oblige with any sexual favours. In the end they never talked; they only argued. He had to get pissed and/or high to make love to her, he dreaded going back to his own place, and spent more and more time out with his mates and skating.

One day, she announced she was pregnant and although shocked, he said he would stick by her, and support her and the baby. They celebrated the pending birth in the pub with all his friends and for a while their relationship improved. However, temptation and the pull of the park with his band of playmates was too great to resist, and he soon fell back into his self-indulgent ways.

Needless to say, this caused more friction which reached boiling point when she announced that she had got rid of the baby because she couldn't see him as a committed partner or future father. He told her to leave, but with nowhere to go, things went from bad to worse when finally, one morning he got back from a night's work and found the place empty!

They had bought a lot of the stuff together, so he was stunned and angry when all she had left him with was a knife, fork, spoon, plate and cup! However, when he had time to think it through, he was so relieved that she had gone, he wrote off the stuff considering it a small price to pay for getting his life back.

With the danger averted, they resumed the monotonous toing and froing, up one aisle and down the next, when out of the blue in the distance, right at the end of the aisle they had just turned into, Kate thought she saw her sister!

'Oh, look there's my sister,' she said with an element of surprise in her voice.

Luke was still looking over his shoulder for "the bitch's parents".

'Where?' he asked.

'There,' Kate answered pointing to a lady in beige coming towards them, Kate thought her description was sufficient for him to pick her out.

Luke could see a lady in beige about fifty meters away but he doubted that it was any relation of Kate's; this person was stockily built with grey hair, dowdily dressed, void of makeup and frumpy.

'Who do you mean?' he said.

'The lady in the beige jacket and brown scarf,' Kate repeated adding the detail of the scarf.

'Blimey! She doesn't look anything like you!' he couldn't disguise the disbelief in his voice.

'You're right; everyone says that.'

Kate didn't wave to draw her sister's attention, she didn't see any point as they were gradually approaching each other anyway.

'Oh, bugger! I have to go back to aisle two,' Luke said, 'Forgotten something. Won't be a second.'

'Okay, hurry up! I want to introduce you.'

'Yeah, yeah.' And he disappeared around the end of the rows of canned vegetables.

This shopping trip was turning into a nightmare for him. The last thing he wanted was to cope with Kate's sister. He wasn't prepared. He wouldn't know what to say. Part of her attraction was her lack of relatives. He liked his women to be unattached and if possible bereft of any family members who could cause complications or come knocking on the door at a later date accusing him of god knows what.

His present situation reminded him of the films he had seen about French Resistance fighters evading the Gestapo, and although his life wasn't in danger, he was beginning to perspire with the stress of having to avoid confrontation. Kate's sister looked quite formidable and he had convinced himself that he would not meet with her approval.

'Hello, Kate. Doing your weekly shop?' she said looking in the trolley. She would have no idea of Kate's shopping habits as they rarely spoke to each other and if they did, the conversation would never have revealed such mundane details of Kate's life.

'No, this is mostly Luke's stuff,' Kate said with some sense of satisfaction as she wanted her sister to know that she was helping with his shopping and to see them as a "couple". She wanted to show him off especially as he was so much younger than herself. She was proud of the fact that she could still "pull" a man and one that didn't resemble a decrepit, middle-aged, grey-haired, pot-bellied moron.

'Luke?' Pat said inquisitively.

'Yes, my new man.' Kate explained puffing herself up like some kind of proud mother bird, 'He'll be back in a minute, he had to go back for something.'

They carried on chatting about Christmas, the weather and other banalities while waiting for Luke's return. However, he was hovering at a safe distance, just out of view, but from where he could watch and wait for Kate's sister to depart, as he had no intention of meeting her.

'Well, I had better get on,' Pat said eventually, having run out of small talk, 'I can't stand hear chatting all day.'

'Yes, he does seem to be taking a long time – I wonder what he's looking for? Never mind we might bump into each other again. Happy New Year! Just in case I forget later.'

'Yes, you too,' Pat returned the greeting and disappeared into the neighbouring aisle of crisps and nibbles.

Meanwhile, just as Kate was starting to get irritated by his absence, there he was – standing next to her.

'Where have you been? Pat couldn't wait. Did you find what you were looking for?' she noticed that he wasn't carrying anything.

'No, I asked one of the assistants and you know what they are like, she went off to look for it and took an absolute age, so I went looking for *her* and then we missed each other, and when we finally found each other again it was to tell me that they didn't have any in stock! Anyway, I'm sorry it took so long, I was looking forward to meeting your sister.'

'Never mind, we might see her again.'

'Not if I can help it,' he thought.

'Anyway, what was it you couldn't find?'

Luckily, he had been prepared for that question, 'Panch phoron,' he said unflinchingly.

'What?' Kate asked, never having heard of it.

'Panch phoron,' he repeated.

'What on earth is that?'

'It's an Indian spice – I use it all the time. Now you know one of my trade secrets,' he looked pleased with himself, having avoided meeting her sister, and convincing Kate that he had genuinely gone in search of an obscure spice.

Kate followed him round the end of the aisle trying to keep up; she had never seen him act like this before, but then they hadn't been to the supermarket together before. His entire focus was on avoiding the old couple and Kate's sister – shopping came to a standstill and didn't resume until he was sure that they had left. The whole episode left her thoroughly bemused; she had never played 'cat and mouse' in a supermarket before!

Chapter 22

Intelligent Rats

Megan had been so wrapped up in catering for her daughter and grandson that she hadn't missed Kate's company so much, this in turn, had allowed Kate the freedom to completely dedicate herself to Luke and their time together without a guilty conscience.

Life returned to 'normal' on the Tuesday; Kate went back to teaching and then met Megan for the Salsa class, but this time they went for a drink afterwards as Jason was going to be at his dad's and Kate sensed they needed time together.

'It's certainly a good workout,' Megan said unstrapping her shoes.

'Yes, it's fun too,' Kate agreed.

'It certainly is; I really enjoy it! Where shall we go – the usual place?

'Yes, we can have a football match and beat the quiz machine!' Kate sounded like an excited child being allowed to go to the fair, and Megan laughed at her enthusiasm.

'Agreed, and this time I'll thrash you!'

Kate chuckled knowing that it was unlikely – she always won at football; it was sometimes very close but she had a more aggressive technique that she had picked up from an ex-boyfriend.

However, Megan got more answers right on the quiz machine for someone with no higher education; she had great general knowledge and Kate admired her for that. She had seen a kindred spirit in her from the moment they became friends, after all they were both Chinese rats and supposedly "highly intelligent".

According to the legend, all the Chinese animals were arguing about who should appear first in the calendar: the Tiger argued that he was the fiercest; the Buffalo that he was the strongest; the Dragon that he was the most magnificent; each one seemed to have a valid reason, when Buddha, who was looking down on the quarrelling, decided that it could not continue and commanded them to settle it competitively.

He ordered them to line up along the bank of a river and on his command, to swim to the other side; the first to touch the opposite bank would be declared the winner and would start the calendar, and the other years would follow in sequence according to the order in which each animal finished the race.

They all jumped in together and swam as fast as they could, however the water buffalo was out in front right from the start, being used to the water and very powerful. Strangely though, the little old rat was right behind him, although much smaller he was sleek and stream-lined and very determined, and his little legs worked ten to the dozen keeping up with him.

As they neared the opposite side the rat could see that he would never have the strength or speed to overtake the buffalo, so just at the last minute, he caught hold of the buffalo's tail and pulled himself up onto the huge brown back of the animal, ran along the entire length until he reached its nose, and then, right at the last second, it jumped off onto the bank nanoseconds before the enormous beast. Thus, the rat was declared the winner and accredited with being the most intelligence of all the animals!

Of course, Kate was immensely proud of being a Chinese Rat and told everyone she met, it was a way of saying, 'Don't mess with me! I'm smart.' Not only that, they were renowned for their resourcefulness and ability to survive against all odds.

In the corner of the bar, they were making the usual ruckus at the football table, cheering each other on and occasionally hitting the ball right out of play onto the floor. However, no one else seemed to notice as there was an international football game at full volume on the television between England and Italy, so the rest of the customers were completely engrossed in that.

Kate won the best of five games, but knew that Megan would do better at the Quiz, so they moved across with their drinks ready for the challenge. Unfortunately, there was someone else playing on it at the time so they sat down at a nearby table to wait for it to be free, giving them a chance to catch up with the holiday gossip.

'I met Luke's best buddy Keith on New Year's Day,' Kate said a bit smugly as she hadn't been introduced to any of his friends till then. And she went on to tell her about the Frenchman and the fun they had had.

'What have you been up to?' she asked Megan

'Well, Lisa encouraged me to go on a dating website – I wasn't that keen but she said it wouldn't hurt to have a look, so I did!'

'And .....?' Kate asked intrigued.

'Well, I went to meet someone!'

Kate was wide eyed in amazement, she would never in a million years have thought that her timid, unconfident friend would meet a perfect stranger on a blind date.

'You're joking! Where?'

'In that new cafeteria not far from your house; the one with all the retro stuff in it.'

'Okay....and....?'

'And he was very nice.'

'Nice! What does "nice" mean? I need more!' Kate demanded impatiently.

'Well, he had a nice face, he's a bit younger than me, but you wouldn't know it because he's a little overweight.' Kate immediately interpreted that as 'fat'.

'Go on. What does he do?'

'He works for a delivery service.'

'What! You mean he's a van driver?' Kate said disparagingly.

'Hmm, I know, it's not fantastic but he *was* nice and wants to meet again, and it's a start; it's getting me out there and giving me confidence to do it again,' she said with a sheepish smile knowing that she would normally have shared her plans with Kate before going ahead and added defensively, 'I thought I should make the effort now that you have someone and you know how extrovert Lisa is; she convinced me and set the whole thing up. I don't think I would have done it on my own.'

It was true that Kate *did* feel as though her friend had betrayed her by going behind her back, but on the other hand she would probably never have looked around if Kate hadn't found Luke; she couldn't help feeling that she was somehow getting her own back.

When Kate took a moment to think about it she considered Megan's chances of finding anyone decent in the area would be slim, and decided that nothing serious would come of it.

She had a theory that if a man (especially over a certain age) wasn't married then there was something wrong with him, because no woman in her right mind would give up a good man. All the decent men she had met in her forty-five years of dating had been married and there had *always* been something wrong with the single ones. Otherwise she would be happily married herself, as it was, her marriage had lasted three and a half weeks!! And she fell pregnant with twins at forty-three! She had thrown him out after a bout of violence towards her – not knowing that she was pregnant at the time – not that it would have made any difference to her decision as she would put up with a lot; but *not* violence – it was the one thing she wouldn't forgive: that, and injustice

A very astute American friend had told Kate that if she was really serious about finding a husband then she should get work in a nursing home where she would meet all the lovely, visiting husbands who had cared for their wives for years, and who, after their deaths would be looking for a replacement: the younger the better!

'So, when are you seeing him again?' Kate wanted to sound interested.

'On Thursday. He works odd hours.'

'Okay, well good luck with it all,' She felt she had to sound encouraging although deep down she was hoping that it didn't work out, and that her friend and their friendship would stay exactly as it was, or they would never see each other.

She decided to tell Megan about her card reading if only to convince *herself* that her new romance was strong and would continue to flourish.

When she had finished, Megan looked skeptical, 'I would take it with a pinch of salt if I were you. After all you don't know this woman.'

'She was very accurate about my past; there were things that she couldn't possibly have known, so I'm basing it on that,' Kate sounded convinced?

'Just be careful. I don't want to see you get hurt.'

Kate wondered if she really meant it, or was hoping that it would all fall apart and that they could go back to their old routine, when no men were involved.

'Don't worry, I'm just enjoying the attention and the sex,' she said with a laugh, making light of it all. The former was definitely true, she loved the attention he gave her, the latter however, was not much to get excited about – he had probably *heard* of foreplay but that was it. She generally ended up doing most of the work. Luke preferred her on top, he said that he didn't end up 'hurting' so much the next day. Apparently, the day after their first night together his balls had hurt so much he couldn't skate! And his mates had taken the mickey, but it had amused Kate no end.

She hadn't travelled the world without learning *something* about how to satisfy a guy in bed and she hadn't heard him complaining, on the contrary he would lie for hours letting her work her magic until her jaw ached! She wanted to make sure it was the best sensation ever, so that it became a drug that he needed and couldn't live without.

She did it because she adored his company and appreciated his consideration and respect for her, and she was aware that compromises had to be made for a relationship to work. A little pampering was cheap in exchange for the way he had changed her life, so she indulged him like a child. It wouldn't have worried her if she had never had an orgasm again, sex was no adventure to her now, the attraction wore off for her after the first couple of times with a guy. Besides, they made toys that did a better job! She loved him for the person he was and not for his performance in bed. He was different; she couldn't say exactly how, but he made her feel so good about herself she just knew that he was right for her.

Megan could see the change in her friend and had reason to worry, no matter how flippant Kate appeared to be on the surface she knew she was smitten, was letting down her guard and was genuinely concerned for her.

Chapter 23

Father and Son

Meanwhile Luke was enjoying the company of his son – a rare occasion.

'So, you really like this one?' he asked his dad.

'Yes.'

'Is it serious? I mean do you love her?'

'Hmm yeah I think I do.'

'Christ dad, it's been a while since I've heard you say that!' Jason was surprised at his honesty, 'I think you should take it slowly, you know that you don't have a very good track record; remember the last one?' he reminded him.

Luke nodded and had a vision of the empty flat.

'And then there was the one before that – you know the married one? It ended badly for her, in divorce, and without you!'

'Yeah, bad choice, but what a looker!'

'Why do think this won't go the same way?'

'This one ticks all the right boxes,' he said positively.

'Oh yeah, what do you mean by that?'

'Well she owns her own house, her kids are grown up and independent and she won't be able to trap me with pregnancy because she's too old. She is financially solvent and has her own hobbies and evening activities, so she doesn't rely on me for entertainment. She's happy doing her own thing and isn't resentful when we can't see each other. Besides she probably can't believe her luck landing a young dude like me!' he said arrogantly, '*And* she's got half a brain whereas the others have been airheads.'

'Okay... That solves *your* side but suppose she really falls for you, what then? What happens come the spring when you are so busy skating and fishing and seeing the lads that you don't have time for her?'

'She'll understand. She's a busy lady she'll probably be glad of the free time by then,' he said complacently, leaning back into the sofa.

'It sounds good, I hope it all works out for you,' Jason was sincere, as he would have liked to see his dad find a partner who would stay with him for more than a few months.

The following evening Kate went round to Luke's after the Rock n' Roll session. Normally she would have gone for a drink with Megan, but Luke had messaged her and asked to go round after her class.

She was glad he missed her, it made her feel important in his life; something that had been lacking for years ever since the boys hit fourteen and she had been going out with an insensitive warthog.

She had felt used and abused for years in her previous relationship by all three of them – two selfish teenagers who thought she was out of touch, and a Neanderthal who wondered why she wasn't constantly cooking, cleaning and baking for him! It had been one of the most depressing times of her life – she had done nothing for her own pleasure; all she did was try to keep everyone else happy which almost led to disaster when one night she found a way through to the railway line and was going to wait for the first train to pass by, because she had had enough and couldn't see any point in prolonging her misery; besides she didn't believe that anyone would miss her because she was convinced that none of them had an ounce of love in their hearts for anyone except themselves. Fortunately, (or not), a man out early was walking his dog (probably a shift worker), saw her, and suspecting something amiss, managed to persuade her that there was help and that she should see her doctor.

By the time she got home the moment had passed, so as soon as the surgery opened she made an appointment, and the doctor put her on a course of antidepressants, which kept her going for the next couple of years. But it wasn't until she managed to get rid of the asshole in her life and the boys moved out that she began to feel human again.

That was when she had enrolled in a life-drawing course, and began to do things for her own pleasure without feeling guilty! It was a strange sensation at first and she had to convince herself that she was allowed to do things for her own gratification, but thanks to the support of her friends she pulled herself out of a dark place.

She had been cured of men, having believed all her adult life that they would be the answer to everything, but realising that they had been the problem! The misconception that a man was the answer to a woman's happiness had almost certainly been instilled in her by her parents' apparently 'perfect' marriage, which she had tried to emulate for the last forty odd years and failed.

But that was all in the past, now she had a life! She was doing the things she loved and somehow, unexpectedly, she had found a man who seemed to adore her, and more importantly respected and admired her! She found it hard to believe and still had to pinch herself to make sure. She even went back to the card reader for reassurance who said that he loved her and would do anything for her, and that they would get married! Also, she loved his honest approach, and that he didn't hide anything from her.

He wasn't asking her to give anything up or to cook for him, or to do *anything* for him. As far as she was concerned life would carry on as normal and his love for her would supersede his love for anything else, and nothing would really change. She had found the perfect man and the perfect relationship after all these years. Life was good!

Chapter 24

A New Project

Life was good, until February, when Luke threw himself into some sort of building project with his friends (the ones that Kate had seen in his cards a couple of months earlier). She didn't know what it was all about but he was working very hard, doing a lot of physical work involving a mechanical digger and cementing. He was absolutely exhausted, coming off nights and flinging himself straight into work with no sleep.

When Kate managed to see him or talk to him he sounded upbeat and positive, and said that it was all in preparation for something that would make him financially solvent for the rest of his life.

'Just bear with me for the next couple of weeks sweetie and you'll see how all of this will eventually pay off, and we'll live like millionaires, and I will be able to treat you like a *real* princess!'

Kate would look at the exhaustion on his face and said that he already treated her like a princess and how happy she was, and that she didn't need or want anything more. But she also saw how it had no effect on him whatsoever; he was going to see this through at all costs, besides, he "couldn't let his mates down, they were in it together" (whatever "it" was), and it would be split three ways.

Kate knew it was useless to argue; once he had a bee in his bonnet there would be no persuading him otherwise, but the others didn't work nights, they got a good night's sleep and were fit and able to do a day of physical work.

He was pushing himself to the limit and she didn't think he would be able to carry on without it having a detrimental effect on his health.

'*Please* take some time off to get some sleep. You can't go on like this – you'll make yourself ill,' she pleaded with him one evening spooning on the sofa in front of the fire.

'I am fine sweetheart. You don't have to worry. Yeah I feel tired, sure, but it's a good tiredness and we're nearly there. The floor's down and we've built the walls, all that's left is to make it secure with a good, solid door and security system. It'll be a good place for me to store all my tools too because now they're all over the place and stuff goes astray.'

'But what's it all for? It seems like a lot of work and expense for the tools,' Kate asked because she had been wondering for a while what it was about.

'Best you don't know hon. The less you know the better. But believe me I wouldn't be doing this unless it was essential to securing my future.

Chapter 25

Told You So

Luke was either so busy or too exhausted to see her for the next week and she couldn't wait for the work to be completed.

It was Friday evening and Kate was packing her bag for the night as neither of them had anything organized and were going to watch a DVD by the fire, when she heard a message come through on her phone, 'Sorry, sweetheart but I am not feeling 100% can we leave it tonight, speak tomorrow xxx'

Kate looked at the message and wondered if there was a hidden agenda, 'What's wrong?' she immediately messaged back.

'Nothing – just tired – need an early night to catch up. Speak tomorrow, don't worry – love you xxx' he reassured her.

She felt deflated and strange sitting at home on her own with Cat, watching a regular TV programme, and hoped that a good night's sleep was all that was needed.

They didn't have what Kate could describe as a physically, passionate relationship, but she enjoyed his company and she always came away feeling good, which she hoped was reciprocal.

Past relationships based solely on physical attraction or neediness had been transient and hollow, and she had long ago realised that having sex had little (or nothing) to do with love. However, this one had crept up on her unexpectedly and she was surprised by the depth of feeling she found herself capable of after so many failures. Three months earlier she would have described herself as a complete cynic concerning "true love" – a non-convert, but she had been 'caught' and was strangely grateful for the opportunity to experience the unfamiliar mixture of agony and ecstasy. It was painfully wonderful and she wondered why she was willingly putting herself through this "torture" and questioned whether this 'love' of suffering was not masochistic?

The next morning, she texted early to see how he was.

'Not too good – think it might be a cold xxx'

Kate looked at the phone wondering how to respond. 'Can we meet xxx' she sent.

'Not a good idea, I don't want you do get it xxx.' And he added a sad face emoji.

'Can I get you anything?'

'No. Just need rest – got medication – I'll be fine – speak soon xxx'

Well, she thought, what do I do with myself now? She had planned to spend the weekend with him and was now at a loose end. She picked up the phone and rang Megan, 'Hiya! What are up to?'

'Brad's got the weekend off so we've planned a couple of outings – I've discovered that he doesn't know the area very well. What about you? Has Luke finished his project yet?'

'Yes, virtually, but he's gone down with something.'

'You said that would happen. Men – they never bloody listen! So what are your plans?'

'Well, I don't really have any. Luke and I had planned the weekend together. I suppose it will give me a chance to catch up on housework and plan some lessons. I'm pretty annoyed though.'

'I can imagine,' Megan sympathized.

She wandered around the house shifting piles of stuff from one place to another. She opened a bunch of letters and sorted them making new piles of stuff.

She went down the town and spent money unnecessarily, and finally went home again and watched TV, 'Pride and Prejudice' for the umpteenth time!

She texted, 'How are you feeling? xxx'

'Pretty rough xxx'

'What, no better at all? xxx'

'No, not really xxx' he added a sick face sucking a thermometer.

'I miss you. Want to see you xxx' followed by a sad face.

'I know sweetie, I miss you too, but don't want to pass this on xxx'

'Okay xxx' and she added tearful faced emoji.

Messages went back and forth all week. Valentine's day came and went with a beautiful bunch of red roses and a wonderful card declaring his love for her, and although she drew some comfort from them, they were no substitute for the real thing. She had grown used to his company and couldn't stand the separation, it was driving her crazy!

She was driving Megan crazy with more texts to answer than usual and Megan had not progressed to a smart phone so it took her ages to reply. Also, she was spending more time with her new man so Kate had to find free slots to chat or see her.

The weather was improving and although she managed to get out each day to the Polish café, life seemed lusterless without him. She wondered how he could bear it, but then realised he was probably feeling too sorry for himself to consider anyone else, so she texted two or three times a day to make sure he couldn't forget her.

'Good morning! How are you today?'

'Yeah, loads better thanks. The weather helps. Jason's off work and we might go skating,' he sent a smiley face.

Skating! Kate looked at the text in amazement. How could he go skating? she said to herself.

'Are you sure you're up to it?' she immediately wrote back, 'I think you should take it slowly, get your strength back xxx'

'Don't worry babe, feel so much better, got to get out, so fed up with being indoors, can't stand it any longer xxx'

'Okay, I understand, but I beg you – don't overdo it! Xxx'

'No, I won't xxx'

'Can we meet up? Where are you going? Xxx' Kate had some free time before her lessons and now he was better she wanted to catch up with lost ground.

'Don't know yet hon, haven't decided. Let u know later xxx,' adding another smiley face.

Kate frowned at the screen. She wasn't happy with that. She wasn't jealous of his wanting to go skating with his son; she had never felt jealousy in her life – she didn't know what it was nor did she understand it in others. She had suffered jealousy all her life from work colleagues, friends and relations – mainly from her sister, who had planned and plotted to make her suffer, practically from the day she was born.

Chapter 26

Egotism takes Over

Kate texted Luke in the middle of the day in the hope of meeting up somewhere but he didn't answer, she assumed he was too busy skating so she left it till the evening.

'Hi, how did the skating go xxx?'

'Yeah, smashing thanks – So good to get out in the sunshine. What was yours like xxx?' he followed with a smiling sun face emoji.

'Not bad thanks – glad you enjoyed the skating. Shall I come over xxx?' Kate presumed that he would no longer be contagious.

'Can we leave it till tomorrow, I'm really tired from the skate, been out ALL DAY and need to recover xxx'

She looked at this last message and was annoyed and disturbed by the fact that the first thing he did when he felt better was go skating and not meet up with her, and then, when he got back he said he was too tired!

'Just for a short while, I won't stay long xxx'

'Sorry hon, going to bed soon – tomorrow xxx'

She wasn't happy, so when the doorbell rang and Megan was there to give her a lift to their Lindy hop class she was not in a good mood.

'What's up?' Megan could sense there was something wrong.

'He's been out skating all day with his son and is too bloody tired to see me!' Kate replied in an irritated voice.

'Oh, so he's better then?'

'Yes, it would seem so.'

'How long has he been feeling okay?'

'This is the first day he's been out.'

'It sounds as though he might have overdone things.'

'Yes, more than likely. I told him to take it easy. As if he's going to listen to me.'

'Well you know what men are like, they never grow up.'

'Hmm,' Kate sounded totally fed up and her mood was not improved by Megan's cheerfulness on how well her own relationship was developing.

'Rick took me out to dinner on Valentine's Day.'

'Really,' Kate tried to sound interested although the word came out flat without intonation, and she reflected on her own, non-eventful one.

'Luke sent me a beautiful bunch of red roses.'

'Yes, Brad got me some flowers and a box of chocolates too.'

Kate thought that it was beginning to get competitive and let it drop, besides she wasn't interested in hearing about anyone else's men. She had been patient for nearly two weeks waiting for Luke to get better and then he goes skating and wears himself out so she can't see him!

Megan could tell that she was tetchy so switched on the radio, confident that her mood would lighten once they started dancing.

'Feeling better?' she asked in the car on the way home.

'Yes, thanks,' Kate's voice had regained some of its cheerfulness and by the time Megan dropped her off she was back to her old self.

Early the next day she sent a text to Luke, 'How are you feeling xxx?' But half an hour later she still hadn't had a reply. Concerned, she sent it again and waited, but still he didn't answer.

'Are you receiving my messages?' she couldn't leave it and wondered if she should go and see him when suddenly he answered, 'Text you later xxx'

'Are you Okay xxx?' Kate was obviously worried.

'Yeah, all good, no worries – speak soon xxx'

Kate looked out of the window and could see that it was going to be another lovely day so she couldn't help herself adding, 'Please take it easy today. Don't do too much – give yourself a chance to completely recuperate, *please* xxx'

'Yeah, no probs, don't worry, will do xxx'

Well, all seems okay, she thought, so with four lessons ahead of her to teach that day, she set about preparing the work. She wouldn't suggest meeting for lunch because she was going to strapped for time; she'd see him in the evening and it would wonderful to spend time together. She couldn't wait.

When Kate had said goodbye to the last student she rushed back to find her phone and immediately texted him, 'Hi! How's everything? Shall I come over?' and kept it close by as she waited for his answer. Half an hour later and nothing so she sent it again adding, 'I am not going dancing tonight – kept it free so we could see each other xxx.' Smiley face.

Another half hour had passed and still nothing so she decided to text Jason just to make sure there was nothing seriously wrong.

'Hi there! It's Kate, sorry to trouble you but I sent your dad a text and no answer, is everything alright?'

She immediately received a reply, 'Dad's asleep. Went out skating again today – don't know when he'll wake. Best leave it till tmrw maybe xxx'

'What!' She said aloud to herself. Cat woke up and looked at her quizzically thinking that she must be talking to her. 'Bloody hell!' she went on, *now* she was angry! Hadn't she told him to take it easy? Selfish pig!

'OK.' Was all she was capable of texting because she didn't trust herself to say anything else while expelling smoke from her nostrils.

She was furious. She had cancelled her dance class for nothing, 'Men!' she shouted at the top of her voice. Cat, certain that she had done something wrong, jumped off the chair that she had been sleeping on and tore out of the room just in case. Kate noticed but was so angry left her cowering under a table.

'Bugger, bugger, bugger!' she didn't normally use that kind of language, but occasionally she felt it was warranted, and this was one of those occasions.

She opened a bottle of wine looking for something to help sooth her mood and drank the first glass far too quickly, but she had enjoyed it.

She switched on the tele as a distraction – she needed a good film. While she was scrolling down she remembered a DVD of 'Mama Mia' that Megan had lent her. She looked through the pile on the floor and soon had it up on the screen, so pouring herself another glass of wine she sat on the sofa and indulged herself. Cat felt that the moment had defused and risked jumping up on his mistress's lap, where strokes and tickles told him that whatever he had done was forgotten, so there they both sat, Kate singing along to all the Abba songs and Cat curled up purring in contentment.

Kate awoke the next morning feeling a little worse for wear; gone were the days when she could drink everyone else under the table. She wasn't used to alcohol and always had her wine watered down in a spritzer, or if she drank at home she would have low alcohol. However, yesterday she had ignored the rules and now she was going to have pay for it!

She couldn't do anything until she had finished her second cup of coffee, then she reached for her phone and texted, 'Good morning!' she wanted to sound cheerful and certainly didn't want him to know that his skating had annoyed her, 'How are you today? Xxx'

'Not too good xxx'

'What do u mean? Xxx'

'I don't feel good. Bad head – shivering xxx' he added a sad face with thermometer.

'Do you think it's a relapse? Is it the same as before? Xxx' she wasn't feeling 100% herself and hadn't been expecting this.

'I don't know, just bad all over, everything's aching xxx' sad face.

'Shit! Shit!' she shouted putting Cat on alert again. This was too much! Her head was hurting; already vulnerable from the alcohol and now the stress of coping with his stupidity. She restrained herself from replying too quickly having regretted it in the past. Texting in anger had done her no favours.

She had asked him not to go back to skating too quickly and to take it easy!

'Oh, bugger!' She said to herself, 'Leave him to it – it's his own stupid fault. I don't care. He messed up Valentine's, and now he's going to do the same to my birthday. Selfish bastard.'

He had booked tickets for the theatre and a hotel in London for Kate's birthday, as it happened to fall on a Saturday, and she had been really looking forward to it. All her friends had seen "The

Phantom of the Opera" and she been wanting to see it since forever.

'Ah, well, it was only Tuesday so maybe he would be better by the weekend,' she thought.

She didn't bother to text back, there was no point, if she gave him advice he wouldn't take it.

She had had a life before Luke and she had plenty to keep her occupied so she pushed him to the back of her mind and got on with life. Anger had a wonderful way of motivating her.

She texted in the evening and found no improvement but managed to wish him well, it was perfunctory more than anything else as she was still annoyed by his selfish behaviour.

When she received no reply she texted Jason who told her that his dad was feeling very poorly and had a temperature, and that maybe she should try again in the morning.

This did nothing to lift her mood as the following day would be Thursday and all the time getting closer to the weekend. Meanwhile her sons had asked her if she would like to go out to lunch on the Saturday which would obviously need booking and she had had to put her answer on hold until she knew for sure how Luke was going to be feeling. The whole business was so infuriating, and what irritated her the most was that it could easily have been avoided.

She decided to wait until Friday morning before letting the boys know; aware that it was the last minute but it couldn't be helped, optimistically, she was still hoping that Luke would make a miraculous recovery!

Friday made absolutely no difference at all, according to Jason he was still indisposed. She'd had it! Enough was enough! She told the boys to book somewhere for Saturday and was grateful to be going *anywhere* in the end, even if she did find their company overbearing and exhausting.

Kate was finding it hard to be sympathetic as she was convinced that it had all been self-inflicted. She kept thinking of how he could have avoided everything if only he had got more sleep instead of running himself into the ground with the building work at the beginning. And then, just as he was getting better, he had to go and destroy all the good work by skating for two whole days in February! She wondered if he would learn any lessons from it all.

Probably not, she concluded, if past experience was anything to go by. She had yet to meet a man who considered his health, most of them stuffed themselves full with red meat, bread and potatoes and avoided the doctor like the plague, especially if it required pulling down their trousers!

Chapter 27

Happy Birthday Kate

In the end, she had accepted the boys' offer to take her to lunch because she couldn't stand the indecision, and knew that if nothing were planned then she would end up sitting at home on her own.

Unexpectedly, on the Saturday morning, Luke texted her saying he wanted her to go round and open the presents he had for her!

She had planned to take the morning easy, wash her hair, do her nails and get ready for lunch with no pressure; but no, now she was going to have to allocate at least an hour to spend at his place, because she couldn't just go round, open them and scarper.

'Are you sure you feel well enough? We could leave it till tomorrow if you like? Xxx' she tried, in the hope of putting him off till the next day.

'No, I am feeling much better thanks. Really want to see you. Want to wish you Happy Birthday and give you your presents. Xxx' he added a line of celebratory emojis: candles, champagne bottle, a wrapped present etc.,

Kate wondered whether things would finally go back to how they had been before February.

'OK. See you about midday xxx' and wondered why she wasn't feeling more excited about seeing him again after more than three week's separation.

The doorbell rang and it was Megan, laden with gifts and a beautiful bunch of flowers, singing Happy Birthday.

Kate ushered her in as quickly as possible because she didn't want anyone passing by to see her in a semi-state of undress and with wet hair. She put the kettle on and asked her to make the coffee while she quickly dried her hair.

By the time she emerged from the bathroom Megan was chatting to Cat and there were two steaming cups of coffee on the table.

'Ooo, lovely, thanks. I'm sorry but I'm a bit under pressure now 'cos Luke wants me to call in before I have lunch with the boys,' she said reaching for the bottle of base coat for her nails.

'Don't worry, I won't stay long, but I had to come and say Happy Birthday to my best mate and bring you these,' she gestured to the beautifully wrapped gifts on the table.

'Oh, Meg, you shouldn't have. I feel thoroughly spoilt.'

'You deserve it. We've been through a lot together.'

Kate waited for the base coat to dry and then carefully opened each one. Her friend knew her so well that they were all perfect, a mixture of practical and pampering.

'They are perfect, thank you!' and she kissed her on the cheek.

'Good, I'm glad you like them. Now I had better push off and let you get on. I hope you have a lovely day. Where are you going for lunch?

'The Michelin Star one on the bay'

'Wow! They're really pushing the boat out!'

'At last,' Kate smiled.

'Good. Don't get up – I'll see myself out,' and with that Megan got up, ruffled the fur on the top of Cat's head, said goodbye to both of them and left.

Kate decided to get dressed and put on her shoes before applying the colour to her nails, previous disasters had shown her the error of her ways.

When she saw that time was running short and that she had forgotten to extract her car keys from the depths of her handbag before starting the operation, she didn't dare risk scrambling through the contents and she couldn't see them anywhere near the top so she looked around for something to hook them out with. Luckily her eyes fell on the kitchen tongs – perfect! She thought as she removed everything on the surface until she was able to locate them. As long as she took care in the car, they would be dry by the time she got to Luke's, she thought.

How she had missed Koko and Kiki! So, when they rushed out to greet her, she made as much of a fuss of them as she could. Luke kissed her on the cheek saying it was better to be safe than sorry, and how he had missed her. Kate was relieved to see that he looked no worse for wear after three weeks of confinement and gave him a long, hard hug which he reciprocated. It made her realise how much she had missed the physical contact and if she hadn't spent hours preparing for lunch she would have taken everything off and gone to bed for the afternoon.

'Hey, steady,' he said pulling away from her, 'Or you may have to cancel lunch,' he laughed.

She looked at her watch and wondered if they could fit in a quickie, although it wouldn't be, so they went into the living room.

Nothing had changed, except that there were several beautifully wrapped parcels of different sizes lying on the sofa.

'Ooh, someone's been busy!' she said kissing him (again on the cheek) and sitting down next to the gifts, 'Which one should I open first?'

'Leave that one till last,' he said pointing to smallest and he sat down so close to her that she could feel the warmth of his body down the length of her back, his chin resting on her shoulder so he could watch her. Koko lay at her feet. She was happy to be back and tried to forget the last three weeks persuading herself that it had just been a glitch and normal service had resumed.

She was in no hurry to open them as she wanted to savour the moment.

In recent years, her birthdays had been and gone with little or no celebration and although all her friends from abroad had sent her cards, her egotistical ex and her sons hadn't bothered to make a fuss so she was loving the attention and was impressed by the thought and care he had put into his choice of gifts.

Kate showed her appreciation each time with a kiss and by saying how clever he had been at finding just the right things, and how she loved each one and the reasons why.

Luke seemed pleased that his consideration had paid off and couldn't wait for her to open the last one.

She was quite disappointed when she only had one left to open so, as she pulled at the pretty pink ribbon and peeled open the shiny wrapping she wondered what she would find inside the small box. Half wishing, half hoping, she slowly opened it peeping under the lid. Inside, there was a quite delightful, small, diamond-studded cat brooch set in silver; it was gorgeous and she loved it and knew she would wear it, in fact she pinned it straight onto her dress.

'I love it,' she said giving him a hug, 'I feel totally spoilt.'

'Good, and so you should be, it's your birthday. I'm only sorry that I had to cancel London,' He leant over and kissed her on the neck, one of her vulnerable spots, and designed to break down her defenses.

She looked at her watch and regretted not having arranged to see him later in the day so that she didn't have to rush off.

'I wish I didn't have to go,' she said with regret.

'Me too,' he snuggled up close.

She knew she was already late so she sent a text to one of the boys saying she was on her way.

Luke's face was saying, 'don't go' but she didn't have a choice. Her sons didn't treat her very often so she didn't want to mess it up by being late.

She left him standing on the doorstep sandwiched between Koko and Kiki as she reluctantly pulled away, and, as she drove to the restaurant she thought about the intimacy of the moment they had spent together, and how, thankfully, nothing between them seemed to have changed. She was sure that life would return to normal and the episode of illness would be forgotten.

Kate had hoped for a ring but was not disappointed with the cat brooch. She had faith in Sylvia and her predictions and although they had been through a rough patch, she was certain that they were back on track now and the future looked rosy.

She was on cloud number nine when she got to the restaurant and found the boys waiting outside for her.

'Sorry mum they're fully booked, but we can go somewhere else,' Ricky said cheerfully.

Under normal circumstances she would have been really pissed off by them not having booked; she would have told them to forget it and gone home fuming, but (luckily for them) getting back with

Luke had mollified her and she agreed, 'So what do you have in mind?'

There was silence for a while as they both tried to think of a suitable alternative.

Suggestions came and went, they finally settled on a hotel on the seafront as they could see that their mother had made a special effort and was looking particularly elegant.

Kate had inherited her dress sense from her mother who had always been so smartly dressed that she used to turn heads in the street. And Kate could remember having her own picture taken for the local paper, in the 1960s, when she had been spotted in the street in red PVC! It wasn't elegant but it was really cool at the time. She was wearing a short red PVC jacket with mini-skirt to match, and red PVC boots! PVC was the latest fashion statement and she looked outrageously good!

For her birthday she had chosen to wear the same red, Italian dress with fitted sleeveless top that she had worn for dinner on her first date with Luke, so she was confident of 'the look' it created.

Fortunately, when they got to the hotel there was space available in the restaurant so once installed, Kate really started to relax.

'Order whatever you want mum,' Ricky said magnanimously.

'Yeah, whatever your little heart desires,' Charlie chipped in.

They had brought her presents and cards, and although not terribly original, she was touched by the thought.

The boys were on form, laughing and cracking jokes and making her laugh too, so when she closed the door later that afternoon and switched on the tele, she felt wonderfully content and simply wanted to enjoy the sensation, as the last three weeks had been so full of uncertainty and self-deprecation. On reflection, it was one of the best birthdays she could remember.

She was stroking Cat on the sofa when she had a text alert on her mobile from Luke, 'I hope you had a lovely day sweetie, can we meet for lunch tomorrow?'

'Yes of course!' she replied instantaneously. What more could she wish for!

Chapter 28

Megan Takes the Plunge

The next day, they met at the top of her lane and they went to her favourite pub for a roast, being a Sunday. Luke was on form, teasing her in an endearing way, and they played darts and pool and went for a stroll along the top of the cliffs with the dogs.

'Do you want to come over tonight?' he said giving her hand a squeeze.

'There's nothing I would love more,' she said with that smile that had disarmed him from the start.

She couldn't wait to tell Megan. Life was perfect.

'I'll cook something – nothing special,'

'Can't wait. I'll be over about eight if that's okay?'

'You're still doing your ballroom dancing then?'

'Yes, I had to keep busy while you were ill. It was driving me crazy not seeing you!'

'Yeah, me too hon,' and before they went their separate ways, he kissed her– leaving her wanting.

She practically flew down the lane to her house. Cat looked at her suspiciously as she seemed happy? She was!

The evening went exactly as she would have planned; they had dinner on the floor in front of the fire (the nights were still chilly), watched a video and went to bed. And, of course, the following day started flawlessly with breakfast in bed!

Kate went home to prepare lessons having arranged to meet for lunch as usual. She would text Megan and catch up. But her mobile buzzed before she had a chance: 'Hi! Hope you had a GREAT Sunday? Bradley was here last night and we did it!' Megan read the message again, 'Did it! Does she mean....?' Kate couldn't wait for a text as it took an age on Megan's old phone – she had to ring her.

'Hello there!'

Megan could tell by her tone of voice that she was smiling with anticipation.

'Hello!'

'Well.... Tell me! Did I understand correctly? Don't keep me in suspense!'

'Yes, you understood.'

'So...how?'

'Well, I cooked him a nice dinner and we both got completely pissed, and he led me into the bedroom and ripped my clothes off.'

'What literally?!'

'Yes!'

'And.....?'

'Well, he certainly knows what he's doing. Not like Harry. But I think it's my fault; I have so many hang ups from before that I couldn't climax, whatever that means as I never did with Harry.'

'I'm sure he understood, didn't he? Did he?'

'Oh, yes, he had no problem. He managed it twice.'

'Yeah, well that's men for you. Don't worry about it, it'll happen when it's supposed to. Do you want to borrow some toys?'

'No, I don't think that's a good idea, at least not at the moment, it might make him feel inadequate.'

'Hey, look! We should celebrate! We have to go for a drink tonight after Zumba! My treat – prosecco?!'

'Sounds good, but don't forget I'm driving.'

'Yes, but you could have one glass?'

'Yes, they have those little bottles at the bar on the front.'

'Perfect! And hey; congratulations!'

'Thanks.'

'Well, well, well!' Kate said aloud to Cat who woke up and looked at her, she assumed that as her mistress didn't have any company that she had to be talking to her.

Kate couldn't have been happier for her friend; it was about bloody time – all those years with no sex seemed unimaginable to her. She would probably have raped someone out of frustration! No, she wouldn't have needed to – there had always been men on tap in Kate's life!

She sent a quick text to Luke warning him that she would be a bit late that evening and explained why.

The evening came round pretty quickly and before she had time to eat anything Megan was tooting the horn to let her know that she was there.

'Hi!' Kate said as she jumped in the car, 'And congrats again.'

'Thanks.'

'Do you feel any different?'

'Yes, sort of.'

'Good different?'

'Yes!'

'Whoopy!'

The Zumba class was exhausting but fun and they were on good form when they got to the hotel bar. The barman immediately recognised them, 'Two white wine spritzers with soda and no ice in large glasses?' he said proudly, the regulars liked to think they were special, and one way was to remember their orders.

'Not today Jann, we're celebrating! Two prosecco!' Kate said with a flourish.

'Oh, lovely. Is it someone's birthday?' he enquired in a silky, Slavic accent through the sexiest of smiles.

'In a way, yes.' Megan glared at her and kicked her lightly on the ankle.

'Oh?' he said expectantly.

'I'm celebrating losing my virginity!' Kate said with a smile.

They could both see that Jann wasn't quite sure whether he had understood or whether it was the good old English sense of humour, so Kate put him out of his agony.

'Joke!' she said and they all laughed.

So, none the wiser, he opened two small bottles and as he placed them on the counter with glasses he said, 'I hope you enjoy!'

Kate paid and they took a seat near the window from where they could see the lights of France.

'Cheers!' Kate held up her glass.

'Cheers!' and the clink of glass against glass rang through the virtually empty bar.

'Let's drink to success!' Kate said optimistically.

'To success in all its forms' Megan reciprocated.

Chapter 29

Kate's Treat

The week went by without incident and Kate regained a feeling of stability in her life. Luke was ultra-attentive and she was confident of his sentiments towards her.

He had promised somehow to make up for not taking her to the theatre in London and asked her if there were any exhibitions or places that she really wanted to visit. She had always wanted to see the Cabinet War Rooms in Westminster having passed the sign so many times, but she had never had enough time to fit it in. So Luke made her promise not to arrange anything for the following Sunday and she agreed.

The weather was fine so they walked from Victoria to Whitehall, stopping on the way for a French pastry and coffee in the most delightful, cosy, family-run café. As far as she could tell everyone working there was French, and Kate felt momentarily transported to her favourite country; she was sure that she had been French in a previous life.

Her pastry was filled with the most delicious thick, yellow, cream that she had eaten so many times on the Continent, but never figured out how to make.

It took her back to when she had lived in Rome and she and her boyfriend would walk home from the jazz club in the early hours of a Sunday morning, passing a bakery that was making all the bread and pastries for the next day.

The bakers would leave the metal security blind open about a meter from the ground probably to allow some cool air in, and as she and Luciano walked past, the smell was impossible to ignore so they would duck under the shutter and beg to be sold an early, 'freschissimo' pastry filled with the most amazing yellow pastry cream imaginable.

Had she eaten the same pastry in a café in Pembleton, in the middle of the afternoon it would not have been so memorable; it was the combination of walking through the deserted streets of Rome in the early hours, and of catching the aroma of the fresh baking, and then being allowed to creep under the shutter and watch the bakers busily pulling trays of pastries and loaves of bread from the ovens as though it was perfectly natural for them to be there, made them feel special – it was!

If you tried to buy anything from a baker in England by sneaking under the metal security shutter they would probably call the police, but the Italians greeted them with, 'Buongiorno' and smiles.

When they had paid, they would wander slowly back home munching their way through the bag of creamy pastries, with a stop to wash them down with coffee or cappuccino.

Sometimes, they were so revived from the pastries and coffee that they would keep going all Sunday and just have an afternoon nap. At other times the pastries and coffee had a soporific effect and they would flop straight into bed and sleep until midday.

She had made some long-lasting friendships and done many exciting things and absolutely adored the Italians and their country, but she hadn't spent long enough there having left prematurely due to a vicious attack on her by a taxi driver.

Chapter 30

The War Rooms

When Luke had finished his *second* pastry they walked on through the back streets to Parliament Square taking in the elegant grandeur of the surrounding buildings. They peered along Downing Street and wondered if the Prime Minister was carving the Sunday roast, and stood in front of the guards on horseback and trying in vain, to make them laugh. They passed The Cenotaph and turned off following the signs to the Cabinet War Rooms, and after descending a short flight of steps found themselves in a bustling reception area where they joined the queue for tickets.

Kate had no expectations whatsoever, all she knew was that the underground labyrinth of offices had played a strategic part in saving the country from German occupation, so, when she finally emerged at the other end, she couldn't believe how quickly the time had passed; the experience had been so engrossing that they had spent three and half hours underground! She wondered how many people knew that there had been a secret communications centre in Selfridges!

As they stepped out from the underground maze, the dazzling winter day that they had left behind at the entrance had turned to night, the streets lit artificially, they walked under Admiralty Arch into Trafalgar Square.

Luke wanted to take her to his favourite oriental restaurant before catching the train back, which she thought would make a perfect end to a perfect day and readily agreed, even if it did mean more walking. So, they set off down The Strand, and after about five hundred meters Kate asked if it was much further.

'No, it's literally where you see that sign,' and he pointed to a bright red neon sign in oriental writing,

'You'll love this place, it's so authentic.'

Kate was really hungry and looked forward to her meal.

As they turned the corner (the door was not on the main road), it was obvious that it was closed; there were no lights on and a very clear sign saying "closed".

'Well, we come here all the time on Sundays. I can't understand it!' he sounded genuinely puzzled.

'We?' Kate inquired.

'The skaters. This is *so* annoying.'

'Well never mind, there are loads of places open. Let's go somewhere else?' she suggested.

Luke stood looking at the restaurant willing the sign to change and for the lights to suddenly go on, and Kate knew it would be best to wait until he was ready for a new plan, he didn't like ideas not going to plan. Finally, he said, 'Yeah, Okay.'

So they walked back again in the direction of the station and ended up in a commercial place with absolutely no atmosphere offering pseudo-Italian food for tourists. Kate could see that he was not happy with their choice, but as they were both hungry and didn't want to walk for miles, they had settled for less than second best.

They ate because they were hungry, but it had not been the perfect ending.

Chapter 31

Normal Service

The lunches together resumed, and Kate noticed how the conversation always ended up with Luke talking about skating moves and how much practice he had put in. She knew that he could practice for hours, all day, doing the same move over and over and even then he wouldn't be happy; he would go back to the park the next day and repeat the same thing all over again. It was an obsession and if the weather was inclement then he would use the kitchen.

He explained each move in detail using his hands to imitate the blades, and she just let him talk as he was totally oblivious of how uninterested or bored she was. There were so many different names for the moves: The Swan (a kind of circular movement), Eagle Cross, Eagle Royal Cross, reverse Eagle Criss-Cross, Mabrouk, Chap Chap, Crab, Kasatchok, Toe Wheeling, Heel Wheeling, Gregfit (done with cones) – cones seemed to be an essential part of an inline skater's equipment. They were a set of mini-sized cones about twelve centimeters high in fluorescent colours, presumably so that skating could continue after dark!

As a teacher she made a good listener and made all the right sounds, even though she hadn't a clue what he was on about. Sometimes she would go and watch him, although there were only so many times a person could watch the same thing. She surprised herself by her tolerance, and put it down to the fact that he was not demanding or expecting anything from her.

Since her return to England all she had met were "chancers", "fraudsters" or "users" and her last relationship (of 11 years) had left totally disillusioned.

Strangely though, once she had got used to being on her own, instead of it depressing her, she experienced a satisfying sense of freedom. Liberated from the thought (instilled in her from birth) that, she had to have a male partner to feel fulfilled as a woman. She had begun to enjoy life by indulging in all the things that she had given up for motherhood and men. Then, just as she had found her new philosophy on life, Luke had come along and rocked her determination never to get involved with a man again. And now it was too late, because she had opened the door to her heart and let him in.

It had happened imperceptibly as neither of them had been looking for romance; on the contrary they were both non-believers, skeptics and yet...

It was the last Friday in March and Kate was going to spend the night at Luke's after a special rock 'n roll session, so it was late when she let herself in (he had given her a set of keys weeks ago which had heightened her feeling of security in their relationship). He was watching television when she opened the door to the living room.

'Hiya!' she bent down and gave him an affectionate kiss, 'How did the skating go?' She knew that he always went over to a sports venue and met a bunch of friends on a Friday night.

'I didn't go.'

Kate immediately sensed a problem from his tone, 'Why not?' she asked, wondering if it was something that he would be able to disclose.

'Too angry and pissed off!'

'Hey, that's not like you. What's happened?' And she sat down next to him putting an arm around his shoulder in support.

'You know all that work that we did preparing the building?'

'Yes.'

'Well it's been a bloody waste! A waste of time, energy and money!'

'That sounds hard to believe.'

'Believe it! It's true! That stupid dull-witted oaf Karl went and told his air-head girlfriend everything and she's got a mouth like an open flood gate, so the whole thing's off now – cancelled, aborted – all that work, all my plans, three years of planning this has taken, and it's all for nothing! That was my retirement and our future, all down the Suwanee.' She had never heard him sound so negative.

'Are you sure it can't be salvaged?' Kate said desperate to help in some way.

'Na, forget it! Too dangerous, that stupid cow won't be able to keep it to herself, especially once the money starts to roll in. I can't believe that he told her, he knew how important it was to keep schtum. I can't tell you how angry I am. I was sick for nearly three weeks doing all that work!'

'Yes, I know, this seems so unfair. Can't you just go ahead without him?'

'Na, it won't work, that'd probably be worse, he'd go squealing to the law out of spite and Guy has a family to think of – it's his place, he can't afford to have the fuzz up there.'

There didn't seem to be any appeasing him; he rejected all her suggestions and she had run out of ideas. She had never seen him so down (except maybe when he had been sick) and she couldn't seem to lift his spirits.

'I don't think that you should write it off too quickly, you never know you may come up with a solution later on.'

She was pretty sure that it was all connected to some sort of drug business, and had narrowed it down to the growing of Marijuana, because it was a large surface area that had to be secure. She had tried to find out more, but knew that he wasn't going to disclose anything.

'I don't think so sweetie,' he said glumly.

She didn't know whether it would help, but she put both arms around him and gave him a hug saying that she would put her thinking hat on.

His mood was no better in the morning. There had been no lovemaking, even her eggs looked sad, and she left without any plans made for the weekend.

It was a beautiful spring day so Kate dedicated the morning to washing and hung it out in the sunshine – the first time that year. She left the back door open and Cat went crazy tearing in and out. She texted Luke to see how he was feeling, but it was a while before he replied. She kept checking her phone while she pottered in the garden, there was so much to do having virtually left it to run wild over the winter months. Normally she would avoid gardening at all costs but the warm weather encouraged her to blitz it.

She felt her phone buzz in her pocket, 'Hi Sweetie, going over to Cliffe-on-Sea xx'. Kate knew that that was his normal venue on a Saturday so she wasn't surprised, also the two kisses told her that he was still down.

'Do you want to meet later? xxx' she didn't expect a positive response but tried anyway.

He replied, 'I might stay over xx'

She knew it was an excuse because he would have to feed and walk the dogs, but she wasn't going to pursue it.

'Okay xxx' and she added a smiley face, 'Try and relax if you can.' She desperately wanted to be with him but wasn't going to put him under any pressure.

Kate woke early the next morning even though it was Sunday and the first thing she did was check her phone – nothing, so she decided to do another load of washing and hang it in the garden. She sent a 'Good morning! xxx' with a smiley face and got on with life; he would probably get back to her later. She had been groomed during his illness to chill when he didn't reply.

When she had had enough domesticity, she texted Megan on the off chance that she would be free to enjoy the spring weather with her, but, of course, Bradley was there and she was 'seeing to him', whatever that meant?

The last time they had seen each other she had asked Kate to explain how to give a blow job, assuming that she was an expert! Kate did her best, but with no vegetables at hand to demonstrate on (being in the pub at the time) she resorted to a saltcellar which was entirely the wrong size and shape, and if they hadn't been such good customers and friends with the owner they would probably have been asked to leave for indecent behaviour. Anyway, it was a hysterical evening and they laughed so much that their sides ached. Kate told her to go home and practice on a carrot! Reminding her that if she left teeth marks he would probably end up in hospital.

Chapter 32

Cooling Off?

It was a perfect day for a long walk by the sea, so Kate picked up her MP3 player and left the house listening to Greek (a language she was determined to master). Luckily, she had always enjoyed her own company so she had no problem amusing herself or keeping busy and it would have been a crime to spend the day indoors. Even so she did miss him.

She kept checking her phone, but found no communication from Luke.

She was trying to understand; okay, all his dreams had been shattered, but *she* hadn't walked out on the relationship, she was still there trying to support him; but somehow she felt that 'they' had become secondary to the calamity that had befallen his mysterious business. It was difficult for her to properly comprehend what was going on not knowing all the facts, but she had seen the effect it had had on his mood and disposition. Give it time, she said to herself, it would all blow over and everything would be the same as before.

She was on her way back to the house when a text came through from Luke, finally!

'Hi hon, wanna meet me on the front? Xxx' The front always meant the sea front.

'So, he's out, probably walking Koko,' she thought. 'Whereabouts are you? xxx' she replied instantly.

'By the café xxx'. It meant backtracking about a quarter of a mile but the weather was so lovely she didn't mind. However, when she turned the bend there was no sign of Koko, just Luke weaving in and out of his mini cones doing his tricks, to an audience! She felt like a groupie! She walked slowly towards him wondering what on earth she was doing there, after all she'd seen it all *so many* times before.

'Hi, sweetie!' he broke off from his performance as soon as he saw her, skated over to where she was standing and gave her a kiss, which for some reason it didn't make her feel special only cheap! She was uncomfortable there as he went back to his tricks. Did he expect her to stand there and 'Ooh' and 'Aah' with the rest of them? Sometimes they broke into applause!

'Bugger this,' she muttered under her breath and walked up the steps to the café. She was not happy, she'd been hoping to go for a peaceful stroll with Koko, just like they used to do, not stand and cheer on the sidelines like some sort of star-struck teenager. She ordered a pot of tea and sat on the terrace looking out to sea and tried to overcome her irritation. After about twenty minutes he appeared in trainers carrying his skates. Kate forced a smile, 'Hello.'

'I could just do with a cup of tea,' he said taking a sip from hers.

'I'll get you a pot,' she said getting up.

'Yeah, thanks sweetie.' Kate disappeared into the café and reappeared with a small tray that she placed on the table. She had calmed down a little now that they were alone and the crowds had dispersed.

'You're feeling a bit better then?'

'Well, no good crying over spilt milk,' he smiled.

'Have you found a solution?'

'No, just not going to let it worry me. The weather's better so at least I can skate.'

Oh goodie, goodie! Thought Kate sarcastically.

'And then there's the fishing – the boys will be starting that this week.'

'Well, you seem to have everything sorted?' she said in a resentful tone which went unnoticed.

'Yeah, pretty much, just have to get on with life.'

Kate wondered how much she would be included in his plans.

When the pots of tea were empty they left and headed back up the cliffs. Luke rabbited on about how he had nearly perfected a move that involved a series of ninety degree turns while crossing skates and changing weight from one skate to the other, the name of which Kate knew she would never retain. She listened but wasn't taking it in, and wondered whether he was talking simply to break the silence although she knew that wasn't necessary, at least not as far as she was concerned; their relationship had transcended the need for perpetual conversation.

When they reached the top they went their separate ways, Luke said he wanted to get back to watch the motor racing so he left her at the end of her lane and headed off. They had made no arrangements to meet up later in the evening and although things seemed to be back on track, a feeling of uncertainty niggled away at her.

Cat was all over her as soon as she opened the door and followed her through the living room out to the garden at the back. Kate felt the clothes that she had hung out earlier.

'Ah, perfectly dry!' she said to Cat who looked up intelligently; she proceeded to unclip the pegs and put them in the bag. She inhaled deeply, holding each freshly laundered item up to her nose; there was no substitute for that fresh air smell, and it would pervade the living room until she put them away.

The horizon was streaked orange and pink with not a breath of wind, so after having dealt with the laundry she poured herself a glass of rosé and sat outside to watch the sun disappear, while Cat unsuccessfully hunted butterflies and bumblebees.

She hoped for a text from Luke, willing him to miss her, but when nothing arrived she sent *him* one, 'I am glad that you are not letting the 'business' get to you. Shall we meet for lunch tomorrow? xxx'

'Can't tomorrow babe, loads to do xxx' followed by a sad face. 'Maybe later in the evening?'

'OK xxx' smiley face, she tried to sound nonchalant.

She spent the rest of the evening searching the guide for the best programmes on the box and busied herself preparing work for the coming week.

The next day, Kate went to lunch by herself, more for the exercise than anything else because she hated being in the house the whole day long. Just before her first pupil arrived, Megan rang to say that she couldn't make the dance class but would see her the following evening for salsa. Kate wasn't too put out over it, and when she finished teaching, messaged Luke, 'Hey, what are you up to? xxx'

'On the front – want to meet me? Xxx'

'OK – same place? Xxx'

'Yeah xxx'

She quickly changed shoes and walked briskly down the slope towards the front.

He was in a cheerful mood as he skated alongside her, 'Do you want some chips?' he asked her as they approached a fish and chip shop. She liked the idea of sitting by the harbour with some chips, so he got two portions and they sat on the harbour wall watching people work on their boats and yachts, getting them ready for the season ahead.

They chatted about the pros and cons of life on the ocean wave and agreed that it wasn't for them. Kate said that she would prefer the freedom of a camper van and Luke said that if he had the money and the space to park one he'd like the idea too. They talked about the kinds of places they would visit if they didn't have to work, and Kate realised how ignorant she was of her own country.

On the way back they reached Luke's place first having taken another route, so Kate suggested she stay, however Luke's reaction was unexpected – he didn't seem to be against her staying, but neither was he over-joyed.

Kate ignored his lack of enthusiasm; it had been too long since they had enjoyed each other in bed and she was in need of some reassurance.

She stayed, certain in the thought that all would be well once they got into bed together.

She made the first move and he responded predictably, and although Kate knew she had satisfied him, she was left wanting. She could hear from his steady breathing that he was asleep so she turned on her side and eventually joined him; she would have to wait till the morning

Chapter 33

It's Over

She woke to sounds of activity in the kitchen, so with her eyes still closed, she reached over the side of the bed for her tea, and on finding nothing, assumed it was on its way. She checked the time and saw it was early, only six o'clock. Flopping back onto the pillow she waited, however, after ten minutes, when there was no sign of anything she got up and wandered into the kitchen. When she opened the door she found Luke cleaning!

'Morning! Shall I make some tea?' she said.

'Yes, help yourself sweetie, I don't need another cup. Didn't want to wake you.'

Kate made her tea and went back into the bedroom. She walked over to the window and peeked through the curtains – the sky was a flawless blue and the sun streamed in through the crack between them. It was still chilly in the mornings even if the sunshine was testimony to the day ahead, so she got back into bed to warm up and finish her tea. She put on her clothes and looked in at the kitchen again but there was no sign of breakfast, instead she found him on the floor with newspaper spread out in front of him with his skates in pieces.

'What are you doing?' she asked.

'I'm cleaning them. Haven't done anything to them all winter and they need an overhaul; it should improve performance, and I need to get all this done so I can get out today and make the most of the fine weather.'

She could see all kinds of tools, a small bottle of clear oil and a tin lid containing ball bearings which she assumed had come from his skates. She could see that he was completely engrossed in the task, so she offered to cook breakfast; but he said he would be in the way and that he would do it later.

Kate went back to the bedroom, and on reflection could not see any point in hanging around so she gathered up her stuff, popped her head around the kitchen door, and said,'Okay, I'll be off then.'

'Hey, hang on hon, there's no need to go, I won't be long and then I'll cook breakfast.'

Kate looked at the array of stuff and knew that it was going to be a while before everything was reassembled, and was not prepared to hang around. What did he think she was going to do for the next 45 minutes to an hour? Sit and watch him? Make small talk? Tell him how clever he was? So, this was the way it would be from now on, she thought to herself, second fiddle to a pair of skates! She wondered if that came higher or lower on the scale to a dog?

She thought she detected a look of regret on his face, although she might have imagined it.

At least he had the decency to see her to the front door where he gave her a perfunctory kiss, brief and emotionless, after which she left without looking back.

It was a brilliant, clear April morning with not a breath of wind, so Kate was quite happy to be out of the house walking. He had made her feel unwanted, a nuisance, and she had a sick feeling of rejection in the pit of her stomach. She needed to get home, away from him, to think things through. It was less than half a mile to her place and she was enjoying the stillness of the early morning.

There was no denying that she was upset by his behaviour and that nothing had gone as she had imagined; instead of improving their relationship, it had just made her feel worse.

Cat came straight up to her as soon as she got inside and, she found the attention comforting – at least he loved her!

She made herself a cup of coffee and prepared some lessons for later in the day, by which time the feeling of rejection had turned to anger. He knew she was awake before he had started on his skates so why not get breakfast out of the way first? Then they could have parted on good terms; he could have got on with his skate-cleaning and Kate would have gone home feeling less demoralised.

As it was she felt like shit, for the first time in their relationship he had made her feel like the last one – that awful man who had treated her like a piece of furniture, a commodity!

Had Luke been pretending all along? The promises – "I want to take care of you," – all shit? Had she fallen for the crap *again*? How could she have been so stupid? She wasn't going to walk away without telling him what she thought; she'd had enough.

She broke her rule and texted in anger, 'I had to leave because if I had stayed it might have got nasty and I could see that you were *far* too preoccupied with your beautiful skates to give me the time of day, not to mention breakfast! If it was your intention to make me feel like a piece of worthless shit then you succeeded brilliantly! Don't worry, I won't be staying again.' She pressed 'send' then she rang Megan to make sure that she hadn't forgotten all their dance dates for the week ahead.

'Hiya! Are you still alright for Zumba tonight?'

'Yes, of course, we arranged that ages ago!'

'And the rest of the week?'

'Yes, I said I was, weren't you listening? Are you all right?' Megan sensed there was something wrong.

'Yes and no. It's complicated – I'll explain later when we see each other.'

'Are you sure you're all right?' Kate didn't usually call early in the morning.

'Yes, don't worry, we'll talk later.'

Meanwhile, Luke had replied to her text, 'Sorry you feel that way – not intended – just had a lot planned, besides you invited yourself remember? I never complained about all your dancing and stuff, did I?'

His message incensed her all the more, 'You told me that you didn't want me to give any of it up! You said that you liked me dancing and drawing! And if you hadn't wanted me to stay then you should have said instead of ignoring me like shit!'

'I think you are over-reacting. I was going to cook breakfast but *you* wanted to leave.'

Kate knew there was no point in trying to justify herself; he had probably had this sort of argument many times before and was well rehearsed in responses. It would have been futile to retaliate; it would only create more bad feeling. Anyway, this sort of thing made her ill – she wasn't into bickering, she liked a balanced, harmonious life, that's why so much went unsaid for fear of causing trouble. She would rather shut up and put up than create discord, but sometimes she just needed to stand up for herself. Besides, he didn't seem to realise when he had hurt someone, she had seen him pass a couple of very insensitive remarks to his son and had seen the hurt on Josh's face, but it had gone completely over Luke's head. On one occasion she had intervened with, 'Oh, I'm sure your Dad didn't really mean that.' For Luke to come back with, 'Yeah, I did.'!She couldn't believe it!

Chapter 34

Reconciliation or Revenge

At about midday while she was browsing through a new Spanish course book she saw a text flash up on her phone. It was from Luke, 'Are you feeling any better? Xxx'

"Feeling better?" What did he mean by that? Why did men do that – make out that it was all the woman's fault because obviously she wasn't well! What the f*** did he think was wrong with her? It couldn't be PMS at her age, so .... the change? She wanted to reply "suffering from menitis", but thought better of it, so she didn't text anything.

After a while, not having had a reply he texted again, 'Do you want to meet? Xxx'

Kate stared at the screen. Meet for what? Why? she thought. The last thing she wanted was to go back over the events of the morning, apportioning blame or listening to self-righteous justification.

'What time? xxx' she punched in the question out of curiosity.

'I could fit you in at about six? xxx'

Kate stared at the message – she couldn't believe it!

'Fit me in! Fit me in!' she said out loud, 'How dare he!' shouting. 'It's not a bloody doctor's appointment! Besides he knows I'm always busy teaching at that time.' Cat stood to attention wondering what he had done.

She was furious and didn't reply. She knew she wouldn't be seeing him at six and certainly wasn't going to be 'fitted into' his schedule.

'Fuck him!' she said loudly – Cat bolted.

She was really happy to hear Megan pull up outside at around seven thirty; she needed the distraction of the Zumba class and to get rid of her pent-up anger.

They went on to the Pub for a drink as Brad was working a late shift and Megan was in no hurry to go home.

Once they had their drinks and had found a quiet corner Kate told Megan about the morning's events and the text message that had so infuriated her.

'What! He said he would "fit you in"? Bloody cheek! I would have been furious too!' Megan agreed.

Kate was grateful for her moral support.

'What did you answer?'

'I didn't!'

'Don't blame you. I wouldn't have either. So how have you left it?'

'I don't know. I don't really want to speak to him, in fact, I think it's over.'

'Christ! are you serious?

'Yes, I don't want to be "fitted in", except I don't want him to get away with this either.'

'What do mean?'

'Well, this is what he does. He takes up with a girl in the late autumn when the skating peters out, and then dumps them in the Spring when the weather improves again. He's told me about two of them but I'm sure there have been more. I know that the last one felt very bitter because she emptied the flat when he wasn't there. Anyway, he should know better than mess with me because I've warned him what will happen.'

Megan looked quizzically at her.

'I am sure I've told you about all the people who have done things to hurt me.'

'Hmm, I think you have – maybe a couple.'

Kate believed that there was someone (call it a guardian angel for want of another name) who 'looked after her,' as everyone who had ever hurt her or treated her badly out of spite, jealousy or pure nastiness had always been repaid threefold. So, Kate was confident that everyone eventually got what was coming to them even if she had to wait a couple of years, by which time she would have forgotten all about them. Then one day, someone would come up to her in the street and say 'Did you know that so-and-so died?'or 'so-and-so had a stroke' and she would think, 'Yes! Finally!'

At first, she thought it was a coincidence but later she began to rely on justice being served without her needing to lift a finger.

'I could just sit back and wait and he will be dealt with, but this time I don't want to wait for poetic justice, he needs to be taught a lesson. And *now,* not *later.*'

Megan could tell that her friend was angry and she didn't blame her, after all, he had promised her the earth, moon and stars knowing it wouldn't last and like she said, his life seemed to follow a pattern of finding a female playmate for the winter and dumping them once the weather improved. And yet Kate had been perfectly happy before *he* had appeared on the scene, 'man-less'. Somehow he had managed to beguile her into falling in love with him although Megan could see none of his charm.

'So, what do you have in mind?'

'I don't know yet, I'll have to think about it. It will have to be something that spoils his skating; that's the one thing he loves more than anything or anyone!'

'What, you mean steal his skates?'

'No, he would just get another pair. Anyway, I don't want to spoil our evening talking about him, I can work this out any time. How's Brad and the sex?' She wanted an update on their love life.

'Yes good, I think, but then I'm no expert, in fact there's something you could help me with.'

'Of course, if I can. What is it?' Kate said willingly.

'I need more advice on blow jobs. I don't want to do the wrong thing,' she remembered the salt cellar episode in the bar and blushed.

'Have you tried?'

'No! Harry never let me touch him! He thought it was "dirty"!'

'Crumbs.'

'Yes, that's why I need help.'

'Have you looked on the internet?'

'No, won't it come under porn?'

'No, I don't think so. Let's have a look!' Kate punched in "How to give a blow job" and immediately came up with a list of sites which she read out to her. "How to blow his mind", "Oral sex techniques", "Earth-shattering blow jobs", "The most satisfy.......'

'Stop!' Megan put her hand over the screen and was blushing.

'But there's stacks of sites here, I hadn't realised, maybe I could learn a trick or two?'

'You! You could open your own site!'

'I'm not sure how to take that.'

'It was meant as a compliment.'

'Okay......Let's have a look at one.'

'Not here!'

'Why not? It's pretty quiet. I'll turn off the sound just in case it's a video.'

'No please, can we go to your place?'

'Yes, of course.' Kate was intrigued to see what they were all about, so they finished their drinks and left.

Once inside the privacy of Kate's house, she uncorked a bottle of rosé and poured them both a large glass of wine, then she brought the sites up on the laptop.

'Bigger is better,' she said with a giggle. Megan looked nervous. 'Have a drink,' Kate said as she clicked away at the keyboard, 'I think we'll try this one.' And she opened a site with an attractive American lady in her mid-thirties and a realistic rubber penis. 'Aw, not the real thing.' Kate sounded disappointed.

'Don't worry, that's fine – I don't need the real thing,'

They watched as the lady talked them through how to hold it, how much pressure to apply and where; tongue techniques, rhythm, speed, and how to combine them all. They sat and watched in silence, mesmerized by the cool, unemotional way the lady explained everything. There was absolutely no passion involved so once it was finished Kate added a few tips of her own about how she should expect him to react.

She ran upstairs and reappeared with a couple of sex toys.

'You can practice on these,' Kate said sliding them across the table towards her.

'You have to be joking! Where have they been?'

Kate reassured her, 'Don't worry, they have been sterilized.'

Megan tentatively picked one up and inspected it, accidentally switching it on, which made her drop it in surprise, and Cat jumped off the table and shot out of the room. They laughed and had more wine and Kate showed Megan what to do on one while she imitated her on the other. In the end Megan had to stop from laughing as Kate had added a realistic panting and groaning sound track.

'Hey, you can't stop – he hasn't come yet!'

By now Cat had returned and was sitting on the table watching and wondering about all the activity – her mistress's lessons were never normally so noisy and certainly didn't involve long objects of vibrating rubber.

'I think I might have to go into training to develop my jaw muscles.' Megan gave her mouth a stretch, massaging the sides with her hands.

'No you won't, he'll probably come the minute you put your mouth around it!'

'Ugh! What does it taste like?'

'Awful, you have to lay down some ground rules first. Just tell him he's not allowed to come in your mouth, and always have a towel handy so when he does it doesn't go everywhere.'

'There's a lot to remember.'

'Not really, it's like everything else, practice makes perfect,' and she took a large bite off the end of her carrot.

'Ouch!' exclaimed Megan, 'Was that symbolic?'

'I don't think Luke will be getting any more from me,' Kate said thoughtfully munching her way through the rest of the carrot.

'I think I'd better go,' Megan looked at the clock which read nearly midnight, 'Brad will be back soon.' Although officially employed as a driver Brad augmented his income by working in the stock room, restocking the shelves, putting orders together, or any other job that would provide him with a few extra hours of shift work which meant he often worked to midnight.

'Are you all right to drive? You're over the limit.'

'Yes, I'll be fine.' She got up stroking Cat on the way out.

As Kate waved goodbye she wondered if Brad was in for a treat.

Lying in bed that night, uncharacteristically she turned her thoughts to revenge. In the past, she had allowed the laws of the universe to run their course. What would be, would be. It was a philosophy that had always worked, even though she no religious credence she *did* believe that people reaped what they sowed. She coped (where possible) by distancing herself from harmful or damaging influences.

She had left jobs in the past rather than confront a situation, and she found it easier to leave a relationship than try to convince someone that it was worth salvaging; if a man had to be convinced then she didn't think he was worth fighting for.

For some inexplicable reason this time was different, she didn't want to wait for retribution, maybe it was her age or maybe she was simply fed up with men doing and acting exactly as they felt fit, either way, one thing was for sure – she wasn't going to let Luke get away "Scott free"; he needed to be taught a lesson, but how?

She needed guidance but she no longer trusted the forecasts made by the card reader that had opened a business near her house; things had not turned out the way she predicted. She would contact an old friend who she trusted, she had always been accurate and Kate regretted not having gone to her months ago then maybe she wouldn't be in this predicament.

The next morning looked very grey and rain was forecast so of course she found a text, 'Hi sweetie! Meet for lunch? Xxx' Just as though nothing had happened! But if it was going to be wet then he would be at a loose end, so why not find a playmate? Kate didn't feel like seeing him; she wanted to keep away until she had thought of a solution. She wouldn't be able to think logically in his company, and was still smarting from his offhand treatment of the other day.

She didn't answer until she had finished her cup of coffee, and something told her to be amiable.

'OK. Same place, same time? Xxx' superficially adding three kisses – not meaning any of it!

'Yeah, see you later xxx'

He was already at the café when Kate arrived. He got up and gave her a kiss so she went along with it and reciprocated, and once they were served he chatted non-stop about skating. About what he had done, was going to do and was doing! About how annoyed he was with the weather but how the forecast was good for the following day, anyway he could practise in the kitchen until then.

Kate simulated interest, she wanted at least to keep the peace until she had decided how to deal with him. He seemed to be so

172

sure of himself.

They parted on what appeared to be 'friendly' terms, however no plans were made to see each other. Normally she would have gone round to his flat after her Salsa lesson so she texted him later to test the ground, but he said he was going fishing.

Megan dropped her off at home because Brad was waiting and she was hoping to give him her first oral treat having practised on various vegetables for a couple of days, and having sat transfixed to her laptop watching the most brazen demonstrations of oral sex. It was becoming addictive and she had found herself rating them!

Sometimes Megan would have flash backs to her life pre-Kate, and asked herself if she had been happy. She came to the conclusion that she didn't know! She wasn't even sure if she knew what happiness was?

Life had been predictable and 'safe' with Harry, even if he hadn't always been there; but *so* boring. There had been times that she had regretted splitting with him, and questioned whether it had all been worth it. She wasn't a loner like Kate, she liked to have someone to do for, and she *loved* cooking and could see no point in doing it for herself.

There was no doubt about it – Kate entering her life had transformed it; they had had *so much* 'fun' and she had given her an entirely new perspective. Megan felt that she had been given a chance to recapture lost opportunities and experiences that had been denied her or repressed by her marriage to Harry. The strange thing was that she still loved him because whatever his faults he was a kind and thoughtful person and he had always shown compassion, and supported her in times of bereavement or need. They had rubbed along 'all right' for more than 35 years, but she had been sexually deprived and frustrated and Kate had shown her how to open Pandora's Box.

And then, of course, they started doing 'stuff' together in the evenings because Megan needed the company

Chapter 35

A Plan

Kate switched on the television and started to prepare lessons for the next day. She thought that actually sitting down to watch anything was a waste of time and rarely indulged in the activity, besides, it took the edge off the monotony of photocopying.

Cat would sit on the table nearby in the hope of an occasional stroke.

When she felt she could do no more she got ready for bed, fed Cat and went upstairs. She always watched some television in bed, it was her little luxury and, as long as she avoided all horror films, it relaxed her.

She woke at about three o'clock for a drink of water and starting thinking about Luke. She lay awake going back over the relationship and trying to figure out when and how it had all started to go wrong. There were so many mitigating factors: the strenuous building work; the illness; the relapse of illness brought on by stupid selfishness; the ruined birthday because of it; the betrayal of one of his partners and the good weather!

She switched on the radio, low. Radio four (the World Service at that time of night) usually lulled her back to sleep – not because it was boring, quite the opposite, generally it was so interesting that it took her mind off whatever it was that was keeping her awake. There was someone talking about computer chips and Kate thought of her nephew and his research in that area and wondered whether they all knew each other. The man on the radio was describing a situation that had caused a bad accident all due to a flaw in programming. Luckily, no one had been badly injured or killed but he was trying to emphasise the care that was needed when implementing new technology and the rigorous testing that should be adhered to.

She thought about the word 'accident' – what had her nephew said about chips in things at Christmas? She wished she had paid more attention.

She was wide awake now, she'd had at least three hours sleep – Margaret Thatcher regularly survived on that. She switched on the light and decided to make a cup of decaffeinated tea.

When she got downstairs Cat, who was curled up on his usual chair, lifted his head in surprise, and if Kate hadn't known any better she would have sworn he could read the clock. He didn't even get up to say 'hello' like he did in the morning, so somehow he knew she would be going back upstairs, 'uncanny,' she thought; so intuitive – that's why she was a cat person.

She switched everything off and went back up to bed with her cup. There was a new voice on the radio and as Kate sat and sipped her tea she made a mental note that she had to ring her nephew first thing in the morning. She was intrigue by an idea which could help her get over Luke, but she needed to speak to Rob before she could allow herself to get too excited about it. Anyway it was a plan, which was more than she had before, and with that in mind she lay back down and slept through to the alarm.

As soon as she had made a cup of tea and fed Cat, she sent a text to Rob to see when it would be convenient to speak to him.

He texted back almost immediately, 'Hello! Good to hear from you – I'll ring you around midday if you're free then? x'

'Yes, perfect thanks x'

Kate busied herself all morning – she always had plenty to do but now she was impatient to find out whether she could put her idea into practice, and she couldn't stop looking at her watch. The phone rang bang on twelve, of course – he was a scientist.

'Hello! Thanks for ringing.'

'Not a problem. It's nice to hear from you, we don't speak often enough.'

'Yes, you're right, we don't.'

'What can I do for you?'

'Well, do you remember the conversation we had at Christmas

when we came over for dinner?'

'Remind me?'

'You were telling me about chips that you were using as teaching aids.'

'Yes, it's going really well, we are expanding their use all the time. What did you have in mind?'

'Well, I have a friend who teaches skating, rollerblading to be precise and I remember you saying that you were able to use the chips in football boots to help in training?'

'Yes, that's right and we're getting some good feedback on it.'

'So, I was thinking that maybe he would be able to fit them into the skate boots to help the children practice the correct movements; you know it's quite a complicated sport and some of the stuff can be very complex, especially at a higher level.'

'Yes, I don't see why not, basically, they all work on the same principal.'

'This sounds great!' Kate couldn't help sounding enthusiastic.

'I'm glad that you sound so positive, let's hope that your friend agrees.'

'Oh yes, I'm sure he will. What happens next? How much will it all cost? And will we have to meet or can you post it?'

'I can post it. Each pack comes with full instructions and as long as he has basic computer skills he should be able to set it up by himself. Anyway, there's a help line he can call if there's a problem, and as we are still at the research stage so it's all free. Besides, this is an area that hasn't been used before so the feedback will be valuable to us.'

'Wow, even better, I can't wait to tell him!' She was elated by the news.

'If he is half as excited as you are then it will a positive response,' he said laughing.

'Sorry,' Kate wondered whether she had sounded too keen.

'No, I'm pleased, it's good to hear such enthusiasm, we face a lot of scepticism in this business so it's refreshing to hear someone who needs no convincing.'

'Oh, no, You don't have to convince me – I have faith.'

'Brilliant! I shall get a pack sorted for your friend as soon as possible. How many children are we looking at, I presume he has classes of small groups?'

'Yes, groups of about six.'

'Okay, I'll sort it out myself. He'll need a chip for each boot, plus a few spares 'cos they're always getting lost. Where shall I send it?'

'You can send it to my address if you like as he isn't always in.'

'Okay, will do.'

'You're wonderful, thank you, and thank you from him too.'

'No, thank *you* because we need the feedback for our research. All we ask is for him to fill out some forms on a regular basis to let us know how it's going.'

'Yes, no problem, that's the least he can do. I'll make sure he does that. Honestly Rob I know he's going to be over the moon with this.'

'Good. It should be with you in a couple of days.'

'Perfect and thanks again.'

'Speak soon.'

'Yes, I'll text you to let you know when it has arrived. Bye for now!'

'Bye!'

Kate's heart was pounding with nervous excitement. She couldn't wait to tell Megan. Was she pleased with herself or what?

'I can't believe I thought of this!' she exclaimed in a loud voice as she picked up Cat holding him aloft and spinning him around in circles celebrating her moment of success. He looked bewildered by his mistress's behaviour and hung around in case he was needed again, brushing up against her legs and causing her to stumble.

Her mind was racing now and she started to plan ahead – how was she going to fit them into his boots without him finding out? Rob had said they were tiny, so maybe she would be able to hide them in the lining? Anyway, she wouldn't be able to do anything until the package arrived. She couldn't wait to tell Megan.

One thing was for sure – she would have to keep seeing Luke and put up with being 'fitted in' and act like she was grateful for sparing her a few minutes of his time. She would have to pretend that nothing had changed and that she still loved him as much as before; but he had hurt her badly and now the trust was gone. What made it worse was that he didn't seem to realise how much he had hurt, betrayed and let her down. He had led her to believe that he was different when actually he was just like all the rest – treating women like commodities – using and abusing them and then finally dumping them. And then getting on with life as if it were all perfectly normal! Either you learned to fit into their plans and lifestyle or move on.

Megan picked her up right on time as usual.

'Hi! You Okay?'

'Yes, fine and you?'

'Absolutely spiffing!'

'Wow! What's happened? You're in a good mood. Don't tell me – you and Luke are getting married?'

'Don't be daft! It's over, I told you that; I'm not a glutton for punishment. There'll be no going back now.'

'So ...?'

'So, I had a brainwave – last night, at about three o'clock.'

'Crumbs, I was fast asleep or listening to Brad snoring; he's good at that.'

'By the way how's the practice going or have you moved on to the real thing?'

'Moved on.'

'What!!' Kate could see that she was looking pleased with herself even if she was blushing.

'Well come on, tell me! I want to know everything – blow for blow! Pardon the pun.'

'Well, obviously I went home and practiced like you said and I watched some more sites, in fact it became quite addictive.'

'Yes, I know. And.....?'

'Last night I made sure we had both had plenty to drink – me especially, I needed it.'

'And....?' Kate was impatient to hear the rest.

'Well, I started with my hand because I had seen on line that they didn't get straight into it, and I could tell that he was enjoying it so I moved in slowly, and you were right he came almost immediately! I think he was in shock. Anyway, I was prepared with a towel. I had another go later and he lasted a bit longer, and then, of course, in the morning again.'

'And....?'

'Well, I'm not nervous any more, but I reckon I still need loads of practice. But you're right it is more exciting, and it is different to feel in control.'

'See, I told you. Look what you've been missing all these years. Make the most of it girl! Well done! I think this merits another celebration, don't you? I bet he's walking around all day with a hard on and he'll be ripping those clothes off as soon as you get in the door!' They both laughed imagining the moment.

'Not tonight, he's on lates and won't be in until midnight again, but I'll be ready and waiting,' Megan smiled wryly.

'Yeh!' exclaimed Kate and she punched the air, 'I'm proud of you! Now all you need are a few toys.'

Megan was proud of herself, but she wasn't as wild and adventurous as Kate, 'Let me get the hang of this first!'

'Okay, but let me know when you get bored and want to move on.'

'That won't be for a while. But you haven't told me about your brainwave?'

'Right, yes – sorry, I had to hear about your initiation – got sidetracked. As I said, I woke around three and started thinking about "that pig". I couldn't get back to sleep, so made tea, took it back to bed and remembered something Rob had told me when we were at my sister's for dinner on New Year's.'

'He's in I.T., isn't he?'

'Yes, research, and doing pioneering stuff by the sound of it. Didn't I tell you about it?'

'No, I don't think so. I know you said that it was pretty boring but I don't remember anything else.'

'That's probably because it didn't seem significant at the time, but it is now.'

'Why's that?'

Kate described as best she could the kind of work he and his team were working on.

'Hmm, you're right it does sound interesting *and* educational which has my approval because I am sick and tired of all these games, they are such a distraction. But go on – how does it affect you? Are you going to use it for your work?'

'No, not at the moment anyway, maybe later. I have a far more important use for it'

'Okay....can I guess?'

'You can try,' Kate watched as her friend pondered the challenge while concentrating on the road.

'I know! You're going to use the chips in sex toys!' Megan sounded confident that she'd found it.

'Hell no. You've got sex on the brain! Is that going to be your sole source of conversation from now on?'

'Well, who do you think my teacher is?'

'Yeah, yeah, okay; actually it's not a bad idea. But it will have to wait. I have more important fish to fry.'

'Come on then, don't keep me waiting.'

'I'm going to put them in his skates!'

Megan didn't answer for a while as she was negotiating a busy crossroad, but once they were on a straight stretch of road again she said, 'What do you mean?'

'Well, remember I explained to you how they are being used to help children with learning difficulties, and for training in various sports?'

'Yes.'

'I'm going to fit them into his skate boots, but not to help him. I will programme them to do the opposite; I want to spoil the experience. I want to ruin it for him.'

Again, Megan didn't say anything immediately, not because of the traffic but because she was trying to assimilate what Kate had just told her.

'I think I understand,' she said, although she couldn't envisage the result, 'But I thought it was against your belief – taking revenge?'

'Yes, you're right, it is. You know that I don't normally bother – I just leave it up to the powers that be and it always works – but this time it's different, there's an urgency about it that I can't explain; I can't let him get away with it. I don't see why he should spend his summer outside skating around, having the time of his life, without a care in the world while I sit at home trying to get over him and

180

feeling miserable. To tell you the truth I feel very bitter, which is not like me. I would have managed to get through the summer if he had dedicated just ONE evening a week to us; that would have been enough. I think it was when he said he could "fit me in" that it all started. It would be different if he hadn't made promises and gone on about "the future" making out that he really cared and making *me* care; if it had only been for sex it wouldn't matter – he'd just be another dick – water under the bridge bla, bla; but he made out that it was more than that, and then there was that bloody card reader, she didn't help.'

Megan could hear the distress and anger in her voice and felt sorry that it had turned out the way it had, and wasn't sure if she should encourage her to pursue the idea of 'planting' chips in his skates, it sounded like espionage and she worried about where it would lead.

'When you get these things, how are you going to "plant" them? Because you told me the relationship was over?'

'Don't worry, I still have a key and anyway I'm not going to let *him* think it's over. I don't have any qualms about being dishonest now; this is self-preservation, this is to keep me sane. All my life I have walked away from relationships rather than confront them, but not this time; I have to see this one through. And I'm not just thinking of myself – what about all the others whose lives and emotions he's messed with? I need this. *He* needs this.'

Megan pulled into the car park and they dropped the subject, they could hear the music way before they opened the door; it was well attended because of the live group that had been booked. Some people had driven two hours to get there and Kate appreciated living so near.

The evening was a great success. They danced practically every number, had a good laugh, flirted with the company and drove home on a high – Megan back to experimental sex and Kate back to planning her next move in "Operation Chip Control".

Kate kept in touch with Luke and went along to wherever he was skating to be 'nice'. She tried to act as though there was nothing wrong, asked about Jason and the dogs, and pretended to be interested in all the skating tricks he was doing. It was like listening to a kid of fifteen (luckily she had had plenty of practice in that!) as he insisted on demonstrating and explaining in detail how to perform each one. But she couldn't wait for the package from Rob to arrive.

Chapter 36

The Package

The doorbell rang, Kate looked at her watch and thought 'postman'; sure enough, when she opened the door there was a nicely weather-beaten chappy on the doorstep, 'Parcel to sign for?' he said in a toneless voice as he handed her a screen and stylus. She did her best but it looked nothing like her signature, she reckoned that a chimpanzee could have done a better job and she apologized as she handed it back; but the postman seemed to find it quite acceptable.

She eagerly took hold of the package, (a box measuring about 30cm x 20cm x 15cm) as though it were a gift from above, and felt a ripple of anticipation. She went straight to the 'classroom' and conquering her desire to tear the box apart with her hands, she carefully slit through the tape on the joins with a craft knife leaving the box intact and reusable.

Having removed the bubble wrap, she placed everything on the table in front of her and checked each item off on the list in the instruction leaflet. It was all there so she decided to study the leaflet in detail before anything else.

It seemed to be fairly straightforward as long as she followed the instructions step by step. It would appear that once the chips were planted they could be manipulated by using a handheld device very similar to the ones that she had seen the boys using for video games and the X box.

From what she understood she would be able to monitor everything on her computer. He had even included a note to say that he had made some adjustments for use with skates, one of which being a speed control, not necessary for sports like tennis where technique was the main point of focus. In any event, it was optional and could be switched off.

Kate wished that she didn't have any classes later as she was dying to try out her new gadget, but duty would not allow her the luxury of taking time off to 'play', so she packed it all carefully.

Chapter 37

Start of Play

She had trouble focusing on her classes more than usual that evening, finding herself continually glancing up at the box on the shelf. She could not wait to get it set up and have a go.

Once she seen off her last couple of students with an 'Au revoir' she rang Megan to see if she wanted to come and observe. If she were honest with herself she was really looking for moral support.

'Guten Abend!' She often used a bit of German to remind Megan that she used to be quite good at it.

'Guten Abend!' came the reply with a chuckle, 'And how are you today?'

'Me? I am absolutely fine, in fact I am feeling great!'

'Let me guess – the parcel has arrived, hasn't it?'

'Damn! Yes. Am I so transparent?'

'Sometimes.'

'Are you free to play tonight?'

'I could be, but I would have to be back by eleven.'

'That's loads of time! Shall I come up or do you want to come here?'

'Have you got any wine?'

'Yes, of course.'

'Okay, I'll come down to you; I need to get out, I've been in all day.'

'Great, see you in a bit.'

Kate changed her shoes, slipped on a jacket, grabbed her bag and went out to the convenience store across the road. She had lied about the wine because she did not want Megan to buy it and anyway it would only take her a couple of minutes. She had been so grateful that they had opened up a late night store literally minutes from her house. It was one of the reasons that she didn't want to move. As she got older she was becoming more aware of the importance of living near to town and conveniences. She chose a bottle of white so they could make spritzers. No sooner had she opened it and put two glasses and a bottle of soda on the table, than the doorbell rang.

Megan looked flushed and Kate wondered if she had overdone the fun in bed! She asked her how it was going and Megan surprised her with her unvarnished, enlightening account of the last couple of sessions.

'Wow! You're talking like a pro!' Kate was impressed by the sudden progress in her friend's sexual experience.

'No, I don't think so, I'm learning. Anyway, where's this piece of high tech equipment?'

Kate took the package down from the top shelf, placed it on the table, and while Megan poured them two spritzers, she carefully removed the contents.

'What are these?' Megan held up a small polythene, zip-lock envelope containing what looked like a blister sheet of tablets, but on closer inspection were too small and didn't look like something she would want to swallow.

'I'm not really sure what anything is yet, but I think they are the chips. Let's see.... Item label BTZ02.' Kate scanned the paper work that had come along with the contents, 'Yes, here it is – "BTZ02, blister sheet of twelve chips".'

'They are really small!' Megan said squinting slightly and holding them up to the light to get a better look at them through the slightly opaque blisters.

Kate looked up at the sheet and agreed, 'You're right, they *are* small – tiny in fact! Well that's good – all the better to conceal!' she said like the wolf from Red Riding Hood, 'And this is obviously the control gadget,' she said with authority extracting the rectangular box from its polystyrene packaging.

'That looks familiar,' Megan remarked as Kate laid it on the table, 'It looks just like those things your boys used to use with those racing games they played all the time on the tele.'

'Yes, you're right.'

'What are those two levers for?'

Kate consulted the instruction manual, 'It looks like one is for direction and the other for speed, so .... not *too* complicated.' She was reading on down the page when Megan interrupted, 'Don't you think we should try one out?'

'Yes, I'd love to, but I think it all has to be connected to the laptop first.'

'Well, come on then, let's have a go,' Megan said encouragingly.

'Okay, it's always good to have a bit of moral support, and two heads are better than one,' she smiled and lifted her glass. They both took a couple of swigs from their glasses before Kate picked up the instruction booklet again, and opened it at page one.

Rob had been right when he said that it was straightforward, in fact, with Megan reading it out to her, Kate had been able to set everything up in half an hour and they were ready to try it out. Kate didn't have any skates so it would have to be on a boot or a shoe.

The instructions advised the user to stick the minute chips to a strong adhesive tape and not to try and pick them up, in that way, they could not be dropped or lost and could be applied directly to the front of whatever footwear was being used. There was tape included in the box although any strong adhesive tape could be used.

Kate cautiously opened a blister containing a chip which looked like a minute, silver battery and pressed a square of tape onto it. She then stuck the tape and chip onto the front of Megan's boot at ankle height. She asked her to stand up and walk to the middle of the room.

'Wow!'

'What?' Megan asked.

'I don't know how it works but I can see where you are and where you are going. Walk around a bit.'

Megan walked around and Kate was able to track her on the laptop screen.

'This is really cool!' Kate shouted out to her as she had moved into another room, I can see exactly where you are! It's amazing!' She moved the lever surrounded by arrows and she heard Megan shouting, 'Hey! Stop! What are you doing?'

'Why? What's the matter?'

'I can't control my right boot, it keeps wanting to turn right, I'm going around in a circle! What have you done?' True enough, when Kate checked the screen she could see her turning around in the same direction, but as soon as she moved it back Megan was walking normally.

'Is that better now?'

'Yes, that's fine – back to normal.' And she reappeared in the classroom.

Kate noticed a button marked "stop" so she pressed it.

'Aagh!'

'What's wrong?' Kate asked, although she was fairly sure that she knew what was happening.

'I can't move my foot!'

'Which one?' Kate asked trying not to laugh.

'My right one. The one with this thing on. I'm going to take it off!'

'No! don't!' Kate depressed the "stop" button and Megan came back into the classroom, sat down, and had a few gulps of spritzer.

'That was a really surreal experience! It's very disconcerting losing control of a part of your body and even worse having it take control of itself!'

'Hmm, yes, I can imagine,' Kate didn't sound too concerned, her mind was racing with the thought of endless possibilities for this new gadget and couldn't wait to get the chips fitted into Luke's skates.

'I think *you* should have the experience, here,' and Megan peeled the tape off her boot and passed it to Kate. 'Stick it on *your* boot and I will show *you* what it's like.'

'Yes, I will, but not tonight. Look it's coming up to eleven, didn't you say that Brad would be back?'

'Crikes! Yes. I must go.' She downed the rest of her spritzer and put on her jacket. 'When do you think you'll "plant" these things?'

'I'm not sure, I'll have to wait and see when I can get access. I think he's working the night after next. I could volunteer to help walk the dogs.'

'Well, let me know if you want moral support, I think Brad's on nights too.'

'Yes, thanks.' Kate stood on the doorstep and waved her friend off till she turned the corner.

When she got back she found Cat sitting on the laptop – he liked the warmth; it was a habit of his. Sometimes, in the winter, Kate would make him a not too hot-water bottle in a fluffy cover to sit on. It was like a mini-waterbed and he would knead it for ages before settling down – he knew it was a treat and loved it!

'No Cat!' he immediately jumped off; he knew that tone of voice meant "move".

Kate cleared everything away and texted Luke as she would each night, 'Did you have a good day? xxx'

'Yes, loads of skating – getting real good at the new move I made up but don't know what to call it yet xxx'

'Sounds great. I'll try and get down tomorrow and you can show me,' she left a smiley face,

'Going to bed now. Night xxx' She didn't like being hypocritical, but fire had to be fought with fire.

'Nite hon, sweet dreams zzz xxx'

Kate had her first good night's sleep for ages. She wanted him to think that there was nothing wrong and that she was 'cool' about him having no time to see her, and she felt she had achieved that.

Chapter 38

The Plant

Kate's life carried on the same as it had before she met Luke: she prepared classes and tidied up in the mornings; went down to the Polish café for lunch (alone); taught in the afternoons and early evening and went exercising or dancing in the evenings with Megan.

She was waiting for the opportunity to plant the chips but didn't have to wait long. Luke texted her to say that he had to go up north and could she walk and feed Koko and Kiki for one night the following week.

She couldn't wait, and the time seemed to drag, but Tuesday was suddenly there and she and Megan were trying to calm the dogs as they fought their way past them into Luke's flat.

It was the first time Megan had been there so while Kate fed them Megan had a nose around.

'Hmm, it's quite spacious and I love these high Victorian ceilings, and he's meticulously clean!'

'Yes, obsessively so in my opinion, but then you know what I think of housework,' Kate said disdainfully.

Megan was aware that Kate did the very minimum; she kept the classroom in order, vacuumed regularly, and made sure that she always looked smart and clean, but hardly ever cooked or dusted. Her favourite quote was from Quentin Crisp who said "After five years the dust doesn't get any thicker" and her fridge was covered in magnets of the same ilk: "Only boring people have tidy houses", "Creative people have untidy desks".

Megan volunteered to take the dogs out for their evening walk, she loved animals and used to have two dogs herself, so during their absence Kate began thinking about where she was going to conceal the chips.

She picked up one of his boots and noticed how worn and battered it looked, something that had escaped her all the time he had been wearing them. She had never needed to inspect them at close quarters until now, and it was quite a revelation. She could see that they had been repaired in several places, some professional, some not so, which made her feel a lot better about 'tampering' with them.

She heard Megan coming back with the dogs that came sniffing around Kate and wanted to know what was going on.

'Hi, how's it going? Have you figured out what to do yet?' Megan inquired as she wandered into the kitchen and found Kate at the kitchen table inspecting his skates.

'Kind of, I don't think I'll have a problem hiding them. Have you seen the state they're in?'

Megan walked over and picked one up, 'Yikes! This has done some work!'

'Yes, I know, they both have, but I can understand why he doesn't want to change them. I loved my old ice-skates and never really got used to the new ones.'

'So where are you thinking of putting these little beauties?' she said holding up the blister pack of chips.

'In here,' and Kate pointed to a decorative logo on the Velcro strap across the front of the boot. It had tiny metal studs embedded in the leather so she planned to replace one with a chip which, luckily, was of similar size, shape and colour and reckoned that no one would ever see the difference. She had brought a whole bunch of equipment with her, including a surgical scalpel!

'Where did you get this?' Megan carefully held it up examining the blade, 'It looks dangerous!'

'Only in the wrong hands,' Kate said in a sinister voice making her friend laugh.

'I didn't know if there would be any booze in the house so I bought this,' Megan said pulling a bottle of chilled white from a plastic bag and putting it on the table.

'Good thinking, there might be some 2% beer somewhere, he used to get it in for me, although I haven't been around for a while and he doesn't drink. There's plenty of weed though if you feel like a spliff.'

'What's that?'

'A joint.'

'What me? I've never touched the stuff!'

'Well you can try it now if you like, he's got stacks and won't miss it.' Kate didn't look up as she was concentrating on trying to prize one of the metal studs out of the logo on Luke's left boot with the point of the scalpel. When she had finished she got up, went to one of the kitchen cupboards, brought out a metal box and placed it on the table with the lid open.

Megan was curious and peered inside. It had a familiar smell, she had smelt it around certain people in the town – their clothes, skin and hair. There was a strange looking little gadget inside the tin that she had never seen before, 'What's this for?' she held it up.

'Hang on a sec,' Kate was removing one of the minute chips from its blister with a pair of tweezers and locating it in the hole vacated by the stud. When she was satisfied that it wasn't going anywhere she looked up.

'That's some kind of grinding device. You put some weed in there and grind it into a fine powder.'

'Why?'

'You're asking me?' Kate replied in astonishment.

'Well yes! You seem to know what it's all about.'

'Not really. I've just seen him doing it. Maybe it's more concentrated and easier to carry around or maybe he sniffs it like coke, who knows? He usually mixes it with normal tobacco.'

'What – this stuff?' and she held up a pouch of shop tobacco.

'Yes. Go ahead and roll yourself one if you want to try it. I have to concentrate now.' She had removed a metal stud and was carefully applying a minute drop of superglue to the cavity where she would place a chip.

'Do you think I should?'

'What do you mean?'

'Well, I've never had it before.'

'What! Not even a puff of someone else's?' Kate had finished the operation and looked up at her friend in astonishment.

'No, nothing, never!'

'You continue to amaze me.' Kate said almost in admiration.

'Is that good?'

'It's different.'

'I'll settle for that. But you still haven't answered my question.'

'Yes, definitely – it doesn't have to be strong – make a weak one.'

'What about you? Are you joining me?'

'No thanks, I've tried it several times and it doesn't do anything for me. I've never tried his stuff mind you.'

'Okay, so what do I do?'

'Come here, I'll show you.'

With that Kate pulled the tin towards her, took a paper out of the packet, laid it flat on the table, she spread a pinch of tobacco from the pouch down the centre and topped it with a quantity of weed, and then carefully rolled it up.

Handing it to Megan she asked, 'You used to smoke, didn't you?'

'Yes, but that was years ago.'

'Doesn't matter – same principle, just take your time and inhale.'

'Okay, here goes.' Megan lit it up and started puffing while Kate inserted the other chip.

Now that Kate had done all the delicate work she had a look around for some alcohol and found a couple of cans of 2% beer; she opened one and smiled at Megan as she sipped on her second glass of wine and puffed away on her joint which, from time to time, she would look at curiously as though she was figuring out how a bit of rolled up 'stuff' could make her feel so good.

'So, how is it?' Kate was also curious.

'Hmm, it's good, much better than a normal smoke. Is it addictive?'

'Not as far as I'm concerned it isn't, but then as I said it does nothing for me. It's different for everyone I suppose. Luke has at least one a day – every evening. I've known quite a few men who smoked one every evening; I think it has the same effect as alcohol has for me. And don't forget alcohol can have an adverse effect on some people – it can make them very aggressive whereas I think this is supposed to be relaxing, so maybe a spliff is their answer to a drink. They all seem to prefer one or the other. At least the ones I've known.'

While they chatted, catching up on any unshared gossip, the dogs lay asleep on their mat occasionally twitching an ear and sighing.

'Right, I'm ready to test these out now!' Kate said decisively. 'Have you finished that thing?'

'Nearly. What do you mean? Surely you don't want me to put them on!? I can't skate Kate. Hey, that rhymes! I can't skate Kate. Can't skate Kate ...' Megan was laughing as she spun around the room repeating the words over and over.

'Uh, Oh,' Megan was wondering whether it had been such a good idea to introduce her friend to the world of recreational drugs, as the spinning had turned into leaps and wobbly arabesques.

'Hey! Darcey Bussell. Take your ballet shoes off and put your skates on!'

'I can't skate Kate, I can't skate...' Megan carried on performing wild and exaggerated movements with her arms and legs so Kate just sat back, sipped her 2% beer and enjoyed her friend's performance.

All the whirling and twirling had woken the dogs who were sitting up, wide eyed in astonishment. They were used to people watching television in the evening, not gyrating and leaping about

Kate waited until Megan had exhausted herself and flopped into the armchair.

'I should have been a ballet dancer – I *love* dancing and I was good you know, when I was young.'

'Yes. I know, you told me all about it.'

In fact, Megan had competed in ballroom competitions all over the county, and to all accounts had done really well. Kate had seen some photos of her and her partner receiving medals and trophies and looking extremely glamorous.

'*You* were good too, weren't you Kate?'

'Yes.' That was also true, Kate loved dancing and had done all kinds when she was at school: tap-dancing, modern stage, ballet and ballroom and had medals for all of them. That was one of the reasons they understood each other so well, through their love of dancing.

'Do you feel like helping me now with these skates? And don't worry I don't want you to put them on, at least not on your feet because I know you can't skate.'

'Er, okay then, as long as I don't have to skate Kate.' And she started to laugh again.

'No, just put your hands inside them and put them on the floor.'

'What! You want me to put my hands inside those smelly, old things?'

Kate picked one up, looked inside and then held it up to her nose, maybe Megan had a point.

'Here, we'll put these inside,' Kate got up and pulled two plastic bags from a drawer, pushed them into the boots and handed them back to her.

'Okay,' Megan still sounded hesitant, but she managed to get a skate on each hand and balance them upright on the floor. The bags had been a good idea anyway as they fitted better around her small hands and filled up some of the space.

'Christ knows how he stays upright on these things,' she said wobbling madly and struggling to keep them straight, 'I won't be able to keep this up for long,' she warned.

'Don't worry it won't take long, I just need to know if they work.' She couldn't help smiling at her friend bent forward with her hands on the floor and her bum in the air.

'Ready?' Kate asked.

'Yes,' Megan answered innocently, giving Kate permission she gently moved the right-hand lever forward, this in turn, moved the right skate.

'Woooh, hang on, what about the other one?' Megan looked liked a wonky kangaroo on all fours, so Kate moved the other skate up next to it and Megan caught up with her legs.

'The blood is rushing to my head.'

'Try crouching.'

'Yes, that's better,' she agreed as she bent her legs into a squatting position, 'I feel much safer like this.'

'Right, I'm going to try something else, ready?'

'Yes.'

Kate tried maneuvering both skates to the left and as they turned Megan went with them,

'That's clever!' she was clearly impressed as she shuffled along behind them.

Kate carried on experimenting with various moves for as long as Megan was willing to crouch on the floor, which she probably wouldn't have agreed to do without the spliff.

Finally, Megan pleaded with her to stop as she needed to stand and stretch her legs, reminding her friend of how old they were.

'Yes of course, and thanks, I couldn't have done this without you,' Kate really appreciated having her as a collaborator.

'What are friends for but to stick their hands into a stranger's smelly skates and crawl around the floor after them?!' they both laughed and took a swig from their glasses.

Kate cleared everything up and made sure the skates were left in exactly the same place as she had found them.

She made a fuss of Koko and Kiki told them to be good until Luke came back. They seemed to understand as they settled back down and watched as she and Megan let themselves out.

Megan dropped Kate off and went straight home as Brad would be back from work and she wanted to get there before him. She didn't seem to be any worse for wear from the effects of the spliff or Kate would not have allowed her to drive.

At home, Kate put the box of 'tricks' carefully away on a high shelf in the classroom and smiled to herself when she thought about Megan's antics; she didn't know that Kate had videoed her dance routine – she would keep that for another day. The evening had gone more or less as planned, the entertainment had been a bonus, she had accomplished what she wanted; all she had to do now was wait until Luke got on his skates again. She wouldn't have to wait long.

Chapter 39

The First Trial

The next morning Kate found a text from Luke thanking her for looking after Koko and Kiki; he obviously hadn't noticed anything else or he would have mentioned it.

'It was no trouble at all. What are you up to today? Want to meet for lunch? xxx' she left a friendly text.

'Sorry hon, I need some shuteye and then if the weather holds I'll be skating xxx'

She hadn't expected him to be free, but had asked anyway.

'Okay, enjoy xxx,' she replied in an offhand manner but she was delighted! She was going to test out her handy-work from the night before.

It was just after nine and she reckoned he would be asleep till about midday (he never slept much more than three hours in the day time) so that would give her a couple of hours to play on the 'gadget' before her first lesson; as long as he didn't hang around at home.

Kate watched the clock all morning and would normally have gone down to the Polish café at lunch time but she didn't want to miss an opportunity to use the chip control, so she made herself a sandwich at home instead.

She had everything set up and glanced at the laptop from time to time to check for movement.

Suddenly she noticed a change of scene – it looked like Luke had picked his skates up and was walking towards the front door with them.

Kate's heart raced with anticipation; she wanted to mess with his skating but at the same time she couldn't help feeling apprehensive as she wasn't very adept at using Rob's gadget yet and didn't want to cause a serious accident.

She sat down in front of the laptop, and watched and waited.

He had put them on the back seat of his car and Kate knew that his usual skating venue, the sea-front promenade, was only a few minutes' drive from his flat so she quickly made herself a coffee as she didn't want to have any interruptions when he had his skates on.

It took him seconds to change from his trainers, and once in motion Kate felt like a miniature passenger on a fairground ride about twenty centimeters from the ground. She was weaving around legs, dogs and pushchairs as they rushed towards her at what seemed to be an incredible speed! It was fascinating, not at all like the experience in Luke's flat when Megan had worn them on her hands.

Shoes, boots and wheels of various shapes and sizes, balls and bicycles all flashed past .

She was mesmerised, and for a while completely forgot the reason why she was sitting in front of the screen, until he started to slow down. She could see his hand (up close), placing bright orange cones on the ground about a meter apart, they looked enormous although she knew that they were only about twelve centimeters high.

'This was how Gulliver must have felt in the Land of Lilliput,' she thought

Soon, Kate found herself weaving in and out of the cones, the sensation was similar to watching a three D film, however, when he began turning and spinning she started to feel quite nauseous.

All the while that he was moving in different directions Kate wasn't sure how to manipulate the skates so she thought she would just try the speed control and slowed them down very slightly. She waited for him to react but there was nothing, so she moved the dial further towards 'slow' and noticed that he broke off from all his 'tricks' and skated over to the railings. He had lifted his right skate up to knee height and was spinning the wheels with his left hand as though checking them out.

'He must have noticed there was something wrong,' she thought, 'Good, that means it's working.' She put all the controls back to neutral as she felt a headache coming on probably caused by the stress she had put herself through, knowing that it had been a make or break moment, so she left the laptop open and watched him practice the same trick over and over again for two hours.

He occasionally stopped to chat and explain some techniques to interested passers by especially if it involved another rollerblader, otherwise he dedicated every minute to thinking, breathing, doing rollerblading.

Kate was a strong advocate of physically active pastimes, she used to encourage the boys to participate in any sporting activity that took their fancy, as she could see not only the physical benefits, but the social ones too. However, there was participation and then there was obsession, and *isolated* obsession, which was how she saw Luke's attitude to his own activity.

She had only met one of his friends and although he talked about others, he never seemed to spend a great deal of time with them. The only time that he had spent time in the company of other men was when they had been renovating the barn for the project that was to turn his life around financially, but had been abandoned due to his mate's stupidity and indiscretion, after which, he never mentioned them again.

He was still working hard at the same 'move' at three thirty when Kate had to switch off surveillance because she had a student arriving for a lesson, and she suspected he would still be there at sundown. She had never understood how he could repeat the same thing over and over again for hours on end; sometimes for days!

Anyway, she couldn't spend her every waking moment watching him perform to the public; now she knew it worked she would switch it on when it was convenient.

Chapter 40

Skating Scuttled

Megan found herself at a loose end that Friday evening as Brad was working and there was no dancing, so Kate said she would rustle up a light dinner and they could enjoy a film together, although she did have some other entertainment in mind.

As soon as Megan stepped through the door Kate poured the white wine spritzers and then put a huge bowl of Salad Niçoise down in front of them to pick at. If they were still hungry afterwards there was cheese and French bread.

They ate and watched 'Love Actually'; the third time for Kate but she didn't mind.

It was only just after nine o'clock when the credits came up and as Megan didn't want to go back to an empty house she suggested playing a game (they would often play word games in the evening until it was late) but Kate said she had a better idea, 'Why don't we play with skates?'

'What do you mean? Oh no, don't tell me, you've gone and bought yourself a pair of skates?'

'No, don't be daft! I mean let's play with *his* skates!'

'Is he skating in the dark?'

'No, he'll be at the rink.'

'Okay, let's see. You told me the thing works, so I wouldn't mind seeing it in action.'

'Right. Give me a second.' And Kate got the box from the top shelf and set it up with the laptop, and when the screen lit up Megan felt like a fly stuck to the front of his skates, travelling along a highly polished floor at a steady speed alongside other skaters.

'Wow! It's really sharp! I had no idea that it worked so well!'

Megan was genuinely impressed, and she picked up the instruction booklet that had come in the box.

While she flicked through the pages, Kate saw an empty space to Luke's right so she thought she'd try redirecting him and used the levers to direct both skates off to the right, but unused to their sensitivity she overdid it, and they hit the barrier at the edge. Kate laughed and Megan looked up, 'What's up? What have you done?'

'Well, I thought I'd try using the direction controls and he seems to have hit the edge,' Kate giggled as Megan leaned over to look at the screen. His skates were not moving much, they were up close to the barrier and there were other skates nearby acting concerned.

'Don't you want to listen to what's going on?' Megan asked.

'I don't think I can.'

'Sure you can – look – it says here in the book "volume control",' Megan pointed to the subheading.

'Yes, you're right, let me see...' Kate took hold of the book and studied the page, she punched a key on the laptop and a menu came up, and when she clicked on 'sound' immediately tuned into voices which she adjusted with 'volume control', and soon they could hear everything that was being said.

'What do you mean when you say the skates just headed towards the barrier?' They heard one of his mates inquiring.

'It was like I couldn't control them! Like they did their own thing!' She recognised Luke's voice.

'Na, you're always in control. You're the best skater here Luke, you gotta be mistaken man.'

'No. I'm not kidding you man, I tell you, the skates did it on their own. You know me mate I wouldn't bash into the barrier on purpose.'

'No, no of course not mate. So what about now? How do they feel now?'

Kate and Megan could see him moving a skate back and forth on the spot.

'Yeah seems okay,' and after he had tried the other one he gingerly took a few steps forward and, of course, everything was fine as Kate had moved all the controls back to neutral.

'What d'ya think?' one of his mates shouted over to him.

'Yeah, sweet – all good,' and from Kate's viewpoint everything seemed to be running normally; he was weaving his way in and out of the other skaters, joking and laughing and was probably thinking that it was all in his head.

'It really does work then.' Megan said in near disbelief.

'Yeah, it really does!'

'It's brilliant! I can see these things making a fortune once they go on the market. Just imagine all the uses that they could be adapted to?'

'Yes, I'm sure you're right, although I don't think that just *anyone* will be able to get their hands on them.'

'Hmm, no, too dangerous. Does that mean that you will be able to use it as spy ware? If you keep the camera and sound on will you be able to listen to everything he says and does?'

'I suppose so, as long as the skates are with him, or near enough to pick up the sound.'

'Wow....'and Megan sat looking into space as she envisaged a myriad of possible situations, 'You are really lucky that Rob is working on this – what a brainwave!'

'Do you mean him or me? Because I thought I had a brainwave when I thought of adapting it to this?' Kate felt she deserved some sort of acknowledgement for having found such an ingenious solution to curbing his skating pleasure.

'Oh, yeah, you too. Genius idea! It's brilliant!'

'You have to promise me Megan that you don't breathe a word of this to anyone else; at least not until the whole business is over and finished with.'

'Yes, of course, I promise. Lips sealed,' and she put her finger up to her mouth. 'Are you going to have another go?'

'No, not tonight. I don't want him to become suspicious. The last thing I need is for him to get them checked out and for someone to find the chips.'

'Yes, you're right.'

'This has to be done in small doses and subtly.'

'Here's to the success of "Operation Chip Control"!' Megan raised her glass.

'Yes, cheers!'

They sat and watched the screen and listened to the banter that went on between Luke and his mates, and Kate seethed as he flirted with a young girl who he obviously knew well.

He was skating backwards in front of her so they were face to face, not that Kate could see their faces, but she could tell that she was very young by the timbre of her voice, and the distance and position of their skates denoted close proximity.

Kate heard him invite her for a drink after the session and she accepted, so she decided to press the 'stop' button which meant he came to an abrupt stop falling over onto his back with her on top of him!

'Aah! What on earth are you playing at?' she shouted the words into his face even though they were only millimetres from each other, and she didn't want people to think that *she* had caused the accident.

'I don't know, it's these skates tonight, they're doing weird things – they just suddenly stopped! I mean all by themselves!'

'Yeah, yeah. You really expect me to believe that?' she said disentangling herself from the compromising position she was in. 'Just because I agreed to have a drink with you, doesn't give you permission to take liberties.'

'No, you're right, and I wouldn't, I'm telling you it's these skates, there's definitely something wrong with them. Are you Okay?'

'No. I think I've sprained my wrist,' and skated off leaving him sitting on the floor looking at his skates in dismay, while the others skated by making jokes and teasing him, not for one moment thinking that there was anything wrong; they just thought that he was messing around.

He finally scrambled to his feet and made his way over to the exit and sat down in one of the seats rubbing his right elbow which must have taken most of his weight as he fell.

'You alright mate?' Keith had seen him sitting out and had been concerned.

'Yeah, no probs, just don't know what's going on with these skates?'

'What's up?'

'That's the problem, you won't believe me when I say they seem to be doing their own thing.'

'Well, yeah, sure mate I believe you, I mean you're the king – there ain't no one here better than you. So what do you think the problem is?'

By then, Luke had taken one of them off to have a closer look, 'I dunno mate, they seem fine now, that's the weird thing,' he was obviously holding it up and inspecting it at close quarters because Kate was getting glimpses of Luke's face.

'This is much better than tele,' remarked Megan who had been riveted to the screen.

'Yes, I know and more fun – I am *so* enjoying myself!' and they raised their glasses again.

Keith asked him if he was going back out, 'Na, I think I'll call it a day mate. Two accidents in one night – too much, especially as I don't know how they happened.'

'Yeah, I understand man, but I think I'll do some more, there's a real cutie out there and I think she's warming.'

'Sure, go ahead, and good luck!' By this time Kate could see that he had removed both skates and was putting his trainers on and she was getting a good view of the others skaters. She could see a few very attractive girls and tried to pick out the one Luke had been flirting with so she asked for Megan's help; they had fun picking out girls but couldn't agree, and as she was probably keeping her distance since the incident, they would never know.

'I think the fun is over, don't you?' Kate said.

'Yes, pity,' Megan sounded a bit glum, 'but I can see you having a lot more with this.'

'Not half,' and they smiled and drank. Megan left just before midnight so she would be back before Brad finished his shift, and Kate went straight to bed as she had an early lesson the next morning

Chapter 41

Hidden Forces

The following day after her lesson she sent Luke a text, 'Good morning! Hope you enjoyed your skate last night? Are you free for lunch? Xxx' She wasn't expecting him to say 'yes' because the sun was streaming through her windows.

He instantly replied, 'Hi hon, so so, yeah meet same place, say 1.00? xxx'

'Wow!' Kate exclaimed aloud startling Cat, 'maybe this little gadget has more power than I had envisaged?'

And she walked around the flat chuckling to herself and rubbing her hands together with delight.

She checked her makeup and hair and changed into something that she knew would please him, then eagerly walked down to the café.

The town was buzzing with groups of teenagers, couples and families with pushchairs all out enjoying the warm spring sunshine, and all straddling the pavements, forming human barriers. It was extraordinary how groups of four or five people seemed to think it was fine to stop right in the middle of the pavement, and chat to a family with a pushchair forcing passing pedestrians into the road.

As she turned the corner she could see him already seated by the window although he hadn't ordered anything to eat yet.

'Hiya!' Kate bent forward and gave him a kiss that he responded to, she had a good feeling about this.

'Hello hon, you alright?' he was the first to ask.

'Yes, on top form, and you?'

'So, so.'

'Aah, not ill again I hope? Or is it the dogs?'

'No, nothing like that.'

'Oh good. So what's up?'

'Well, last night's skating ...'

'Oh...?' Kate was doing her best to keep a straight face and to sound genuinely interested.

'Yeah, I don't really know what the problem is but my skates seemed to have taken on a life of their own.'

'What? What do you mean by that? That's impossible! Do you realise what you've just said?' Kate was trying hard to adopt a tone of incredulity and surprise.

'Yeah, yeah I know it sounds mad but that's exactly what it felt like.'

'So, what happened?'

Luke recounted the details of the two incidents except for the bit about the girl falling on top of him, even though Kate gave him the opportunity by asking whether anyone else was involved or hurt.

'Well, it all sounds very strange. Are you sure you hadn't had too much to smoke?'

'No, I never smoke when I skate and besides I had to drive home so I wouldn't touch it.'

'Okaay....' Kate said as though she was contemplating the problem, 'I'm really not sure what to say. Have you had a look at them? Are they alright today? Maybe when you took them apart you left something out?' She was pretty sure that even if he had inspected them that he wouldn't find the chips because he would have looked at the mechanics not the boot. Besides, she had been so careful to camouflage them that even Megan hadn't been able see them, and she had known where to look!

'No, I've done that a hundred times and they should be running better They seem fine at the moment. I shall go out later, but of course, I'm a bit nervous now.'

'Try and put it behind you. It's just one of those things. I'm sure it won't happen again.'

Hmm, I was thinking .... you know what you told me about how everyone who hurts you or who does you harm is always revenged by unknown forces?'

'Yes,'

'Well, you don't suppose that there are unknown forces playing around with me, do you?'

'Yes, it's possible, although it doesn't normally manifest so quickly. But then you have to admit that you have been pretty nasty recently.'

'Nasty? Do you really mean that? In what way? I know that I haven't had much time for you but I thought you understood, you always seemed to be busy doing your dancing and stuff.'

'Yes, but nothing has changed in my life since I met you – I've always done that. You're the one who's changed – the last time you made love (or should I say "fucked") it was mechanical, like I was a piece of meat; you made it blatantly obvious that you didn't want me there. You made me feel like shit.'

'Gee, I'm sorry, I didn't realise.'

'Hmm, I don't agree, I think you knew exactly what you were doing. I think you've done it before – it's a pattern. You do it to get rid of the women interfering with your skating schedule once the sunny weather starts. Also, there have been times when you haven't noticed that you upset me or Josh, it's as though you just don't see or feel when you hurt someone.'

'Really? I was unaware.'

'Yes, I know. Anyway, it's all water under the bridge now. I think we've both moved on. At least I know I have. '

'Well, at least let me buy you some lunch?' he offered.

How magnanimous! Kate thought, a measly bowl of soup for three pounds fifty.

'No. It's alright, I'll get my own thanks.' Kate got up and went to the counter not bothering to ask him if he wanted anything.

He followed her with a hangdog expression on his face and ordered a panini and they paid separately.

Kate was grateful for something to keep her mouth occupied as she didn't really have very much to say, and imagined that he didn't either. The atmosphere was quite stained, and she would be glad to say goodbye and get back home.

She found it hard to believe how someone, who little more than a month ago had promised her the earth, could have changed so much. It was obvious from their conversation that he was only worried about himself and his skating and that he thought that some kind of 'hex' that had been put on him.

In a way he was right although there was nothing supernatural about it, and Kate had the power to remove it if she wanted, whereas had it been a true 'force' she wouldn't have had any control over it.

Anyway, she didn't like the sleazy way he was making time for her and trying to be nice in the hope that "the powers that be" would look down kindly on him and would leave him alone.

'No chance!' she thought, 'I'm going to make your life as uncomfortable as I can. You made me fall in love with you and then dumped me, knowing that you had done it before. It's probably like a game to you. Well, I can play games too.' It wasn't really in her character to do this sort of thing but she was making an exception because she reckoned he deserved a lesson!

As she sipped her soup she had a brainwave.

'You know, I think your life would improve if you treated me better; maybe if you weren't so selfish about your skating and fishing, and watching motor racing on tele when you could record it instead. And if you treated me with respect in bed, and cooked me breakfast the way you used to.'

'Ha! Ha! Good try!' he laughed, 'Now I know you're messing with me. You really want me to believe that you can control what happens?'

'Well, I can talk to the people who do,' she smiled at him wryly, leaving him wondering; but he wasn't going to be intimidated.

'Yeah, Okay, you do that – then we'll see.'

'Ah, no – that's not the way it works I'm afraid.'

'No? Explain! How *does* it work then?' he mocked, in between mouthfuls of panini.

'Well, the improvement has to come from you first because you have a lot to make amends for; you have a history of callous, selfish behaviour where women are concerned, from what I understand.'

He shrugged his shoulders, as though it was of no consequence, and Kate knew that he had dismissed the advice as a load of rubbish.

She knew of at least two other girlfriends who had tried to make him understand the damage done when he dumped them in the spring; not to mention his wife who ended up being sectioned, permanently parted from her children, and mentally damaged for life! He had learned nothing, if anything he had become more insensitive and less compassionate.

It was going to take Kate months, maybe longer, to get over his callousness because she didn't give her heart easily. However, now that she had her hands on the technology, she was determined to try and teach him a lesson or two.

The atmosphere was pretty 'cool' between them for the rest of the lunch session, and as they went their separate ways Kate watched him swagger down the hill with an air of 'untouchable'.

Indoors, she pulled the 'Chip Control' console from the shelf and switched it on, as he had said that he was going out later. While she waited, Kate busied herself preparing some lessons for the following day, at the same time keeping an eye on the laptop in case Luke decided to go skating.

She could see that he had left the skates resting against the wall in the hallway, but she heard him air his concerns to his mate on the phone about how he thought that Kate had put some kind of spell on them, and because he had put the phone on speaker she also heard his mate tell him not to be ridiculous.

She smiled to herself thinking that no one was going to believe him. Ordinary people didn't believe in witches and spells and the more he went on about it, the more people were going to think that he was losing it.

Finally, he hung up and she realised that he was on the move as he grabbed hold of his skates and left.

She carried on with her work knowing that she had about fifteen minutes before any action.

She had no idea what mischief she would create, but she was looking forward to causing him trouble. "What goes around comes around" so the saying tells us, only this time it's coming around a bit more quickly than usual, she thought.

Chapter 42

More Fun and Games

The next time she looked at the screen she could see the miniature cones laid out at regular intervals in front of him and he was zig-zagging cleanly in between them, forwards and backwards. People were stopping in admiration as he added more and more bits to the zig-zag, turning it into a complex, skillful routine.

Kate waited until there was a sizeable audience before intervening. She thought she would try stopping one skate. The performance came to an untimely end, as instead of executing a combination of smooth curves and turns in between the cones, he ended up spinning around on the spot on one skate while knocking the cones in all directions with the other one. Kate could hear the people laughing. Embarrassed, he decided to call it a day, 'Sorry folks – technical hitch. Been having trouble with my skates lately,' and he skated on one foot back to the car where he changed back into his trainers.

Once he had removed the skates he picked up the one that had been causing him trouble and tested the wheels by running his hand along them, of course he could find no fault because Kate had disengaged the controls.

Anyway, she was satisfied that she had ruined his session because normally he would have been out there for another four or five hours.

After about an hour she noticed a text from him, 'Hi hon, how about I rustle up a light dinner and we watch a film xxx'

' Well, well, well! *Something* has got through to him then?' she muttered to herself.

In the past she would have jumped at the chance, but she didn't see why she should comply too quickly. Why should it go his way?

She was hurt and didn't trust him, *or herself.* She didn't want him using his charms to try and win her over or weaken her reserve. And she resented being used as a fill-in for what would otherwise have been a day of rollerblading.

'Sorry, not tonight – other plans. But I would accept an invitation to dinner at an intimate restaurant, followed by a night of physical pampering leaving me in a state of total satisfaction x,' she had deliberately reduced the kisses. What was the point of three kisses? They were barely friends now; she would keep in touch but never again was she going to be available for his convenience. She had put herself out for him time and time again, but that was the past; annoyed with herself for having fallen for his beguiling ways and magnetism.

He came back with, 'Dream on sweetie! x'

She hadn't loved him for the promises of a better life (with all the money he would have acquired from his mysterious, abandoned business) it had been his easygoing, engaging personality; his (apparent) transparency; his apparent 'thoughtfulness' and respect for her; all of which seemed to have dissipated since his illness and the advent of warm spring sunshine. She had been *so* stupid having vowed never to get involved with the opposite sex again.

She had recovered and repaired herself from 'the bastards' so many times before that she thought it could never happen again, and even if it did, she told herself that she would cope just as she had in the past – "pick herself up, brush herself off and start all over again" as in the words of the song. But it seemed harder this time, and she couldn't work out why. Had she trusted too much, or loved too deeply? The clairvoyant's first reading had been so convincing that she had let down her defenses and barriers, naively assuming that she was right.

She left the camera on so she could keep track of what he was doing and saw that he had taken the skates to pieces on the kitchen table *again!*

Kate laughed at the thought of all the extra work he was putting into cleaning them, when they had recently been done. She watched as he picked up his mobile, 'Hi man. You going fishing tonight?'

'No, sorry mate next week, depending on the weather.'

'So, what'ya up to?'

'I'm taking Janice out for a meal.' (Janice was his mate's girlfriend).

'Okay. Enjoy – speak soon. Give her a kiss from me.'

'Yeah, speak soon.'

She saw him put the tin on the table, and roll himself a spliff.

Kate couldn't help smiling, because she knew that he didn't like having his routine or plans upset.

'Good,' she thought aloud, 'at least I have managed to mess up one day,' although, even as she said it she had mixed feelings: mildly uncomfortable about being vindictive, and yet pleased with her ability to manipulate his skating.

Kate had to turn off her laptop as her first student was at the door and she would be busy for the next couple of hours, in any case he wouldn't be going anywhere because he would need to reassemble his skates. She would turn it back on later to see what was happening.

The next few days were busy for her so she left Luke alone apart from answering his texts which were arriving more frequently. It was obvious that her words had had some effect, and he was probably thinking that it would be better to keep friendly contact than aggravate the situation

Luke didn't speak about his concerns to his friends because they would have thought that he was going crazy, but he privately harboured a fear that there were forces working against him. She had told him of *so many* incidents in the past when weirdly anyone who had hurt her (emotionally or physically) had always been paid back – and not equally, but threefold – at least! He wished he had taken it more seriously. In fact he wished that he had never met her. He tried to analyse his behaviour – What had he done that was so wrong? he asked himself. She knew that he was going to be more occupied in the summer, he'd explained that to her, hadn't he? Yeah, okay, he didn't find her sexy any more, but was that his fault?

After a few uneventful days Luke had put the skating incidents behind him and had been making the most of the fine weather. The sun was shining, he had made it up with Kate (or so he thought) and his skates were perfect.

Kate, for her part, had been busy teaching, dancing and exercising and celebrating birthdays, as most of her friends seemed to be born in April and May.

Come Sunday, when life became less hectic and Megan was entertaining 'her man', Kate thought that maybe she could have more fun with the chip control gadget – the temptation was simply too strong to ignore.

So down came the box from the shelf. It took minutes to set up and connect; now she had the hang of it.

Chapter 43

Interested Parties

Kate's mobile buzzed and she picked up to speak to Megan, 'Hi there!'

'Hello! What you up to?'

'Just messing with his skating session in London,' she chuckled.

'Any luck?'

'Yes. I've completely ruined his day!' Kate said with satisfaction.

'Well done – success then?'

'Oh yes and very satisfying. Anyway, to what do I owe the pleasure?'

'Well, do you remember Susie?'

'Do you mean Susie married to the golf fanatic?'

'Yes, she's totally fed up with the golf – it's taken over; he's even talking about a golfing holiday with his mates where she can sit and watch! Or should I say admire?'

'Hmm, sounds painful.'

'Exactly! So I was thinking of talking to her about the chips? I mean he does exactly what he wants, when he wants: he expects the food on the table, a clean house, clean laundry, grocery shopping done, and the sex on tap! *And* he complains if it isn't all done to perfection! He makes such a fuss if she wants to have a day out with the W I and isn't back exactly on time, that she says it isn't worth the hassle.'

'Nice.' Kate squeezed in sarcastically, remembering why she was divorced.

'Anyway, what do you think? Can we help her? I would really like to. I am so sick of all my friends being used as unpaid housekeepers and prostitutes, just to keep the peace.'

'It would mean letting her in on our secret?' Kate said sceptically.

'Yes, I know, it's asking a lot, but I've known her for more than thirty years and she can be trusted, believe me.'

Kate knew Megan to be a pretty good judge of character especially where her old friends were concerned, and she had had her fill of women being exploited by their husbands with the self-deluded idea that the female sex had nothing better to do than "keep their men happy", so she agreed.

'Thanks Kate, you're a saviour – I can't wait to tell Susie, she's so depressed.'

'No problem, but I think we need to have a meeting because obviously I'll have to get another console and chips under some pretext, and she'll need some guidance.'

'Yes, of course. I just want to stop her slashing her wrists. She's desperate.'

'Okay, I'll let you know as soon as the package arrives, and then we can set things up?'

'I can't thank you enough Kate, for Susie.'

'Just glad to help; I know what some of them are going through.'

'Do you want to come up this evening for a light supper and watch something ? Brad's on 'lates', and won't be back till after midnight.'

'Yes, thanks, that would be nice.'

Kate spent the rest of the afternoon photocopying material for the next day, after which she fed Cat, and walked over to the corner shop to get a bottle of wine to take to Megan, then drove the few miles to her little bungalow behind the hills.

They ate the rest of the roast that Megan had cooked earlier accompanied by the bottle of rosé and watched a series with Tom Hiddleston that Megan had recorded. Kate left before midnight replete with food, wine, good company and images of Tom.

First thing the following day, Kate sent a text to Rob under the pretext that one of her students was a golf instructor who thought that using the chips could help some of his beginners with their strokes; apart from the data that could be added to Rob's research figures.

He replied almost immediately saying that he would have it put straight in the post, and added that they had developed an app for smartphones and tablets, and would text Kate the details. This was good news as it meant that she would no longer be restricted to using the laptop.

No sooner had she downloaded the app when she saw a text from Luke inviting her to dinner at one of the most exclusive restaurants in the town.

'Ha, ha!' she exclaimed, 'It seems I'm getting a result!' Cat's ears pricked up but that was all, as he was used to her outbursts and didn't think it warranted more attention; nothing had been thrown and no doors slammed.

She didn't waste any time in replying, 'Yes, that would be lovely. I am free Friday x' She had chosen Friday knowing full well that it was the one evening when he usually joined his mates skating, and that would be the most inconvenient. She waited for his reaction.

He didn't reply immediately and Kate could picture him frowning at the phone figuring out how to handle the situation. He would be working out how to do both: keep her happy *and* go skating. Kate had done this to test him, and wondered how much he believed in what had recently happened. Would he forego his usual evening of skating with all his pals?

There was always plenty to do in the morning so she didn't hover over the phone waiting for a reply, instead: she whizzed around feeding Cat; clearing up; getting showered; putting on makeup; making boring calls and eating a late breakfast.

When she had finished, she glanced at the screen and saw a couple of messages – one from his lordship!

'Yes, Friday is fine. Pick you up at 7.30. OK? x '

Kate thought about it. She knew that the skating was late on a Friday, so maybe he was hoping to dine her first and then get some skating in afterwards, because the late session was from 10.00 to midnight? If they left a bit later he would not be able to fit everything in, bearing in mind that he had a forty drive to get to the skating venue.

'Sorry, it will have to be 8.00 as I have a class till 7.45 x' She didn't, but it was always a good excuse.

She imagined him swearing at the screen, and smiled. He had

probably discussed it with Keith and they had solved the dilemma together, and now Kate had moved the goal posts!

After a while (having resigned himself to a no-skating night) he texted back agreeing, and Kate silently punched the air while doing a little victory dance. She would eek out the evening to make it last as long as possible, just in case he was planning to eat quickly and still get away in time for an evening of fun and games. Anyway, he could rely on five days of hassle-free skating because she would leave him alone until after Friday, and then, depending how "the night" went, she would reassess the situation. Oh yes, life was sweet and so was revenge!

A couple of days later, as soon as 'the package' arrived, Kate sent Megan a text so they could set up a meeting with her friend Susie, who had been checking her phone in anticipation and who, of course, wanted to meet up straight away.

Kate had to explain that they would need the golf clubs and that the only times she would be free would be the mornings or evenings after 8.00 pm. Susie knew it would be impossible in the morning as her husband would probably be using them, however he was out most evenings playing darts, poker or cribbage. So they arranged to meet the following evening.

Megan drove, and they appeared on the doorstep plus golf clubs and wine!

Kate had never handled golf clubs before, and hadn't realised just how heavy a full set in a bag weighed, 'Wow!' she said as she took the clubs off Susie, 'No wonder, they go round in those little buggies – I wouldn't want to carry those any distance!'

She put them upright in the corner of the classroom and unpacked the control unit and chips. Rob had slipped a handwritten note inside reminding them that they had to use the extra strong adhesive (enclosed) as there was so much impact involved in the game that the chips could easily become dislodged.

Kate laid everything out on the table and saw that there were at least twenty chips, 'Hmm, I wonder why there are so many?' she thought aloud.

'Well, there are at least fourteen clubs,' Susie suggested.

'Really!?' Megan and Kate chimed in unison; they had both learnt something.

'I'm surprised that it hasn't come up in a quiz,' Megan added.

'Useful to know if it does though,' Kate made mental note of it. 'Did you bring your laptop Susie?'

Susie pulled an Apple laptop from her bag and laid it on the table, and Kate got to work connecting cables and punching keys. Meanwhile, Susie and Megan stuck the chips under the lower edge of the grip. Kate had shown them how to lift it up and slide one underneath out of sight, holding it in place with a tiny spot of adhesive.

Megan had poured three glasses of the wine and once all the clubs had been chipped, they had a toast to success.

'Now all you have to do is learn how to use the controls – you may have to practice a bit,' Kate advised her, 'Megan used to play a bit so you could have a practice run now if you want?'

'Oh, right – me guinea-pig again!' Megan said more in jest than annoyance, 'Right here goes,' she stood up and grabbed a club.' What about a ball?'

'Sorry, there might be enough room to swing a club, but I draw the line at hard projectiles being propelled at high speed around my room!'

'There's a ping-pong ball over there on the shelf; will that do?' Susie had spotted the ball in between some books.

'Well done! I had forgotten I had that. It's Cat's – he won't mind.'

So Megan took up the stance of a true golfer, shifted her feet slightly and then slowly lifted the club high above and behind her head in preparation for the shot.

Kate offered her advice, ' You can see all this on the screen,' she pointed to Susie's laptop, 'So you'll need to get ready once the club is in this position to take control on the way down.'

'Rrriight,' Susie confirmed somewhat nervously, taking hold of the controls with a look of concentration on her face.

Megan brought the club down like a practiced amateur and sent the ball straight down the "fairway". Kate clapped, 'Well done! Good shot!'

'Yes, too good. What happened Susie? I'm not supposed to be

doing so well!'

'Yes, I know, I'm sorry; it all happened so quickly! Can we try again?'

'No problem!' Megan dropped the club on the carpet and went in search of the ball.

'I *did* say that you would need quite a bit of practice,' Kate repeated, 'and the controls are really sensitive so don't go mad with them! I have an idea – why don't we start with putting – it's slower?'

'Yes!' they both agreed before lifting their glasses and having a couple of sips.

So, once again Megan took up her stance in front of the ping-pong ball, judging the distance between the hole (a circle of black paper) and the ball. She pretended to pick tiny obstacles out of the way, and lifted a finger to judge which way the wind was blowing. She had seen them on television lying the putter on the ground in line with the hole and getting down on their hands and knees; she wasn't quite sure how it helped, but she did it anyway.

Kate had indulged her playing the part up to then, 'Hey! Tiger Woods! Get on with it!'

'Just making it authentic, that's all,' she smiled.

'Right, Susie are you ready? And Meg, try and go slow.'

Megan slowly drew the club away from the ball to a distance of about fifteen centimeters and then took the stroke, but this time it went off at a sixty degree angle to the left.

'Hooray! Success! I presume that was your doing Susie?' Kate was well impressed.

'Yes, I didn't mean for it to be so dramatic though, you're right it needs a very light touch. Can we try again?'

'You'd better ask Rory Mc Ilroy over there,' Kate said pointing towards Megan who was still playing the part of the bewildered golfer inspecting her putter to see if there was something wrong.

With a couple of glasses of wine in her Megan was up for most things, so the session continued with Susie gaining more and more confidence, and they soon progressed to using woods and a driver by which time they were on their second bottle of wine.

'I can't thank you enough Kate; I know this will change my life. I just want a bit of respect and acknowledgement. I don't think it's asking too much?'

'It's no more than you deserve and should have had it years ago. Glad to have been able to help.' This was followed by more raising and clinking of glasses.

The practicing deteriorated the more they drank, and turned into an evening of laughter and rushing to the loo, so they called it a day and gathered everything up. Susie put the control unit into the bag that she took to her exercise class because her husband never looked in there, and when all the kissing was done they got into Megan's car and disappeared around the top of the road.

As Kate wandered around clearing up she smiled, pleased with the evening's activity, and the thought of winning Susie more freedom.

Chapter 44

Complete Control

Friday evening came around pretty quickly. Kate got ready before her lessons, and everyone asked where she was going as they had noticed that she looked exceptionally attractive.

'Just out to dinner,' she said nonchalantly.

Luke's text came through at exactly eight o'clock to let her know that he was at the end of the road.

'Hello, have you had a good week?' she asked as she jumped into the front seat.

'Yeah, not bad at all, thanks. And you?'

'Good, thanks – Megan's on good form; we've had a few laughs.'

'Sounds like you've enjoyed yourselves. I've had some excellent skating.'

'Yes, I'd noticed the weather's been good for it, and I said things would get better as soon as your attitude towards me changed,' she glanced to see his reaction. He looked back and smiled saying nothing.

During the meal he was his old chatty, witty self, reminiscent of the winter. He paid her a compliment on her appearance, and generally made her feel good about herself. Everything seemed to be working out as planned. She thoroughly enjoyed the food, taking her time, as she had no intention of giving him the opportunity of leaving in time to go skating, noting how quickly he had finished his dish of spaghetti carbonara. Unusually, she ordered a dessert, stretching out the process even further, and she noticed him look at his watch.

'Shall we have a coffee?' Kate suggested.

'Not for me,' he said emphatically.

In the "old" days he would have added: "But don't let me stop you, if you want one."

Not that night; he was trying to convey the message that it would not be a good idea, which of course, only provoked her the more.

'I think I'll have one if that's alright?' she said lightheartedly, smiling.

He couldn't contain himself any longer, 'You could have one at home; besides it's just an excuse to add another three pounds to the bill.'

She had been wondering how long he was going to be able to keep it up, although she knew that he would do almost anything to preserve his wonderful world of skating.

'Yes, you're right, and your coffee is excellent, *and* you have decaffeinated,' she knew that he didn't mean *his* home, but she wanted to see him suffer.

'I meant *your* home sweetie.'

'Oh, that's a disappointment; here was I thinking that we were going back to your place to make mad, passionate love.' Kate was trying hard not to sound mocking, but as she said the words his mouth dropped open and then quickly closed again.

'I don't think so, at least not tonight.'

'But I am really in the mood, and I thought you were too, or is this little gesture just a token to keep me happy so I don't mess up your skating again?'

'No, nothing like that. I have to go and pick up a car and deliver it to Norfolk.'

'Oh, you should've said; I'm sorry I hadn't realised,' she said as authentically as possible.

She doubted very much that it was the truth, but went along with it for the moment. She had nothing else to do after he dropped her off, so she had decided she would follow him.

They parted amicably; she even eked a kiss out him – probably guilt driven.

She made a pretext of opening her front door, but as soon as he drove away she jumped into her own car. It took moments for her to pull out, and she knew that she would only have to follow him to the motorway to know where he was going as the skating would take him in completely the opposite direction to his mate's car depot.

Sure enough, a few minutes later, he took the coast direction to the skating venue, and there were no exits for miles which confirmed her suspicions. She had no problem with that as he would be the one to suffer. However, she did wonder how long it was going take him to realise who was in control. She did a three hundred and sixty degree turn around the roundabout and headed home, knowing exactly how she was going to spend the remainder of her evening.

It would take him at least forty minutes to reach the leisure centre, so she got changed, fed Cat and poured herself a glass of wine, then she switched on the laptop, and saw immediately that his skates were in the car.

'Crafty devil,' she thought, but not surprised; she was *so* looking forward to later.

The TV was on catch up because she had missed an episode of a french detective series that she had become involved with and she couldn't wait to see, besides, it was filling in the time until he got his skates on. In any case, she had become so adept at using the equipment that she could keep an eye on both and still create havoc.

He arrived more than half an hour late, but an hour and a half of selfish enjoyment was obviously worth the sacrifice, and he would be going on to a pub or bar afterwards with the others.

Kate watched as he took to the floor, greetings were exchanged and questions asked:

'Hey, you're late! Car trouble?'

'What happened? Overslept?'

He ignored them all and skated around warming up. Keith joined him and they chatted; she heard him say, 'I had to take the bitch out to keep her happy, she seems to think that she has some sort of control over my skating,' he laughed.

'Hmm, so that's how he sees things, is it?' she thought, seething, she pushed the control to "stop" on one skate. This caused him to trip himself up and do a somersault, landing in a crumpled, embarrassed heap in the middle of the floor. Everyone looked around because he never stumbled, let alone cause a major incident

'Hey, mate, are you okay? What on earth happened there?' Keith turned around and stopped.

Luke was sitting up in shock, trying to work out what had gone on.

'Anything broken?' Keith said half joking, although he was aware that it could be possible having seen the way he had fallen. There had been a few broken bones during the sessions, and none so dramatically.

'No, I think I'm okay thanks – just stunned. I'll probably have a few bruises though,' he grinned and skated off to sit down. A couple of people shouted comments: 'Drinking again!', 'Too many spliffs Luke!' Neither of which Luke touched while he was skating, and they knew it.

The first thought that entered his head was Kate – she had obviously been hoping to make night of it. Was this his punishment? Now, he was even more convinced that there were forces beyond anyone's control, in control of *him,* because Kate had no idea that he was skating; as far as she was concerned he was on his way to the car depot. He sat and contemplated his situation and couldn't decide whether to have another go or not. He was still smarting from the fall, on the other hand he had not driven all that way just to sit and watch everyone else having fun.

Finally, he got fed up with all his mates having a go at him, so he went to join them. Tentatively and uncertain he took to the floor anticipating disaster. This was alien to him having always been so confident on his skates, admired for his skill executing combinations of tricks, the others looked to him for help and advice, he was the roller blading guru.

After completing a couple of laps, he appeared to regain his self-assurance and started twisting and turning in between the other skaters. Kate watched for a while and couldn't help but admire his style, it made her quite nostalgic for the ice rink, she missed it *so* much but there was no way she could risk a bad accident at her age, especially being self-employed.

Suddenly, as he passed a young girl (half his age) he grabbed her hand and swung around in front of her smiling – she laughed. There was no doubt that they were on fairly intimate terms from the way they touched each other, and this was not the same girl as last time. Kate was not going to tolerate that for long – it was one thing having a bit of a skate with the guys, but going to flirt (having lied to her), that was something else.

She took the controls and forced an abrupt stop repeating the accident of a couple of weeks earlier with the other girl. Again he fell on his back with no warning so she landed on top of him, and accidentally or otherwise kneed him in the balls while trying to disentangle herself. This left him bent double on his side, writhing in pain in the middle of the floor like a helpless, wounded animal. Kate had seen men hit there before and they all made the same fuss, concluding that they were all great big cry babies with low pain thresholds.. She didn't have any male genitalia so she would never find out how painful it really was, however, she did make a note of how effective it seemed to be for future use.

Two or three of his friends hovered around to see if they could help, but he just lay on his side groaning until the pain was manageable enough to allow him to stand; even then he staggered to the exist nearly bent double. Kate smiled contentedly, 'Another good job done,' she said aloud on her way to the kitchen to pour herself a celebratory drink.

She heard the clock in the hall chime eleven. 'Good,' she thought again, ' he won't be going back out there now.'

As she wandered back into the other room her mobile pinged – it was a text from Luke, 'Hi, sweetie, I felt bad about leaving you tonight. Do you want to come over tomorrow for dinner and stay? Xxx'

'Ah! Finally, he's getting the message,' Kate picked Cat up (who complained loudly about being disturbed) and did a few turns around the room with him. She did not know whether cats got giddy, but when she put him down he stood motionless as if disorientated, and then bolted from the room. He was great company – pity he can't talk and make love to her, then she wouldn't have to bother with men.

She replied, 'Sorry, but I have other plans – big dance.' It was true, she had arranged with Megan to go to an exceptional rock 'n roll evening. A few weeks ago she would have foregone the dance for his invitation: not any more, things had changed; she had wasted too much time trying to keep him and other men happy, and where had it got her? Another text came back, she could see him sitting out at the side of the rink on his phone, looking pretty miserable.

'How's about coming round after? I can cook you breakfast and then go for a walk with the dogs? Xxx'

'It will be late? 11.30?x'

'Yeah. No problem. You still have a key – let yourself in xxx'

'Okay x'

He sent a thumbs up and a smiley face, and she smiled to herself as she thought about the changes ahead, starting with his performance in bed!

Chapter 45

All Change

By the time Megan had dropped her off the following evening it was gone midnight. As she turned the key in his door, the dogs went berserk as usual, and she fought her way to the bedroom as they jostled for favour. They obediently sat outside as she slipped silently around the gap in the open door. Luke had left the corner light on low, just enough for her to see the faint outlines of the furniture and the shape of his body under the covers. She assumed from the rhythmical deep breathing that he was in a deep sleep, so carefully putting her overnight bag in the corner where no one would trip over it, and removing the essentials, went to the bathroom.

The shower felt wonderful as it washed away the sticky night of dancing, but she didn't linger, because asleep or otherwise, she was determined to get her long overdue quota of foreplay.

Refreshed and ready for some pampering, she crept back into the bedroom. So far she had given and not received – things were about to change!

With his back towards her she gently stroked the smooth, flawless skin, coaxing the sleepy response, 'Hello sweetie. Good night?'

'Yes, excellent, but I am wide awake,' she said kissing him on the shoulder, figuring he would need a bit of encouragement to stir him into action.

Finally, after applying all of her persuasive expertise, he turned over and smiled.

'Right,' she thought as she rolled onto her back puling him with her, so that he unexpectedly landed on top of her; a position that he had avoided in the past during their love-making.

'Your turn,' she said with conviction.

He parted her legs with his and moved to penetrate her; she knew he was thinking that he could make quick work of it and get back to sleep.

'Uh, Uh, I'm not ready yet,' she protested pushing hard on his shoulders, leaving him in no doubt as to what she wanted. She didn't care whether he used his tongue or his finger just as long as he satisfied her.

She felt him reluctantly change position and go down on her.

She gasped as his tongue made contact, and an involuntary shudder shot through her; it had been so long that it felt like a new experience, and she willingly surrendered. She knew that he was only pleasuring her in the hope of incident free skating, but she didn't care in a way it made it more exciting, the thrill of being in control, having the power to manipulate and not be the victim was a real turn on! She was going to make the sensation last, because she knew that as soon as she came he would penetrate her, and it would all be over.

For the first time since they had met she felt as though he had made an effort, and she was satisfied! It didn't take him long to climax; after which they lay separately, each to their side of the bed. He had never held her after sex – it seemed to be just a physical process with him, almost a task. At first It had hurt and worried her, she would have loved to have fallen asleep in his arms, but when it was over it was over, there was no tenderness. It was quite primeval. She remembered once putting her arm around him only to have it removed, and turn his back to her with a perfunctory, 'Good night!'

All of that romantic stuff didn't matter to her any more because her emotions were in a different place. Love had been replaced with revenge; she was still hurting but now she could make him hurt too, and that made it easier to stomach.

He wasn't going to like *having* to keep her happy but that was irrelevant, in her mind now he was 'a thing' to be used if possible, and it was amusing her. What she was doing was completely out of character and she surprised herself with her ruthlessness, but she was secretly quite proud of how she had handled everything. She still regretted allowing herself to fall so completely for his charming bullshit, and she reminded herself that he hadn't only hurt *her*; she was doing this for the others too, the ones who had come before.

It wasn't long before the deep, regular breathing told her he was asleep, so she put in her earphones and tuned to radio four in the certainty that she would shortly join him.

The next morning was like they had never rowed. She was woken with a piping hot cup of tea, followed by eggs sunny side up, cooked exactly the way she liked them.

'How did the delivery go?' she asked him innocently as he handed her the plate.

'Delivery?' he repeated quizzically. She had caught him off guard.

'Yes, the car you delivered the night before last?' She could see that he was confused.

Coming to his senses he replied, 'Oh yeah, yeah, good thanks – no problems.'

'Where was it again?'

'The Midlands.'

'Oh, really? Funny, I thought you said somewhere else.'

He thought he had said somewhere else as well, but he couldn't bloody remember, that was the problem with lying.

'F***ing Liar,' Kate thought to herself, 'and he can't even do that properly! I'm glad I made him pay for that.'

It was a cloudless sky and she was so looking forward to a long, leisurely walk with the dogs by the sea, maybe stopping for a drink and a snack. It was as though they had a sixth sense because they stuck to her like glue as she went around gathering up her bits and pieces. They kept brushing up against her, or standing right in front, determined not to be forgotten, tails wagging furiously. And if dogs could smile – she would have sworn they were smiling.

Her phoned was buzzing – it was a call from Megan. Luke was busy in the Kitchen so she closed the bedroom door and answered it, 'Hello.'

'Hi! How are you? How did it go?'

'Great. Perfect. Couldn't be better.' She didn't need to ask Megan because her love life had been on an even keel for weeks.

'Wonderful! I have more good news,' Megan continued,' Susie is over the moon with her "stuff".She told me that she's never had so much fun in her life. Apparently, the first day he came back from the golf course in a foul mood, and the second day an even worse one. Susie told him that if he helped around the house his game would improve, but he just laughed and said it had nothing to do with it.'

'So what is she going to do?'

'Nothing! She's going to carry on messing with his game until he conforms.'

'That could take a while,' Kate remarked sceptically.

'Yes, but she's enjoying herself so much that she doesn't mind; she said she hasn't laughed so much for ages. Her favourite is landing him in a bunker and watching him trying to get out of it. She said there was sand flying everywhere, and he came home covered in it! You can picture it can't you?'

'Oh yes, maybe we could go and watch too – make it a lunch party – open a bottle?' Kate didn't need an excuse to have a drink although she preferred to do it in good company

'I'll ask her; I'm sure she'll agree. It *would* be fun.'

The bedroom door opened. It was Luke, 'You ready sweetie?'

Megan had heard him, 'Okay, you'd better go. I'll get in touch with Susie and arrange something.'

Kate said her goodbyes, hung up and she went to join Luke.

Chapter 46

Golf, Lunch and Laughter

'Come in! Come on through to the conservatory, I've put out some cold snacks and salad. I see you've bought your own wine,' Susie said cheerfully leading the way.

Kate noticed how much brighter and more positive she sounded since the last time they had spoken, and was sure that she looked younger; her hair had been cropped and tinted, and she looked just like Tamsin Greig from Episodes. The new style enhanced her superb bone structure that her husband had found so attractive forty years previously. She was tall and slim but had never bothered to make the most of herself. Now, in an off-the-shoulder white sleeveless blouse and the clingiest of jeans she looked stunning, and Kate wondered whether her husband had gone blind.

It was the first time that Kate had been to Susie's house, as they walked through to the conservatory there was a magnificent view of a well kept garden with raised beds jam-packed with colour, an ornate birdbath, a gazebo, and a shed that looked like a guest chalet.

They sat at a long twelve-seater, teak table, and Megan took seconds to open the wine and fill the glasses. Kate topped hers up with fizzy water to make a spritzer.

'Cheers!' they said in unison as they raised their glasses.

'Please help yourselves,' Susie gestured to an array of plates loaded with finger food, so they sipped and nibbled while she tuned in on the laptop.

'I have had such a good time with this, but I expect Megan has told you?'

'Yes, we chatted the other day, and it sounds as though you've really mastered it?'

'I don't know about that, but I seem to be able to accomplish what I want,' she chuckled.

'Let's drink to success!' Kate suggested.

'To success!' they both replied.

They huddled around the computer as the view of a local golf club came up. Susie had put a couple of chips in her husband's golf bag so she could view his reaction to his missed shots as well as take control of his strokes.

He was on the fourth tee waiting for his friends to tee off.

'Good shot Howie!'

'Nice one Geoff!'

They were each others' fans. Roger (Susie's husband) took his stance on the tee, and went through the motions of practising his swing, then he squared up to his ball on the little orange peg, raised the club up and backwards way above him, bringing it down with remarkable force and speed, but due to Susie's minute adjustment he missed the ball entirely swinging the club all the way around over his left shoulder and knocking himself off balance, inelegantly stumbling backwards.

'Shit! What the fuck? Don't tell me it's started again!' he sounded well angry, but the girls were impressed.

'Wow, that was really well done Susie,' Kate praised her skilful handling of the controls.

'Well, as I said I've had a lot of practice, and the thing that annoys him most is completely missing the ball because it makes him look such a fool. I love it! It gives me such power. At last I feel like I am getting my own back, and I might get through to him.'

'So what have you said to him?' Kate was slightly worried that Susie might have given the game away.

'I told him that I had a local witch put a spell on him, and that until he pulls his weight at home his game will deteriorate.'

'Brilliant! And how did he react?'

'He said it was a load of rubbish and didn't believe a word of it, and that it was a phase that would pass.'

They carried on eating and sipping the chilled rosé. Kate was impressed with the food that Susie had made from scratch; there was a home made quiche with all her favourite ingredients that Kate was having a third helping.

And they laughed and laughed. Not all the blunders were as dramatic as the first one, in fact most of them were very subtle. Susie could steer the shot slightly off course so that he never managed par. Sometimes she made him spend ages on the green putting the ball backwards and forwards and each time narrowly missing the hole by millimetres. It amused the ladies no end watching him trying to keep calm, but eventually losing it.

They watched until he finally told the others that he'd had enough and would meet them in the club house later.

'He knows that all he has to do is help around the house by doing his share so I can get out more, and have dinner ready for me when I get back from the occasional trip with the ladies.' Susie explained.

'Too right! I hope he comes round soon,' Kate added.

'Me too. On the other hand I shall kind of miss the fun it's giving me – it has changed my life already.'

'You don't need to worry, even if he does conform, there'll always be relapses, especially when he thinks it's all stopped. And even if he doesn't relapse, you can do it just for the hell of it occasionally'

'Yes, that's true,' she said more cheerfully.

When they had emptied the bottle and nearly cleared the dishes, Kate and Megan said their goodbyes thanking Susie for the afternoon's entertainment.

The next time Kate would hear from her would be to tell her that Roger had started to give her a hand with the cleaning, shopping and loading the dishwasher. It was a start, and Susie had reduced the punishment on the golf course although it was 'work in progress'. Susie arranged a day out for 'the girls' to the Tate in London to thank Kate properly, and Roger had promised to have dinner ready for when she got back.

The word soon spread, and when the other ladies heard about the change in Roger they started asking questions, and Kate began to receive a lot of enquiries: 'Could we please have the same "formula to freedom" as Susie.'

She didn't know any of the women (she and Susie moved in completely different circles) their only mutual friend was Megan.

She texted Susie, 'Hello there! I hope life is treating you well and that Roger is being a good boy? x'

She received a response almost immediately, 'Yes, as good as gold, thanks to you x'

'By the way, I've been getting a lot messages from women I don't know. I don't suppose you have any idea who all these women are? x'

'Oh, I hope you don't mind? They are all desperate for a life, and they couldn't help but remark on Roger's change in attitude, and my new found freedom! Obviously, they wanted to know how it had happened, so I said you had helped, and they would have to ask you? x'

Kate couldn't text any more; she needed to talk, so she said she would ring her and punched in Susie's number, 'Sorry, Susie I can't be doing with texting – I need to know exactly what you have told them?'

'Hello, yes of course, I'm sorry, I only gave your number to two people. How many calls have you had?'

'About five missed calls, and three or four texts.'

'Blimey! Word must have spread. I'm really sorry.'

'I would have appreciated it if you had asked me first,' Kate was trying not to sound too angry.

'Yes, I know you are quite right, I'm sorry; they seemed so desperate and I just didn't think.'

Kate wasn't terribly surprised as she hadn't struck her as the most intelligent of Megan's friends, although a little consideration wouldn't have gone amiss.

'What did you tell them?' Kate asked again.

'I just said that you had helped me – I didn't give them any more details, except that it would be up to you,' Susie sounded apologetic, realising that she had acted thoughtlessly.

'Hmm, well I don't know what I'm going to do about it, because it's got out of hand. You'll have to tell them that I can't reply immediately. There are too many of them. I need to think this through.'

'Yes, of course, no problem, just send me their names and numbers – I'll sort it, promise.'

'Okay, thanks. I'm not saying "no", I just don't know how to handle it. Give me a couple of days to think this through. I can't ask Rob for seven or eight boxes all at once; he'll get suspicious. By the way are you sending him regular feedback on the progress of your "pupil"?'

'Yes, absolutely. I am leaving feedback every week on line, just like you said.'

'Okay, well done. I will send you any names and numbers, and please say that I am not ignoring them. I will think of a way around it. Sorry, I have to go now. Speak soon. Bye'

'Bye Kate, and sorry again for being so thoughtless.'

'No worries, I'll sort it,' she said and hung up.

She went to the kitchen and switched on the kettle for coffee, and as she waited for it to boil she made a list of all the people who had contacted her and sent them to Susie, then she sat down at her desk and thought about the problem in hand. She phoned Megan and explained it to her. She apologised for her friend's lack of consideration and said she would put on her thinking hat.

Kate was sure that they would come up with a solution between them Megan was full of ideas.

Chapter 47

Join the Club

About four hours later Kate saw a text from Megan: 'I have an idea! Shall come round later with a bottle to discuss? x'

Kate wasted no time replying, 'Yes, please x' and added a smiley.

It was about seven thirty when Megan arrived with bottle, and Kate showed her through to her office (she was printing something and didn't want to leave it in the middle). She had already thought of glasses, which Megan immediately filled.

'Well, come on then, don't keep me in suspense,' Kate couldn't help her impatience.

'These ladies all know each other, right?' Megan was making a statement.

'I think so, I'm not sure, I would have to check that with Sue. But they are friends of friends.'

'Well, friends or not, I thought that they could share the equipment; maybe form a club?'

Kate did not answer immediately, she was thinking over the logistics of Megan's idea.

'Go on,' she said finally hoping that Megan had worked it all out.

'One of them (Linda) has a pretty large studio, purpose built for all her artwork, and her husband never goes in there; I know because she attends my Thursday class and we sometimes go back to her place afterwards.'

'And.....?' Kate wanted more.

'About four of them have husbands that play golf, and one or two of the others fish together and so on, so if they play together, the ladies could take it in turns using the same controls, couldn't they?'

'Hmm, that's not impossible. They are made so you can switch between different people in a group; they were designed for use in schools. It would require more programming, but it's all in the booklet that Rob sent me, and it's been pretty straightforward so far. The only problem I can see is keeping this from the men, because I don't know how we are going to keep the lid on it.'

'Yes, I agree, but I have an idea about that too,' Megan said quite smugly.

'Okay, carry on,' Kate was putting the printed sheets of paper into orderly piles, and was happy to listen to any suggestions. She took a couple of sips of wine and carried on printing.

'We could form a club, like a secret society, the men have their pathetic boys' club, don't they?' She was referring to The Masons, 'We could ask them all to sign something, swearing them to secrecy; after all said and done we have the weaponry to make their lives misery if they don't,' she smiled and drank to the thought.

'I like it. I think it would work, even if I only order two to begin with; they could work in shifts. I could order some more later by degrees, but where would we meet? I don't have room here.'

'We can meet at Linda's; I've already tested the water about using her studio for something, and she had no objections because she'll probably be using the equipment too.'

Yes, well done Megan – another stroke of genius, I have to say. I shall have to appoint someone as secretary to do all the emailing etc and I think we ought to start charging a nominal fee for usage, say a pound a session, it would pay for coffee and biscuits, *and* stationery. And there is less likelihood of the equipment being discovered if it's all in one place, because people can be careless.'

'So we need to call a meeting once the boxes arrive?' Megan had her organising hat on.

'Yes, do you think you and Susie can organise that? And could you ask her to tell them not to contact me any more. I have enough on my plate with my classes and monitoring my own man – I really didn't mean for this to escalate the way it has.'

'Yes, absolutely. You have enough to do – we'll handle it. Come on, let's drink to the WTC!' She raised her glass.

'The WTC ?'

'Yes – Women Take Control.'

'Okay – not very original,' Kate wasn't impressed.

'Won't it do for now?'

'Yes.'

Megan changed the subject and asked about Luke.

'I'm leaving him alone for a while, I think he realises now that he has to be available when I feel like a bit of pampering, he suffered for days after the last accident, whinging about his wrist, shoulder and back; he made out he had done it that morning – lying bastard. I told him so to his face. I said that I knew he had been skating the night before and that it had happened there with a girl, who I described in detail. You should have seen his face – it was an absolute picture, he didn't dare refute any of it because he couldn't, not without digging himself in deeper. So then I told him to pay me some attention in bed, he's been used to getting it all his own way. He lied outright to me about skating that night, and I made him suffer for it. I felt great afterwards. He thinks I've paid someone to wreck his skating. Anyway, enough of him. How's your love life?'

'It's calming down a bit, it hasn't reached the boring stage yet, but it might if I don't think of some ways to spice it up.'

'You can always borrow my box of toys,' Kate offered.

'I might take you up on that.' They drank to it. 'Hey! I've just had another brilliant idea!' Megan was not known for her humility where inspiration was concerned.

'Let me be the judge of that, go on,' Kate encouraged her.

'Why don't we set up an exchange for sex toys, all we would need would be loads of disinfectant?'

'That's not a bad one, however I think we have enough on our plate at the moment, don't you?'

Megan nodded.

They finished the wine, then Megan left; but Kate felt a lot more optimistic about the future for Chip Control, *and* for the ladies who needed to 'get a life'.

The next couple of days were fairly uneventful, Kate had plenty of work although she did remind Luke who was 'boss' by giving him a 'skate scare' from time to time. She also insisted on being wined and dined every Friday night with a stop over so that he could 'look after her' the way she liked. She added that if he flirted with anyone at the skating venues she would ruin the sessions for him, and he believed it – why wouldn't he? – she had managed it before. He didn't have a clue how, and that was even more worrying. He knew that she had joined a witches' coven years ago, but he didn't believe in that sort of "hocus pocus" and would not allow himself to think that it could affect his skating. He was certain that she had some kind of collaborator where he skated – someone who threw 'stuff' on the ground that somehow jammed his skates. This was his reasoning, although he had thoroughly inspected the area each time and found nothing, nor had he seen anyone suspicious hanging around. He had asked his friends to inspect his skates, and they had found nothing either – he was completely baffled.

Also, his friends were beginning to use the word "paranoia" which had him really worried. He had accused his wife of that, and she had ended up sectioned!

Kate said she would talk to "the forces" and ask them to leave his skating alone just as long as he behaved himself and looked after her in bed, which was working well for her – not so for Luke, who felt trapped and confused. Worst still he had lost control, and that was driving him mad!

Chapter 48

The First Meeting

The boxes arrived and Kate asked Megan and Susie to send out emails to everyone so they could agree on a date when most of them were free, preferably a morning, when their husbands would be on the golf course, or the river bank and they could get 'hands on' experience, so to speak.

It did not take long for Susie to get back to her as the women were willing to forego any classes or former commitments in order to get control over their partners. They had seen the change in Roger and could not wait to get started on transforming their own husbands, so the meeting was set for the following Monday.

Kate was the last to arrive as she had had an early lesson. She entered Linda's garden from the back of the house, and as she approached the studio across the lawn she could hear the excited chatter of anticipation through the open windows. On opening the door she was really surprised by the numbers – what had been seven had become at least twelve! The minute she entered the room everyone clapped and cheered. Kate felt slightly overwhelmed, and found herself blushing.

'I didn't expect so many of you,' she said as soon as the noise had dissipated.

Someone handed her a cup of coffee and a tin of posh biscuits.

Susie took charge by asking everyone to find a seat. Luckily, Linda's work table comfortably sat twelve, and by squeezing up they managed to fit everyone in.

To Kate's relief Susie had agreed to chair the meeting, and Megan said she would take the minutes.

Susie had worked in the legal department for an insurance company in the city before retirement, and was well qualified to direct the proceedings. She had also drawn up a contract binding them to complete secrecy, and that each had to read through carefully, agree to and sign, before anything was revealed. So the next half an hour was spent reading it through, working together in pairs, and occasionally asking Susie to clarify something.

She began by taking a list of everyone's names, and asked for a contribution of two pounds towards the coffee, biscuits and admin, which she handed straight to Linda, formerly an accountant, who had volunteered to be treasurer. She said that she would prepare a name tag for everyone to wear for the next meeting.

Susie had brought along a couple of golf clubs to demonstrate where and how to hide the chips. She showed them how to carefully lift the grip with a knife or flat screwdriver, and slide the chip underneath out of sight holding it securely in place. She then followed the same procedure with the fishing rods, darts, squash rackets and table tennis bats (the ladies had brought along whatever they could lay their hands on); she volunteered to visit and help anyone who was unsure of how to do it by themselves.

Megan had ordered a whole load of chips on the pretext of sudden popular demand, and replacement due to loss. Rob had warned her that many of them became dislodged and lost, especially during the more rigorous games like rugby and football. She went around distributing an adequate number (in zip-lock bags) to each person, after which Susie gave a demonstration of how to use the programme and the controls at one end of the table, while Kate showed the rest of the ladies at her end. Fortunately, both Roger and Luke were out doing their 'thing', which provided an ideal opportunity for the ladies to get 'hands on' experience.

There was a lot of giggling and exclamatory language, interspersed with gasps and squeals of delight, as each of them tentatively took a turn. It meant that Luke's and Roger's morning was completely disrupted with the ladies' interference – nothing too dramatic as the women were overly nervous and only caused minor mishaps; but it resulted in Luke abandoning his session, and Roger drowning his sorrows in the club house bar, sending Susie a text asking her what he had done to upset her?

The meeting concluded with Linda setting up a timetable for small groups to take it in turns using her laptop and one of the boxes, while Susie agreed to take the pressure off by taking another group, and Kate said she could help out when she wasn't teaching.

The ladies appeared to be delighted with the morning's activities, leaving animated and motivated.

When the last of them had gone, having thanked their hostesses profusely, Kate, Megan, Susie and Linda opened a bottle of Prosecco to celebrate.

'Here's to a very successful meeting!' Megan toasted and they all raised their glasses.

'To a very successful meeting!' they chanted, clinking glasses and sipping the sparkling wine.

The system worked well, especially once the ladies got to grips with the controls, and they soon had their husbands eating out of their hands! With their newfound freedom and power they hired coaches and organised trips to theatres, stately homes, museums and art galleries. They booked trips to France, Oxford, Cambridge and took boat trips along the coast and up the Thames. They were finally allowed to really enjoy retirement.

The men commiserated among themselves whenever they could get together, occasionally getting to the pub.

'I don't believe in this shit about a witch, do you?' one of them said over his pint.

'Na, me neither, but I had my racquet checked out and they couldn't find a thing wrong with it. I'm blowed if I can figure it; what worries me more is Janet having this power, it's not natural. It's like I'm being held to ransom, and she's *never* at home.'

'Yeah, I know what you mean, it's not right. I've never done so much housework in my life, and you won't believe what she's asking me to do in bed!'

At that point they all had something to say about the demands being made on them under the duvet.

'She's told me to watch videos on what to do – imagine! At my age! And she's bought some battery run toys because she says they are more stimulating than me! It's humiliating.'

There were a lot of grunts of agreement and similar stories.

They sat round a large table staring into their pints trying to think of solutions, and feeling pretty sorry for themselves. The other locals had noticed a change in their demeanour too; the otherwise raucous, boisterous group had become miserable and subdued. It was almost as if they were suffering from some kind of illness.

'What's up with the old boys?' the man serving behind the bar asked the other one.

'I don't know, they've been like that for the last couple of times, they don't drink much any more either. It used to be difficult to keep them under control, now I wish one of them would crack a joke. I haven't heard any of them laugh in ages. I've asked them what the problem is, but they said they were fine, and didn't understand what I was on about?'

None of the men were prepared to explain to anyone outside the group what was happening for fear of sounding stupid, or worst still mad! So they decided to make the most of their stress free days. They had noticed that when the ladies went on a day trip together that they could expect less turmoil, even though the women had an app on their phones and could cause considerable disruption when warranted.

It was uncanny how they always seemed to know what they had been up to, even when they weren't practising their sports, the women knew their every move. Little did they know that some of the more controlling wives had sewn chips into their jackets too, in order to keep track of them!

It was infuriating, and most of them had come to the conclusion that they were being followed, although they never found any evidence. Richard (ex-security) thought the women were hiring illegal immigrants for cheap money to somehow sabotage their sport, and report back on what they were finding. They came up with all kinds of theories but couldn't find any evidence. There was a bunch of philanderers among them who used to enjoy chatting up the girls in the club bar, but they had had to call a halt to all that, as their partners would give them such a hard time afterwards. Roger said it was like wearing a tag on probation.

One of the ladies had gone to the extreme of sewing a chip into every pair of her husband's underpants, as he spent too much time sitting around watching sport on television, or in the pub. So whenever she felt like moving him off his arse she would send a little shock through to his groin making him jump out of his seat. This caused no end of amusement with the other ladies, especially as she would then send him a text saying that a bit of hoovering would ease it, and succeeded in getting him to clean the house instead of being a coach potato; he was even beginning to lose weight.

The women were laughing and smiling more, and people not in the "know" remarked on how much they had changed; that they were looking and acting younger; that they had more "joie de vivre", and they had!

Meanwhile, Luke had obviously been missing his skating on a Friday night, as he asked for the following Friday off in exchange for a Tuesday. As it happened it suited Kate because there was a group booked at the Rock 'n Roll venue, and both she and Megan wanted to go. She wasn't going to tell Luke anything about it, because she wanted him to feel as though she was doing him a favour, and if there hadn't been any dancing it would have given her a reason to get the box down from the shelf and have a bit of fun. He had been so "good" and attentive lately that she had all but forgotten its existence.

In any case she was far too busy on the Friday evening dancing, to cause chaos at the skating rink. Saturday as well, as the girls had arranged a day in France and there was too much going on to waste time on him. The others checked up on their partners from time to time, but they all seemed to be behaving themselves; it was amazing how they had learnt to tow the line. A couple of them had actually taken up cookery classes, and *were enjoying* it! The others resorted to takeaways, ready meals or roast dinner, which Kate reckoned any idiot could produce, after all what was it? a lump of meat thrown in the oven, Bisto gravy, Aunt Betsy's roast potatoes and ready made Yorkshire puddings and a few boiled (to death) vegetables? Some of them never wanted to see a roast dinner again, and had forbidden it.

Come Sunday, when life became less hectic and Megan was

entertaining 'her man', Kate thought that maybe she could have more fun with the chip control gadget – the temptation was simply too strong to ignore.

So down came the box from the shelf.

At first, she couldn't figure out where he was; she saw pavement and plenty of people but as the camera range was low she was having difficulty in placing the location.

Finally, she recognized Keith's voice and worked out that it had to be London and they were doing 'The Stroll'.

She should have guessed that earlier, as once the weather improved they always went to London on a Sunday to meet up with all their fellow-skaters.

'Ooh, this could be good,' she said to Cat who was sitting next to her on the table supervising the proceedings.

Kate sat watching them as they skillfully wove their way through people and cars, thinking that it was almost as good as actually participating – less the danger!

She waited until an opportunity arose for her to create as much chaos as possible. She did not have to wait long, as not too far ahead she could see the group enter a narrow lane full of pedestrians, so she very gradually began to lift Luke's right leg upwards and outwards while maintaining a steady speed on his other skate. She executed everything slowly so that he could keep his balance, but now he was skating on his left leg with his right one sticking out nearly at right angles to one side. He heard another skater shout out to him, 'Hey! Luke! Very clever but watch out for the people!'

'Yeah. I know mate. I can see them but I don't have any control – can't stop and can't put my leg down!'

'Stop messing around! What you're doing is dangerous mate!'

A family in front pressed themselves flat against the wall and Luke missed them by millimetres even though his shoulder was brushing the wall on the other side. He could hear the dad shouting after him, 'You crazy idiot! What do you think you're playing at?'

There were a couple of marshals skating along with the group to make sure that everyone kept together, but they were out of range paying attention to the new-comers as they assumed that seasoned skaters like Luke knew what they were doing.

Luke was shouting at people to get out of the way but they didn't understand and a large black guy (taken by surprise) threw himself flat on the ground as Luke's leg went over his prostrate body. He could hear people behind him swearing and calling him names as they ducked out of his way.

He considered deliberately falling down, but he was going at quite a pace (something else that he seemed to have no control over) and not only could he cause considerable damage to himself but also to the other skaters behind him who could trip over his body. He decided that there was nothing he could do until he got out of the alley.

A family with a large dog were ahead so Kate decided to bring the drama to a close, as she really did not want to see an innocent member of the public hurt. So far she had been having fun, but the thought of causing injury to anyone apart from Luke was not on her agenda, so before Luke reached the family she brought his leg down alongside the left one and switched off the control, allowing him to skate unhindered and in bewilderment as to what had just happened.

'Hey mate, what was going on?' the guy behind had drawn alongside him.

'You won't believe me if I say I don't know,' Luke was skating normally and couldn't have explained the incident logically even if he had wanted to.

'No mate, not really, you're bloody lucky the marshals didn't see you.'

'Yeah, right,' Luke was trying not to show it but he had been badly shaken by the incident. He could have easily injured someone, or himself, so when he saw an empty bench he skated straight over to it and sat down. He was relieved to be off his feet; his legs and hands were shaking.

Keith had come back to look for him, 'You Okay mate?' he asked concerned.

'I don't know – just had a bit of a shock.'

Keith sat down next to him, 'How's that then?'

Luke explained the sequence of events as best as he could, but even as he heard himself speak he thought it all sounded too surreal.

'Have you been smoking mate?' Keith thought the only explanation for it all had to be that he was high on something.

'Absolutely not! You should know me better than that!' Luke responded indignantly.

' Anything else?'

'No, mate, nothing except water! Stu was behind me – he saw the whole thing.'

Keith could see that his friend was suffering from shock: all the colour had drained from his face and his hands were shaking.

'You'd best sit here a while. I'll get you a cup of tea from Lucy's.'

'Thanks, and something sweet, please!' he shouted after him, and saw Keith raise his hand in acknowledgement.

Minutes later, Luke was sipping some sweet tea and munching his way through some sort of commercially produced, chocolate covered, sponge cake in a wrapper.

'Thanks,' Luke put his hand on Keith's shoulder, 'I think I'll call it a day,' and he reached into his backpack for his trainers.

'Hey! What's going on? This ain't like you mate; we've got nearly the whole afternoon left.'

'Yeah, I know but I just don't feel up to it. But don't let me stop you – you'd better hurry if you want to catch the others up.'

'I don't really want to leave you like this,' Keith was genuinely worried because Luke had never dropped out of the Stroll, and he didn't want to leave him on his own. 'If you're not going to carry on then I think I'll join you.'

'No, please don't. I'm fine really – I just need a break.'

'Yeah, well I feel like a break too, so I think I'll stay.'

They sat in silence for a while, in the spring sunshine, just watching the general public get on with their lives. There were families with dogs, couples on the cusp of romance, couples over the cusp and lost in romance, groups of youths talking far too loudly in the self-obsessed belief that they were the only people in the world, and that everyone else would surely be interested in their conversation!

It was the old couples who still held hands that fascinated Keith the most. He wanted to ask them how long they had been married, and how they had managed to overcome everything that life had thrown at them. Not the ones who were just hanging on in there out of habit or because there was no alternative, but the ones who still looked at each other the same as the day they got married, and who, when one died, the other shortly followed: such was the strength of the bond between them. Would others replace them? Or did you have to survive war and hardship to realise the true meaning of love in this increasingly materialistic, throwaway world? He had heard his parents talk about the war and how his mother's wedding dress had been made from a used parachute!

He visualised a very different demographic in fifty years time – no one knew the value of anything any more. The motto of the young was: "Replace with new; preferably with a label". Deep in thought he sighed, inadvertently.

'What's up mate?' Keith asked.

'No, nothing, just thinking about life.'

'Ah, you don't want to do that.'

'Na – you're right.'

'Do you feel like moving?' Keith suggested.

'Yeah,' Luke got to his feet and walked at a leisurely pace through the park, while Keith skated along beside him. He was grateful for Keith's company and pleased that he had insisted on staying

Chapter 49

Cat Control

She watched as they approached St James's; Luke with his skates in his backpack, and Keith skating alongside him.

When the doorbell rang Kate reluctantly got up to see who it was. She opened the door to find her neighbour on the doorstep who wanted to talk to her about cutting down a tree that overhung his property, and was beginning to block light to one of his windows. She stood and listened to his concerns and told him that she would have it trimmed back before the summer foliage got too thick, promising more drastic action in the winter.

He was renowned for his ability to talk, so now that he had her attention he was determined to keep it, and seemed to have saved up a number of past issues to chat about. The "conversation" was completely one sided, with Kate agreeing to everything he said in the assumption that he would soon run out of topics. He didn't; so in the end she made up an imaginary visitor who she had abandoned in order to answer the door, and excused herself saying that she absolutely had to get back to them, and would he mind if they carried on their conversation at a later date.

When she finally managed to close the door, she hurried back to the 'classroom' taking up where she had left off, but found Cat sitting on the controls!

'Off!' she shouted clapping her hands. Cat instantly jumped off as he knew that the tone of voice accompanied by loud clapping meant 'move quickly', but when Kate glanced at the screen all she could see and hear was chaos!

The scenery had changed from the green serenity of the park to what looked like a crowded main road. There was no rhythmic pattern of pedestrians and cars flashing past, Luke was stationary and, as far as Kate could make out, lying on the ground. They were a lot of people all talking at once – a cacophony of voices amongst which she thought she heard someone say, 'Look for a pulse!'

She caught glimpses of faces none of which she recognised, but she realised that he must have put his skates back on (probably while she had been listening to her neighbour) otherwise how would she be able to view what was happening.

Then she recognized a familiar voice – it was Keith's, 'Luke! Luke! Hey Luke man – wake up!' there was a kind of desperation in his voice, and she imagined him shaking his friend, or patting his face. What was going on? Had he lost consciousness? She asked herself.

Kate was glued to the screen but was not unduly worried as she knew how many bad falls he had taken in the past, and had always got up limping or hobbling away. He was a tough cookie; she had seen the bumps, bruises and grazes that he had always made light of. "Hazards of the trade" he called them.

Riveted, she kept watching, she had to make sure that he was alright. She could not understand it – she had left him leisurely strolling through a park and within minutes (what seemed like minutes), he was lying unconscious on a road! She wondered how long her neighbour had kept her on the doorstep.

'There's a pulse!' someone said, 'It's Okay, he's alive!' It all sounded very dramatic to Kate. What did they mean by "he's alive", surely it wasn't that bad? They had to be exaggerating?

She tried to keep calm, she remembered shooing Cat off the controls when she came back from answering the door and tried to recollect what position he had pushed them in. All she could remember was putting them back to neutral.

She went around the table and picked him up, 'What did you do puss? Anyway, it's not your fault – it's mine, all mine, I shouldn't have left the control unattended – my fault, all my fault. You're the best puddy in the whole world and I love you lots.' She could hear him purring loudly as she settled him down on his favourite chair.

When she had got up to answer the door Cat had seemed quite settled and content and it had never for one moment occurred to

Kate that he would move, let alone sit on the control box!

Now she could hear sirens approaching; a vehicle stopped and doors opened.

'Stand aside! Let us through please!' She was still getting glimpses of movement – faces, hands, she saw a box (possibly medical), hi vis jackets and voices of people who sounded as though they knew what they were doing.

There were two men working in unison; each seemed to know instinctively what was needed.

'Neck stabilized,' one of them said.

'Okay, together – one, two three ....'Kate had to imagine what was happening as the chips in the skates were obscured by a cover of some description, but she got the feeling that maybe something was being slid underneath him, because she then heard one of them counting again, 'One, two, three –Steady mate, nice and steady.'

Now, it was obvious that he was being carried to a waiting ambulance.

She heard Keith say, 'Can I come too mate – I'm his friend?'

'Yeah, Okay, maybe you can give us some details. What's his name?'

'Luke Johnson,' Keith answered the paramedic's questions while he watched the other one connect his friend up to all kinds of dials and machines with flashing led lights. He also filled a syringe and emptied the contents into Luke's right arm. All the while he lay motionless.

'He's going to be all right, yeah?'

'Hard to tell mate. You'll have to wait till he gets to hospital. They'll do all the tests and let you know,' the paramedic carried on with his questions, 'Next of kin?'

'His son, Joshua.'

'Surname?'

'Same, Johnson.'

'Have you got a contact number for him?'

'Yeah sure,' Keith pulled out his mobile and dictated the number to the man while the other one loosened the binding on Luke's skates before carefully removing them as he could not be sure whether he had sustained any injuries to his feet or ankles.

'Do you want to hang on to these?' he said and passed them to Keith who had his ear to his ringing phone.

'Yeah, of course,' Keith had given up with the call and was leaving a text message for Josh.

'Do you know his date of birth?'

'Who Josh?'

'No, your friend here, Luke.'

'8th August 1958'

'Really? He doesn't look it!' the paramedic was surprised as most men in their fifties were overweight, with receding, grey hair, and Luke was the antithesis of that image.

'Well, he's real active – the skating – it keeps you young.'

'Yes, it seems to work, apart from the hazards involved.'

'Yeah, that's a real mystery, he's the best skater I know, I can't figure out how it happened.'

'I expect the police report will tell you all that. They were there interviewing the driver when we left.'

'The driver?'

'Yes, it looked like your friend here had a collision with a vehicle. The driver looked pretty shaken up.'

'I can't believe that, we've done The Stroll hundreds of times together and nothing even close to that has happened!' Keith watched the dials and the lights.

'Well, that's definitely what it looks like at the moment. I expect there were witnesses. You didn't see anything then?'

'No, I was up ahead, had my back to him – more's the pity because normally we skate together. I might have been able to stop it.'

'Hey, don't beat yourself up, accidents happen, count yourself lucky that you *weren't* there or you might be lying over there next to him. I'd better take your name and contact too only because I gave you his property. They'll probably ask again in A&E.'

'Sure, no probs,' and Keith willingly gave them all his contact details, 'How's he doing?'

'He's stable for the moment and we're nearly there so depending on internal injuries he's doing okay for now. Have you got in touch with his son?'

'No, I've been trying – left a message – waiting for a reply.'

The ambulance pulled up abruptly.

'Okay, sorry mate, have to ask you to move.' Keith moved to one side leaving the exit clear, someone outside had already flung open the doors and the two paramedics had Luke on the move; outside there were arms and hands outstretched to receive him. Keith jumped out to follow as his friend was whisked away on a trolley, and as swing doors opened and closed behind him he found himself enveloped in uniforms adorned with stethoscopes and watches and a strong smell of surgical alcohol.

The paramedics were passing on information that sounded like a foreign language except for BP which he interpreted as "blood pressure", although the numbers after it had absolutely no significance; he could only remember having his blood pressure taken the once, and the nurse told him some numbers (something over something) followed by, 'A little high, but nothing to worry about,' so Keith left none the wiser, but reassured that he would not collapse with a stroke in the near future.

As Luke was taken through some more doors a nurse asked Keith to wait outside indicating a row of chairs.

'We'll let you know as soon as we have more information, meanwhile would you mind reporting to reception.'

Keith answered as many questions as he could, but he knew absolutely nothing about Luke's medical history – he didn't even know if he had a doctor! And while he sat there, he wondered how much Luke would have known about *him* had the roles been reversed. It had never occurred to him how little close friends really knew about each other.

The thought crossed his mind: maybe we should all be tattooed with our National Health Insurance numbers as babies so that, in case of an accident, the doctors can find out all about us.

There was a lot of activity, a very worried looking mum came in with her daughter who was cradling her left arm with her right one and whimpered incessantly. The mother was doing what she could to console her but it was as though the child couldn't hear her. She could only focus on the pain in her arm.

The child and mother were dealt with almost immediately, 'probably priority due to her age,' Keith thought and picked up a magazine from the table next to him. Flicking through the pages he stopped at "How to Deal with Body Hair" and read on out of curiosity, as it had never occurred to him that it would warrant an article covering two whole pages. Unfortunately, as soon as he started the first paragraph he saw Luke being wheeled out, so he jumped up, 'Where are they taking him?'

'Who are you?' a young doctor asked.

'His closest friend, I came with him in the ambulance.'

'Right. Well, we're taking him for a scan – need to find out what's happening, or happened, inside. You can come with him if you like.'

As Keith approached the trolley he saw that Luke's eyes were open, 'He's come round! Is he alright?'

'He's conscious but we won't know the full extent of his injuries until he's had the scan.'

'Hello mate. How's it going? How ya feelin?' Keith took hold of Luke's hand which was lying outside the cover and squeezed it reassuringly, and although he felt no response his friend did manage a faint smile and an 'Okay mate.'

Kate was so relieved to hear Luke's voice and so grateful for the chips in the boots that had kept her in touch with everything that had happened; she desperately needed a hot drink but didn't dare leave the screen in case she missed a vital piece of information, so she switched to the app on her phone while she waited for the kettle to boil.

All the time Keith had the boots with him Kate would have an insight into what was going on, and she thanked her lucky stars that it was Sunday and that she didn't have to switch off in order to teach.

She was amazed at how quickly she watched him being rolled out again and back up to A&E. Keith asked all the same questions but was calmly told to wait at A&E, and they would let him know in due course.

Keith's phone rang – it was Joshua – he had already rehearsed what to say, 'Hi Josh!'

'Hey, mate. You okay? You wanted me to ring you?'

'Yeah, I'm fine, it's your dad...'

'Dad? What's up mate – sprained an ankle or lost his phone again?' Joshua said jokingly.

'No, neither of those, well not a sprained ankle, it's a bit more serious than that.'

'More serious?' Joshua repeated and added, 'How serious?'

'Well that's the point no one seems to know yet. I'm at the hospital now. He's been for a scan and he's back in A&E where I'm waiting for an update.'

'Hospital!' Kate could hear the shock in Joshua's voice so she guessed that Keith had the boots hanging round his neck. 'You didn't mention anything about hospital in your text? Jesus! Keith what happened?'

'Yeah, I'm sorry mate but I wasn't sure how bad it was and I didn't want to alarm you over nothing, although it doesn't look like nothing now. At least I still don't know for sure, I'm waiting to hear about the scan.'

'Do you think I should come up?'

'I don't know mate. It's up to you. You could wait until they let me know the results of the scan.'

'Well it sounds pretty bad already, even if they let him out I shouldn't think he'll want to get the train back. I'd better come up anyway.'

'I think it's a good idea because they need to talk to family, they don't seem to be keen on telling me too much.'

'No probs, I'll be there in a couple of hours, so if you get to speak to him tell him I'm on my way, please. Which hospital is it?'

'The Westminster.'

'Okay mate, see you soon.'

'Yeah, see ya and drive careful!' Keith ended the call just as the same young doctor who spoke to him earlier came through the swing doors.

'Hello, Mr Mitchel?' The doctor asked extending his right hand.

'Yes.' They shook hands. 'Please, call me Keith.'

'I'm Doctor Lewis, I've been treating your friend since he arrived...'

'Yes, I know, I saw you before. How is he doctor? Have you found anything from the scan?'

'Yes, we know quite a bit more now but he may be here a while, until we know the full extent of his injuries.'

'Yes, I understand, so what do you think – overnight?'

'No, I'm afraid that he may be here some time, we can't say for sure, but it will be at least a couple of weeks.'

'Weeks!'

'Yes, I should say minimum two weeks, it's always difficult to give an accurate time in cases like these.'

'Cases like..?' Keith was hoping for some more details.

'We understand that Mr Johnson has a son, is that correct?'

'Yes, he's on his way. He should be here soon, depending on the traffic – he's coming from Sussex.'

'Well, if you don't mind I shall wait until he gets here as normal procedure is to tell the family first.'

'Oh yes, of course, I quite understand. Can I see him?'

'I'm sorry, I don't think that would be wise at the moment. I would ask you to be patient until Mr. Johnson's son arrives. I can assure that although critical, he is stable and not in any pain.'

'Yes, of course, thank you doctor,' Keith found it strange hearing Luke being referred to as "Mr. Johnson" and went in search of a drink dispenser, also he had a few texts to answer as the other skaters were concerned and needed updating. So he installed himself in the row of chairs next to the emergency room and waited for Joshua's arrival.

Keith woke to someone saying his name and shaking him gently on the shoulder, 'Hey Keith! Wake up mate!'

'Oh! Hello! Good to see you Josh, maybe we can find out what's happening now, they didn't want to tell me anything until you arrived, you'd better let them know you're here.'

Joshua spoke to one of the ladies at the reception desk, who picked up the phone to pass on the information, however, before he had time to sit back down next to Keith, Dr. Lewis had reappeared.

'Mr. Johnson?'

'Yes,' Joshua and the doctor shook hands.

'I am currently treating your father, and was here when he was first admitted.'

'Good to meet you doctor. Can you tell us exactly what's wrong?'

'Yes, please would you like to follow me,' and Dr. Lewis led them into a small anti-room with comfortable chairs.

'Please, take a seat,' they sat facing each other, 'As far as we can establish, it would appear that your father has sustained a broken collar bone, broken right tibia and fibula, fractured Ulna and Radius in the right arm, four broken ribs and considerable damage to vertebrae at the top of his spine.'

For a moment no one spoke, then Keith said, 'It all sounds quite serious doctor?'

'Yes, I can't deny that he is in a serious but stable condition.'

'How on earth did he get all those injuries just skating?' Joshua asked in semi-shock.

'Well, they believe there was a vehicle involved. It was not a simple skating accident, the police are waiting to interview him about a collision.'

'Christ, Keith, did you know about this?'

'No, well not really. I didn't see how it happened. There was a car there but I thought he had stopped to help. It never occurred to me that he was involved. The paramedics mentioned something but they weren't sure either, they were just worried about getting him here alive I think. But it would make sense, otherwise how did he get all those injuries?'

'God almighty, what happens now? Can I see him?' Keith had never heard Joshua sound so stressed.

'Yes, of course, although he is not aware as to just how serious his injuries are, but I will be in there, in the background if you need me to clarify anything.'

'When you say serious doctor, what do mean by that? Obviously he has broken bones but how long do you think he will be here?' Joshua sounded no calmer.

'I'm afraid I can't answer that question at the moment. We will know more in a few days' time when the bruising has settled and we have done more tests.'

'But surely it's just a question of plaster casts and crutches, isn't it?' Joshua was urging the doctor to reply positively.

'No, I'm afraid it won't be as simple as that. There is the damage to the spine to consider.'

'What is that?'

'Well, as I said we really can't tell the extent of that immediately as everything could be different in a couple of days, but it does mean that he has to be kept under observation with restricted movement until we are able assess the full extent of the damage.'

'I think I understand doctor. Can we see him now?'

'Yes, of course, please...' said Dr. Lewis who got up first, opened the door and showed them across the waiting area to the emergency section where Luke was lying on a trolley, hooked up to tubes and surrounded by bleeping machines displaying LED patterns of light.'

'Dad,' Joshua's voice faltered and Keith thought he might be near to tears. Tears of shock.

'Hello son. What ya doin' ere? Long way to come for a bit of an accident,' he managed a smile.

'Just thought you might like a lift home,' Joshua wanted to put a hand on his shoulder but he couldn't remember which was the broken collar bone besides he was encased in a sort of support that went around his torso, neck and shoulders.

Dr. Lewis noticed the concerned expression on Joshua's face so he went over to explain, 'The brace is to make sure that there is no movement in the spine. It will be necessary for a while until we are sure what exactly is happening in that area, but we shall make him as comfortable as possible and free of pain.'

'That's good, thank you doctor. We are grateful.'

'Yeah, very grateful,' Keith added and turning to Luke, 'Stupid question I know mate but how are you feeling?'

'Not too bad mate, can't feel much at all really.'

'Good, no pain then?'

'No.'

'Do you remember what happened?' Keith was curious to find out how he had sustained such serious injuries.

'Not really, it all happened so quick, but I am sure that those skates caused it, just like the other times – they seemed to have a will of their own – they just seemed to take off in the wrong direction! I know it sounds mad but they were uncontrollable!'

'What does he mean by "just like the other times"?' Joshua turned to Keith for an explanation, 'What's been going on?'

'Yeah, he's convinced there's something wrong with his skates, and that they have been causing him problems, because he has had a couple of mishaps at the rink,' then turning to Luke he asked, 'Do you want me to check them out?'

'Yeah, please man. Have they said when I can go home?'

'No, I don't think they know themselves. They need to keep you in for observation and more tests which makes sense to me.'

'Yes, me too dad, I think you're in the best place at the moment. They know what they're doing and Dr. Lewis seems more than competent.' Joshua tried to sound reassuring.

'Yeah, I suppose you're right,' Luke managed a resigned smile.

'The police are waiting to have a quick word so could I ask you to come back later?' the doctor requested.

'Yes, of course, no problem,' they replied almost in unison.

'Just be careful what you say mate – don't admit anything!' Keith said over his shoulder.

'We'll see you later Dad,' Joshua raised his hand.

'Yeah, later mate.' And they both reluctantly left the room.

'We'll get a drink, yeah?' Keith put his hand on Josh's shoulder.

'Yeah, good idea.' As they walked along the corridor two uniformed police officers were approaching from the other direction.

Keith could see that Joshua was shaken by his father's accident; it was the last thing in the world that he would have expected, his father was an ace on his skates, and he had never had more than a few bumps and bruises, all self-inflicted learning new tricks. He had been doing the Stroll for years and had never injured himself. The whole thing was baffling.

'Are you okay with coffee, or do you want something stronger?' Keith asked as they headed towards the vending machines.

'I don't know. What are you having?'

'I think you could do with a bit of a booster,' Keith offered his advice, 'My shout.'

'Yeah, okay then. Where shall we go?'

'I noticed a pub across the road – it would be good to get out of here for a spell – I need a change of scene.'

Kate looked at her watch and noticed that it was nearly eight o'clock, 'Where on earth has the time gone?' she said aloud to her only audience Cat, who was lying fast asleep on his favourite chair.

She didn't need to eavesdrop any more on Josh and Keith, although she did leave the laptop connected and on loud speaker so she would be alerted when they returned to the hospital.

She switched on the television as she didn't want to miss the last in a series that had been totally enthralling. She knew that Luke wasn't going anywhere, and she could keep an eye on the screen.

They spent a good half hour in the pub, and then Kate saw movement, so she had to turn the volume down on the TV. When they looked into the room where they had left Luke, the staff were treating someone else!

Josh looked alarmed, 'Jesus Keith, you don't think....'

'Na, they've just moved him. Come on reception will know where.'

Kate heard them being directed to Intensive Care and watched as they took the lift and then seemed to walk for miles, eventually arriving at another smaller reception and led to where Luke was hooked up to just as many monitors, drips and machines as before.

'Just a short visit please as he is very drowsy – all the drugs you know, and he does need to rest,' the nurse smiled and left them alone.

'Hi dad,' Kate noticed that Joshua sounded slightly calmer.

'Hi son,' and Luke managed another smile, 'Did you get out a bit?'

'Yeah, we went over the road.'

'Good.'

'Have you spoken to the police?' Josh was concerned about what his dad had told them.

'Na, not really, I just told them my version – I feel sorry for the driver of the car, it wasn't his fault.'

'Well, I don't think you're really in any condition to say that yet dad. You didn't tell the police that, did you?'

'I don't know, I'm not sure.'

'Well, I don't think that they should have been allowed to see you so soon. You need to have time to think about what happened and, I mean you're pumped full of drugs – you can't be thinking coherently.' Joshua sounded indignant, 'Don't you agree Keith?'

'Yeah, absolutely. Too right!' he could see that Joshua needed the support.

'Well, we can get that sorted later. There must have been loads of witnesses.' Joshua added.

'Yeah, later,' Luke said sleepily.

Keith and Joshua exchanged glances which conveyed the same thought. It was obvious how tired he was, but before they left Joshua made his dad promise not to speak to the police again without a solicitor present.

'We're going to go now dad, but I'll be back tomorrow, okay?'

'Yeah, thanks, best get going to miss the traffic eh?' He had no idea of the time.

'Yes,' Joshua bent over and gave his dad a kiss on the forehead like he would to a sick child. Keith felt moved by his action and very helpless, 'Cheers mate. Have a good night!' he said as cheerfully as possible, and once again they slowly left the ward.

Kate noticed that Josh had picked up Luke's mobile so she thought of texting him (Luke) as that would look perfectly normal.

'Hi! Hope you enjoyed The Stroll? Great weather for it! Do you want to meet for lunch tmrw? Xxx'

She didn't expect an answer immediately because he would have all the other texts to answer first. There would have been loads of them from the other skaters, who would be unaware that Luke couldn't reply. But she was wrong, her phone buzzed after a few minutes; 'Hello Kate, Keith here. Luke's had a bit of an accident, and we've had to leave him here in hospital x'

She immediately texted back sounding as panicky as possible, 'Hospital! What do you mean???? And who are "we"? x'

Again almost instantly, 'It's complicated. I will ring you later. Josh and I are driving back now x'

Kate had to sound genuinely concerned, 'Okay, but I don't understand – can I speak to Josh? Really worried – need to know what happened. It must be serious?'

'She wants to speak to you mate, freaking out a bit by the looks of it.'

'OK. Can you call her and put it on loudspeaker,' Joshua suggested, concentrating on the London traffic.

Kate had only just put the phone on her desk when it rang, 'Hello!'

'Yeah, hi Kate it's Josh,' he spoke into the phone while Keith held it as near as he could, 'we've just seen your message and Josh said you wanted to know what's going on?

'Yes, *please* Keith.'

He went on to tell her everything, not realising that she was already in the picture, although Kate made sure that she asked the right questions in the right places, feigning ignorance. She asked about visiting hours but he said he wasn't sure as he was in intensive care, and although Joshua was allowed to visit any time (as next of kin), he wasn't sure about friends.

'I'm going up tomorrow so I'll keep you updated, and I'm going to have to get a timetable together so everyone else can visit when they want to. He's pretty drugged up at the moment and not entirely with it. He's even talking about it being his fault; he's got a crazy idea in his head that his skates did it!'

'Well, I don't think you should take any notice of that, but he may need a solicitor if there was a car involved.'

'Yes, you're right, we haven't thought that far ahead yet.'

Anyway, look, I expect you're both tired, so, love to you both, and please tell Luke that I love him and I am thinking of him.'She hoped she sounded sincere and wondered whether she would be punished for her deceit.

'Yes of course and you take care – speak soon, bye.'

'Bye,' and Kate hung up but she still kept the laptop switched on just in case she missed anything important however all she could hear was music, and she suspected that Keith had fallen asleep.

Kate simply had to tell Megan, so she took the house phone as she had a flat rate on it.

'Hello!' Brad answered.

'Hello Brad, how are you?' Kate asked quiet coolly and out of politeness, as she still wasn't sure what his intentions were towards Megan; she was very suspicious, as Megan could be considered as "a good catch" – financially.

'Yes, fine thanks and yourself?'

'Yes thanks, could I speak to Megan please.'

'Yes, I'm passing her the phone as I speak.'

'Hiya! Have you had a good Sunday?' Megan sounded upbeat and on form.

'Different.'

'How's that?'

'Well, Luke's had a skating accident and is in hospital in London.'

'Jesus! Megan what did you do?'

'Me, myself nothing, but Cat sat on the control box,'.

'What do you mean? How? Why did you let him do that?'

'I didn't *let* him – it was an accident. There was someone at the door, and while I was there he decided to move and knocked the controls which caused a bit of an accident involving a car.'

'A car!' Megan echoed, alarmed.

'Yes, unfortunately whatever Cat did sent him into the path of an oncoming vehicle.'

'Christ! What's happened? I mean how bad is it?' Kate gave Megan a list of the injuries as she remembered them.

'God almighty, he's lucky to be alive!' Megan exclaimed, 'How do you feel about it? I mean this is what you wanted, isn't it?'

'Yes and no. I wanted to disrupt his skating but a broken ankle or torn ligament would have sufficed. I never intended for him to be completely incapacitated!'

'No, I guess not, but don't you see it as fate? Maybe he deserved this? I know how much he hurt you with his egotistical, self-indulgent attitude. And we know he's done it before.'

'I don't know Megan, I'm a bit in shock myself. I suppose time will tell; and there's nothing I or anyone can do about it.'

'So, will you be going up there?'

'Yes, but not immediately. Keith is organizing a rota so the visiting is staggered. I think he's going to need lots of sleep for a while with all the drugs he's on.'

'Yes, I suppose so, anyway we're seeing each other tomorrow, aren't we?'

'Yes, definitely. I'll need to get out and relax. Pick me up the same as usual?'

'Yes, I'll be there; then you can catch me up.'

'Okay, see you tomorrow.'

'Yes, night,' and they both hung up. Kate glanced at the clock – it was nearly ten thirty – she wondered where the time had gone. When she went back to check her laptop she saw that Joshua had put Luke's skates in the hallway and was on the phone to people letting them know the news.

Kate didn't want to hear it all again so she closed it up, put the chip control box away on the shelf and decided to get an early night, then she could prepare her lessons first thing in the morning. She fed Cat, switched off all the lights and went upstairs to bed.

As she settled down to read her book she thought of Luke lying in hospital, and although she knew that she hadn't actually caused the accident, she had acquired the chip control with intent to disrupt his life – especially his skating. She had wanted him to suffer but maybe not quite as much. And Megan was right, sometimes fate takes over and then it has to be left in the lap of the gods

Chapter 50

Post Accident

Kate woke to brilliant sunshine streaming in through the window and the birds in the garden having a field day. It was six o'clock, she was wide awake and ready to tackle a new day.

The first thing on her list was to prepare her classes for the afternoon and evening so she would have time free to focus on texting Joshua and Keith in order to keep in touch with the news from the hospital.

She was surprised, because although she had woken early, she had had a good night's sleep, uninterrupted and with no dreams; at least none that she could remember.

Over her cup of tea, she reasoned with herself, Megan was right – it had been fate. Okay, she was aware that she had left the controls unattended but she had no idea that Cat was going to move, and even less of an inkling that he would cause such a disaster. She had to believe that fate had taken over and maybe it was payback time for all those past misdemeanors, many of which Kate didn't know about. But he shouldn't have chosen Kate's heart to break –she had warned him.

In some ways she wished that she had never met him, but she had been flattered that a man fifteen years her younger had found her attractive enough to "love". Most women of her age would have had to pay for it. She believed that he had had a retirement plan and that it went tits up due to a blabbermouth, but that was irreversible now, and the casual way that he treated her following his illness was unforgivable. How can you tell someone you love them, promise them the earth, say you want to take care of them and then treat them like an inconvenience?

One thing was for certain, Kate had never had control of what happened to her life or of those around her, she just knew that if anyone behaved vindictively towards her they always seemed to suffer for it in the end, and that was why she tried to be a law-abiding person because she knew it worked both ways. She had proof of that.

She had never intentionally been nasty to anyone, as far as she could remember, because it wasn't in her nature and she had done her best to avoid nastiness because she didn't like aggression, and only resorted to it when cornered.

As her (clairvoyant) friend in The States had said, 'You didn't deserve it.'

'She's right,' Kate said aloud, 'I didn't deserve it,' and as usual Cat sat up and looked at her for an explanation.

Kate patted her on the head, 'It's okay puss, don't worry, it'll all be alright again.'

It was eight fifteen by the time she had done all her preparation and filed it away, so she sent a friendly good morning text to Joshua to ask him how he was doing and whether he had any news on his dad's condition.

'Good morning, Kate! No I haven't; I'm just on my way out, and will know more once I've spoken to the doctor. I shall probably spend most of the day up there. Could you do me a huge favour and give the dogs a quick walk at about midday? You still have a key, don't you? x'

Kate responded immediately, 'Yes, of course, no problem, please let me know if I can help in any way. I would be grateful if you could keep me updated about Luke. And give him my love x'

'Yeah absolutely, thanks for that – be in touch x'

She was pleased that Joshua trusted her and had asked her to help. With the sun shining she would make the most of it, and take them both for a nice long walk. She enjoyed their company, and they were such obedient and intelligent dogs; it was a delight to walk them.

She ate a hasty breakfast, put on her trainers and a light jacket and walked around to Luke's, knowing that by the time she got there Joshua would be on his way.

Koko and Kiki met her with all of their usual buoyant enthusiasm;

she loved it.

'Ooh, steady,' Kate said gently as Koko put his front paws on her waist in the hope of getting to within licking distance of her face. 'Down now,' she didn't need to shout or even raise her voice because they did exactly as they were told.

'Good boys,' she chatted to them, as they followed her around looking for the skates. Luke had always left them in the same place in the hall, but Joshua would have dumped them anywhere, so she switched on the app on her phone to help her locate them. She thought she recognised the kitchen, and sure enough they were lying on the kitchen table so, with her scalpel, she quickly extracted the tiny chips and replaced them with the metal studs that she had removed about a month ago, carefully storing them in small, transparent zip-lock envelope in her handbag. Then, taking the leads off the hook in the hall, she headed towards the front door with the dogs hot on her heels; they knew that the minute that she unhooked them that it was walkies.

They must have walked five miles, right along the sea front, up onto the cliffs, where Kate enjoyed a cup of tea and a snack overlooking the sea, and back again. The sun was unusually warm for May and she prudently applied sun block to her nose and forehead, her two most vulnerable areas.

The rest of the day became routine, although she felt invigorated from the fresh air and exercise, and seemed to approach her lessons with renewed vitality and a mental plan to go for a serious walk with the dogs every day, for as long as the weather permitted.

Joshua left a message on her mobile later that afternoon, 'Hello, just letting you know the latest news. They've set his leg and arm but can't do anything with the collar bone yet although they seem to think it's good because he's lying flat and the bone is together so should be alright. He's still in the contraption and heavily drugged up and that's basically it. One thing, he doesn't seem to be able to feel anything in his legs (sad emoji face) – doctors say not to worry – early days. Contact me if you have any questions x'

Kate had a ten minute gap between classes so she texted straight back, 'Thanks so much. It sounds satisfactory. Are you going tomorrow? x'

'No, I need to go to work but Keith is going up and maybe Aunt Sue and cousin Emily. I'll tell him to let you know what's happening x'

'Thanks. They should perk him up. They are all good company x'

'Yeah, it's all worrying though.'

'Yes, I know it is Josh, but like the doctors say, it's early days and he was in really good shape before the accident so he has every chance of a full recovery, at least that's how I see it x'

'Yeah I know you're right. We must all try and be positive. By the way, thanks for taking the dogs out, you must have walked miles they're exhausted. Speak soon x'

'Actually I enjoyed the exercise, do you mind if I do it again tomorrow? x'

'Please, be my guest – it'll be doing me a favour – thanks x'

'OK x'

Kate turned off the sound on her phone because she had to start another lesson and a couple of hours later when she closed the door on the last pupil Megan pulled up to drive them to their regular rock n' roll session.

Of course she was dying to hear everything so they went to the pub afterwards for a drink and a chat. She kept saying she couldn't believe it. Kate was finding it difficult to believe too, 'In a way it's a disappointment,' she said over her spritzer.

'What do you mean "a disappointment"? Did you want him dead?!' Megan sounded shocked.

'No, of course not, nothing like that. It's disappointing because I was having fun controlling his skates, and he was beginning to give me what I wanted in bed.'

'Oh, I see. Yes, I suppose it is. I doubt if he will be back skating this summer.'

'Hmm,' Kate agreed, then in a more cheerful tone, 'I'm taking the dogs out every day for a nice long walk – I think it will do us all good, and I can get a snack at the beach café because they take dogs. Also, it takes the pressure off Joshua, so he has one less thing to worry about.'

'That's a good idea, I might join you sometimes.'

'Yes, that would be great,' Kate liked walking alone but she enjoyed Megan's company too and was in need of support. She knew that she hadn't actually caused the accident, but still felt somewhat to blame for not having foreseen Cat's actions.

They finished their drinks under a bit of a cloud and Megan dropped Kate off earlier than usual.

The week seemed to drag even though Kate had plenty to do. She just wanted the weekend to come as she desperately needed to see Luke and find out just how serious his injuries were.

She had decided to go up on the Sunday around midday as his mates wouldn't turn up till much later, but as she approached the hospital entrance she hesitated. Even though there had been plenty of time to reflect on the events of the previous week, she was not looking forward to this visit and was fighting a mild feeling of panic growing inside her chest. She took some deep breaths in the hope of calming the palpitations, and sat for a while in the sunshine on a nearby bench watching people.

The short 'time out' seemed to do the trick, and she soon found herself in the reception area staring at a colour-coded plan similar to the one at St. Thomas's.

It took a while to reach Intensive Care as there were stairs and endless corridors, but finally she reached the reception. She looked at her watch, it was three pm, Joshua said that it would be a good time to turn up. She asked the nurse who was sitting at a computer screen where to go, and was shown to his cubicle.

She managed to suppress a gasp as she turned the corner, faced with all the machines and apparatus connected to, and surrounding him. He looked very small and vulnerable.

'Hello!' Kate bent over to kiss him trying to sound cheerful and hoping that her voice didn't betray her true feelings.

'Hello sweetie,' he sounded hoarse.

'You sound a bit croaky. Are you alright? Stupid question – of course you aren't alright; I mean have you got a sore throat?'

'It's the tube – makes me sound like this.'

With all the tubes and wires she hadn't noticed the one in his throat, 'Ah, right, yes I can see it now.'

'And what about the pain? Are they managing it?'

'Yes, That's the one hanging up there,' and he indicated with a slight movement of his head a drip hanging from a flimsy looking metal stand to the left of the bed.

Kate was relieved to see that he could move his head, 'Good, and apart from that, are you comfortable?'

'Yeah, can't really feel much and not allowed to move. Don't know how long I can put up with this though; you know I can't stand not being active, and no one can tell me anything.'

'Have any of your friends been to see you?

'Yeah, a couple, I expect they'll be quite a few in later after The Stroll, but Joshua and Keith have been taking it in turns to come in every day. By the way, thanks for walking the dogs, Joshua says it helps him a lot.'

'It's not a problem – I enjoy taking them out – they're good company and so obedient, and besides now the weather has improved it means that I get some fresh air and exercise.'

Luke smiled, 'What do you have in the bag?' Kate had laid a plastic bag on his bed when she came in.

'Some fruit and those sticky, gooey, spongy things that you like.'

'Hmm, sounds good. The food's pretty bland here; but I don't eat much anyway.'

They talked about the hospital food and Kate teased him about the pretty nurses; she chatted about her classes and the funny things that the dogs had done on their walks, like dragging a huge stick along the ground for ages in the hope of getting it home, until abandoning it in exhaustion. And Koko (the more adventurous of the two) getting his snout stuck in a paper cup. Kate showed Luke the photos which actually made him chuckle.

She heard a voice over her shoulder say, 'Hello Kate,' and turned to see Joshua.

'Hello!' she was genuinely surprised and very pleased to see him and they kissed, continental style, on both cheeks.

'Have you just arrived or did you get here earlier?' she asked him.

'I came up this morning with Keith; he's gone skating, but will be in later with some of the others.'

'Okay, I'll probably be gone by then. I've been showing your dad some photos of Koko and the crazy things he does.'

'Oh yeah, I know he is funny – he has me in stitches. If you don't mind I'll let you two catch up – I have a couple of things to do in town, and you probably have quite a lot to talk about.'

Kate would have preferred him to stay, as a sparring partner; there was only so much she could chat about, and she didn't want to run out of stimulating conversation, also, trying to lift his mood could be quite demanding.

She stayed until the skaters turned up which meant she could catch an early train back and go to a special rock 'n roll night with Megan.

Unable to focus on her book on the journey back, she looked up from time to time and stare at the regimental rows of hops and fruit trees. She brooded about her visit, and how defenseless he had seemed surrounded by all the flashing, bleeping gadgetry. She tried to analyse her feelings and found that they were mixed; wishing more than anything that it hadn't happened, especially as they seemed to have come to a mutually satisfactory arrangement. Then she considered that it might have happened anyway, with or without Cat's intervention.

The club had paid for a well known singer and backing group from London, and enthusiasts came from miles away; it was usually packed and more fun than the regular sessions, and it meant net petticoats and dresses. Kate loved watching the circular skirts swirl, revealing slender legs and layers of net, and the men in bootlace ties, waistcoats and winkle pickers. She could just about remember the end of the rock 'n roll scene, but just as she was approaching the age when she could have joined in, it went out of fashion and 'The Twist' took over, so she missed out on the pretty flouncy skirts. That was the reason why she and Megan took advantage of every opportunity to revive the fifties, even if it was only for a couple of hours.

Even though she had left London fairly early, she hadn't left herself much time to get ready, so she was still applying makeup in the car on the way, while she told Megan all about her hospital visit.

'It sounds as though he'll be there for a while; a few weeks at least,' was all Megan could think of saying, and Kate agreed.

'Do you think he'll recover? I mean do you think he'll ever get back to normal, like before the accident?'

'I don't know, and I don't even think that the doctors know yet. I think it all depends on the spinal injury.'

'How do you feel about it all' Megan asked.

'Pretty bad. I know that I didn't actually flip the lever, but in a way I feel culpable.'

'Don't!' her friend commanded, 'It was fate, at least that is how I see it: you were called to the front door for a reason, and Cat was left alone for a reason. It was all meant to happen, the fact that you provided the means is neither here nor there, you did nothing intentionally – you only meant to disrupt his skating *not* put him in hospital. You mustn't feel guilty. This was *meant* to happen. He needed a lesson, and the hand of fate dealt him one. The powers that be obviously thought that just inconveniencing his skating wasn't enough. If Cat hadn't caused this accident something else would have happened to him, and who knows it might have been worse, he might have died somehow.'

'Hmm, you could be right,' Kate said thoughtfully, 'anyway I'm not going to dwell on it tonight; we're going to dance our little socks off and have fun, yeah?'

'Yeah!' and they high-fived.

The music and company were just what Kate needed to lift her spirits..

When she got home she was not in the mood for bed, so she sat up with Cat on her lap watching Out of Africa for the umpteenth time; she could have watched it just for the music – she loved the haunting strains of John Barry's sound track and sometimes put it on loop in the bedroom to fall asleep to.

As the credits rolled up it was nearly three, and although she still wasn't tired she went up to bed knowing that a couple of pages of her book would act as a sedative.

The next day was cloudless blue sky as far as the eye could see and even though she had only had four and a half hour's sleep she was wide awake and raring to go; she would get the washing on the line, pick up the dogs (if Josh was in London) and go for a long walk along the cliffs.

June went by: teaching, dancing, walking dogs and visiting Luke in hospital. Once his situation improved; his bones had set and he no longer needed intensive medical care he was transferred to a hospital more convenient for friends and family, although Joshua had left for Europe where he worked every summer chartering his yacht around the Mediterranean; Luke had insisted, so Keith had taken over and promised to keep him up to date.

Luke's bones had mended, but he was left paralysed from the neck down and could do nothing for himself. The hospital was hoping to move him to a rehabilitation centre or a convalescent home but there were no available beds, or they were not equipped to cope with such a severe case, so he stayed in hospital.

Finally, Kate suggested taking him to her place. There was an office on the ground floor that she could quite easily turn into a bedroom and the N.H.S. would provide a special bed and arrange visits from nurses etc. Also, as his official carer it would mean extra cash to help pay for food and such.

Joshua couldn't believe her generosity of spirit and kept asking her if she was sure that she knew what she was letting herself in for, and how much responsibility it would be.

She reassured him that with all the help and support, she was sure that she would be able to cope.

She had practically adopted Koko and Kiki, and Cat had reluctantly accepted that he was going to have to share his mistress with two enormous, brown, woolly canines and after a few initial scuffles resulting in a couple of nasty scratches on Koko's nose; they learned to accept one another.

Preparations to adapt the office started almost immediately after a visit from social services who had to approve the suitability of the room and location; right next to a toilet and bathroom, which could prove invaluable if ever Luke started to regain mobility, and for emptying and cleaning medical equipment.

Keith helped move some furniture and Kate packed up the books which meant she could collapse the shelving making more space for the special bed and various apparatus, and chairs for visitors.

Megan had told her that she was mad to even be considering taking him in, but Kate was adamant; she needed to do this, it would help them both.

Chapter 51

Delivery

They decided to move him on a Saturday as Kate had no students and it would be less disruptive, and she would have all weekend to settle him in.

So, at 11.00 o'clock on Saturday an ambulance drew up outside her house and two muscular paramedics brought Luke through the hall, into the office/bedroom, and with well-practiced coordination placed him in the hospital bed facing the window with a view of the garden. They installed a monitor, a drip and a machine to help him breathe which apparently was one of the complications of paralysis.

Social services had given her some information in leaflet form about what to expect, although there would be nurses and physical therapists coming in to assist and advise.

There would be problems such as constipation, bladder control and bed sores that all had be checked and managed; even though local services had been set up to take the pressure off Kate as much as possible, she would still have to learn to administer certain drugs and treatment, but she did not envisage any insurmountable problems.

She had had to shut the dogs in another room during Luke's arrival anticipating they would go crazy the minute they saw their master, and Kate thought there would be enough excitement without introducing a couple of yelping, bouncing, bundles of brown fur. She would let them in later once the ambulance had left and Luke felt up to it.

The next visitor was the nurse, a cheerful, attractive woman in her thirties, full of energy and positive vibes. She looked like an illustration from a children's book: rather plump with ruddy cheeks.

She showed Kate how to empty Luke's colostomy and urostomy bag (poo and pee), how to treat his bed sores, and avoid more developing. She also left Kate with a list of medication and a timetable for taking it, and a list of foods to avoid along with some recipes that looked like baby food! The top of the bedside table was covered in bottles, jars, packets and tubes of cream. She said she would be back later in the evening to check on him and to show Kate how to move him to change the sheets, and how to wash him down.

When everyone had left Kate felt a bit overwhelmed, and for the first time questioned herself and the decision she had made. Until that moment Luke had hardly said a word, 'Are you sure you want to take this on? It's a lot of work and I just feel like a nuisance being here.'

'I'm positive. I am sure that it won't be forever, and I think we can both learn lessons from this. I'll go and get the dogs, they've been so patient.'

She brought them through keeping a firm hand on each of their collars to prevent them from jumping on top of Luke. It was hard holding them back as they were clearly overjoyed to see their master, so she let them put front paws on the bed and lick his hand and arm. Kate loved watching the reunion which brought a broad smile to Luke's face. When the wagging and whimpering had subsided, they finally settled on the floor where Kate was forced to tether them so they couldn't climb on the bed.

'Would you like to watch tele?' she asked before leaving the room.

'Na, think I'll rest; it's all been quite tiring. Though I wouldn't mind some music.'

'Yes, of course,' she placed his earphones over his head and switched on his MP3 player, adjusting the volume, 'just shout if you need anything,'she said as she went to the classroom to sort out papers and mark homework that someone had dropped through the letterbox.

One of her regular weekend tasks was sorting all the mail; she had five piles: one for each of the boys; one for her own important stuff (bank statements etc.,); one for complete junk (magazines, unwanted publicity etc.,) and one for 'interesting' stuff – anything that she might order or read before throwing it away. When she had divided it all up, each pile had a home either in a drawer or in a box under a table or chair! She noticed that the 'order or read ' pile was growing and getting out of control probably because she was simply too busy to look at it.

She had just sorted all the post when the landline rang and as she picked it up she saw Megan's name on the screen.

'Hello there! How's the patient?'

'Well, I think; what I mean is – as well as can be expected. He's here, installed, and the dogs are lying on the floor next to the bed, so all good at the moment.'

'I bet they were pleased to see each other?'

'Yes, definitely.'

'So, what are your plans? Are you allowed out? It's a lovely day out there.'

'I'll be taking the dogs for a walk soon. Do you want to join us?'

'Where are you thinking of going?'

'The usual – along the cliffs.'

'Are you allowed to leave him on his own?'

'I bloody well hope so. Anyway, what can happen? He can't move, so he can't get up and fall over, and he's connected to all his stuff. Besides no one has said that I can't leave him on his own,' she justified herself.

'Okay, then we can catch up – say half an hour, in the car park?'

'Perfect.'

Kate opened the rear nearside door and both the dogs bounced out, ears flapping, tails wagging to greet Megan, who was already there.

'Hey! Calm down you!' she said laughing. Their exuberant greeting made her feel special, they probably did it to everyone, but she took it as a personal compliment. They could wriggle, wag *and* lick all at the same time like windup toys.

Suddenly Koko shot off up a grassy knoll, having spotted a couple of large seagulls pulling worms, with Kiki in hot pursuit. They were allowed to run freely off the lead on that part of the cliff although they never strayed far, constantly glancing back to check that Kate and Megan were still there. They followed at a leisurely pace, it was warm and there didn't seem to be any point in hurrying.

'Will you be able to leave him a lot?'

'I can't see why not. He was listening to his music when I left and it's not as though he can go anywhere, I mean he's completely confined to bed because it's a properly adapted one with barriers on both sides, so even if he did suddenly regain any kind of movement he couldn't fall out'

'Apart from that how are you?'

'Well, I have to admit that I had a bit of a wobble when I looked at all the medication and machinery, and the list of dos and don'ts, but I suppose it's a bit like looking after a baby.'

'Yes, I suppose it is, but do you want that? Isn't it going to be tying?'

'I don't know yet, remember I'm doing this for a couple of reasons: one is as a kind of penance, and the other is guilt.'

'I suppose I understand ....but at least you have taught him a lesson?'

'I don't know, I think he was beginning to relate his behaviour to the accidents, and he had started to treat me better; I had just got him trained in bed. He just thinks that it was an accident caused by malfunction of his skates. If he were able to skate he would be back up there flirting with all and sundry, and selecting a new victim.'

'So how are you going to get through to him that he kind of brought it upon himself? Will you tell him how it happened?'

'No way! It was never my intention – I never envisaged this! No, I shall have to think of something more subtle. Any ideas?'

'Hmm. Let me think,' Megan said and they walked on in silence for a while taking in the magnificent view from the top of the cliffs. They could clearly pick out the coast of France fringing a sheet of cobalt blue, where brilliant, white, triangular sails darted back and forth as the dingy club practised the art of tacking.

They both appreciated the benefits of living on the coast: the freshness of the air; the infinite number of designated walking routes; the cool sea breezes that made the hot summer days more bearable; and the newly renovated harbour area offering countless restaurants, bars and outdoor entertainment for the weekends, when they wanted a change

Megan broke the silence first, 'Didn't you say that before you planted the chips he treated you badly?'

'Yes, that's an understatement! He treated me like shit! Especially in bed, like it was an obligation, and like I was a nuisance! There was no tenderness involved – quite the opposite and I got nothing out of it, but then he never satisfied me – I was always the one who did all the work and made sure that *he* was happy. But from what he told me he treated all the women that he wanted to ditch with the same contempt. He said about one of them (she didn't have her own place to go to) that he had to get pissed and smoke a couple of joints before he could make love to her.

He made it pretty obvious I was in the way – an inconvenience, interrupting his skating, fishing and grand prix watching routine. Superfluous to his needs and to be gotten rid of. I remember sending him a text telling him how bad he made me feel, and he phoned me back (he rarely spoke on the phone because he used Pay as you Go and it was too pricey!) screaming and shouting, and blaming me for everything. He brought up stuff which was completely irrelevant; trying to find reasons to be angry with me. I didn't recognize him. It was like listening to an irate stranger; I saw a completely different side to him, and not a nice one. Or maybe it was the real him and the other one was false? Anyway, I would never be sure after that. It took a lot of effort to pretend that nothing had happened and see him again, and be "nice" just so I could plant those chips. I tell you I didn't like pretending – that's not me, but I had to, at least for a while.'

'Yes, I know. I remember how upset and hurt you were. He really did hurt you! And he had no conscience about it. All that mattered was that he could do his skating! You're right. Anyway you know how I feel – I think he deserves what happened and anything else that's coming to him! He goes on my list of arseholes. Hey, I've had an idea!'

'What's that?'

'Have you ever seen the film "Misery"?'

'Yeah,' Kate answered uneasily as she knew how Megan's mind worked, and she wondered what was coming next, 'Jesus! Meg you aren't seriously suggesting that I should torture him!'

Well, not physically maybe and we could drop the word "torture", but a bit of mental and emotional torment might make you feel good.'

'Hmm, I don't know, I think he's probably suffered enough. What did you have in mind?'

She had to ask out of curiosity. One thing Kate could rely on was Megan's imagination; she could have some very singular ideas.

'Well, for starters, it's summer so you could wander around with nothing on; get a brazilian – you told me he liked that. Or you could wear some of that ultra-sexy underwear that I've seen.'

'I don't think there's any point when he can't get it up any more.'

'Are you sure about that? I've seen all kinds of stimuli on the internet, even for paraplegics. You remember Christopher Reeve – he used them after his accident.'

'Well, get you! But even if they worked, he wouldn't actually feel anything, or get any physical pleasure from it.'

'Darling, I wasn't thinking about *him*!' Megan said, amazed that it hadn't occurred to Kate earlier.

'What you mean me? Like get on top? It seems a bit macabre, don't you think?'

'Well whatever turns you on!'

'That's the point, I'm not sure it would. I did it for *so* long, just to keep him happy.'

'Okay, I get it. But his tongue still works doesn't it? You could still get some satisfaction there?'

'Hmm, yes, but he would have to be willing.'

'Why wouldn't he? After all you've done for him. You got him out of the hospital, and you're dedicating one of your rooms, and most of your time to his recovery. I would have thought it was the least he could do.'

'It's early days Meg, and let's face it he wouldn't be in this situation if I had been more vigilant.'

Megan shrugged in a non-committal way, throwing a ball for the dogs.

They enjoyed the rest of the walk without mentioning Luke or sex again.

Chapter 52

Solutions all Round

Megan spent more time at Kate's due to her lack of freedom, and the ladies of the WTC were enjoying more days out than ever now that most of their husbands were towing the line; about once a fortnight they all met at Linda's to catch up on progress, and to introduce any new members.

It was always a great morning with the ladies sharing videos of the pranks they had played on their partners; there were darts that never reached the dartboard, fishing rods that acted as though they had caught something but hadn't; squash balls that kept hitting the opponent; golf balls that refused to leave bunkers and got lost in shrubbery, and golf clubs that did their own thing. The laughter was a tonic. There was no doubt that the chips had changed their lives *and* their personalities: they had more confidence; more conversation; more interests; more fun and freedom!

Luke's accident had made them aware of their limitations, and Kate had held a meeting warning everyone of the dangers of leaving the controls alone with a pet or small child in the room.

Sometimes, on warm, sunny evenings a few of them would gather in Kate's garden, open a couple bottles of wine, and cook up a barbecue. They invented a code so that Luke could not understand through the open window whenever they referred to 'Chip Control'. Some of them volunteered to 'babysit' Luke to give Kate a break; she had even managed to get away to London for the day.

Life for the girls was generally good: not so for the guys – they spent their lives comparing notes on housework, quick and easy ways to satisfy their women in bed, and calamities involving sporting activities. They had looked up local witches and wizards on line, and found none within a thirty mile radius, so there was constant speculation as to how the ladies were managing to control them. Even when they were 'allowed' out they never truly relaxed and enjoyed themselves, knowing that their every move was being monitored. Their universe had become disordered and unruly, and they had become frustrated and bewildered, no longer in control of their own personal cosmos.

Kate and Megan still exercised and danced as much as possible; leaving Luke alone for a couple of hours in the evenings was no problem, as long as he had something to watch on television or some music to listen to.

There was only one dance class that Kate did on her own, and that was ballroom. It had been easy to take up again having taken lessons as a child. However, she had just received a text message to tell her it had been can, cancelled because she had been looking forward to it, she scanned the list of other classes available to see whether she could find an alternative, just for one evening.

There was a class listed, for the next level, but because it would be a one off she was sure she would be able to manage. She would prefer to be challenged than to be bored out of her mind by going over basic steps in a beginners' class; the only other possibility. So, leaving plenty of time to drive there and to change, she set off at 7.00 – dance bag in hand.

There was a look of surprise on the teacher's face when she arrived so Kate went straight over to explain why she had turned up unexpectedly. Fortunately, the teacher (who knew Kate) agreed that she would probably be able to cope with the higher class, and was happy for her to stay and try it out. So she changed her shoes and said hello to some of the other dancers, none of whom she recognised.

It came as no surprise to her to see a surplus of females – there were always fewer men than women in all the dance classes, that was just the way it was, and most of the men who attended were attached to a woman who had no intention of sharing! This usually meant that the women without partners had to take it in turns to dance with the instructor, sometimes leaving two females having to sit out at the same time.

Kate was aware that her presence had exacerbated the problem and she apologized to the young woman sitting next to her as they both watched the other couples "shuffle' around the floor to a quickstep. (The average age of the class must have been sixty, hence the use of the word 'shuffle'). They were all fairly adept at the dance, incorporating as many of the new sequences of steps as they could and occasionally breaking out into a little run diagonally across the floor, or a kind of hop and skip movement, both of which lasted but a few seconds and were always followed by a series of slower, less energetic ones allowing them to catch their breath and recover.

Kate noticed that one couple had sat out, and that the lady was fanning herself feverishly with a paper fan decorated with flamenco dancers, probably acquired on holiday in Spain. Her husband was offering her a drink from the bottle of water, after having taken a couple of gulps himself. She reckoned that they were hitting eighty and was not surprised that the quickstep had got the better of them.

The girl started the conversation, 'Are you from here?'

'Just along the coast – Pembleton,' Kate replied.

'Oh, yes, I know it quite well, my parents live there.'

'Really? It's not a bad town – there has been quite a lot of redevelopment and the fast rail link to London has made a huge difference. I've only come along tonight because my other class was cancelled,' Kate felt that she needed to explain her sudden appearance.

'I understand, that's happened to me a couple of times and I really missed it,' she empathized.

They sat for a while just watching the dancers and listening to the music. Kate was the first to begin the conversation again, 'Do you live here?'

'Yes, on the seafront; it's a wonderful place to bring up the children.'

'How many do you have?' Kate saw a common ground.

'Two boys.'

'Me too! I have two boys – twins.'

'That was lucky!'

'Hmm, yes and no.'

'Oh, I know what you mean.'

'How old are they?' Kate wasn't expecting them to be very old as she guessed her to be in her early thirties.

'Eight and ten.'

'So the eldest is taking the 11 plus?' Kate was always interested in children's education and progress.

'No, we decided it wasn't for him because he's autistic, he has a form of Asperger's.'

'Oh, that's a shame,' Kate had heard of it but wasn't sure what it meant.

When she had done her teaching practice one of the schools had a "Special Needs Department" that she visited, but it seemed that the pupils were all playing games on computers! It was only her impression and probably wasn't that at all, but she knew that sometimes children were taken out of lessons to attend the unit. That was her only exposure to "learning difficulties" during her training so she had assumed, that as a teacher, any children with learning difficulties would be spotted and 'taken care of', so she had never given it another thought.

'What exactly is that?' she felt that it didn't matter if she showed her ignorance because the young lady didn't know that she was a teacher.

'It's quite complicated because there are different levels; some are highly intelligent and learn to hide it, and may not ever be diagnosed. My husband is one of those and we didn't find out until later when the boys showed signs

'Crumbs! How did you find out?'

'Luckily the school spotted it.'

'What exactly does it mean? I've heard of it, but I'm not sure of how it manifests.'

'There are many signs, but one of the main ones is a lack of social skills – avoiding eye contact. They can be loners, or only feel comfortable with people that they know really well like family or close friends. They lack natural empathy or understanding in distressing or emotional situations although, the more intelligent ones watch other people's reactions and learn what to say and do. I have terrible trouble organizing any sort of get-together at the house; it's only recently, and with a lot of coaxing, that I have persuaded my husband to come out of the back room and say "hello" to my friends when they visit.'

'Gosh, that must have been difficult?' Kate sympathized.

'Yes, it has been. But there is so much more, for example: he can't read faces, so if I am upset or distressed he just doesn't notice because it doesn't register; it's the same with the boys.

I can't count the number of times that he has asked me to *tell* him what I am feeling, and how angry he gets (probably with himself). Also, he can spend hours on the same task. He can repeat the same thing over and over and never seem satisfied; he is such a perfectionist! For example, if he cooks something and it doesn't turn out exactly the way he wants, he chucks it! Don't get me wrong, he's highly intelligent! Luckily he has a job where they leave him alone and they recognize his ability, because he is what they call a "high functioning" Asperger, and quite honestly it's too late to really do anything to change his behaviour. The boys however, are getting help now it's been identified, but it's not been easy coping with it all. There have been several times when I wanted to walk away.'

Kate sat and listened and tried to empathize, and added that she didn't think that she would have been able to do it in her place.

'How about reading? Do they like reading?' she was curious.

'The boys *have to* read because they are set it at school but they would never pick up a book of their own accord, and as for Sam, he's never read a book in his life! It's a miracle that he's done so well, but he's a wizz at maths, and accountancy is perfect for him. It's only because he's so intelligent that he has learnt how to react in certain circumstances and what to say, by watching and learning from other people and the television, but it isn't instinctive.'

As Kate listened to all his idiosyncrasies it began to dawn on her that the girl could have been describing Luke!

She thought back to about what he had told her about his school days and how, in secondary school, he played truant as often as he could. He had hated it and, except for art and music, most of the teachers had given up on him. So, to encourage attendance they had let him do as much art as he wanted; he spent all day, every day in the art room where he kept himself to himself, and churned out work much of which was hung on the walls around the school. It kept him busy and out of trouble.

The more Sofie (that was her name) described her husband the more characteristics Kate found in common with Luke.

They exchanged phone numbers, that was Kate's idea because she thought the girl might be able to help in some way. She had already helped – she had opened her eyes and answered so many of Kate's unanswered questions.

They both danced the next one (a foxtrot) and didn't get the chance to chat again, but Kate's mind was not on the steps, and had to apologise for the mistakes she was making. She kept repeating "Asperger's" over and over in her mind, 'That's why,' she said to herself. She considered the word "autism", it encompassed so much, maybe he had other forms too? His spelling was appalling! Was dyslexia part of it, or was that a separate issue? She envisaged hours of research on her laptop.

But more than anything she felt guilty. Why hadn't she thought of it herself? She was a teacher for Christ's sake! She was supposed to know about these things. Hadn't she heard somewhere (on the radio) that *all* men had a form of autism to some degree? That would explain a lot!

When the class had finished she changed and said her goodbyes as quickly as possible.

As she turned the key in the ignition she wished that she hadn't travelled so far to the class; she needed to get back and explain to Luke. The journey was too long, and was giving her too much time to think – he couldn't help it, she thought, because he didn't know. It wasn't his fault.

The sun was setting and the sheep looked so peaceful in the fields, and all Kate could think about was how she wished she had found out earlier. Why hadn't she seen it? Why hadn't she thought about it?

Because she had been hurting so much that was all she could think about, that, and how to feel better and how to hurt him; to pay him back, how to get over him and all the other men who had treated her like a commodity.

She thought about them and recognized traits of autism in them as well. Had they *all* had problems? She wondered, why had she met so many? Maybe it was her problem? She started to analyse herself – had she chosen them? No, some maybe, but most of them had approached her – why? Had they seen a kindred spirit, or had it just been physical. Do Asperger's attract Asperger's? She was sure now that she had it too!

She cast her mind back to her childhood, to school. She hadn't taken it seriously until she was twelve and then, when she decided to apply herself she excelled in everything! No one was more surprised than herself!

She had always thought of herself as "average", but as soon as she had put some effort into her work she shot to the top. It had been like flicking a switch, and she enjoyed succeeding; after years of playing second fiddle to her sister and believing that she could never do as well as her, she was suddenly excelling at everything!

Unfortunately, the headmaster and her parents decided that she was being held back so, just before the new year began in September, they told her that she would be skipping a year. This meant joining a class of strangers, even if she recognized their faces she didn't "know" them. She floundered (especially in mathematics), she found herself struggling and she suffered.

What made it worse was there was no help on offer; she was somehow supposed to catch up on her own! Doing so well the previous year had not helped her at all, everyone thought that she was some kind of budding genius and would not need any help. Her sister could have helped (especially with the algebra and geometry) but instead delighted in seeing her suffer, she hated the thought of Kate being good at *anything*, except art and dance as they were not "proper" subjects, so they didn't count. Eventually, after a couple of years, Kate caught up and did well in her exams, with an A* in Mathematics, much to her sister's chagrin.

She had never really made friends, except for the girl who had skipped a class with her and another 'new girl' who joined later. It didn't worry her, she had always had to rely on herself, one or two friends were enough for her, besides she didn't think that they took friendship as seriously as Kate. Once, there had been an incident at school when Kate had asked for backup from one of her so called 'friends' who completely let her down being too 'weak' to take sides.

So, from that moment on, Kate's attitude towards her changed, and in a weird way she was relieved because she didn't want to waste her loyalty and friendship on someone who wasn't going to be there for her. She just knew that had the roles been reversed then she would have been there one hundred per cent to support her friend and was grateful that she had shown her true colours or she might always have referred to her as 'her best friend'. Whereas now, in Kate's eyes she wasn't worthy of her friendship and from that moment on barely two words passed between them. Kate even took a different route to school, leaving earlier so as to avoid her. It would not be the last time in her life that she would walk away from a relationship because of betrayal and disappointment.

She was annoyed and upset with herself for not having recognised Luke's problem; she had tried to hurt him instead of helping, and now she couldn't help the tears.

She looked around for a tissue – there weren't any, so she used the back of her hand.

The more she thought about her past relationships the more she was beginning to understand why they hadn't lasted; she kept choosing the same kind of man! In fact, the one before Luke, the one that had lasted eleven years (on and off) had probably been worse!

She remembered a time when she had a broken bone in her foot and he just stood and watched her struggle on a slippery, fine gravel slope leading down to a beach (they were on holiday in France) until, in the end, she had to slowly turn around and climb back up on all fours in agony! Not *once* did he hold out his hand or offer support – he just stood there not saying or doing anything! She wanted to get in the car and leave him there and get on the first plane back, but she would have ruined the holiday for the boys, so she stuck it out.

She had tried to get rid of him several times as she was aware of how damaging he was for her, but he kept turning up like a bad penny. It wasn't until (thankfully) he found someone else that she finally saw the back of him.

Skirting the hills now, the town lay outstretched and twinkling below as she began the descent.

She couldn't help going over the problems peculiar to sufferers of Asperger's that Sophie had listed in the class, and as she searched through the brief history of her relationship with Luke in her mind she kept finding (or imagining) similarities.

The more she compared, the more convinced she became that Luke was a sufferer. Although *had he* suffered? She asked herself, or had he just caused suffering in those closest to him, like an alcoholic or a gambler, happy enough in their own little world and oblivious to their effect on others?

'So, none of it is his fault?' she thought aloud, 'And they wouldn't even have heard about it when he was at school. No wonder he was so obsessive about skating! And other stuff!'

She felt guilty. Why hadn't she seen it? Because she knew little to nothing about it – it wasn't her domain. It was a speciality. She would have to look it up and find out more. But how would that help them now? The damage had been done – she had to repair it!

She remembered reading something in the paper about Zebra fish being able to repair their own spinal cords and a study taking place in North Carolina; it was very positive as they had discovered a healing protein that helped to bridge the gap in severed spinal cord tissue. She would contact them and get help. If necessary, they would go to North Carolina! He would be able to walk *and* skate again – she was going to fix it. It would be her mission and she wouldn't give up!

Panic was taking over as she turned into the lane and negotiated the narrow opening between the posts of the drive; she could feel a tightening in her chest making her feel nauseous and dizzy.

In her distress, she dropped the keys getting out of the car. Her hands were shaking, she felt light-headed, and her body had suddenly become too heavy for her legs.

Stumbling into the hallway, she dropped everything on the floor as she headed straight to Luke's room. All she could say was, 'I'm sorry,' over, and over again.

'What for, hon?' he asked in bewilderment.

The End

About the Author

Unfulfilled as a newly qualified Fine Arts graduate working for a newspaper in London; P J Swift left to live and work abroad in order to pursue a desire for travel and to learn languages.

Her 'odyssey' took her to Italy, Spain, France, Germany, The USA and The Bahamas; teaching herself the languages as she travelled.

On her return to the UK, fourteen years later, she qualified as a teacher and brought up a family.

Having optimistically entered into several romantic relationships, and abandoning all hope of ever finding a 'partner for life', she found solace in writing, which ultimately brought her the contentment she had been seeking.'